Hope you enjoy this, my debut
novel. If so, please tell others.

ventureb@telus.net

Reflections
of
Indigo

Twyla Enns

Vanessa, may a rainbow always brighten your sky.

Twyla Enns

iUniverse, Inc.

New York   Bloomington

Reflections of Indigo

Copyright © 2009 by Twyla Enns

This is a work of fiction. All of the characters, names, incidents, organizations, and dialogue in this novel are either the products of the author's imagination or are used fictitiously.

iUniverse books may be ordered through booksellers or by contacting:

iUniverse
1663 Liberty Drive
Bloomington, IN 47403
www.iuniverse.com
1-800-Authors (1-800-288-4677)

Because of the dynamic nature of the Internet, any Web addresses or links contained in this book may have changed since publication and may no longer be valid. The views expressed in this work are solely those of the author and do not necessarily reflect the views of the publisher, and the publisher hereby disclaims any responsibility for them.

ISBN: 978-0-595-52121-0 (pbk)
ISBN: 978-0-595-51105-1 (cloth)
ISBN: 978-0-595-62185-9 (ebk)

Printed in the United States of America

iUniverse rev. date: 7/7/09

Reflections of Indigo is dedicated to my best friend and loving husband, Vern, who gave me the time and consideration to write this novel, and to my beautiful daughter, Jodi, who will always be my inspiration.

It is easy in the world to live after the world's opinion; it is easy in solitude to live after our own; but the great man is he who in the midst of the crowd keeps with perfect sweetness the independence of solitude.

Ralph Waldo Emerson

Part One

A Time For Changes

Chapter One

To every thing there is a season, and a time to every
purpose under the heaven... A time to get, and a time
to lose, a time to keep, and a time to cast away.

Ecclesiastes 3:1 & 6
King James Version

As her fingers slid along the cool, beveled edges of the crystal
wall plaque she again so carefully had unwrapped, a mixture of
contradictory emotions—as unsettling as the weather—stirred
within her. The morning's bright sun and the darkening ridge in the
western sky had promised a chinook. The long thick branches of the
old spruce tree, heavy with cones, were shifting slightly to nature's
peculiar springtime pulse until finally, succumbing to the warm
gusts, they drooped onto the short wooden pickets of the front fence.
Now the heavens were sullen, the air as frigid as her tolerance.

From the corner of her eye Desiree could see the unopened
vial of tablets she had left that morning on the trestle table. There
were only five in the small plastic container, but that was more than
enough she had been told. And how easily she had acquired them.

Her initial intentions, bold and unbelievable, still clouded her mind and nipped once again at the core of her integrity. Yes, the tiny white pellets were almost possessing her now.

Apparently she had already committed the perfect crime, the ultimate sin. A death had definitely occurred; but no arrests, charges, trial, jury, or sentence had been given her even to this day—despite resentment still being able to wrap its horrid essence around her. She had power now, however, because that unexpected prescription truly held her destiny. She knew to wait just a little longer to erase all doubt. The right answer would come to her. It always did. What would everyone think of her then?

She sat at the old upright piano, its grand hue shining softly, her rough hands dropping onto the cold worn keys. She wasn't normally so insensitive to such discordance. Music was her life. Since her fifth birthday the piano had been a close friend, a never-failing source of strength. Lately she had often played an entire sonata for herself or an impromptu ditty for her daughter, who would prance into the living room to gingerly align her favorite dolls around the hearth before stopping to listen to the unfamiliar tune. For Desiree her love of music had filled many long winter hours with total contentment. But today as she sat alone in the large open space, that same piano held little interest for her and her round blue eyes, as pale as arctic ice, grew somber.

Slowly her favorite tune by The Byrds, "Turn! Turn! Turn! (A Time for Every Season)" came gently to her mind. She stood up and lovingly eyed the plaque as she hung it above the piano before crossing the room and letting her tired, aching body fall onto the loveseat.

Soon she was oblivious to her surroundings—those ugly papered walls she had stripped and recovered with new eggshell paint in the softest hue of bronze, the large bound Persian tapestry still draped over the two leather wing chairs in the corner, the unframed sketch of Jason she had left on the coffee table, and, outside, the tall decorative oil lamp swaying in the chilly March wind, casting long flickering shadows across the room. Even the golden glow from the thick marble fireplace along the front wall didn't seem to grant her any stimulation that early evening, and while the burning logs crackled and hissed she closed her eyes and let her mind drift into thoughts of other times, earlier times… Turn! Turn! Turn!

After picking up the last tiny pieces of a saucer she had broken while trying to slide it under some cereal bowls in her aunt's tiny cupboard, Desiree turned around and touched the grimy doorknob to the wooden spice rack above the gas stove. Through its tiny windows she noticed the masking tape someone had sloppily wrapped around one particular jar. The word *ginger* had been scribbled on it. But she didn't have to open it. She knew what was inside. Yes, there had been careful thought in her aunt's preparations for her family's short visit that weekend and Desiree gave a tiny sigh. Salt, pepper, ginger, allspice, nutmeg, and cinnamon were the only spices her mother was allowed to use at home. Garlic of any kind was forbidden. And she knew her aunt loved to cook Mediterranean dishes, especially for a crowd. It was her one true passion.

"So why, here, in your very own home, should you be concerned with your brother's strange demands?" She was talking out loud, as though her Aunt Julia were nearby. "Why should you feel obligated to make such bland meals for everyone?" She had ripped off the masking tape, wanting to crumple it up and throw it into the trashcan under the sink but decided to re-tape the spice jar instead. "And how can you look so content when dishing them out?" Perhaps it was their *special* secret, and Desiree knew better than to ask her father such a question. She glanced at the stove timer and then walked into the living room.

There was an eerie familiarity in the air as the scent of Aunt Julia's lavender perfume lingered and now, only needing to slip into her new navy blue suit before accompanying her older sister to a small house party, Desiree sat on the deep velvet cushion of the sofa, yanked a crocheted toss cushion from behind her, and let it fall onto the worn carpet.

She noticed a tiny book behind the end table and after picking up the already dog-eared paperback copy of the current bestselling novel *Valley of the Dolls*, by Jacqueline Susann, she remembered hearing a recent comment on her favorite radio station about the novelist's unusual, almost outrageous writing style, and no doubt because of it the book had become an instant sensation.

Desiree studied the paperback's glossy binding as her mind centered on the lengthy article she had read in that morning's paper about the intensifying radical attitude of the 60s' youth—total renouncement. The idea held her in quiet wonder, until an unexpected twinge of jealousy coursed her veins. How many times had she been compared to a porcelain doll? Just like a Royal Doulton figurine—so delicate, apparently too fragile to touch—like an innocent statuette suddenly coming to life on a skating rink somewhere as the sight of her lithe slender body stopped all other activity around her. Or playing the piano where her long nimble fingers could excite a choir of angels. But from what she could understand, the world was beginning to perceive its youth as an ever-growing army of tin soldiers. Determined. Resilient. Proud. Anti-establishment. Desiree felt like neither a statuette nor a soldier. Not even the little girl next door. More like Raggedy Ann.

She caressed the deep soft finish of the sofa's arm as her thoughts continued. How she wanted to be more sophisticated, just like her sister. Yes, Erin, now a college graduate, was the soldier in the family—and not the lowly private for any longer than needed. Tall, dark, and self-assured, no doubt she would soon be stepping out of the bedroom, making her usual grand entrance, just to model her latest outfit. Fashion-conscious Erin spent every spare penny on the latest fads. On their last visit together, wasn't she wearing granny glasses, and a see-through blouse?

But there seemed to be something different between them now. Since leaving home to attend college, Erin's usual acceptance and encouragement concerning her younger sister's affairs had waned considerably. The recent graduate had even admitted over the phone just last week that she was tired of the single life. Her boyfriend, Brian, had taken a vacation trip to Switzerland that spring and only recently advised her that if he found a teaching position in Geneva, he would want to stay there for a few years. Erin apparently had taken the news with much chagrin. She was going to try and wait for him, apparently. Just recently she started to send résumés to various publishers. Her journalism certificate had already been copied dozens of times and was framed now, wrapped carefully in sheets of tissue paper, and placed in her old cedar chest back home. She was hoping to have a worthwhile job this fall, getting paid well for her efforts, and then being able to afford her own spacious apartment. She had been looking at a brand-new car, too—a candy apple red Mustang convertible. Yes, she would be starting a new life no longer near her ever-dependent Aunt Julia. Soon, she had said, she would be living.

Desiree straightened some loose pages and tucked the novel under her arm before going down the hall to see her sister.

"You didn't hide this novel very well, Erin." The young blonde gently closed the bedroom door behind her and heard a loud sigh as her sister reached for a tiny ashtray on the dresser's edge.

"Oh, gads. Thank goodness *you* found it. This isn't anything like those Harlequin romances you have to smuggle between textbooks or binders, and then hide under the mattress every night. I bet you'd have the silver to polish, or the stove to clean again, and absolutely be forbidden to go over to your friend Lynda's for at least a week, if a novel like this were ever found in Mom and Dad's house."

Her sister had perfectly visualized the scenes at home. "Good girls don't read books like that, you know," Desiree could surmise her mother saying repeatedly. A fast reader, the teenager had almost memorized all of her father's *Time* magazines, but she had become easily unimpressed with the steady supply of history books he had recently given her.

Erin leaned forward, took the book being offered her, and dropped it into the bottom drawer of the old walnut dresser. "This gem of a book has been through countless readings already, as you can see. I just finished the first chapter again, and had to throw it under the sofa when I saw you and the folks at the front door yesterday. Thanks, Sis." A hint of mischief played in her dark green eyes, as she settled her lean body into the corner vanity chair. "Isn't it odd, Desiree? You and I graduating in the same year?" she added moments later.

"Yeah, it is a little, I guess. But you know your journalism certificate is a lot bigger deal than my high school diploma."

"Yes, I *do* know that. And I got honors, yet. Now, don't you ever forget that!"

A distinct tone of contempt rang in Erin's voice and Desiree grabbed the doorknob behind her with both hands in a weak effort to look nonchalant, casual, as she watched her sister light up an oddly-shaped cigarette. Its smell was new to Desiree and made her feel suddenly queasy. She had heard about marijuana in school, had read about it in newspapers and magazines, but she didn't care at all to see Erin smoking it. She rejected the toke being offered her.

"Come on. It'll help you relax for the party tonight." With a careless shrug, Erin continued. "But, gads, it's good to see you again. And Mom and Dad, I guess. Too bad they couldn't have visited *here* a little while longer instead of taking Aunt Julia to the cabin to get it ready for another winter. Seems all they ever do when they come to this little domain is cater to *her*. Obviously she still hasn't accepted any part of Uncle William's death even after all these years. And why she kept that old place in the woods when she sold the rest of the farm is beyond me."

Desiree's mouth was watering; she felt dizzy, flushed. Anticipating an unwanted dash down the hall, she opened the bedroom door. She tried to concentrate on watching Erin, who had taken another slow drag before putting on her black stretch-lace boots. The black denim knickers, with matching midi-vest and shirred satin shirt, made her look so trendy. And of course the latest hairdo, a short geometric Vidal Sassoon cut to the thick reddish-brown hair, added just the right touch of sophistication to her easy style.

"Have you found an office job yet, Des? Bet you haven't even started looking for one."

"I'm still teaching piano. You know that keeps me busy." She took a deep breath, soon wishing that she hadn't, because now her head was aching.

"Teaching just during the day, still, I suppose. So you won't bother Dad."

"I don't bother Dad. He knows my new schedule now."

"Bingo! And is he ever home then?"

"No," Desiree sighed. She sat on the edge of the single bed and fingered the delicate knit of the mottled spread, its once-bright colors now faded, much like her expectations of the coming weekend. After the awards ceremonies that previous afternoon she had wanted her entire family to go to the cabin. She had purposely packed her oldest pair of jeans and a wool plaid shirt so she could walk, in warmth, with Erin along the stony shores of the nearby river to that secluded cove hidden in a thicket of young balsam fir. She had been looking forward to their time together for quite a while.

"Still afraid to leave the nest, aren't you?"

Desiree picked at some fallen hairs on the long sleeve of her cotton blouse. "I have three new students now."

"Well, good for you, but I'll bet since Lynda has moved down east, you don't have a close friend anymore."

"I know lots of people, Erin."

"Perhaps. But do any of them really know *you*? I don't understand why you aren't aching to get your own place. I was so glad to finally move out. Thank goodness for Uncle William's small inheritance so I could come up here to attend college. And to think you spent yours on more music lessons. Is any of it left?"

"No."

"Gads! That's so hard for me to believe."

"Why, Sis? You know I love music beyond anything." Today, however, thoughts of being with her family at the cabin seemed more appealing to Desiree. She was still here, however, alone with her sister who was stinking up Aunt Julia's matchbox house. With increasing intensity she wished that she hadn't accepted Erin's invitation so quickly that morning but, hoping for another glimpse of her sister's fascinating lifestyle, Desiree couldn't resist such an unexpected and flattering request. Suddenly, though, the thought of curling up in a big soft chair and reading that worn paperback seemed more enjoyable, more relaxing.

"But you can't stay with the folks forever you know, and moving out isn't cheap." Erin took another slow drag.

Desiree twisted her thick milky-blonde hair and pinned it loosely at the crown while watching Erin carefully apply makeup to her sallow skin and deep-set dark green eyes. Getting up from the bed she whisked a small brush of peach blush over her high cheekbones, suddenly conscious of the few cosmetics she used even for special occasions. Then, just a hint of light blue eye shadow and dark brown mascara, and she was finished. That was all she felt she needed, being so much more than she knew she could get away with at home.

"Maybe Aunt Julia will give you her old piano," Erin volunteered. "You know it only collects dust here. Why don't you ask her for it?"

"That's an antique now, Sis. She would never part with it. Grandpa had it shipped here all the way from Oslo for her and Uncle William as their wedding present."

"I know that. But really, I think it would help you both. There'd be a lot more space in that tiny living room without it. You could leave home, start teaching in your own place and finally spread your stiff little wings."

As she stared into the large mirror of the vanity and saw the pleasing reflection, a sudden surge of importance overcame the young blonde. She felt suddenly glamorous, special, included in something outside of herself, yet not that foreign in her own imagination. She set the brush on the vanity and carefully took her new bouclé-knit suit from its hanger in the closet.

"Oh, gads! I hope you're not planning to wear that tonight!" Erin snapped. "Just because I was stuck in an ugly beige suit that Aunt Julia and the folks insisted I wear yesterday at the ceremonies doesn't mean you have to look stuffy tonight. We are going to a house party, not a church tea. Mom and Dad won't be with us, so why not try to dress just a little more stylishly? Here, put this skirt on. It's a bit snug for me now but the suede is still so soft. And this silk blouse should fit you perfectly. You can take it home with you tomorrow, if you want. Brian gave me this outfit before he went to Europe. Isn't it sexy?"

"It's beautiful." Desiree touched the tiny pearl buttons of the creamy blouse and slipped into the softness of the caramel suede. She had only dreamed of wearing something so luxurious, perhaps strutting down the catwalk in New York City right behind Twiggy, who again was stealing the limelight because of her awesome beauty, her unusual spaghetti thinness, and that shocking pink shortest of shorts with a wide leather belt that appeared to require the same yardage to create. But as attractive as the blouse and skirt were, the outfit made her feel even younger than her seventeen years, and as always, Desiree wanted to look as elegant and striking as her sister.

"Ohhh, this is so short, Erin. I can't wear this tonight."

"It's just those mile-long legs of yours. Come on, now. You should want to show off that beautiful tan. For once, why don't you try to look like "The Girl from Ipanema" and not just the little girl next door?"

Erin gently pulled out the large hairpin and started brushing Desiree's long, soft curls.

"There! Much better already. Now just a little squirt of my favorite perfume, and presto! But don't stand there looking so damn prudish. Tonight I'd like you to open up a little and maybe get noticed by some handsome and promising young man. Who knows, maybe we'll both find someone special tonight…"

Ever-scheming Erin, Desiree thought, as she sat at the edge of the bed and picked at a loose thread of its knitted covering. "But you told me…"

"Yes, I know I told you that I would wait for Brian. But I don't think I can wait *that* long for him, or anybody, for that matter." There had been a deepening tone of disappointment in her voice. Erin twisted her lean body, reached for the ashtray, and took another long, slow drag. "Mom wanted a boy, you know."

Desiree sat up straight. "Wow! Where on earth did that come from?" She instantly noticed an odd, rather cynical look on her sister's face and for a fleeting moment a colorful image formed in Desiree's mind. Had Erin's portrayal of the independent, happy-go-lucky coed been a total façade these past few years? Had she been cloaking some ugly fibers of jealousy towards her younger sister?

And had those threads just started to tighten their weave? Had her nonchalance towards Desiree's genuine naiveté been only a game?

"Mom wanted you to be her *first and only son,* you know."

"Huh?" Her thoughts were slow in returning to her actual surroundings. "What are you talking about, Sis?"

"Well, after adopting me, that is," Erin started. "Neither of them really cared which gender I was. They just wanted a baby so much. But then, when Mom was pregnant with *you,* she decided that her first *conceived* child should keep the Bjornson name, and she honestly thought she was carrying a boy."

"Why was I named *Desiree,* then?" She picked up a large orange comb from the narrow headboard and started fingering its hard plastic teeth. "Desiree means *a much wanted girl,* you know."

"Really? Trust *you* to look something like that up." Erin played with the distinct crease in her black denim knickers before continuing. "Well, maybe Mom was hoping to be carrying a boy and just didn't want to bother Dad with her own wishes."

"You know Mom doesn't keep anything from Dad."

"Yeah, sure. Just like *you* don't. And how then do you think you got the nickname *Jam?*"

"I have no idea, Erin. How?" There was a disturbing tone in Desiree's voice now. A few bright orange teeth were suddenly in her other hand and she let them fall onto the bed.

"Let me give you a hint. What are the first letters in each of the names James, Allen, and Matthew?"

"J-A-M, of course. But what does that have to do with any of this?"

"Well, actually, I think the whole concept was brilliant on Mom's part. I never thought she could think up such an original idea."

"You're confusing me, Sis.

"You see, Mom wanted to name her son James Allen Matthew."

"Three given names to our single ones. Hmmm. But what's wrong with that?"

"Nothing, of course. Think about it, though. You are always her little *Jam* when you win each and every music award or when you win each and every skating trophy. But you are just little *Desiree* when you drop a plate or screech their new car to a sudden stop. *Jam. Jam.* You know, I like that nickname. And it suits you. Wish I had thought of it myself."

Desiree tried to remember when she was last called *Jam.* Was it while dressing for her high school graduation ceremonies last May? Or was it when modeling the bouclé suit she had designed and sewn especially for this weekend? She really could not remember. "You know, I don't believe one thing you've just said. When did Mom tell you all this anyway? And why wouldn't she have let me know about it?" The comb was toothless now, mutilated by her fumbling fingers.

There was a sudden odd cackle from Erin's throat, which seemed to have caught even *her* off guard, and she quickly turned toward the small window to hide any surprise showing on her face.

Desiree wanted to believe only part of her sister's unexpected comments. She was hoping the tiny seed of retribution that had just been planted in her own psyche was only another of Erin's many zany and inventive schemes. *Yes, look how content and satisfied Erin seems now,* her thoughts announced.

"Gads! You still take life so seriously, don't you? And until you move out and get away from such puritanical parents, how can that change? But I wouldn't worry about it." Erin stuffed a compact and small package of Kleenex into her black leather shoulder bag. "I just might be embellishing things a little." A tiny smirk curved the corners of her mouth.

"And why would you want to do that?"

"I might clue you in later." Satisfaction glistened in Erin's green eyes as she noticed her sister picking up the broken teeth of the comb. "I meant to buy some more jasmine incense today. It smothers this smell. Oh, well, I could just tell the folks that I'm trying a new scent. They wouldn't know the difference anyway."

"Of course they would."

"And how on earth would Mom and Dad, or Aunt Julia, know what this smell really is?" She snapped her bag shut before glancing at her watch. "Let's see now. If we leave in ten minutes, we'll only be half an hour late. Can't look too eager now, can we?"

En route to the party in Erin's old blue Falcon, its dented rear bumper clanking erratically over the rough old pavement to the radio's various Beatles' tunes, Desiree leaned back in the passenger seat and stretched her long exposed legs. The thought of seeing Todd and Sara again brought a tiny smile to her lips. They were the only couple she had met since Erin left home and they were such warm, easy company.

As her sister shifted gears and pressed her foot further down on the gas pedal, Desiree concentrated on the simple words to "Turn! Turn! Turn!", which were now blaring on the radio. She had memorized those exact words at her first week ever in a summer Bible school camp and, as she thumbed through various books of the Bible, for some reason this particular verse had caught her instant attention and apprehension. It had been one of the easiest passages for her to learn. And now there was a song, a beautiful tune with easy biblical lyrics, making it to the top of the current pop charts.

"That's too nice a song to have so loud, Erin."

Erin twisted the broken knob, and a sudden thought warmed Desiree. She smiled. That entire album had been played repeatedly on the stereo in Lynda's bedroom where the chubby redhead had taught her the various steps to the waltz, the jive, the twist, and the bossa nova.

"You're a quick study, Desiree. Just follow the lead, and it shouldn't take you long to learn any of these dances," Lynda had insisted while twirling her friend around again and again. "Always act as if you were exactly where you should be," Lynda had reminded her so often. "It'll help you to feel more confident, girl. Every time. Every place."

Turn! Turn! Turn!

The low, fading sunlight spread a hazy blanket of amber around the large ranch-style house, and after getting out of the car Desiree eyed the elaborate landscaping with quiet reflection. Massive weeping willows, letting the tips of their lower branches tickle the greenness below, dominated the sloping yard. An array of white sweet alyssum, smothered in a tiny rock garden near the sidewalk, seemed to be weeping for a single moment of acknowledgment. With the slightest of breeze, mauve chrysanthemums kissed the edge of the old stone steps. Various climbing rose bushes, in a riot of pastels, waltzed along the red brick façade in perfect rhythm to the gentle breeze. She sighed as she thought of her mother's longing for such loveliness back home and of the allergies that kept her from their garden.

Desiree touched the velvet moistness of a tiny petal poking through the wrought iron railing while Erin rang the doorbell and pulled at the broken stem of a rosebud that was draped over the top step. She tucked it behind her ear. When the front door opened, the expected wide smile and firm embrace from Todd Remmings greeted them both.

Inside, the scent of freshly picked sweet peas permeated the large foyer as their tall, burly, craggy-faced host guided them down the spiraling oak staircase nearby.

Soon unfamiliar voices and short fits of laughter from beyond the French doors to her left made Desiree's entire body stiffen, so unlike those previous times when she and Erin had been the only guests. Despite Todd's unrivaled congeniality and Erin's usual search for adventure, the atmosphere seemed so different, somewhat tense tonight. She knew she looked *en vogue* wearing her stunning mini skirt, and the small leather purse that matched the open-toed shoes her sister had lent her for the evening perfectly completed the ensemble. She could feel her long blonde hair draped down her back and over the silky softness of the blouse. Tonight she was hoping to be included, accepted, to feel special, but for some reason it now seemed that sitting in the cozy alcove and perhaps reading a popular book like *Valley of the Dolls* might be more enjoyable. No one would really know that she was there, and no one would even have to care.

Through the French doors she could see the recent renovating Todd had done to the rumpus room; its floor and walls were splattered with black and white tiles. Lipstick-red vinyl bar stools at the other end of the room broke some of the checkered layout, as did the mirrors and chrome-framed pictures of popular '50s Fords and Chevrolets which hung above the brightly lit jukebox over in one corner. Tiny strobe lights flickered everywhere. As unique as the rumpus room looked, Desiree preferred the subdued quality of this smaller, cozier area.

Glancing around after being guided into the larger room, Desiree pressed the soft kid leather of her clutch purse against her hip and made a quick study of the oak pool table in one corner. At the long counter nearby various liquor bottles had been arranged, as if on display. The entire scene was so foreign to her. She felt Todd's large hand squeezing her elbow and she smiled shyly as casual introductions were made. When a chorus of murmurs concerning yesterday's awards ceremonies produced a circle of toothy smiles and wide, curious eyes, a rare moment of composure overtook the young blonde and she followed her sister and Todd to the bar. Waiting for the glasses of wine her sister had immediately requested, Desiree eyed the guests gathering around the jukebox.

She felt so uncomfortable, so over-exposed, while everyone else looked so confident, so chic. She was like an ugly green caterpillar, soon to emerge, she realized, but into what? A sovereign Monarch butterfly, she was hoping, or would she be just an ordinary brown moth? To soften her fixed smile when suddenly sensing curious eyes watching her, she concentrated on folding the small stack of paper napkins in front of her. They were very soft, as thick as linen, lap-size and white, with tiny scalloped edges. To herself she said: *Todd, do you have any more of these for me to fold? Oh, Lynda, looking confident and feeling comfortable aren't easy. How were you always able to do both?*

She could remember her sister often exuding that same smooth capacity. Having already offered to help Todd behind the bar later, Erin was poking Desiree's bare thigh in a quiet attempt to catch her attention and Desiree sighed faintly, smiling sweetly at them both.

"Is Sara in the hospital already, Todd?" Erin asked quickly. "I didn't think she was due for another month or so."

"Five weeks today, apparently, but she decided to leave the puppies with her mother for the evening. Crowds still excite them. I just hope they're house-trained before the baby comes." The slight ring of laughter in his baritone voice and the twinkle in his pale gray eyes belied Todd's burliness. He felt the moist cork before tasting the dry white wine and, satisfied, filled two crystal glasses. "Sara should be here at any moment."

"I wish I could see those Samoyeds. I hear they're such little darlings." Erin gracefully took one glass of wine and handed the other to Desiree.

"I think I'd rather just have some Coke right now, Erin," she whispered, carefully putting the glass onto the counter. "This wine might be a little too dry for me."

Erin glared at her sister and quickly pulled her away from the bar. "Don't embarrass me in front of everyone here. Gads! Desiree, you know you don't come to parties like this one and drink soda pop!" She quickly finished her wine and mumbled something to herself.

"Pardon?" Desiree sat at the edge of a recliner and pulled at the hem of her short skirt as she tried to heed Lynda's words once again.

"Oh, never mind, Sis. Just don't look so tense. *Please!*" Erin took the full glass of wine left on the counter and carefully set it on the chrome table beside her sister while loud fits of laughter from the other side of the opened French doors quickly ended the room's various conversations.

Erin turned, waiting expectantly. "Now there's a guy I'd like to meet again. Jonathon Sommers is far too high-strung for you, Sis, but I'll take him any time." Erin quickly straightened the hang of her denim vest. "Looks like he came solo tonight. Hmmm," she said pertly. "This might be easier than I ever thought."

"Shhh. He might hear you. Can't look too eager now, can we, Sis?" Desiree quickly took a tiny sip of the wine and *let* her lips pucker.

While the newcomer acknowledged other guests with a loud cheer or brisk salute Erin smoothed her short dark hair. She approached him with a polished flair and as the young man's warm dark brown eyes caught her attention he smiled spontaneously, displaying the straightness of his white teeth and the slight cleft in his strong chin.

Almost mesmerized by the perfect maleness of the new arrival, Desiree remained seated in the deep Naugahyde recliner and felt the cold stiff material before squeezing the long crystal stem of the wine glass beside her, hoping not to break it, trying to get her thoughts on something less affecting than that late guest. Flawlessly sculptured, he was handsome beyond any romance novel imagery, and he was standing just a few feet in front of her now, while her bare legs were sticking to the seat.

Another group of guests thundered down the stairs but the tall newcomer was ignoring them all. His eyes were focused only on Desiree.

Who is that sweetheart sitting there? Jon Sommers wondered. *Who is that girl with the deep dark tan and such hauntingly pale blue eyes? I think she's "The Girl from Ipanema". Yes, she has to be ...* But, no. She was Erin's sister, he was now so hurriedly being told. Erin. So outspoken, so self-assured. *But what are you like, little sister?* He wanted to know. His eyes darted across the room and when he saw more friends on the dance floor acknowledging him he stepped forward.

Desiree pressed both hands against the arms of the recliner. There was a different feeling now in her abdomen—an odd twitching, as though a hummingbird were fluttering inside, and she hoped that her initial gaze had gone unnoticed. She pulled at the hem of her skirt. Looking up again, however, the azure haze of her longing eyes was caught in the quiet seduction of his, and the moment was held in a beautiful liquid hush.

Flames of anger, however, were almost shooting from Erin's narrowing eyes. She grabbed Jon's arm and pulled him onto the dance floor.

And Jon let Erin's firm body press tightly against his. He let her warm hands squeeze his neck and shoulders and back, but he refused to let his eyes stray too far from the beautiful young blonde he had just met.

He had watched Desiree's slender, voluptuous body settle into the recliner, had noticed one delicate hand ever-pressed on the hem of that very short skirt, and had seen the other tighten around the glass of wine. He loved how those endless legs seemed to glide across the tiled floor to the bar where she sat near the wall and studied the paper napkins with feigned interest. And still those eyes, those distinctive silvery-blue and mysterious eyes, were focused elsewhere as though hiding from him. Had his easy smile startled her?

Staring at her glass again, wishing it contained something just a little sweeter, Desiree could still sense those dusky ravenous eyes almost seducing her with their intensity. Jon was a statue of the finest Italian marble—hard, polished, and dark-veined—chiseled to perfection. And such a magnificent specimen of manliness had noticed her in the crowd, apparently comfortable with what he had found. She was slowly getting caught up in the splendor.

But he was still dancing with Erin. Desiree could see the longing look on her sister's face, could almost feel the beautiful sensations she knew were whirling through Erin's supple body. She turned towards the counter.

Brown wavy hair, slightly mussed and graying at the temples, framed Todd's ample face, his constant smile enhancing the twinkle in his pale smoky-blue eyes. His thick, strong fingers tapped against the countertop while the upbeat music kept the dance floor crowded. Only he and Desiree remained seated now.

"Can I fix you another drink? A Bloody Mary? Weak with lots of ice?" Not expecting an answer, he put her wine glass into the sink and reached for a clean tumbler. "Erin seems rather pleased with herself tonight, doesn't she?" His words were soft, almost a whisper.

Desiree smiled.

"And Jon's quite the charmer, isn't he?"

"Pardon?"

Todd sent her an odd almost-knowing look as he handed her the fresh drink. "Trouble is, Desiree, Jon knows his own attraction and he expects your full attention before night's end."

"What?" She had trouble shifting her weight in the thickly padded bar stool. "I think they make a perfect couple. See how nice they look dancing together."

"Their temperaments are certainly well-matched."

"What do you mean by that?" His words puzzled her, and for some reason, almost offended her.

"I don't think a frying pan would be left in the kitchen cupboards if Jon ever got out of line around her. Erin wouldn't put up with his erratic behavior for a single moment."

"Of course I know about my sister's occasional impulsiveness, but I haven't got that impression of Jon yet."

Todd squeezed her hand gently and looked her straight in the eye as a twinge of concern narrowed the arch of his bushy brows. "Desiree, I hope you never do."

There was a slightly ominous tone to his voice and for a fleeting moment her entire body quivered. She suddenly wanted to go home, or to the cabin, or over to Lynda's. *Lynda, you were my best friend, my only true friend. Why did you move away? If you had come with us this weekend, right now we could be walking to the hollow behind the cabin. We could be finding that old knotty stump we discovered years ago. Remember? We could be sitting on the mossy ground, eating our freshly picked crabapples, and watching the warblers scurrying along the ground. It would be fun. Like always.*

She had panicked. She smiled sheepishly at Todd who had just been asked to freshen a few drinks at the other end of the long bar. Again she looked around the room. Erin must have gone upstairs for something and now Jon was approaching her. Quickly tucking the slight flair of soft leather under her legs, she turned away. She lifted her tumbler and took a slow, tiny sip.

"Too strong for you, huh?" Jon's deep voice was casual, despite a large knot forming in the back of his throat. Uneasiness swelled within him. He was amazed in that crowded, noisy room by Desiree's prolonged act of indifference. He wanted to show her off as his own. Hadn't she smiled so sweetly at him earlier? Why would she be looking elsewhere now?

Pleased by the faint scent of Chanel No. 5 around her, he studied her softness, the perfect hang of the silk blouse against her full, perky breasts. So many buttons, like tiny pearls, cascaded from her throat. Her utter beauty, her stillness, her continued aloofness took him. She was pulling at her short skirt again and staring at the crystal tumbler in front of her. How could anyone be so unconcerned when so close to him? As the moments lingered, Jon's eyes sparkled like black onyx as he quietly watched her caressing the crystal, touching it so carefully. Slowly. Methodically. Up and down. Up and down, again and again. She had aroused every cell, every pore, and every vein in his body.

"Here you go, Jon," Todd interrupted. "Bacardi and coke … Are you all right, Desiree?"

She had wanted to be so relaxed that evening, unruffled by anything or anyone. How long had she been stroking that tumbler just to have something to do? While that heavenly man sat so close, the very core of her was dancing in a whirlpool of wonderful sensations. Loving the intoxication, she had only started to question her weakening restraint. And Erin would certainly disapprove. *Can't look too eager now, can we, Sis?*

"I really think I should make you another drink."

"Pardon? Oh, no, no. This one's all right. But a few more ice cubes would be nice." *Erin, where did you go? Lynda, why did you move so far away? And Jon, why are you doing this to me?*

There was a soothing lull to her voice and Jon loved its fervid affect.

"Let *me* get that ice for you. Todd's been serving drinks all night." He took her drink and stepped behind the bar as she again searched the room for Erin.

"Here's your new drink. A virgin Bloody Mary with lots of ice. I think I got carried away with the Tabasco sauce, though." He gave her a deep throaty laugh and winked as he stirred the tomato juice and spices with a fresh celery stick.

When his large hand touched the laced cuff of her blouse she eluded the path of his heated gaze, that delicious silent enticement, by purposely recalling Todd's unexpected remarks. Slowly the tender interchange waned. When Jon asked her for a dance she was able to refuse him.

"P-l-e-a-s-e?" There was a slight pressing edge to his bass voice as the curve of his lips widened.

"But …" *Erin wants you, too, Jon,* she wanted to admit, but she couldn't just then. She took her glass and felt its coldness against her palm.

"But what? If you don't know how to dance, I'll be glad to teach you."

"No, not now, Jon. Please let me finish this drink. It's quite tasty, actually. Then maybe we…" *Then maybe—nothing,* her thoughts continued. *Sitting here with you, Jon, is innocent enough, but Erin would be furious if she saw us now. She wouldn't understand. Where are you Erin? Get back here quick and claim this man before it's too late.*

"Your sister and I are just friends, you know. Business friends at that. Now, please, may I have this dance?"

"How did you know that I was going to…?" How quickly she had questioned him. Surprised at his comment, she was more upset now at her own transparency. But he continued talking and only when he mentioned that he would be going up north in a month to work on the seismic rigs again that year did she feel disappointed. Trying to hide her emotions, she asked, "Where did you meet my sister?"

He laughed softly at her blushing face. More at ease now with her exceptional modesty, he took her hand in his and squeezed it gently. Her simplicity fascinated him. Her pureness and quiet dignity had such magnificent appeal. So solitary, so dainty, so quietly stunning was his new acquaintance. *Desiree, I want you. I want you now.* "There're still a few weeks before I have to leave. We can enjoy ourselves 'til then."

A warm rush enveloped her but realization soon cooled the veneer. "But I'm going home tomorrow. With my folks."

"I didn't think it would be quite that soon."

There was an unexpected softness in his voice now, a slight strain of disappointment, which caught her immediate attention. He had aroused her sensitivity again and she frowned at the thought. She must get control of herself, somehow. "You still haven't told me where you first met my sister. I really would like to know."

"In Jasper, last year. She was covering a ski event."

"Oh, yeah. I remember now. She wanted me to be there with her but I was more concerned about my mid-term exams." Desiree took another tiny sip of her drink and caught the glint of his dark widening eyes.

"Wish you had decided to come. The skiing was perfect. The weather was sensational. But we've only seen each other once or twice since then. It's been nothing more than that, really. Do you ski?" He was squeezing her hand with a firmer hold now.

"No, I've never tried it."

"What? An avid skier like Erin hasn't talked you into it yet? Maybe you both could meet me there some weekend and ..."

Desiree's feigned reserve was quickly fading and the noisy interruption from more latecomers was a welcome respite. Erin stood amongst them, talking and laughing, and her sister eagerly waved to her but when their eyes met Erin quickly broke away from the small crowd. Her green eyes, once shining like emeralds, narrowed to dull slits above her twitching cheeks and the rosebud she had picked earlier, now limp and faded, fell from her hair as she marched towards the couple.

"Gads! I don't believe this."

"Pardon?"

"Desiree. It seems that I can't leave you alone for even a moment to freshen up, without you taking control of everything." She was talking between her teeth and her hot, piercing stare had Desiree sinking deeper into the sticky vinyl seat.

Erin turned her body to face the dance floor. "Jon. I like this song. Let's dance."

"No, Erin. I already asked Desiree for this one. I'll dance with you a little later."

"Oh, I don't think so." She grabbed his drink and slammed it back onto the counter. Her sleeve was now wet. "I want this dance, Jon. Right now!! My sister can find another partner ... can't you, Desiree?" The tiny copper speckles in Erin's eyes darkened to an intense shade of sorrel as her body straightened. Both hands were raised to shoulder height, exposing long needle-sharp fingernails.

Suddenly Erin was like a powerful leopard—poised, waiting, and ready for the kill.

Jon's brown eyes were glaring, his jugular veins protruding. He locked his arms around Erin's small squirming body and forced her upstairs.

As Todd randomly punched several selections on the jukebox, Desiree's eyes began tearing. Her face flushed as she tried to ignore the curious crowd around her. *Act as if ... Act as if you were exactly where you should be*, her mind kept repeating. *Act as if ...*

She had to talk to Erin. She realized that their usual contention had deepened. There would be a contest between them now, one of wit and will, and Desiree winced at the image. Only the firm press of Todd's huge hand on her shoulder helped to soften her thoughts.

"Let's go upstairs for a cup of coffee. Sara should be back soon," Todd whispered, but when he saw Jon approaching them an eerie, disturbing look arrested his gray eyes. He squeezed Desiree's arm tightly before turning away. "I'll be nearby, okay?"

Jon smiled weakly as he pulled a bar stool against the nearby wall and brought her closer to him. "Your sister is a great one for theatrics, isn't she? Bet she's always been. Knows what she wants and is willing to go all the way for it. Same as me, I guess."

"I'm not helping matters by being here with you right now, Jon. Where is she?"

"I left her in the guest room. Why?"

"I want to talk to her. To take her home."

"Hey, it took some doing for me to get out of there in one piece," he announced as he rubbed the deep scratches on his right arm. "I'd like you to stay here with me, my little girl from Ipanema."

His words chimed like a child's lullaby but they reached Desiree's ears like a boxer's blow below the belt. She had to find Erin. Darting around the dancers she dashed up the staircase, taking them two at a time, and only stopped at the back landing to quickly peek at the bleakness outside. She took a few more steps through the island kitchen and dining room before scurrying beyond the living room and then down the hall. Only one bedroom door was closed. She turned the knob and walked in, but no one was there.

Hearing footsteps in the kitchen, Desiree smiled. Only Jon greeted her there, his dry eyes curious, his full lips parted.

"Jon. She's not here. Help me find Erin. Please help me find my sister." Within seconds they were outside on the front lawn.

"Where's Erin, Jon?" Her voice was raspy and she shivered in the sudden downpour. "Her car is gone."

"We'll find her. Come on. My car's just around the corner."

"But we should tell Todd. And I was hoping to see Sara tonight."

Todd soon met them outside, rushing them off before they all got drenched. When told that Erin's car was nowhere on Aunt Julia's quiet street, Jon continued driving—up various residential streets and back alleys, between the downtown high-rises, over to the university and around the Tech.

Only the rhythmic squeaking of wet wipers broke their silence as the moments went by. With her forehead pressed firmly against the cold side window of the car, Desiree studied each passing vehicle. As she strained to see each driver through the gloomy wetness of the glass, she could see only a blurred stiffness behind the wheel and in each occupied seat, or silhouettes of pedestrians dashing towards their vehicles or some opened doorway. She wondered how many animals were shivering in the deluge and scurrying about to find a parked car or large tree to hide under for some protection.

The ebony blanket of night was lifting gently when Jon again drove up the now-familiar driveway, but still no rusty blue Falcon was parked anywhere on the street.

"I don't see the station wagon here, either. Mom and Dad said they'd be back before midnight."

Jon turned off the ignition of his shiny new Austin Healy but stayed behind the wheel. His grip tightened. Somehow he had to stay awake! And he was hungry, too, but he didn't want to hurry anything between them that early hazy morning. The piercing rain had stopped; the gusting wind had weakened. Desiree's nerves were like bare electrical wires left outside in the storm, yet somehow she had been able to awaken some peaceful, almost childlike spirit from within, and his own prolonged lightheadedness surprised him.

"Where'd your parents go?"

"To the cabin near Smoky River. Aunt Julia insisted they take her there to help clean everything up for the coming winter."

"Well, maybe they got delayed, or just changed their minds because of this unexpected weather."

"No, I don't think so. They both wanted us all back home by noon tomorrow."

"With all this rain, though, I bet they are staying there tonight."

"I wish I could phone them to check things out, but Erin has the only house key. There isn't an extra one hidden anywhere out here that I know of."

"I'm sure everyone is okay but I'm not leaving you alone now, that's for sure. My apartment is across town. You can phone your parents from there."

"But I'd better wait here for Erin."

"I'm sure she's found a place to stay. Somewhere. You shouldn't worry about her. She'll be fine." Jon helped her out of the car.

"The battle of wits has already begun, I see."

"What?" From the slight haze of the nearby streetlight he could see the slow upward curve of Desiree's mouth. He hummed a quiet sigh.

"Oh, nothing. But I'd still like to be here when she returns. Let's break a window. I'll pay Aunt Julia for a new one."

Without hesitation Jon walked along the side of the house and smashed a small basement window with his foot.

"Hey!! What are you two doing there?" A deep, unfamiliar voice startled Desiree and she turned around to see a tall uniformed policeman approaching. His steps were long and quick.

"I'm locked out, sir," she said nervously as she scraped the edge of her shoe on the wet sidewalk.

"Are you the Bjornsons?"

"I'm Desiree Bjornson. This is my Aunt Julia's house. My parents and I are staying here for the weekend but they drove her to the cabin early this morning and I can't find my sister who has the only extra key and ..."

A car door slammed shut. Desiree turned towards the street so Erin could see her. But it wasn't Erin. Instead, a heavyset policeman was nearing them, his large head held straight and his gloved hands kept at his sides. Desiree didn't care for his cool manner.

"Would somebody please tell me what's going on?" She was exhausted and her fearful voice, now faint and squeaky, denoted impatience.

"Miss. There was a motor vehicle accident an hour or so ago and we're …"

"An accident? Where? We didn't see any accident tonight. What happened?"

The officer stepped forward. "Miss …" His bass voice was somewhat softer, but just as pleading. "It was a serious accident and we're trying to locate the next of kin."

"Mom and Dad? Aunt Julia? My sister? Tell me!!" She clutched Jon's arm for support.

"Erin Marie Bjornson. We're trying to locate her next of kin. Can you help us?"

Next of kin. Next of kin. The words resounded in Desiree's mind like an old blow horn being used at a sports arena. "Erin. Where's Erin? Where's my sister?"

"Dead on arrival, miss. The other vehicle made a left turn in front of her. Must have been doing at least eighty miles an hour. And in that horrid weather, she didn't have a chance."

"But we've been driving all over the city tonight looking for her. We didn't see any accident anywhere. There was a roadblock on some downtown street, but we both thought it was because of construction. We couldn't see anything that looked like … Jon!"

Jon quickly pulled the heavier policeman aside while the other offered to contact her parents for them, but Desiree insisted that she do it herself. The uniformed pair left within a few moments.

Once inside the house, however, she smelled the lingering sweetness of marijuana in the air, and all strength escaped Desiree.

"It's all my fault, Jon. If only I had gone to the cabin with them today instead of to Todd's party with her. And how am I going to tell Mom and Dad?"

Jon sat beside her in the tiny cluttered living room and tightly held her cold, shaking hands. He knew the policemen should have made that particular phone call, but it was too late for that now. Later, while making coffee in the kitchen, he fumbled through every messy drawer and cupboard until he found a dog-eared personal directory. He reached for the wall phone.

"No, Jon. Thanks. This is something I must do myself."

Reluctantly he gave her the phone and watched intently as she jerked the numbers on the dial.

"Mom?" Her throat tightened. The few words spoken were jumbled. Dark mascara streaked her cheeks. Shortly, she let Jon take the phone.

Chapter Two

The day after the accident Desiree had been sent home, alone, via the Greyhound bus. Her mother did not want any help in packing Erin's belongings. Aunt Julia had been asked to get some sturdy cardboard boxes and her father had been instructed to take everything to the Salvation Army afterwards. As the crowded bus rolled along the newly paved highway, Desiree often caught herself hugging the old leather satchel she had snuck out of her sister's bedroom. Inside was an almost-full bottle of Chanel No. 5, seven LPs, a few 45s and *Valley of the Dolls*—her sister's prize possessions. And all the way home, one song echoed in her mind…"Turn! Turn! Turn!"

Alone for the next few days, long moments of anger, denial, and erratic streaks of an unusual hatred rarely waned to any degree of peace for Desiree, despite her efforts to keep busy by concentrating on her music students and extending some lessons by another fifteen minutes or so. She had already talked for endless hours over the phone with her friend, Lynda, and had stitched hems on another suit jacket or skirt or dress that she had created while the same record played over and over again on the hi-fi. She thought she could now hear a few tiny skips in the Rolling Stones' hit, "Time Is on My

Side". She had also brought out her oil paints and easel from an old cupboard in the basement, having sorted out some particular tubes of color before placing them on top of her corner dresser. Desiree found it disheartening to know that she had been excluded from planning any part of Erin's funeral. Apparently, her parents had made all the preparations over the phone from Aunt Julia's. They would all be arriving back home just in time to freshen up and change clothes before going to the ceremony that next day.

Desiree had often questioned her parents' Christian beliefs, and lately she was even doubting her own. She felt that her mother and her father somehow needed the calming comfort of their church's beautiful surroundings, the themes of various sermons by the aging pastor, and the comradeship of others when helping to decorate the huge dining room for a specific event. To her it seemed they felt God only surrounded them, or anyone, within the confines of their church. But isn't God ubiquitous, omnipresent? And isn't it the particular calling of every preacher around the world to drill that belief into his own congregation's consciousness?

Since she could remember, Desiree had regularly sensed a divine serenity within her own self, wherever she was. She didn't have to be in church, or anywhere in particular, or perhaps dressed a certain way or on her knees, praying, to sense that soft consolation. It was simply there. She could actually feel it. Her sister had often teased her about that *special* feeling, suggesting perhaps that it was just her *imaginary friend* from childhood who had been keeping her safe all this length of time. Was it that simple, though? No, it was definitely more than that to Desiree—a spiritual connection of some kind. She just couldn't properly explain it.

It was different now, she realized, of course. Her only sister had died in a car accident that should not have ever happened and would not have ever happened if Desiree hadn't … Time, however, was not strengthening the lonely blonde. Relentless disbelief still tugged at Desiree's heart, leaving her sleepless, hopeless, and almost helpless at times, even when praying. Her mind could only envision the light-colored casket at the front of the church as a decorative stand on which to exhibit Erin's most recent diploma, graduation photo, and, of course, that white leather Bible that was her parents' last gift to their adopted daughter. There was no comfort in her present awareness, and Desiree wondered how everything would proceed the next time she was in the neighborhood church.

A huge, bright rainbow, its distinct arc crowning a thick grove of old poplars in the distance, had graced the deepening lavender haze of the late summer sky as she entered the church. Inside, friends, coeds, old neighbors, new neighbors, and almost the entire Sunday's usual congregation shuffled around the rich oak coffin that had been wheeled down the center aisle just before the commemoration. Despite the usual almost-memorized ceremony intoned in the pastor's slow baritone voice, Desiree felt an exceptionally deep warmth inside the chapel, and she often looked around, hoping to perhaps find out why, having to remind herself that she was at her own sister's funeral. It had been years since her sister had last attended any regular Sunday sermon or special event the church might be hosting, but now, sitting in the front pew between her mother and her aunt, Desiree sensed an extra something special, something almost comforting in the air, not the usual sadness or regret which funerals automatically brought. To Desiree it was almost indescribable.

She had never before seen her mother cry, but just as the coffin was to be closed and wheeled outside, Mae Bjornson stepped away from that front pew, walked over to the coffin, bent down, and gently kissed Erin's forehead. Then, after placing a perfect long-stemmed red rose onto the crossed arms, a single tear fell from her cheek. Desiree could almost envision the tiniest of rainbows bursting onto the glossy white satin.

At the ceremony's conclusion, to Desiree's pleasant surprise, the congregation's young organist played an impressive rendition of Erin's favorite song by The Beatles, "Let It Be". Aunt Julia must have mentioned that to her brother, perhaps insisting that it be played sometime that afternoon. "Good for you, Aunt Julia," Desiree whispered as the family was being guided out of the front pew.

And now, pressing the long, heartfelt telegram from Lynda against her bosom, Desiree studied each bouquet of roses and every assortment of carnations, chrysanthemums, lilies, and baby's breath that now filled the Bjornsons' small living room. Such fragrant beauty was a rarity in their house and the lonely teen was held in the hushed reverence. She had been to only one other funeral. Her Uncle William had died of cancer when she was four years old and today all she could remember about the whole affair was that she never saw him again, and never got to ride the horses anymore because Aunt Julia had moved to the city shortly afterwards.

Finally, Desiree realized that her mother's unusual smooth activity that week was a complete façade. Even as the guests bade their farewells to the family with tears of sadness and whispers of consolation, Mae Bjornson stood tall, her eyes sober, her hands steady. Signs of her weakening restraint became apparent only when she was preparing for bed.

"Aspirins would be better for me tonight." There was a slight strain in her mother's voice when a glass of cold water was put onto the wooden nightstand. "I just have a small headache, Desiree. I don't need these sleeping pills. You should know that I'll be given *special* strength for the days to come."

Desiree. She was starting to hate that name. She had so many questions for her mother now. *Oh, Mom. Are you blaming me for all this? Are you mentally preparing your God punishes the sinful speech for me later? But isn't He punishing us all? Not just me, Mom. You and Dad, Erin's friends, and our friends are hurting, too—all of them, all of us. And I don't know why.* As she lightly kissed her mother's forehead, Desiree thought she saw a fine streak of gray in those thinning cocoa-brown tresses.

In the short hallway Desiree eyed the bare walls that were once filled with various family mementos. Her favorite had been a small collage of snaps that she and her sister had taken inside the twenty-five cent photo booth in the downtown Woolworth's store the week before Erin moved away to college. Now shaky fingers slid along the wall, and tears were somehow held back as Desiree poured three cups of coffee before sitting across the kitchen table from Jon and her father. She wished she had taken a couple of those sleeping pills herself. Or three. Maybe four.

"Desiree, what should we do with all these lovely flowers? I wish we could keep them, but you know Mother's allergies are already affected."

"She's quite remarkable, isn't she, Dad?" The words had been forced out of her mouth and she thought perhaps too quickly, almost sarcastically. Wanting to hide her disdain, she took a tiny sip from her cup and tilted her head slightly to improve her peripheral vision. She could still see her father nodding his head.

And usually Christian Bjornson would pop two sugar cubes into his mouth and noisily sip the hot drink as deep lines furrowed above his gold-rimmed glasses. But tonight, instead, he dropped four cubes into his cup, stirring them methodically, never lifting the drink to his lips, as he watched his daughter fingering the thick handle of the cream container. Again he noticed the many similarities between his wife and youngest daughter—not at all concerning their physical features but undoubtedly in their sure and quiet inner strengths.

"Maybe you could all go on a vacation next week. Get away from here for a while."

"Jon!! How can you think like that right now?"

A long quiet moment held each of them.

"Desiree, it's okay," her father finally replied. "I think Jon has the right idea. Something like that would be good for us all. But it just might be too soon to …"

Jon poured more cream into his coffee and, ignoring the tiny spoon beside his cup, stirred it with his index finger. "I think next week would be perfect. I have access to my parents' apartment in Vancouver. It's a beautiful city this time of year and I know it would be the ideal retreat that you all need. My parents use it regularly for their own seclusion but they'll be in New York City for another three weeks so you can stay there as long as you want."

"A week, perhaps?"

"Father!!!" She tipped over the creamer when turning to face him and spilled its last drops into her saucer. Desiree got a dishrag from under the sink and as she sopped up the mess, she noticed his azure eyes misting again, his thin lips quivering. She had to keep quiet. She had to try to somehow endure the present situation.

Turn! Turn! Turn!

Christian took off his glasses and set them on the crisp white doily in front of him while Desiree pulled her chair closer to the table and leaned on her elbows.

"You wouldn't be imposing on anyone, sir. Honest. Now, when should I tell the resident manager there that you would be arriving?"

"Let me think a little longer about that, Jon. Please. I just want to be sure."

❧

The huge cumulus clouds had appeared so light and fluffy from the ground that early autumn morning as Desiree boarded the plane, but now they looked like massive icebergs. She was fascinated at the smooth ride. The plane hadn't crashed into the clouds as she had first thought it would, but she realized too late that she shouldn't have told Jon about this being her very first flight. She was wounded at his obvious disbelief and found it difficult to ignore his constant watch over her as they shuffled down the narrow aisle of the plane and nestled into their seats. She could still sense those piercing ebony eyes focused on her.

"This is your very first flight and your parents have let it be with me. That is just so odd."

Surprise rang in his voice but she had so much more that she needed to tell him. She feared that a crying episode might erupt if she opened her mouth for even a sip of pop from the bottle she had just accepted from the strikingly tall stewardess. She fingered the smooth rim instead. She still didn't know how to tell Jon the whole truth. What her mother had said about him just wasn't fair. Even now her mother's voice, her particular choice of words, and that slight quivering of her thin lips which was so obvious when something important was about to be said, replayed in Desiree's mind ... "You know you'd better watch yourself," her mother had started. "Being alone with Jon, I mean. Your father seems to trust you about that, so I guess I should too." A pout had distorted her lips and Mae Bjornson bowed her head for a moment before continuing. "Because Jon is not one of us, as you are well aware, I don't think it is proper for you to tell anyone that we are letting you go alone to an unfamiliar city with a total stranger. No one in the church or the neighborhood has to know anything about this trip, do they, Desiree?"

The blonde teen took a tiny sip before shifting her body in the narrow seat of the plane. She mumbled something to Jon about her mother's weak heart and absolute fear of flying.

Jon gave her a twisted smile. "And you want me to believe that that's the reason your parents aren't with us now? Your father specifically asked for a different flight because he didn't want your mother to feel embarrassed in front of me?" There was a hint of confusion in his low deep voice.

"Yes, Jon. That's the only reason my parents aren't with us now." She had forced the words out of her dry mouth. "You just assumed we'd all be flying here together and ..." *Together. Together.* She could no longer comprehend what that word truly meant, and again, as intense as ever, thoughts of Erin were spinning a dark, heavy web of guilt in her mind. She pinched the worn piping of the armrest. Of course her mother didn't want another reminder that Erin was gone. That's why Jon was sitting there instead, despite her mother's lack of trust. Her father had purposefully engineered this entire affair. Desiree was to blame for all this. Yes, she had killed her own sister. "We always drove on our vacations, taking our time, stopping to see various landmarks or historical sites," she started to explain, her voice soft with remorse. "We stayed in nice motels, too, and no one ever questioned our means of travel. Not even Erin."

Erin. Erin. You were so beautiful. No, you preferred the word stunning. And you were stunning. Twisting the ivory good luck horn on the thin gold necklace, a graduation present from her sister, Desiree felt the warmth of Jon's large hand squeezing her elbow and she remained silent as the plane soared over the mountains.

Her travel partner found it very difficult to believe that this was her very first plane ride. Jon had been flying long before he could walk. Anticipating the short time they would be alone that day, he had taken careful detail in planning their activities. Desiree was an enigma, a rare find that he wanted all for himself, and his continued vivid imagery kindled him to the very core. How was he going to weave their relationship into a priceless tapestry? Perhaps he should initiate the first change—in himself. It need only be slight. Yes, he could do it! After playing with a long tress of blonde hair at her temple, he carefully tucked it behind her ear.

She looked up at him with sad round eyes, and said, "I'm sorry, Jon."

Ohh, those eyes—the palest blue he had ever seen, lighter than an early morning sky. He leaned closer, softly kissed her quivering mouth, and instantly felt the penetrating warmth. But she soon pulled away from him and looked out the window again. No girl had ever passed up his kiss. Not one. Desiree intrigued him. He wondered just how long she would play out this little game of coyness. How could she resist his new persona, his almost-boyish perceptiveness? How long would her prudence last then? The wait might be fun. And he would wait. It really shouldn't be long.

Near the luggage carousels after a perfectly smooth landing, Desiree called her parents as promised while Jon rented a car. She was pleased to hear that a neighbor had taken her mother shopping after treating her to a country-style breakfast at the White Spot.

"I'm glad that she's keeping busy, Dad."

"And I'm wondering, now, why I let you go alone to a strange city with a man we all have just met. This is a time when the entire family should be together."

"And we will be, Dad. Tonight." Silently she too had questioned her father's unusual liberty, managing somehow to suppress her surprise and finally accepting it as an extreme act of consolation by a very saddened man. "I know you both are going to love it here. And the flight was awesome. Please let Mom know."

"We'll be looking for you and Jon at the airport. Flight 519, remember?"

"Of course, Dad. See you then."

The mid-morning sunlight was pale over the snow-capped peaks of the mountains, but because the fresh air was wonderfully warm, Jon rented a Mustang convertible, candy apple red with a white interior. Desiree had never dreamed of such luxury. The top was soon down and he helped her inside as a sweet, almost impish smile curved his lips. Passersby did a few double takes as they shifted their bodies onto the white leather seats.

She knew Jon's summer tan and striking good looks exemplified the jet set and together, perhaps, they exuded the Ken and Barbie doll image, living the perfect life. This trip was truly exciting and it would be unforgettable. "California Dreaming", by The Mamas and Papas, was blaring from the dashboard as Desiree undid the loose navy bandana from her forehead, shook her head purposefully, and let her long tresses blow freely in the light September wind. Beyond the gray asphalt of the airport, the trillion shades of green that SW Marine Drive displayed all along its scenic route captivated her. Jon seemed content to be absorbed in his own thoughts.

He tried to understand her youthful excitement but his mind was buzzing with questions and he wanted some answers. To play his own game properly he realized that he had to be cautious, patient, and gentle, but he thought he had waited long enough for its initiation. They were approaching Burrard Street and the heavy morning traffic was slowing down somewhat. Maybe now was the right time.

"What kind of job will you be looking for soon?" he asked finally, his tone slightly serious. The game had started. *CHANGES*, he decided to call it. And it was Desiree's play now.

"Oh, I don't know. Secretarial, I guess. I want to go to university next year, majoring in music, but I'd like to have some money saved up to help pay the tuition. Mom and Dad can't afford much of it."

"What instrument do you play? The piano?" He had noticed an old upright in their living room.

"Yes. I've just started to teach beginner students at home this year but some day I'd like to be a concert pianist." She saw the glitter deepen in Jon's dark eyes and she smiled with a rare look of satisfaction as she gently touched his hand. "How 'bout you?"

Shivers were running up his arm and down each rib, warming his insides. He loved this game, *CHANGES.* "I'm working on the rigs for just another year. The money's good. I plan to be an accountant some day. The folks have offered to pay my entire tuition if I become an architect like my father but I don't need their money or their interference."

"I'd like to meet your parents some day."

"No, you wouldn't."

Desiree didn't understand the sudden bitterness in his voice and she twisted her body for more comfort. "Why not?" she asked softly.

"Because they're both snobs. I can put up with my father most of the time but Mother is almost unbearable with her silly tea parties, her art exhibits, her fashion shows. And only the upper echelon is invited, of course. You know the kind. Just her damned fuss about anything and everything would drive you to insanity. She flaunts her power." Both hands gripped the steering wheel now. No, he would not allow that way of life to be any part of his ever again.

He had started to weaken. Damn!! This was supposed to be *his* game. And it was *his* turn again. How could he let disturbing memories influence his stratagem? Determined to win, he corrected the angle of the rearview mirror before continuing. "My mother's inheritance completely paid for the house that Father designed. They tore down the old three-story mansion that was originally on the property and had their own house built in its place."

Thoughts of their differing lifestyles suddenly disturbed Desiree. She had to learn more. "Why do you still live at home if you are so against your folks?"

"I only stay there when I'm taking special summer courses in town because it's hard to find a nice furnished apartment to rent for just two months or so, and I don't like bothering my friends. Besides, that way I can save more money for all the things I want in life."

She was almost afraid to ask. "And what exactly is it that you want in life?"

"Oh, nothing out of the ordinary, really. A house something like Todd's would be super, although I'd hate to have to keep up that beautiful yard in the warmer months, or shovel that long sidewalk in the wintertime."

"That's almost normal to dream about." She herself still had that dream.

"The Cadillac of cabin cruisers would have to come after that. And then, of course, a new Corvette." He shifted gears and turned the corner. "What does your boyfriend think of this whole arrangement?"

Not wanting to reveal too much to Jon that morning, at the nearing red light she purposely focused on the shrubs of different shapes, textures, and colors growing in one corner estate. The gorgeous blue shades of the hydrangea plants scattered throughout the massive yard mesmerized her. The large round clusters of beauty were breathtaking. She could not remember seeing blue flowers so big before—only the tiny wild bluebells along farmers' fields back home.

"What does your boyfriend think about this arrangement," Jon repeated.

"What arrangement?"

"What boyfriend?" was the answer he had wanted. "You and me together this entire week. How's he feel about it?"

She leaned forward and stretched her back. "You're really loaded with some deep questions today, aren't you?"

"I just wanna know. You can take your time telling me. You know, we have a few hours to spare."

His quick smile let her mind go back to her high school years, when a few male friends from church had taken her bowling occasionally, or horseback riding. There wasn't a *boyfriend* to talk about—never had been, and couldn't be until she was eighteen years old. Just another month and five days to go, but then what? She suddenly wasn't sure any more as certain events of her graduation ceremonies last May popped up vividly in her imagination... An hour before the graduation dinner was scheduled, Robert Marks, donned in a navy pinstriped tuxedo, had picked her up in his father's 1964 Chevrolet Impala and proudly admitted to having spent a good portion of that same morning hand-waxing and polishing it. There was a tiny clear-plastic box in his shaky hands, and after struggling to get the silvery-white orchid out of its wrapping he somehow was able to pin the exotic flower onto the bodice of her midnight-blue satin gown.

"Don't forget that Cinderella has to be home by midnight," her mother had stated firmly from the front steps as Robert was helping his pretty partner into the car.

The dinner was held in the school's large cafeteria with its every support beam and ugly beige wall temporarily decorated with pastel-colored crepe paper crocuses and hummingbirds, a sure sign of spring. That was the graduation theme—signs of new things to come. And, as expected, Robert's natural charm comforted Desiree all during the sit-down meal. Later they both wanted to stay for the dance that was being held in the school's gymnasium, but … Instead, they changed clothes at his parents' home, just blocks from the school, and spent the rest of their evening together at a newly-opened roller skating rink where hand in hand they glided in their ill-fitting skates over the shiny hardwood floor. And, about fifteen minutes past the stroke of midnight Robert brought his beautiful escort back home. He then put both hands around her tiny waist and drew her closer to him. His mouth opened slightly as he bent his head. The kiss was long and soft. It was her first, and she liked it … But they were just friends. Good friends. And she wanted it to stay that way. Then, after waving back to Robert as he drove off she tiptoed inside. The hallway light flickered off immediately and she could hear her parents' bedroom door close.

As Jon shifted gears and sped around a corner, Desiree's body slid against the door and she wondered if that was his silent way of announcing his growing impatience with her. Yes, she had been reminiscing—purposely stalling—but was it beyond common courtesy? She undid one more button to her new denim jacket and turned to face Jon.

"I honestly don't have a boyfriend," she finally admitted.

Well, he thought, *she is going to talk to me after all.* "So, I'm not in any trouble?"

She giggled, relieved that her announcement had been taken so casually. "But you and I aren't going to be alone here for much longer, you know." She felt out of breath for some reason, and paused before continuing. "Now, what does your girlfriend think about this trip here with me?"

"I don't have a girlfriend. I mean, not a steady." His reply had been instant. "No girl likes to wait a month or so for a date and my job doesn't give me much choice most times. And there aren't many women that far north." He shifted gears again.

Desiree had had mixed emotions about going to the coast alone with Jon. She wasn't altogether sure about his intentions or about her own power of restraint during their time together but her insight was guiding her now, letting her enjoy an unexpected sensitive side to his somewhat arrogant nature.

"Stanley Park is just up ahead. We still have some time to spare," Jon offered quietly.

They spent a good part of an hour walking through the rather crowded aquarium where, in Jon's slight hurry, his gentle pushing of some playful toddlers just in front of them almost caused a scene. But he had other things on his mind. He wanted to be elsewhere without being too obvious about it.

Because the park's Tea House, one of his favorite restaurants, was booked for the rest of the day, they stayed in line at a concession stand near the outdoor swimming pool, now closed for the season. Jon carefully reshuffled the English-style fries and thick hamburgers, loaded with various extras and condiments, in the paper bag given him and under the shade of a tall lone pine tree just off the main path they ate in silence, satisfied, before continuing their leisure walk. Beyond breaks in the vast greenery around them several rusty freighters and countless sailboats dappled the calm, blue water of English Bay.

They sauntered down a narrow moss-covered path through some low prickly bushes and around neglected deadwood to a picturesque secluded opening. Desiree twirled around and the soft flowing curls of her flaxen hair fanned out perfectly before resting on her shoulders. She smiled in awe. A pale golden haze from the mid-afternoon's sun filtered through the sylvan beauty and cast a soft sheen onto the velvet grass beneath them.

The gentle swaying of lofty evergreens and the thick moist carpet of grass were inviting, but anticipation was teasing Jon. His own desire for change was testing him.

They were totally alone, finally, except for a plump goose and her young family of six. Desiree smiled as she watched the goslings waddling hurriedly in single file and in perfect rhythm towards a tiny pond nearby. At its edge the little ones scurried about, cheeping, as if waiting for their mother to join them. Soon tiny ripples and bobbing heads broke the water's stillness while floating cones, tiny broken twigs, and a variety of leaves, now shriveled and discolored, stirred in their play.

Jon had walked the short distance to an old, forgotten bench. The hacked wood, splattered with various-colored bird droppings, had yielded to years of damp exposure. A front leg had broken and the bench tilted to one side. He covered its seat with the extra paper napkins that Desiree had pulled from the metal container when waiting for their order at the booth. She had insisted they keep them for later. Pleased now that he hadn't disposed of them somewhere along their walk, he sat down, checked the seat's sturdiness, and spread his long legs wide. And he let Desiree be. She was at the pond now, whispering to the goslings. For some reason her nearness hadn't scared them away. She was feeding the chicks, tossing them something she had picked up at the water's edge while the mother stayed nearby but aloof. Desiree totally surprised him in so many different ways like no one else ever had.

Purposely bending her body just enough to look as if she were searching for something, she had been watching him instead. When Jon was spreading those thick paper napkins onto the crooked bench she noticed how his hard, bronzed body so perfectly filled those faded blue jeans and tight white T-shirt, and her entire body warmed. She knew he had been watching her all this time, and she wondered what he was thinking as he sat there. She decided that it had been so different earlier, and much easier, riding in the Mustang with him. The console obviously had been her safety net, separating them subtly from their individual wants and lusts. He was standing now, stretching his long, hard arms towards the sky, and she found it difficult to stay still, to pretend to be occupied with other things.

"Oh, how am I going to find the strength I need to handle all these new sensations and every thought I'm having about you, Jon?" she asked herself, looking up high above the trees for a moment before she approached him.

Growing along the nearby pathway was a lone aster, still thriving, its velvety white petals perfectly curled. Jon pricked off a single stem and carefully placed it in Desiree's hair. He looked at her for a long moment before singing the lyrics to "A Whiter Shade of Pale ", a current hit by Procol Harum. "These petals are as light as your eyes," he whispered. And he loved how she bent her head and smiled shyly, letting him take her hand and guide her back to the main walkway, crowded now with wide-eyed tourists or unhurried locals.

Since elementary school Desiree felt she had been ruthlessly teased about the lack of color in her big round eyes. *Icicle Eyes* had been her nickname for as long as she could remember. But in what seemed like a split second, Jon's deep, smooth bass voice had erased all those moments of ridicule.

"What about marriage?" Jon asked softly after picking a ladybug from her hair and shaking it off his finger.

"Pardon?" He had taken her by surprise and she straightened her shoulders.

"Don't you plan to get married some day?" Curiosity was urging him to ask.

"Of course. Some day. But it would have to be after university and only after I have met the right guy." She was trying not to give herself away with hasty words.

"Haven't met him yet, huh?" Smiling, Jon gently touched her chin.

Yes, yes, yes, her heart was saying. "Maybe I have. Maybe I haven't," she said softly, hoping the topic would soon change. With high school behind her, so many options were available, and she wanted to take her time.

"How about kids? I suppose that you would like three or four, huh?" He took her hand but she quickly pulled it away.

"Hey! What's wrong?" He watched her lean, tanned body step away and a pressing realization slowly deepened its hold within. He was still playing the game *CHANGES,* but somehow the other participant wasn't playing by the rules. He had not expected this. He started running towards her.

"Desiree, I'm so sorry for upsetting you," he began as soon as they were side by side again. "I had no idea that I was asking you such a sensitive question."

"You asked me if I wanted to have any kids and I have to honestly answer that by saying I would prefer to adopt." She spoke flatly, not particularly wanting to divulge her faulty genetic background to him just then. "I think there are too many orphans in this crazy world," she continued, trying to erase her deepening melancholy.

"You're right about that." He straightened the drooping flower in her hair before continuing. "And you know somethin'? I'd like to adopt, too. That way I'd know for sure that my first child would be a girl."

She looked up at him, quite bewildered. *Most couples prefer a son,* she thought. *A son they could call James Allen Matthew, perhaps—a son, who could continue the family business. A son, who could keep the family name. A son, who could ... Jam. Jam. Why haven't you called me that for so long, Mom?* "Why a girl first, Jon?" she finally asked.

"It's a long and strange story about my grandfather's will. I'll tell you about it some day. But let's go to the apartment now and freshen up. We can relax there for a while before having to go back to the airport to pick up your folks." In the verdant splendor she let him take her hand and as they walked back to the car the one vivid thought of finally being alone with Desiree played in his mind.

The telephone started to ring as Jon set the suitcases against the paneled wall of the side foyer. "Look around if you want. I'll only be a few minutes."

He hadn't told her that his parents owned the entire apartment complex. Nor had he described the penthouse suite. The elevator opened directly into their abode. Desiree's wide eyes swept across the huge Chippendale dining room and then the low armchairs of peach cotton chintz that caught the natural light from the greenhouse-sized windows of the living room. She walked into the long, narrow kitchen and touched the thick marble counter of rich dark green. The solarium-style room, with its exterior wall of amber glass block and floor of dark quarry tile, had tall cacti in polished brass planters decorating one corner. She also studied the opposite area with its dark oak billiards table covered in thick hunter green felt, and suddenly thoughts of a particular evening long ago came to mind.

"I don't know who was on the phone. They hung up just when I answered it," Jon stated as he watched Desiree pick up the cue ball. She was holding it gently, as if it were a priceless jeweled ball. "Could I interest you in a game?" he asked.

"Oh, no. I'd be no competition for you."

"Don't play much at home, I guess, hey?"

"There's only a ping pong table allowed downstairs."

"*Allowed* downstairs. What do you mean by that? Billiards is a good game."

"And we'll all go to hell for playing it." Her own uttered thoughts surprised her. She wondered why her mind was focusing so vividly on that evening when she first brought her parents over to Lynda's, when her mother reluctantly had gone downstairs to their games room for a try at snooker. But why should thoughts like this now come to her mind?

"And we'll all go to hell for playing snooker?" Jon's wide eyes were like black agates. "Whoever said that to you?"

"Oh, it shouldn't matter, Jon. And I didn't mean to …"

"Erin's free spirit must have helped her cope with all the restrictions at home. Obviously! No wonder she moved out right after high school." Noticing his attractive guest's wide shoulders stiffen and her suntanned face tighten, Jon realized how insensitive he had been. Again. Somehow he'd have to change the mood. "Would you like to see the other rooms?" he whispered a few moments later.

"Oh, not yet, Jon. These three are quite enough to relish for now. I really would like to take a quick bath, though."

After placing her suitcases in the corner bedroom, Jon showed her to the main bathroom and set the Jacuzzi timer for twenty minutes. He handed her a large, thick towel from the wide open-shelved closet before he stepped out of the room. A short time later he shouted from the living room. "Would you like me to rub your back?"

Her pulse suddenly quickened. "Don't you dare!" She loved the soothing spurts exploding from the jets and decided that if she stayed in the water just a little bit longer there wouldn't be any time left before they'd have to leave for the airport. *How are you doing, Mom? Is the flight smooth like the one Jon and I had this morning? I like flying. I wish you did, too.*

From the glass-enclosed balcony Jon eyed the night's softening stillness over nearby Kitsalano Beach. He could see the waves crashing against the rocky shore of Lighthouse Park, across the way, while the gurgling of water continued from the other end of the apartment. And the bathroom lock was being checked again. He chuckled, realizing that all this was a totally new experience for Desiree. He must remember that.

It wouldn't be long before they would be together, completely alone, for a few more hours and she would be his. He was going to be her first, and he grinned with anticipation when he eyed the hall archway and saw her brushing her silky length of hair. In the soft blue sundress that enhanced her golden tan she was truly the girl from Ipanema—so beautiful, so poised, so close. He loved the flow of the thick blonde curls along her back.

The intoxication was enveloping Desiree, now so mindful of her unusually flirtatious desires, so unaware of Jon's hidden excitement. She turned around and slowly walked across the room where she looked at the wall clock in front of her and lit up one of his cigarettes.

"I didn't know you smoked," he stated.

"Just once in awhile." She had never smoked before in her life. She was starting to choke.

"Just when you're nervous, hey?" *Ohh, any minute now,* he thought. *Any minute.*

She wondered if all men were like Jon. Was he watching her now turn crimson? Did she really want to know? When she finally looked over and saw his dark dreamy eyes fixed on her she was caught in the quiet harmony, and soon her total existence, every ounce of her being, dissolved into a beautiful purple warmth.

The phone rang again but Jon didn't want to answer it. He remained on the settee, still and quiet, mesmerized by the aura of the beautiful young lady in front of him. But as the ringing persisted he finally leaned forward.

"Maybe your parents' flight has been delayed a bit," he whispered, slowly picking up the phone. "Hello." His curious eyes stayed on her as he shifted his weight, holding the phone with both hands.

Desiree wondered who was on the line keeping him so silently engaged. She approached him slowly with open arms but he turned away, and seconds later he let the phone drop into its cradle. A disturbed look filmed his eyes now and he slouched towards the dining room. Wide veins on both wrists bulged as he clasped his large hands behind his back.

"What's wrong?" she asked. "Who was that on the phone?"

"Your father." Jon's voice was weak and he turned to face her but his focus remained on the carpet.

"My father? Why would he be phoning here and getting you so upset? Jon! What's wrong? Tell me!"

"Your mother has had a stroke." He looked at her and saw the anguish and shock in her eyes. His lips quivered as he continued. "Your father said that she was a bit tired after coming home from shopping, so she had a long nap. But later as she was talking on the phone with a good friend of Erin's she suddenly fell to the floor. She gave no warning whatsoever. She just dropped to the floor. Your father was with her and the ambulance arrived quickly. She'll be in the hospital for some time, though. Apparently she's paralyzed on her right side. Her right cheek is sunken and she's having trouble talking. But the doctors are almost certain that the paralysis will be temporary."

Desiree fainted.

Chapter Three

The pale opalescent orb of a nearby streetlight broke the darkness of the living room, where Desiree knelt in front of the old leather recliner and felt her father's cold dry hands. In the muted tight embrace a rush of tears moistened his shoulder.

Mae Bjornson's recovery had been steady because her absolute determination to recuperate quickly and perfectly had granted her an early release from the hospital. Her speech was almost understandable at times and, through extensive therapy and unflagging attention from various caregivers, she was soon able to stand up by herself. With help she could already take a few tiny steps before weakening.

And never before had Christian seemed interested in his home's décor or ambiance, having gratefully accepted whatever he noticed. But during his wife's short stay in the hospital, Christian had become a changed man. Already, he had scheduled a professional crew of carpenters, painters, and a complete maid service to renovate the entire interior of the house—upstairs and down. And he liked what he saw. All the carpets were now thick and soft. The walls were all fresh with the pale colors of an early spring. And every appliance, light fixture, or household gadget sparkled.

Gone were the lingering fumes from the old gas stove, which Mae refused to replace with an electric one, because her husband had purchased an entire case of aerosol air fresheners in various floral fragrances. Hidden from view throughout the house, he would squirt the stale air whenever the moment prompted him and, as Mae's allergies were not affected at all by the different aromas, several baskets and bouquets of colorful silk flowers soon decorated their home. "If Mae can't enjoy the real thing, the least I can do is give her the best substitute," he once admitted to another neighbor who had dropped by.

Making the house comfortable for his family was very important to him now, and, trying not to burden his daughter with any extra responsibilities, after he rushed home from work he tried to be available for his wife by bringing her everything she needed. The money kept in a special metal box above the refrigerator was almost depleted. Their dream vacation to Oslo, Norway, Christian's birthplace, might have to be cancelled, or at least postponed, even though it had long been planned as a celebration of their twenty-fifth wedding anniversary. Already Christian's thinning gray hair had whitened, and he had had to cinch his favorite leather belt tighter again that morning.

Guilt often nipped at Desiree's consciousness. Even at her sewing machine, when taking in her father's pants another inch at the waistline, her concentration was disrupted by gloomy visions of his many teary moments. Again, he had tried to get his wife to take one more step forward, but she couldn't. And he had seen his daughter watching him quickly wiping his face. He would soon retreat into his den down the hall, and would still be there when all the house lights were turned off hours later. The saddened blonde was quickly learning that her father's privacy was an absolute need, not a whimsical desire. It seemed that overnight his freedom had been stolen from him, because of Mae's extra needs, Jon's regular visits, and her own extended teaching hours. Yes, her father was finally letting her teach piano in the evenings, having decided to critique essays or correct exam papers in the school library, or in his own classroom at lunchtime, or during any class break. Before then the den at home had been his working domain, where the *Do Not Disturb* sign so often had been draped over the outside knob, when no one nearby more than whispered.

Now her mother was taking physiotherapy in their living room. Its open space was big enough, and the walk downstairs to the large rumpus room was still too much for Mae to tackle, as the therapist had agreed. At two o'clock each workday afternoon the sessions started, and with her increasing number of students, Desiree sat in the upholstered chair near the piano, listening, guiding, and teaching another student, both just feet away from the exercise mat, the lumbar roll, and the therapist, while her mother occasionally winced as her legs, arms, and back were being pulled, twisted, and stretched beyond comfort.

Jon arrived each night just moments after the kitchen was cleaned up. After the second lesson of any given evening he usually found the discordance from that upright piano too much to bear, and he was quickly ready to help Mae put on her trench coat to go outside for another walk. The usual morning skim of snow had again melted away in the low October sun. The sidewalks were dry and safe by early evening, but the few tiny steps they managed beyond the front yard took more than an hour. By then, Desiree's last student had been sent home, Christian had locked the back door, and Mae was ready for bed.

Jon was pleasantly surprised at the freedom he was given in that tiny bungalow. No one questioned his presence, and he felt no rejection. He assumed his visits were just one of the many interruptions the Bjornsons realized they should get accustomed to. Taking Mae for those short walks was almost expected of him now, and he liked that. He felt comfortably included there, but he often wondered when he could have some time alone with Desiree. Her eyes were now like tarnished silver buttons, sunken from worry, and there was an ugly yellow tinge to her deep summer tan.

The morning was young and the street cleaners could be heard in the distance, but Desiree's tired, dry eyes were still open and her damp hands felt cold as she pulled the thick duvet over her entire body.

As sleep still forsook her, the flickering shadows of night giving her no solace, she forced herself to get up and don her thick, new terry robe. Putting on the matching slippers, she tiptoed out of her room and down the hall into the living room. Carefully she pulled open the new long drapes. Wanting to relax and enjoy some comfort, she sat on the new Beaujolais sofa and rubbed her long fingers over a cushion's smoothness as she stared out the wide front window, still so clean from its recent professional polishing. With the faint scent of rose air freshener lingering, some strange energy was rousing her. She looked around and shivered in the awareness. The living room lacked all familiar decoration now, like the main hallway, but after her mother's unusually slow and painful physiotherapy session that afternoon, Mae had obviously decided to display Erin's graduation portrait somewhere. It had arrived by special delivery earlier that week, packed carefully in thick corrugated cardboard, and now it was on the side table next to the Queen Anne chair by the front door. But what else was there, drawing Desiree's full attention to it, pulling her towards it with such a deepening eeriness?

Desiree's heartbeat quickened as she got up and walked to the table. She lovingly caressed the smooth gilded frame with her fingers, but she hesitated to reach for the item behind it. Desiree had seen that same plain box in Erin's dresser drawer the day before the accident. Inside it was Erin's white leather-bound Bible, her parents' graduation gift, given to her on the day of the awards ceremonies. And it was that very Bible that Mae had taken to the church and placed on Erin's folded arms. Amongst family and friends in the side room near the vestry, just before the coffin was wheeled out to the front of the main altar for the ceremony, she had gingerly picked it up and taken it with her to the front row seat.

Desiree leaned forward and stroked the box in front of her before going back to bed. She did not feel lonesome anymore.

But Jon's restlessness steadily grew as the weeks went by. He missed attending various sports activities and he was getting tired of his daily routine at the Bjornsons'. He felt quite fortunate one day, however, to have been given superb mid-field tickets to a football game between his favorite team and its nemesis. "Now, don't forget that I have fabulous tickets for the game tomorrow afternoon," he had whispered to Desiree that Saturday evening, after her parents had gone to bed and he was about to go home. "Be ready about two. Then we won't have to rush for anything."

Desiree had never been to a professional football game and her eyes glistened with anticipation. "Oh, yes. I'll be ready."

While driving home that particular night, because he had not been alone with Desiree for more than a few minutes since her mother's stroke and the evening piano lessons had started, Jon carefully planned the entire day ahead for just the two of them.

Awakening that next morning, just as the sparrows and starlings began their unique chorus from the lofty evergreens that brushed against the cedar-railed balcony of his bedroom, Jon took his time showering and shaving. Then, tucking in the Oleg Cassini shirt Desiree liked best, he tried to bide all the extra time he didn't have in his usual late awakenings by watching two black squirrels dash across the huge backyard and scamper into the corner garden of various shrubs of fading greens, rusts, yellows, and oranges. A magpie, perched on the edge of a branch in the Japanese maple, cawed loudly at their play.

When no one answered the doorbell at the Bjornson residence, Jon returned to his car. Behind the leather-wrapped steering wheel once again, he turned up the radio. The dials needed adjusting for a stronger base. Already he had driven his Austin Healy around the neighborhood in search of a corner store so he could buy a pack of cigarettes, and he almost hit an old tomcat that suddenly jumped from a neighbor's weeping willow.

Desiree still wasn't home, and the football game would be starting in half an hour. The stereo was blaring now, and Jon saw a neighbor peeking out of his front window because of the noise and steady beat. The defiant young man tried to increase the volume even more, but he couldn't.

Finally, when he saw the blue station wagon in his rearview mirror, he clicked off the radio, yanked at the keys, and got out of the car to get Desiree. His door slammed shut.

"Jon, I'm so sorry for being late. An old friend of Mom's is in town from San Francisco. Mr. Anderson invited us to lunch at the White Spot. I phoned you as soon as we got there, but I was told you had already left. And then, when we were just finishing off our desserts, Mom started getting sick. I had to try and rush her to the washroom. We just made it."

"Oh, that's too bad. But the game's already started. I don't want to waste any more time getting there."

"Help me get Mom into the house. Then we can go."

"But…" Jon hesitated momentarily, and then helped Desiree get Mae out of the car as Christian went to unlock the front door.

Jon's favorite team won by a last-minute converted touchdown, and he was pleased at Desiree's obvious attempt to understand the game.

Back at home, and thrilled with the afternoon's activities with Jon, Desiree started washing the dinner dishes while her parents sipped their usual cup of Earl Grey tea in the dining room.

"Jon can be a rather arrogant cad sometimes, can't he, dear?" There was an unusual cutting tone in her father's bass voice.

Desiree squeezed more dish soap from its plastic container and turned the hot water tap on full, letting the suds rise above the countertop.

"But he seems to have come from great wealth, doesn't he, darling?"

"Why would that interest you, Dad?" She turned to face him.

"Because he could take good care of you."

"You know he already does." The tap was quickly turned again. It was at times like this when Desiree wished she could just throw her parents a quick kiss, put on her wool cardigan, and take the usual two-block walk over to Lynda's to watch *Laugh In*, perhaps. Or maybe she could just stay in Lynda's blue denim bedroom and sit on her new queen-sized waterbed while listening to Roy Orbison, or any of her various Beatles' LPs. Or maybe, if they could stop laughing at each other for any length of time, some basic Yoga positions might be mastered… If she stayed in the kitchen for much longer, Desiree knew her father would insist that she join him in the den to watch that evening's TV special comparing the space walks of the two cosmonauts from the USSR and the USA. Later there was going to be a long documentary on the increasing deaths of American soldiers in Vietnam. She would have to watch that also.

"You're mumbling again, Desiree. I can't hear a word you are saying in there."

She let a ceramic platter drop onto the thinning layer of suds, and now her cotton blouse was wet. "Oh, never mind, Dad. It wasn't important." Maybe she should say a quick "goodnight" before being asked to help her mother to improve her speech by reading out loud from the Bible, or some Christian magazine. Desiree would rather go to her room, turn on her small stereo, and listen to those Roy Orbison albums Lynda had given her. Or maybe she could glance through the latest *Cosmopolitan* magazine her friend had also given her, and dream of owning *anything* modeled by Twiggy. Or she could simply pull out *Valley of the Dolls* from under the bed, and finally read it.

Jon's contrary attitude surfaced one more time later that week when he bellowed over the phone because Desiree didn't think she should cancel any music lessons, despite his having front row tickets for a sold out Procol Harum concert. He had remembered that it was one of her favorite groups and she didn't even notice. He finally admitted, however, to knowing that her mother was having more trouble than usual getting around the house. But nobody had turned him down before. Not for a mother. Not for a father. Not for anyone. Not for anything. He hung up on her and went to the concert alone, but during the intermission he left the noisy, smoky crowd and drove to the familiar bungalow, where Desiree greeted him at the door with a tiny smile and a tight hug.

The tall blonde steadily enchanted him. The longing look in her eyes when he touched her, or her softening voice on the phone once she knew who was on the other end of the line had him wanting her more.

He had never heard anyone play the piano better than Desiree. She could play anything from folk to classical. Chopin was quickly becoming his favorite composer. "Just don't let my folks ever hear you play," he remarked one evening as he sat with Desiree and her parents in front of the old upright piano after all the lessons were finished.

Desiree's lips parted. She got up from the bench and lifted its needlepoint seat. "Why?" she asked softly, trying to hide her disappointment as she rummaged through the various sheet music inside.

"Because they'd never let you stop playing." *Because,* he thought, *they would love you for it, and I don't want either of them to love anything that I love so much.* "You know something? My father gave my mother a baby grand when she was pregnant with me, and to this day she can't find Middle C." He shrugged his shoulders. "Even Ray Charles can find Middle C." He gave a tiny smirk, shaking his head in disbelief. "Then, when I was in first grade, she made me take lessons, but I never practiced. My mother and father were never around long enough to know the difference."

"Didn't they want to hear *anything* you had been taught?" Christian's face showed utter disbelief.

"No. They never asked me to play anything for them, and Theresa, our maid, never tattled on me about not practicing. I could always keep out of her way because I had my own bike, my own baseball and football and basketball equipment. And lots of friends, too. Mother never did forgive me, though, for kicking the piano teacher once when she asked me to sit up straight. Mrs. Knucklebee was her name. I just called her Knucklehead, battle-ax that she was. My parents and every schoolteacher I had were always trying to correct my posture. Who needed the hassle from an old music teacher? Anyway," he continued, looking over at Desiree, "since Mother and Father have been back from New York for a few days already, they want to meet you. I told them that we had other plans, but somehow they ..."

"And I would like to meet your parents, too." *I think.*

"We all would, Jon." Christian shifted his body in the overstuffed recliner. He had sensed his daughter's slight hesitation and he watched her closely now.

"Sir, tomorrow's my last night in town, so we aren't going to visit with my folks. I would like to take her somewhere special for dinner."

"I'd like to meet them tomorrow, Jon. If only for a little while." There was a slight strain in her whisper. She looked over at her parents to see her mother managing a tiny smile and her father nodding his head.

"There'll be another time for all of us to meet. We will wait."

Early that next evening, when Jon opened the wide French doors of the two-story stylish home, Desiree gasped in awe. From the cathedral ceiling in the huge foyer both chandeliers dazzled her. Jon flicked a switch by the doors that turned them both off.

"Theresa must be out. Mother insists the lights be left on when they're all away. But she wanted us here by seven o'clock. Where is everyone? She knows damn well I've made other plans and they didn't involve being anywhere near this place."

"Maybe there's time for me to go back home and change into something a little more suitable. An evening gown, perhaps." To harmonize with the pale blue of her eyes, Desiree had purposely chosen to wear an icy-green dress, slightly flared, of soft chiffon. But the material had been on sale, and she had sewn it herself. Now its simplicity embarrassed her.

"Babe, if only you knew how beautiful you look. Even in blue jeans." His soft kiss erased her tiny frown.

Smiling, she rubbed her hands over the solid oak wall paneling in the oversized living room and absorbed the richness of the opposite wall of white fieldstone surrounding the ceiling-high fireplace. Her feet sank into the deep, lush carpet with each step.

Jon didn't rush her. Someday he would have surroundings that were just as elaborate for the two of them alone, but they would be from his very own efforts, not any inheritance.

Having something much more important to show Desiree, he led her up the curved walnut staircase to the huge conservatory, where she was captivated by a Steinway baby grand of white polished wood.

Dare she sit down and play something? Her fingers almost touched the ivory keys, but she stopped herself and walked towards the wide turreted window as she searched the large peach room with widening eyes.

"This wallpaper was flown in from Paris. Can you believe that?"

She could only surmise the origin of the extravagant furnishings throughout the house, but the piano, that magnificent baby grand, still held her. After Jon pulled some sheet music from its deep velvet seat she carefully put all the pages aside, sat down, and began to play Beethoven's "Sonata No. 14 (Moonlight)". One of her favorite classical pieces, she had memorized each note, the contrasting themes, and the movements. She played the classic piece with easy excellence, and was given an unexpected ovation when nearing the finale.

"That was perfect!" a husky gray-haired man acclaimed as he stepped further into the room. "That piano has been here for some twenty odd years and I've never heard more than a few flat chords from it. Until now."

"Yes, I was told," Desiree said softly with a tiny smile. Awaiting introductions, she stood up and faced the man she knew was Jon's father, their likeness was so remarkable. Only the color of hair and a more creased forehead distinguished father from son. She leaned sideways and smiled at the tall slender figure just behind him who, arrayed in a powder-blue linen suit, was eyeing her with a cool command.

"So, you are Desiree." The unfriendly voice fitted the long scrutiny.

"My son refused to learn how to play the piano." John Sommers interrupted, his deep voice firm. "My wife has no natural talent for it either, but she is a superb horticulturist. Her orchids and tea roses are quite the envy of all her associates."

A pair of deep umber eyes lit up instantly. "Yes, some of my orchids have already started to bloom. I'm sure you would like to see them." Wide shoulders soon straightened.

"Let's all have a cocktail first, Katherine."

In the massive living room again, Desiree took the crystal snifter offered her. Somehow the drink swept along her dry tongue, and her lips puckered from the sharpness.

"What's wrong with your drink, Desiree?"

"Nothing, ma'am."

"Are good liqueurs not availed you at home? What a shame. Everyone should be interested in a few of the finer things in life, don't you think? Are your parents just ordinary people or perhaps just a scant cheap?"

Katherine's sarcasm warmed Desiree's blood and she looked up at Jon for support. "No, they are neither ordinary nor cheap. They just prefer not to have liquor in the house. Not even wine."

"Are they alcoholics?"

Jon snickered softly at that incredible image and reached for Desiree's hand.

"No, sir. They are not."

"What does your father do, Desiree?" There was a tone of arrogance in John Sommers voice now.

"He's a school teacher."

Jon was pulling at her arm. "Come on, Mother. Show Desiree your greenhouse. Then we're out of here."

They went into another area of the house, and Desiree caught the pride in Katherine's elegant animation as the aristocratic woman led them through a dark walnut foyer to a large kidney-shaped swimming pool, with a round marble fountain at its far end. A spectrum of colors was playing in the spray. At the south end of the property, beyond the sauna and exercise rooms, was a huge greenhouse. Having all these luxuries fully enclosed under the same roof that someone called *home* was a wonder in itself to Desiree.

"It has become my practice to save only the best for last. Look over there, Desiree."

Up ahead, through a wide archway of fieldstone, was another cosmos of color. Superbly displayed on the continuing stone staircase was a waterfall of orchids and roses, their delicate scents engulfing the warm, humid room and luring her inside.

"Ohhh, I wish my mother could have some of these in the house. She's allergic to all flowers, but even if a single rose were given to her, she'd suffer for days just to appreciate its loveliness."

"You must see my prize-winning Maxillaria. And the Cattleya are just beginning to flower. I've waited over two years to see their exotic blooms, but, of course, you wouldn't know anything about that, would you, now?"

Still awed by the prismatic nursery and the sweet fragrances, Desiree didn't see the short step in front of her and she tripped onto a low bed of tea roses.

"Desiree! Don't you dare touch those beautiful plants!!"

She was crying before Jon could help her into his car. While she fumbled in her purse for a tissue, opposing thoughts filled Jon's mind. Desiree was perfect for him. She did not need, nor did he want, his parents' acceptance of her.

Still wishing to be somewhere else that evening, somewhere more romantic than out in the chill, and feeling almost shadowed by the glitter still exhibited by the chandeliers of his parents' home, Jon decided he could wait no longer. He reached into his jacket pocket and touched the soft velvet of a tiny box. Inside was a beautifully styled, handcrafted, flawless, two-carat solitaire diamond ring, set in eighteen karat yellow and white gold. His dark eyes shimmered with excitement as he took the box from his pocket and held it open for her. "Desiree," he whispered. "Will you marry me?"

"What?" Had she heard him correctly? Had he just proposed to her? "Oh, Jon. After that scene with your parents, how can you think of such a romantic moment *now*?" She pulled herself away from his tightening embrace and reached for the door handle, but it wouldn't budge, and she squirmed in her seat.

Jon hadn't anticipated this reaction. "I didn't plan anything like this for tonight. I think you know that. I'm madly in love with you, Desiree, and I want you with me for the rest of my life. Will you marry me? Please?" His voice was soft, his words soothing.

"Yes, yes, yes, Jon," she said between kisses. "I will marry you."

Jon carefully slipped the ring onto her finger and they sat nestled in each other's arms, silenced by the passion of the moment.

"Let's get married in December. A couple of weeks before Christmas, maybe," he whispered a short time later. He wanted to find a Justice of the Peace somewhere and marry her the next day, escaping all the restless involvement. Or they could elope and then later, in the foyer of a luxurious hotel, he would sweep her into his arms and carry her up to the honeymoon suite where finally they would ... But Desiree would want a large traditional wedding, with friends and relatives gathered in the celebration. She would have it no other way, and he would let it happen.

"But Jon, that's only a couple of months away. We can't possibly have everything ready by then. There's just so much to do and I want to enjoy all the preparations."

"Honey, as far as I'm concerned, it's a couple of months *too far* away, and I have a hunch you'll have everything ordered and arranged by next week. And you'll love every moment." He brushed a lock of hair behind her ear. "We can honeymoon anywhere you want. A warm exotic place, or maybe some gorgeous winter resort where I can teach you how to ski." He lit up a cigarette and offered it to her but she refused it, as usual. "Mother and Father will be quite upset about our timing, I must admit, but I honestly don't give a damn about how they feel or what they might think about anything. I wouldn't even care if they didn't come to the wedding. And, maybe now, they won't."

"Oh, Jon! Please don't talk like that."

And John and Katherine Sommers were upset. Well after midnight the telephone started ringing in the Bjornson home and Desiree, still awake from the evening's anxiety, dashed out of her bedroom to answer the one in the hallway.

"Yes, Miss Bjornson. Jonathon just told us about your marriage plans and, as my son is as stubborn as I am in so many things, I will not prevent him from going through with it. I do find it rather odd and disturbing, however, that you're planning the wedding so soon. My husband and I are always in Palm Springs at that time of year, visiting our closest friends. We can only assume that you have no choice in the timing." Each word rang with haughty resentment and Katherine often hesitated, as though expecting an argument or sharp reply. When nothing was said from the other end of the line, she continued, "I'll be sending you our guest list immediately, and, with such short notice, I hope it will give everyone enough time to make proper arrangements. Good night now."

"She thinks I'm pregnant." Desiree sighed, as she walked back to her room.

Desiree buttered two pieces of toast and leisurely sprinkled a thick, even layer of cinnamon powder over each, while silently questioning her father's sudden frown.

"I thought you dusted the house yesterday, honey." He had noticed the kitchen counter was cluttered again with various containers of cleansers and furniture polish.

"I left a few smudges on the hutch, though."

All that past week he had also noticed the tiredness in his daughter's eyes, her head nodding while reading to her mother, her falling asleep while watching the five o'clock news. Christian twisted out of his seat, walked over to the refrigerator, and reached for the narrow cupboard doors above it. "Trying to have everything done before Jon comes home, aren't you?"

"I'm so organized with my own plans, but there'll be so many more things to do together with him when …"

"Despite being so busy, you miss him, don't you?"

"Yeah," she sighed. "It seems like a decade since I last saw him. You know he phones here every night, and he never hurries our conversations, but it just isn't the same."

"And with Lynda gone now, too," Mae added softly as she took the toast being offered her.

Christian pulled out a small metal box from the narrow shelf before closing the cupboard door. He smiled as he realized that soon something special could be added to his daughter's rather scanty wardrobe. Since she was twelve years old, her entire baby-sitting money had been spent on patterns, fabrics, or basic notions. It wasn't unusual for his daughter to spend an entire Saturday sewing in her room. His den at the end of the hall was next to it, and all these years, while preparing exams or reading another batch of essays from his English class, he could hear her at the sewing machine. She had been taught to sew on an antique treadle machine until one day an electric Singer had been delivered quite unexpectedly to their front door. It was "just another something" from his sister, who, after many long and frustrating hours, still couldn't follow the detailed instructions, and had decided to give it to someone she knew could make it work. And he remembered how excited Desiree was when its re-taped cardboard box was opened and the machine was brought into her room.

Despite seeing the sparkle in her father's clear blue eyes and the growing upward curve of his mouth as some faded, limp bills were crumpled in his hand, Desiree knew there was little money left in their special fund—those hard-earned savings that were to take her parents to Norway some day—back to her father's roots.

"Desiree, Mother and I want you to go to one of those little shops downtown and pick out the best-looking outfit you can find." He slipped a crisp one-hundred-dollar bill and some old, torn one-dollar bills into his daughter's hand.

"Oh, Dad, Mom. I can't take this. It's your special vacation savings. I'm making enough myself now to buy my own clothes.

"We know, but this is our little gift to you for that exact reason. You are doing so well with all your students, old and new." Christian gave a toothy smile.

"Wouldn't it be nice if one of those boutiques was having a sale right now?"

"That would be perfect, Mom."

And later that same afternoon Desiree was back home, modeling a navy wool-blend tailored skirt suit and navy pumps with a matching leather shoulder bag. She could bring it all on the honeymoon.

"Striking, honey. Just striking."

"Yes, that suit fits you perfectly, Desiree," Mae added with a nod. "It's as if you made it yourself."

Jam. Jam. My nickname is Jam, Mother. That's the special name you gave me years ago. Why can't you call me that again, Mom? When will you ever forgive me?

After the dinner dishes were washed and put away, while her parents sipped their herbal tea in the living room before the evening music lessons began, Desiree quietly folded the remaining few bills she had earlier stuffed into her pants pocket, tucking them into that tiny box her father had opened earlier. She locked it and set it back into the cupboard. They would never know that she had purchased her entire new outfit at a discount store where she had found all her purchases at various sale counters.

"Oh, I almost forgot, Desiree," her father stated several moments later from his leather rocker. "Somebody from a business machines company phoned for you today. Now, where did I put that note?" Christian walked up to the china cabinet and took a torn piece of paper from the hutch. "Here it is. A Dawna Greene called to say a mutual friend told her that you might be looking for a downtown job. Apparently there's an opening at her office for a junior secretary or receptionist, and you could come in for a typing test any time this week. No appointment is necessary."

"But I'm so satisfied with just teaching the piano, and I love all my new students. I really haven't been thinking about getting an *office* job."

"The building is downtown." Mae's eyebrows were arching now. "Your bus would stop just half a block away."

Choosing not to question her parents' thoughts or intentions, late that next morning Desiree sat in the only chair available in the crowded reception area and, fingering a tiny strand of English ivy on the round oak table beside her, she waited anxiously for Dawna Greene, private secretary to the branch manager. With a recent issue of *Reader's Digest* opened on her lap, she kept her head down, inconspicuously listening to the conversation across from her.

"I heard one of the secretaries here was killed this past weekend in a car accident in Hawaii. Yeah, enjoying her exotic vacation, when someone apparently broadsided her rental car. Sad, isn't it? So, what are your credentials? I've been an executive secretary for five years now, but my boss is being transferred to the head office down east, and I don't like his replacement. This company seems to promise good benefits."

"I've got my honors certificate from Henderson's. I've only been working for *two* years though."

Desiree realized that her high school matriculation course, with only tenth grade typing to her credit towards any office job, would not compare to the courses she had just heard about, and she shuffled in her seat. She closed the magazine on her lap, placed both elbows on the arm rests, noticed a large reddish smudge on the wall beside her, and waited. When a small well-manicured hand reached out and a soft conversational voice greeted her, she became a little more at ease.

Moments later she was advised that Todd Remmings was their mutual friend, and then she took the typing test. Afterwards, feeling somewhat uncomfortable with her performance, she waited as instructed in the boardroom, staring out the narrow window. While Dawna Greene and the branch manager discussed her application form in the privacy of his office, she felt dwarfed by the glass-topped boardroom table of thickly varnished teak and the numerous overstuffed black leather armchairs. More nervous now, she wanted to take off her new illusion-heeled leather shoes, rub her aching feet, and then quietly open a window, sneak outside, and scale down the old brick building into an almost barren alleyway. No one would take note. No one would even have to.

The doors of the boardroom finally opened and a tall, straight-shouldered, white-haired man walked over to her. He flattened the pocket flap of his dark blue tweed suit before speaking. "Hello, Miss Bjornson. I'm Sydney Morten, the executive vice president here. But what's in a title?" He smiled quickly and held out his hand. "You came with good recommendations, you know."

"Pardon?"

"Todd Remmings gave me an excellent critique and I'm quite impressed. I think you would be perfect as our receptionist, for starters, Miss Bjornson. Can you start this Monday? At eight-thirty?"

"Uhh. Yes, sir. I can. Thank you."

So unlike the warm reception room the main office of her new employment was a showroom where tall rows of steel shelves displayed the company's various wares. Only the windowed west wall housed the elaborate executives' offices, with their individual secretaries stationed outside each door. Desiree's working area, separated from everything by sliding glass doors, was rich and inviting, as though an interior decorator had spent weeks on its décor. A pale oak coffee table, adorned with various ivies, ferns, and cacti in shiny brass pots, separated the upholstered wicker chairs. She was pleased to have to regularly attend to a mature weeping fig, its longer branches nestling near her pencil tray. The office telephones were unusually quiet, she had been told, and few visitors attended at this time of year so she found it easy to master her specific duties behind her new desk.

She had rescheduled all of her daytime piano lessons, with only mild disappointment from a few students or parents, and despite the basic simplicity of her first office job Desiree took pride in her new work. Her confidence was increasing steadily. As time went by she was thankful to have made a new friend at the office. Already Dawna Greene had taken her out for lunches and casual dinners, and had offered her a substantial raise. Desiree was quite enjoying the outside working world.

⚜

"Still got your headache, love?" Christian sat across the dining room table and watched Desiree rubbing her temples again just after the lunch dishes were cleaned and put away. "I hope you aren't planning to go to the office this afternoon. Are you?"

"I know I should, Dad, but I can't seem to get rid of this throbbing pain. I've already taken four aspirins today." Four aspirins *and* her new birth control pill, she reminded herself in silence. To allow her body proper time before the wedding to adapt to the special hormones, she had started taking her new prescription just two weeks ago. She hadn't expected such a quick and negative reaction to it, however.

"Life has been unusually hectic for you lately, with your evening music lessons, your first office job and, of course, your wedding plans. Maybe you should see Dr. Styles, just to be sure everything's okay."

"It's only a headache, Dad. I know it will go away soon." She had wanted to discuss the new prescription with her parents, but she couldn't seem to find the right moment for that. Her *disturbing the course of nature* would no doubt initiate some endless lectures, and she did not have the patience for anything like that right now. The birth control pill was still new on the market and she wondered what the long-term effects might be. Even Dr. Styles was reluctant to prescribe it to her.

"I prefer to give these to ladies who are of legal age, I want you to know," he had remarked emphatically during her last visit.

Because she and Jon both felt it was the right thing to do, she was determined to get the prescription. "You know I'll be eighteen next month, sir. And for the record, I'll also be a bride in seven weeks."

She quietly finished her coffee while her father glanced through the stack of mail he had left on the counter before lunch.

"There's something here for you from the Sommers, I see."

Desiree ripped open the thick manila envelope and scanned through each calligraphic page with growing apprehension. Over three hundred people had been selected to represent the Sommers on her wedding day. She wondered why the list specifically included each one's occupation—a judge, lawyer, architect, chartered accountant, or university professor.

"What is it, Desiree?"

"Their list of guests for the wedding." She stuffed the envelope and quickly put it behind her back. "I forgot to tell Jon's parents that we want a nice but reasonably small wedding. Just close friends and relatives."

"How many guests are listed? A hundred or so?"

"No. Three hundred and seventy-two, to be exact."

"What?"

"It's mentioned at the bottom here." She handed her father the envelope.

"Oh, my. You know Mother and I want you to have the perfect wedding, but …"

"Don't worry, Dad. Jon will be back next Friday and everything will be straightened out. Just don't tell Mom about it, please?" She rubbed her temples again.

But when Jon phoned at his usual time that evening, her concerns quickly changed. His employer had signed a multi-million dollar contract to start drilling in the Cold Lake area, and just that morning Jon had been offered a new job.

"My salary will double," he said, as he stroked the glossy finish of her graduation portrait, which hung near his bunk. "We could buy our dream home much sooner and maybe go to Europe next year."

"Will I see you next Friday?"

"Well, if I accept this job, I have to be in camp first thing tomorrow. I wasn't given much time to decide, was I?"

"No, and there's …"

Only the soft crackling of static could be heard between them for a few moments.

"You still aren't feeling well, are you, honey?"

"Oh, it's just my usual headache."

"Have you made another doctor's appointment yet?"

"No, but I guess I should. Even Dad is getting concerned now."

"Those birth control pills are giving you the headaches. But you already know that, don't you? Why not throw them away? We'll think of something else when the time comes. Okay? And maybe this should be my last year on the rigs. If I didn't enjoy being up here in the bush so much, I'd probably be the accountant at my foreman's office already. I've shrugged off the idea mainly because of the smaller wage. But maybe now is the time to think about a different job."

"No, Jon. Please don't do that because of me. I'll be fine, really. It's just that your parents' unbelievable guest list came in the mail today and …"

"And I suppose that every judge, doctor, and architect in the country has been invited."

"Well, the list is pretty long and your parents did make a special point of letting us know who is who in their world. I was just hoping that we could discuss it with them. Soon."

There was more static on the line and Desiree thought they had been cut off, but finally she heard his low deep voice again.

"You know something? If Mother and Father insist on such a large celebration, I think we should let them pay for it. For everything. And I mean *everything*! Have you found the perfect material for your dress yet?"

"No, I'm still looking, but …"

"I know you told me that you wanted to make all the dresses yourself, but if you can't find the material soon, there's not going to be enough time for you to finish them. Maybe you should buy them already made."

"But you know it's been a dream of mine, Jon. I've had all the designs in my head for years."

"Well, make sure you get *exactly* what you want. And *everything* you want. The *perfect* material for your dress, a long veil perhaps, comfortable shoes, and any and all the flowers you may have dreamed about, too. Whatever. I don't want to find out later that you got some sale items you *just happened* to have found at Woolworth's. I'm going to phone Mother and Father right away and set things straight. There'll be enough money in your bank account by tomorrow afternoon so that you can have the best of everything. And I mean the *best of everything*. And don't buy any *silk* flowers for the church. I want you to have the real thing, okay?"

"But …"

"Promise me," Jon interrupted, determined to persuade his fiancée that there would be no problem now with financing any part of the wedding. And it was going to be a beautiful one!

"But real flowers won't last for any length of time, and you know about Mom's allergies."

"Oh, I forgot about your mother. Couldn't she take something for them? It is your wedding day, you know. And we can get the flowers preserved. They can last for years."

"I know Mom will understand, and maybe she can get a special prescription. But your parents aren't going to let …"

"Now, I don't want you to worry about my parents, or anything else, for that matter. In less than five minutes Mother and Father will know exactly what you and I think of their guest list, and if they won't change it, they can damn well pay for the entire wedding. I think I might take on that new job. It's only for three more weeks. And remember that I love you."

She threw out the remaining birth control pills and within days the headaches stopped, allowing her enjoyable moments to concentrate on more elaborate wedding plans. She still wanted to make all the gowns, had already cut out the patterns from old newspapers, and wished she could soon find the perfect materials because the tiny beads and detailed hand stitching she wanted on each dress would take hours.

On her eighteenth birthday, she awakened early to the sound of the usual pair of magpies squawking in the poplar tree just outside her bedroom window. Their shadows flickered over the floral motif of the new wallpaper. She was excited about the day's possibilities, having cancelled all her lessons on the assumption that something extra special might have been planned by her parents. And, of course, Jon would phone her later.

But she was alone in the house, and there was no note anywhere. Nor had any scotch tape, scissors, or wrapping paper been left on the kitchen table. Her parents must be shopping for her present, she surmised, and she took her time getting dressed, not sure what to wear, but finally deciding on a pair of denim hipsters she had just bought. As she buttoned an old white cotton blouse, she suddenly heard some commotion outside and then her father's loud voice at the front door.

"Desiree. I need your help. *Now*!!"

"Oh, what's happened to Mom?" she asked herself as she dashed down the hall toward the front foyer.

"Surprise!!" Her best friend, Lynda, was in front of her. As both parents quickly shuffled their bodies out of the way, a freckled face and wide, toothy smile lit up bright blue eyes. Lynda stretched her long arms outward, waiting for a hug. It lasted for minutes.

Later, at a corner table for two in a tiny downtown café, the two friends continued to reminisce. Desiree sipped her hot tea as she once again absorbed the usual friendly charm of her red-haired friend.

"I still cannot believe that Jon asked my father for your new address and phone number, and that he has already talked to you five times."

"Yeah, after our first conversation, he wired me money for my plane ticket here. He even lined up your parents to pick me up at the airport. And this morning they were right there at the gate, waiting for me. I don't think he's missed a thing." Lynda took a long sip of her coffee before continuing. "And, Desiree, he's sent me a small fortune since then."

"Pardon?"

"Yeah. He wants me to take you shopping this weekend, to make sure you get everything you want for the wedding. And I'm pleasantly surprised that he's been so insistent." Lynda slid the empty creamer away from her coffee mug. "I haven't even met him yet and I like him. Keep him, girl. Keep him." She reached for her apple pie before continuing. "Now, young lady, what would you like most for a wedding gift from your best friend?"

"What I want most of all, Lynda, is a spice rack."

"A what?"

"A big and fancy spice rack, with all kinds of spice jars filled to the brim. Yes, I want oregano, basil, parsley, thyme, and garlic. Lots of garlic … Oh, and I'll need a cookbook, too. Maybe one that has the recipes like all those delicious meals you and your mother have cooked for me over the years."

"You'll have no excuse then for not knowing how to cook," Lynda laughed softly. Then her forehead furled. "Did you ever find out why your father doesn't allow garlic in the house? You know your mother always avoided me whenever I questioned her about it."

"All she said once was that his parents back in Norway absolutely refused to have it in *their* home. And obviously, Dad just followed suit."

"I'll buy you a nice spice rack, and find you a good cookbook. All *you* have to do, after that, is just follow the recipe. It's that simple. And as time goes by, you can alter any of them any way you want. Knowing you, you'll be a chef in no time."

Later, at a popular bridal boutique, the two friends spent several hours going through various books and brochures, and looking at numerous floral displays so perfectly displayed throughout the store, finally choosing a varied assortment that thrilled the bride-to-be.

"Remember, Jon flew me here specifically to make sure you choose what you really want," Lynda often had to remind her friend. "Yeah, your face lit up when you first saw that spray of rosebuds. So order it! And get those orchids in the display window, too. Come on, I don't want to let Jon down. He's serious about all this, you know."

Finally persuaded, and knowing exactly what she wanted in her very own Bridal Registry, Desiree listed the linens, flatware, china, crystal, and coordinating patterns and styles for the tableware. She had never dreamed of actually being involved in such elaborate affairs.

Lynda's weekend visit was unforgettable.

As the days passed, however, Desiree was saddened by Lynda's announcement that she couldn't be the maid of honor, and that she wouldn't be attending any part of the ceremonies, because of her father's deteriorating health.

"His brilliant mind is going, Des. He's been diagnosed with dementia. He keeps shooing small children away in his rush to get to the opera. And you know how he truly hates opera. But he's so worried about all the kids around him that he doesn't eat. Has to leave his food for the kids. He's lost fifty-three pounds already. He's so lanky and shapeless now."

"What he used to say *I* looked like. Gumby." She was struggling for the right things to say.

"Yeah, but you were only twelve years old then, don't forget." A nervous laugh broke the softness in Lynda's voice. "Now the doctors are more concerned about Dad's heart. He's already on so many different drugs and he's so tired all the time. I just try to keep remembering that the doctors and nursing staff are doing their best for him."

"Please let him know that I'm thinking about him."

As December neared, Desiree gave her final approval to the four-course meal, the numerous flowers for the church, all the decorations, and the musical arrangements for the reception hall. She finally found the perfect deep green velvet and had already sewn the gowns, staying up past midnight on several occasions because of the intricate beading. She decided to finish Lynda's dress and maybe give it to her at a later date.

She was overjoyed one Saturday afternoon when a bouquet of long-stemmed red roses was delivered to the house. 'Be gorgeous tonight, as usual. We're going out for dinner. Love, Jon'. The words on the attached card surprised her. She hadn't expected him for another three days.

"I can't believe how smoothly everything's going for us," Desiree said over her bowl of cherries jubilee in the dimly lit restaurant. "Only the last-minute things are left to do and there's still a couple of weeks before we ... Jon! Is something wrong?" He'd been tapping his fork on the edge of a saucer.

"No, honey. I'm just getting impatient. Let's get out of here. I have a surprise for you." The surprise was for him as well. He hadn't seen the duplex yet and over a morning cup of coffee, he had only glanced at the layout that Bruce Dunlop, his immediate supervisor, had sketched so quickly on a paper napkin. It belonged to Bruce's friend who had decided to move back to Denver, Colorado, before Christmas. Feeling pressed for time, Jon had signed the mortgage papers the same day they had arrived at the camp.

He breathed a short sigh of relief when he drove up the quiet crescent and parked in front of the large Spanish-style duplex.

Golden-tipped junipers edged the sidewalk and high neatly-manicured caragana bushes divided both sides of the property. Smiling, he picked Desiree up in his arms and carried her inside.

In the sunken living room she danced along the deep wide hearth surrounded by a smooth hardwood floor. She felt the cold red bricks along the feature wall that continued up into the dining room and spread around the archway of the huge hidden kitchen. Wide picture windows at the double sink brightened that country-style room, and upstairs, dark French doors opened into an enormous carpeted bedroom. Beside the papered alcove was a walk-in closet; its mirrored doors perfectly reflected the depth of the rear cedar balcony.

"Well, how do you like it?" He wasn't sure how to admit his haste in buying the property, not having even consulted her about their new home. "This half is ours to keep," he blurted out.

"Oh, Jon. I love it." Loose curls of milky-blonde hair lifted in soft waves as she twirled in front of him. An unexpected rush of excitement surged through her veins. Desiree no longer felt like an ugly brown caterpillar, resting in its cocoon stage, wanting to be released, to be free. There was a young spirit inside her, wanting to explore. Jon was opening a brand new world to her, and she quite liked it.

She walked through every room again and scribbled notes in a tiny notepad she managed to find in her purse. She wanted the approximate size and particular shape of each.

Moments later, through the balcony windows of the master bedroom, they eyed the small, snow-covered evergreens growing near the back gate, and the pile of chopped wood that had been left against the side fence. The cool gusting wind was whirling fallen leaves from the lone poplar beside the patio.

"So, are you sure about not wanting any kids right away?" Jon whispered, after putting his arms around her shoulders and drawing her closer to him.

"I'd like to wait at least a couple of years, like we've already discussed." There was a stubborn catch in her throat. She still hadn't mentioned anything to Jon about her faulty genetic background. She had been given a few good opportunities for that conversation, but still didn't know how to begin. "Why?" she asked softly. "Have you changed your mind?"

"No, no. It's nothing like that. I just don't think we have much choice here anyway. There's only one bedroom." He had noticed the instant twinkle in her eyes, and smiled. "But look at the size of it, honey. It almost takes up the entire floor. We can easily make two rooms out of it if, when we have to." He led her back downstairs where again they eyed the tidy emptiness around them. "Now, what kind of furniture should we buy?"

Over the next two weeks they spent pleasant hours together, discussing styles and fabrics and designs, soon discovering they had the same taste in decor, and again Jon decided to set no limit on the expense. It had taken them little time to find and order all the furnishings and various necessities for a brand new household, their new home, and, despite her already busy schedule, Desiree found the time and the energy to pack her own oil paintings, crocheted and knitted items, and yards upon yards of various material she had collected throughout the years. John was amazed at her creative diversity and Desiree was thrilled.

Chapter Four

Reminiscing over the earlier ringing of laughter from her father's den, the light conversations from the two guest rooms, and all the elaborately wrapped gifts carefully placed wherever there was room for them, Desiree wiped the last matching cup and saucer, set them back into the hutch, and gingerly closed its glass doors. Picking up the torn pieces of wrapping paper from the dining room table, she smiled and thought again of Aunt Julia's delight when the gold necklace and matching bracelet were taken from a soft leather case. The gift was a token of thanks for her assistance in the last-minute preparations. As self-centered as Desiree knew her aunt could be, Julia had been unusually poised and buoyant when catering to the other guests.

Being careful not to get the badly scratched leg caught in the loose weave of the new carpet, she pulled out a cushioned armchair and sat at the dining room table. "It's been a good day, hasn't it, Sara?" Desiree smiled contentedly as she watched Sara Remmings skip with such springy steps around the living room.

Sara's large curious eyes were still scanning the numerous unopened presents that had earlier been placed beside the piano.

Her boyish charm was refreshing, her petite figure such a contrast to her husband's stoutness. "I'm glad so many people came today. But with most of them gone now, it's almost too quiet here. I'm not used to that, you know,"

"I wish you had brought the twins."

"Double trouble is what you'd get with them around, and Todd and I wouldn't let that happen to you, especially the day before your wedding. I wonder how the guys are doing with their rentals. My man isn't used to wearing a tux, you know." Her laugh was sweet.

"Ditto for Jon."

"And I wonder where Dawna is." Sara pulled up the sleeve of her cardigan and glanced at her watch. "I promised to style her hair before the rehearsal, and it's almost four o'clock already."

"I know. It isn't like her to be late. Everybody here today said the roads were good, just a little slippery around our crescent, but that was all. I hope we'll hear the doorbell soon."

"Yeah." There was a crooked twist to Sara's small mouth. "Todd told me you two would hit it off."

"She's fabulous, Sara. She's already recommended another substantial raise for me next month. Or so she says."

"Hey, that *is* a good friend."

Desiree glanced at the wall clock above the sofa. "I reminded Mom that you'd be styling *her* hair too, but she's been on the phone now for quite a while."

"Well, she can't possibly be talking to any other friend or relative. I think they've all been here today."

"And wasn't it nice of them to stay and visit? Mom hasn't talked so clearly since her stroke, and I haven't seen her looking so fresh and radiant since the afternoon of Erin's awards ceremony ..."

Noticing the strained look on Desiree's face, Sara squeezed her friend's hand and whispered, "Let's both help her to stay that way." She had seen a small gift, beautifully wrapped in silver foil and a bright red ribbon, that someone had left beside the piano, between two larger presents. But the tiny crocheted silver bell taped to the envelope almost hid the message someone had written on it. Sara bent down to read it. 'Please do not open until on your honeymoon. Love,

Erin'. It was addressed to Desiree only, and the large handwriting was scrawled, crooked, and off center. Sara remembered Erin's handwriting to be artful, flawless. "Would you show me the dresses you've made for your mother and Dawna?" she asked finally. "And of course, I'd love to peek at your wedding gown, if you'd let me."

Desiree led Sara down the hall into her pale yellow bedroom of floral pastels and narrow stripes, and carefully lifted the soft plastic wrapping from the dark green dresses.

"Wow. They are beautiful! This velvet is so thick. I can't believe they're your own design. And then you sewed them yourself."

"I've had them pictured in my mind for years."

"With all the extra work needed to hand-sew these beautiful pearls on your gown, no doubt you got some help. Was your mother able to?"

"No. Her hands are still too shaky. She keeps pretty well to herself when Dad or the therapists aren't here. She hasn't even seen the material."

"Pardon me?" Sara dropped her thin body onto the edge of the canopy bed and leaned against one of the wooden posts.

"Because of our short engagement ..." Desiree was fumbling for words. She wanted somebody to know about the utter disinterest that had been exhibited by her mother since Jon's hasty proposal. Why not Sara? "We all know that she's been working so hard to improve her walk, and her speech. But I think it's just her special way of letting me know that she's not too keen about this marriage."

"That's so hard for me to believe. I thought she liked Jon."

"Oh, she does, but..." Desiree wasn't sure how much she should reveal about her mother's true disappointment in their relationship. Maybe at another time she could explain it all. "She was hoping I would have my music degree before settling down in a marriage," Desiree blurted out. "And will she ever be shocked tomorrow when she sees what Jon and I have done for the celebration."

"What are you hinting at, Des?"

"The expense, I mean. The total extravagance. I can't believe it myself."

"Ohhh?"

The slight lilt in Sara's high voice tempted Desiree to elaborate, but she decided not to. Everything would be obvious the next day.

"But why are there two bridesmaid dresses? I thought Dawna was your only attendant." A questioning frown was forming on Sara's forehead.

"My best friend in high school was originally going to be my maid of honor, but Lynda had to cancel because her father is ill and the doctors don't expect any quick recovery for him."

"I'm sorry to hear that, Des. I hope everything turns out for them." Sara took the dark green dress from the rod in the open closet and carefully draped it against her body, soon realizing that Lynda was a few sizes larger. "Hmmm," she moaned as she put the dress back and shut the closet door. "I wish the twins were girls so you could make fancy dresses for them, too."

"And I wish Dawna were here so she could model her gown for you. Where is she?"

"Desiree?" There was a tiny quiver in Mae Bjornson's soft voice when she joined them moments later. Quietly she closed the bedroom door behind her.

As quick as an early spring sunset, Desiree saw the rosy color in her mother's cheeks disappear. There was a disturbing dullness in her tiny blue eyes. "What is it, Mother? What's the matter?"

When Mae started to fiddle with the lace trimming on the cuff of her blouse, Desiree sensed something was wrong. Her mother only fidgeted with her clothes because exact words were eluding her when she had something important to discuss. It had been an extraordinarily full day for the entire family and her mother looked so tired now. The explanation would come when the time was right. Desiree would just have to wait.

"Mom, please let me call the church so we can get Dad back here right away. I don't think you should be going out tonight, but I don't want you here feeling lonely either."

"I can wake up Aunt Julia," Sara added.

"No, please don't call anyone yet. And let's let Aunt Julia sleep. She's had quite the time here today, bless her heart." Mae stretched her neck and stood taller. "That was Gordon Greene on the phone just now." She bit her bottom lip and pulled at the cuff of her long sleeve before continuing. "Dawna had a miscarriage late last night."

"What?"

Arms were stretched out and, as emergency sirens could be heard in the distance, Sara stepped back, took off her sweater and flared wool dress, and reached for Dawna's thick velvet gown. Being so careful when sliding it out of the plastic wrapping, she elegantly draped it over her bosom. "Wow! This is simply gorgeous, but you both know it's getting late. I'm sure the men are all waiting for us. I think we should be leaving for the church soon."

"My good friend just lost her baby. I can't go to the church right now. I have to go see her first."

"Dawna needs to rest for the next few days and your visit tonight won't help matters much." Mae's voice was almost a quiver. "She should be alone with her husband now."

"Your mother's right, Des. And you both should be getting ready to go to the rehearsal."

"I didn't even know Dawna was pregnant," Desiree admitted. "She hasn't gained an ounce yet."

"Perhaps she just found out," Sara suggested.

"Yeah. I'm sure she would tell me about something like that as soon as she got the chance."

"Maybe she was purposely waiting until after the rehearsal tonight, to tell all of us together."

"But now it's gone. Dawna has lost her baby." She took her mother's hand and felt the weak, almost forced squeeze in return. *Is it déja vu for you, Mother?* she wondered. *What anguish did each of your miscarriages bring you and Dad?*

Noticing the slight tilt of her daughter's head, the way those pale eyes were almost questioning her about something, Mae quickly straightened up. "I think a nice bouquet of flowers would do wonders for Dawna."

"I would like to take Dawna's place tomorrow," Sara whispered as she slipped into the floor-length gown and gingerly pulled up the back zipper.

Desiree leaned against the carved walnut post of her canopy bed, as deep lines wrinkled her tightly closed eyes.

"Oh, my. What a beautiful dress." Mae leaned forward and touched the soft smooth pile. There was a tiny upright curve to her thin lips. "Now I know why you wouldn't let me or Dad come into your room all these weeks."

"You would have been welcome." *I would have let both of you in here, if you had shown any interest, Mom,* she thought. But not once had either parent tapped on her bedroom door to want a peek at any of her wedding creations. Needing space that her bedroom did not allow, Desiree had initially spread the excessive length of dark green velvet onto the extended dining room table and then let it drape onto the carpet. How could her parents not have seen the yardage? But, she remembered, that particular evening they had returned home late from their usual Bible study class at the church. She had already cut out the dresses, tidied things up, and was in bed before they returned home. And how often had she needed to sleep on the very edge of her double canopy bed because the still-unfinished gowns were spread over it! She was often very thankful for her small wedding party. Where would she have put everything else?

"I can't even imagine what *your* gown looks like," Mae sighed, finally.

Desiree walked over to her closet and carefully pulled out the dress. The long search for the exact shade and softness for its material and the lining was well worth it.

"Oh, my. It is absolutely beautiful." Mae touched the tiny pearl buttons of the short long-sleeved jacket before opening it up to see the entire gown. "I hope you're going to cover this skimpy bodice with the jacket when going down the aisle, though. No one wants to see too much skin in church, you know."

"Skimpy bodice?" Sara offered in surprise. "It's a sleeveless dress. And the neckline couldn't possibly be much higher. Unless it was a turtleneck, of course."

"Yes, but you girls should both know that because it is sleeveless, it is not the right attire for any member of this family to wear in our church.

"But Mrs. Bjornson, brides should be the exception, don't you think?"

"No, Sara. I will not let Desiree be the exception, bride or not."

Silence enveloped the room.

Turn! Turn! Turn!

The bride-to-be had been patiently waiting for any kind of acknowledgement or recognition concerning her recent creativity, but somewhere in the deep recesses of her mind, Desiree had often seen her mother's exact reaction to the wedding gown. The chosen design was not to spite her mother. The bride-to-be simply loved the look.

"But everything has changed now." She couldn't let the embarrassing moment prolong. "With Dawna going through all that she is, I just don't think it is right to…"

"Des." Sara stepped forward with a sudden air of determination about her. "I know exactly what's going through your mind right now, but it's much too late to cancel everything, and I wouldn't be a bit surprised to hear that Dawna was up and around the house. I bet she's trying to persuade Gordon to take her to the rehearsal."

"That's exactly what Gordon said she had been doing all afternoon," Mae began. "She didn't want to let you down, Desiree. But finally she decided it was best to stay home and get some rest. She expects to be at the church tomorrow, but knows she's too weak to be the matron of honor."

"Too weak and heartbroken."

"I think I look pretty good in this gown," Sara said in her own impish way. "This deep green is a perfect color for me. Makes my eyes look darker, even larger somehow, doesn't it? I'll just have to stand on my tiptoes and not breathe too deeply for a few hours or so. But I can manage that. No problem." She made a quick twirl with the dress pressed tightly in front of her. "I just didn't think Dawna was quite this tiny. Or so tall." And moments later she had already hung up Dawna's gown, and was carefully slipping into the one she knew was being saved for Lynda.

"Well, now. Wouldn't you just know it?" Sara shook her head in mock disgust as disappointment quickly dimmed the look in her eyes. "With *this* dress on, I'll just have to walk around in my stocking feet or wear my new pair of slippers. Some super-thick shoulder pads are an absolute necessity and then, of course, half a box of Kleenex in my bra might give me a nice enough look. Now, let's see. Which gown should I choose?"

Even Desiree managed a tiny smile, before offering her spontaneous suggestion. "Making wider seams at the sides of Lynda's gown will be easy to do, but because the back zipper and sleeves are already sewn in, alterations to the neck area will be a little difficult without looking obvious, but maybe I can … Thank you, Sara, for your gracious offer."

"You know you're more than welcome. It's kinda exciting. I'm a *spur of the moment* bridesmaid." She twirled around again, almost bumping her elbow on the corner post.

"Desiree, I'm sure the men are starting to worry about us," Mae said finally as she reached for the doorknob. "Would you please phone Pastor Bailey while I get Sara fitted in Dawna's gown? *I* can have it altered before you get back."

"No, Mom. I won't let you do that. Everything is so well organized for tomorrow. Maybe I can take in the darts and widen a couple of seams later. In the morning I can fiddle with the sleeves and shoulders. And it should only take a few minutes to shorten the dress."

"I don't have to be with you tonight for the rehearsal. I think it is Jon who needs the most instruction." There was a tiny lilt to Mae's voice. The concern in her tired eyes had softened, and the bride-to-be smiled at the subtle encouragement as her mother continued. "Now, please phone the church to have your father come and get you both. It's your wedding day tomorrow, Desiree. Everything is supposed to be perfect for the bride and groom."

How fleeting was that rare moment of solace. After a quick call to the pastor, she started walking down the hall, back to her bedroom. "Why don't you call me *Jam*? Please call me *Jam* again, Mom," Desiree muttered.

"The bride-to-be is talking to herself, I see." The door to the guest room opened suddenly and only a mass of ugly worn terry cloth could be seen below a tiny circle of thick white lotion.

"I thought you were sleeping downstairs, Aunt Julia. I wouldn't have talked so loudly on the phone, if I had known you were up here."

Julia stepped back and closed the door slightly. Then leaning forward, keeping only her white shiny face exposed now, she stated, "On the day before her wedding, a young lady should be able to talk to herself. I guess that's almost to be expected. But what she keeps repeating is a little absurd, don't you think, Desiree? If you are hungry, go get something to eat. There's certainly a lot to choose from."

While granting her mother's earlier request, Desiree reached for the thick wool sweater on the front closet shelf and saw her aunt wiping both hands across her robe before fingering a few gifts that had been piled by the piano. Soon the smallest one was handed to her.

"I don't want this getting opened by accident this weekend, Desiree. When Erin first moved in with me three years ago, she brought this home one afternoon and told me she was saving it specifically for you. This was even before you were dating anyone in particular. Something obviously told her to buy it for you. You know she had that *instinct* thing. Just like you sometimes."

There was a catch in the young blonde's throat as she felt the foil's coolness. *Erin,* she thought. *I miss you so much. You should be here trying on your dress.*

"And this is not to be opened on your wedding day, you know. You are to open it only when you are on your honeymoon, with or without your husband being there. That's what she told me she wanted. And don't ask me why. Your sister even had it gift-wrapped at the store and wouldn't let me peek inside. And I still don't know what it is … Honest."

Being careful not to crush the starched crocheted bell taped to one corner of the delicate package, the bride-to-be held it against her breasts and curled in her shoulders, as though hugging it. "Thank you, Aunt Julia …" She had to take a deep breath before continuing. "Would you mind keeping it with you in the guest room tonight? It's so tiny it could easily get lost or damaged.

"I'll make sure it's safe. Now, go get your mother and Sara ready for the church."

"Mom won't be coming with us tonight. I'm letting her think she has the strength to alter a gown for me. Would you please make sure she gets to bed early?"

"Why should any gown need altering? You've had them finished for over a week already."

"I'll explain everything in the morning. I can see headlights coming down the street now. Dad must be coming to get us."

The delivery truck owned by the bridal boutique had pulled out of the parking lot just as father and daughter walked into the church.

"Thank goodness your mother decided not to come tonight. With all these flowers, I don't think she would be able to sleep a wink because of her allergies."

"She's been taking those new pills, hasn't she, Dad? These flowers are just being dropped off now. They should still be in their cardboard boxes, sealed nice and tight. We didn't want the decorating crew here until the rehearsal was finished. Jon's going to phone them later to get things started." She looked up at her father before continuing. "But Mom will have to be around them for most of the day tomorrow, you know. Here, *and* at the country club. I hope she'll be able to breathe."

"I'll stuff my suit pockets with antihistamines for some added precaution. Don't you get overly concerned about your mother. Now is not the time for you to worry about anything except your wedding. Okay?"

"Thanks, Dad."

Seeing Todd near the altar, Desiree ran into his welcoming arms. "Oh, I'm so glad to see you."

"And ditto for me."

From the copy of the order sheet left them, each attendant helped to count the boxes of various floral arrangements and aisle decorations. Within a few minutes the bride-to-be was satisfied that nothing had been missed.

"They're going to be so beautiful, Jon. I know you'll be pleased."

"Yes, yes. You keep forgetting that Lynda phoned me twice just to say how impressed she was with all of your choices."

"You know I had her help, though. And an unlimited expense account too. What a difference that makes. Thank you again, Jon. The church wouldn't look the same without your parents' help. The entire day would be different if …"

"Never mind, honey. We're all getting what we want."

"I wish Lynda were here right now. She'd be enjoying this as much as I am."

"I offered to fly her here again, you know."

"What?"

"Yes. It was going to be another surprise for you. I wanted her here at least for tomorrow's ceremony, but she was too concerned about her father. He's not doing well at all, apparently. I want to meet her some day. Seems like I already have, in a way."

"You'd like her, Jon."

The rehearsal was easy but no one seemed in a rush to leave the church. Desiree stood behind the old oak altar and, as she read a few verses from the dog-eared pages of Proverbs, her thoughts drifted back to that wintry Sunday when she had first met Pastor Bailey.

As the new assistant-pastor, he had given an exceptionally touching sermon that particular morning. He was very young then, having graduated with honors from the seminary the previous spring, and was eager and sincere in his calling. However, instead of the usual benediction that morning, the aging Reverend Howell had, on behalf of himself and the entire congregation, presented a large leather-bound Bible to the Reverend Michael Bailey. The young man was utterly taken by the gesture.

And his tribute to Erin had been exceptional.

Now, through the clear glass walls of the corner study, Desiree could see the Reverend gesturing repeatedly to Jon, Todd, and her father. Sara was again practicing the traditional walk down the aisle, her long strides still so stiff and jerky. Everyone was occupied, seemingly content, and Desiree could no longer ignore the beautiful Casavant organ behind her. She slowly walked over to it, touched the timeworn finish, and with a swelling pride, she sat down at its long warped bench. She began to play "How Great Thou Art".

Moments later the heavy front doors of the church swung open, gusting in the brisk December wind, and after a hurried shuffling of feet Mr. and Mrs. Sommers marched up to the altar.

"As the bride and groom had not yet arrived at the house for the soiree we are having for them this evening, my good wife insisted that I bring her here. You all should be heading there now, Desiree."

"Where's Jonathon?" Katherine's dark eyes widened above the high collar of her brown sable coat when she saw Desiree's wrists drop onto the organ keys. "Surely you will all be leaving here soon."

Desiree dashed over to the study, rushing Jon out. Soon Jon was in front of his parents, his eyes searing with rage.

"Mother. Father. No one here knows of your party tonight because I didn't tell them about it. As you know, Desiree and I have agreed to open all the wedding gifts at your house on Sunday and I think that should be enough socializing for either of us. More than enough, actually."

"But, son, your mother has spent a great deal of time on each arrangement, assuring that all your important associates be in attendance."

"No, sir. Just *her* friends will be there. A few of yours, no doubt, will be too. But *my* best friends are here with me right now."

Mr. Bjornson quietly took Jon aside. "Don't you think you should go? Just for a little while? This party is really meant for you and Desiree, you know."

"No, Mr. Bjornson," he said firmly, turning around to face his parents again. "No!" His voice was loud now, almost cracking with disgust. "This party is not for the bride and groom. It's just to show everyone here what …"

Katherine glared at both men. "Let it be known, Jonathon, Mr. Bjornson, that it was with great difficulty that some guests could attend tonight. After my numerous telephone calls to Palm Springs, our good associates all agreed to fly in a day early. I have also requested that the caterers prepare your favorite dishes, Jonathon, and they should be setting the tables this very minute."

Jon helped Desiree and Sara with their coats before facing his parents again. "Mother. Father. We will not be going to your house tonight. I told you that right from the start." He opened the wide wooden doors of the church and motioned for Todd and Christian to follow.

"But Jonathon," Katherine Sommers said. "Mr. McMasters will be there."

John caught Desiree's soft squeal of surprise. He faced her, noticing those icy-blue eyes widen. He then turned to face his parents again as both hands dropped heavily to his sides.

"Yes," Katherine remarked. "He cancelled another engagement. We all knew that Desiree would approve. Once she was told who he was, that is."

How could you, Mother? How could you? Jon thought. "Desiree," he whispered forcefully. "Mr. McMasters is the dean of Music at the university. He has strong connections all over the music world."

"Ohhh I know who Mr. McMasters is, Jon," Desiree hummed. "But tonight I couldn't possibly …"

"I know, honey. The day before your wedding isn't the proper time to have your musical premiere, no matter what my mother or *anyone* thinks."

Nodding slowly, Desiree shut her eyes. Tonight could be the turning point of all her dreams—from teaching a few novice youngsters in her home to performing for an attentive full house in Carnegie Hall. She chuckled inwardly at her outrageous thoughts, but couldn't erase them from her mind. If only Jon would understand. With a soft plea in her eyes, she squeezed his arm.

Jon finally turned around, catching the slight nod of Christian's head. He took a deep breath and stepped forward. "Mother. Father. It appears that I am outnumbered here. We all will go to this soiree of yours tonight, but as soon as Desiree has played her piece for Mr. McMasters, I'm going to take her home."

"Yes, son. That would be acceptable. But you should leave soon. The guests will be arriving at the house shortly. And, of course, you all must change your attire. I insisted that tonight's affair be formal."

"No, Mother. Everyone here looks just fine. All the others will be overdressed. Rather obviously overdressed, I might add. After picking up Mrs. Bjornson, we will go straight to your house." He brushed against the sleeve of his mother's fur coat as he bounded up the steps that led to the study, where Reverend Bailey had been watching and listening from the opened doorway.

But Jon hadn't noticed the arresting glare in his parents' eyes quite like his bride-to-be. Clenching her fists inside her coat pockets, she looked over at Sara and Todd who were also trying to ignore those hot stares, their heads turning towards the front doors as if hinting that they all leave soon.

Even later, as the Sommers greeted her in the brightly lit foyer of their home, Desiree could still see that same annoyance in their eyes. But beside them and smiling so proudly, her father's proud stance quickly softened the tightness in her stomach.

When she looked around, she was quite taken with the surrounding beauty. The living room was decorated in a definite Christmas theme, with a striking pyramid of Chinese and variegated holly around the two huge poinsettias in front of the large bay windows. Adorning the round glass-topped brass coffee table was a tall spiral staircase of oriental jade, and miniature white candles set in rose petal holders of delicate crystal graced each step.

"Mother. Where is everyone? I thought you said …"

"Son. You obviously made no attempt to rush anyone here tonight, so I took it upon myself to usher the guests upstairs to the conservatory." Katherine looked at her watch and called for the maid. "Theresa. Please escort Mr. McMasters in here now."

Despite the excitement of meeting Mr. McMasters, a flood of questions filled Desiree's mind. How many newspaper articles had she read, depicting him as a gentle and deliberate man with a keen eye for rare musical talent? Had he actually cancelled another engagement so he could hear her play the piano? Or was it more of an obligation to the Sommers that he socialized *with them* that evening?

He stepped into the archway within moments, a black double-breasted tuxedo enhancing his tall, husky frame. As quickly as the introductions were made, his long arm reached out. "Oh, yes. The little blonde who skipped right across the stage and jumped into her parents' arms."

"Pardon?"

"You were so young then, I'm not the least surprised that you don't remember. You ran off the stage so quickly you forgot to accept the first-place certificate the judge was trying to hand you."

"That was you, sir?" She had been only five years old then and she had been so thrilled about winning her very first serious competition that she hadn't seen the judge stepping forward, hadn't noticed anyone special in the crowded theater, except her parents and her sister, who were seated at the far end of the first row. To be remembered by this distinguished man after all these years was a rather comforting surprise. The slight nod of Mr. McMasters' head and the warmth of his clear, laughing eyes lit up her face.

"And this is for the little blonde who stole the show that evening."

He lifted a green waxy wrapping with three red roses centered in a cloud of baby's breath from the antique curio stand beside him and carefully gave it to her. Desiree whispered a sincere thank you to him and smiled shyly at the others.

"Let Theresa put those in a vase for you while we go upstairs to the conservatory. The other guests have been kept by themselves long enough, I do believe." Katherine turned and stepped into the front foyer. The hollow tapping of her high-heeled shoes against the flagstone floor seemed to be directing the group to follow.

"Real warm atmosphere in this place, hey, everybody?" There was a flush of apology on Jon's face as he reached the top stair. Soon the classic lines of dark tuxedos broke the glitter of sequined gowns, and all conversation stopped as the standing crowd turned in unison towards the new arrivals at the doorway.

Desiree thought Katherine Sommers had already aroused every horrible feeling within her, but now the sea of strangers and their critical study of her face and the loose hang of her short wool dress made her knees start to shake. Thankfully her wedding dress and entire trousseau still nicely fit, despite her having lost five pounds this past week. She let Jon walk her to the piano.

"Ignore everyone here but us, honey. But please start playing something soon, before Mother interferes any more."

The warmth of Jon's hand on her shoulder and the realization that her parents, Mr. McMasters, Todd, and Sara were all so near made her feel more comfortable. She began playing Chopin's "Etude in C Minor" and soon forgot the discerning eyes, the sudden lull in the conservatory.

Then, satisfied with her performance, she smiled. The applause and standing ovation quickly washed away all her uneasiness, but Jon was already pulling her up from the seat and rushing her out of the room and down the stairs. She looked behind her, expecting to see Todd, Sara, and her parents at the upper landing. Instead she saw only an empty expanse of papered walls and dark walnut railing. She heard no familiar voices

"Come on, Des. Let's get out of here. Everyone's waiting for us in the car."

"What? Why aren't they still here? Didn't they even get to...?"

Desiree," Jon started carefully. "Your mother was slipping further into her seat from obvious exhaustion, and her allergies to all the poinsettias and holly around here were making her start to choke and her eyes water. I thought she should be taken home as soon as possible. And, you know it is getting rather late."

"Jonathon!" Katherine's voice was a loud shriek. "Come back here this instant!"

Scowling at his mother, Jon made no attempt to reply. Refusing to look around, he turned the dimmer switch by the front doors to reduce the annoying sparkle from the chandeliers and quickly helped Desiree with her coat. Flinging his jacket over one shoulder, he opened the front doors and guided Desiree outside.

"Jonathon!!"

Chapter Five

Through the clear glass walls of the corner study, the bride looked beyond the congregation where a riot of colorful blossoms adorned the spacious pulpit, where various-sized brass urns and crystal vases embraced the field of white gardenias, orchids, and holly, where clusters of white tea roses and wreaths of lilies covered the dark wooden floor. She could only surmise the elegant aisle decor of more roses, orchids, and lilies, all wrapped delicately in organza lace. She looked for her mother and husband-to-be, but saw only blurry streaks and muted colors.

Her eyes couldn't focus on any one particular person but her mind distinctly envisioned who was seated out there. She was certain the guests were curious and concerned about the young lady who, just the evening before, had been rushed up to the conservatory by the hosts so she could perform for them all and then left just as quickly.

Now, only the warmth of her father's smile, his quiet presence, his loving grasp of her shaky hand, and the thought of Jon somewhere near the altar erased any telltale sleeplessness from Desiree's expectant face.

A braided cord of vivid dark green satin, twisted around white rosebuds and a single cluster of snowberries, had been woven into the bride's loosely knotted upsweep. A delightful nosegay of hybrid Cattleya orchids and baby's breath had been attached to the silver fox muff, its beautiful thick fur hiding all the necessary knots and pins. Gold-edged ribbons of dark green silk exploded against the whiteness of her outfit; its short, long-sleeved jacket was of rare French satin, and a sweep train of the same rich material finished the look.

The radiant bride-to-be turned towards Sara, whose large bouquet of white magnolias and gold-sprinkled ivy hid unsteady hands as she circled the large study, preparing to begin the traditional procession down the long aisle. Her gown fit perfectly.

A tiny frown momentarily wrinkled the corners of Desiree's glossy pale lips as she pictured Erin standing there instead. The younger sibling had always envisioned the two of them walking down the aisle, one behind the other, or, depending on whose wedding it was, one leading the other. The bride could definitely sense her sister's presence in the church that afternoon. Yes, Erin was watching everything. But there was more than that sensation enveloping her again today. Something extra special, almost spiritual, was letting the young bride know its presence and she loved it.

When the organist began playing Roy Orbison's "Evergreen", Sara gave a wry, nervous smile before stepping forward. Desiree nodded her head and smiled back.

"Sara looks like she's preparing to walk down the aisle already," her father stated, looking slightly bewildered.

"Yes, just another moment and then we can follow her."

"But "The Wedding March" hasn't begun yet."

"Dad, this is the song I chose instead. It's one of my many favorites. The lyrics are perfect for today." She smiled lovingly at him. "It won't be long now."

Since childhood, she had acknowledged her father's handsome appearance. Having recently lost so much weight, naturally he looked taller; but there seemed to be a wondrous air of influence about him today, and the rented black pinstriped tuxedo exemplified those striking looks. A hint of nervousness, however, streaked his blue eyes and the bride-to-be stretched upward to kiss his cheek as a marvelous sense of pride swelled within her.

"Are you actually ready for this, Dad?"

He instantly bugged his eyes and she giggled. It had been a long while since she had seen her father so spontaneous, and she was delighted.

"Oh, here we go, Dad."

As if on cue, the low December sun, peeking through the high stained-glass windows, streamed on the beautiful young bride whose milky tresses shone like Australian opals. The removable train cascaded perfectly onto the floor and the simple, elegant gown drifted gracefully with each slow stride, enhancing Desiree's softly curved figure.

And the squeeze of her father's arm as they neared the front pew confirmed so much to her. Instinctively she sensed his relief, his pleasure, and his contentment that wonderful December afternoon.

Impassioned by the moment, Christian Bjornson smiled as he concentrated on the rhythm of the unfamiliar song Desiree had chosen for this particular walk down the aisle. How apropos that melody was. The enormous array of flowers throughout the chapel was not affecting his wife's allergies. He had dropped a brand new packet of antihistamines into the zippered compartment of her purse, and it was still unopened. All the wedding plans were now complete and how perfectly everything seemed to be playing out. And the bride-to-be, his only daughter now, was so happy, so poised, and so utterly beautiful. What more could any man ask for?

As they approached the altar, Desiree's sparkling eyes widened when she saw her mother's straight stature and her obvious attempt to give a proper smile. The tailored suit of soft mint green crepe de chine gave her such a sophisticated look. Dawna, sitting beside the mother of the bride, presented a gracious smile. Her entire countenance was honoring every executed plan while hiding her own present pain. Beside her, Gordon looked tired and worried, his face ashen, his eyes dry. Directly across from them a simultaneous nod, slow and deliberate, greeted her. The Sommers' obvious satisfaction erased her uncertainty and she loosened the nervous grip of her own hands, so tight and warm inside the tiny muff. When she turned and looked up again, Jon was right in front of her, standing so tall, so confident, so comfortable. He was her Rhett Butler, wrapped handsomely in his black Oscar de la Renta tuxedo, and his dark glossy eyes and wide white smile against his tawny face heightened her admiration.

Hoarfrost clung to the long branches of the giant evergreens and naked poplars and to the crooked twigs of various drab shrubs, as the white horse-drawn carriage, appropriately decorated for the yuletide season, bumped along the narrow winding road just outside the city limits. It was bringing the small wedding party to the east properly line of the secluded country club nestled in acres of monochromatic splendor and interrupted only by the surrounding winter-gray forests. The Tudor-style mansion where the bride and groom would later start their new lives together was a few miles up ahead.

"Thanks, you guys," Desiree said, smiling as she slipped her feet back into the white satin heels that had once seemed much more comfortable. "Thank you all for giving me such a perfect day."

"This is so beautiful, *Mr. and Mrs. Sommers,*" Sara sang teasingly as she put her arm around Todd and eyed him lovingly. "If Todd and I had spent an entire year on preparations, we could not have arranged such an awesome day."

It had been an exceptionally smooth photo session, taken near the altar and in the church's huge atrium, with several poses having the mountainside mural, the large brick fireplace, or the fieldstone fountain as the backdrop. Jon had taken particular notice of the photographer who purposely used various lenses, filters, and accessories to get a wide assortment of pictures and images.

As a Christmas gift he initially had wanted to mail a framed picture to each and every guest. But as more floral arrangements were being shuffled around the fountain before the photo session continued, he realized there wouldn't be time to have *any* of the photos developed, framed, wrapped, and mailed out again before Christmas Day.

"I could rush things for you," Dennis, their photographer had offered. "I could airmail all the proofs to Lake Tahoe for you."

"That might work. Yes, let's do it that way." Jon smiled. "Now, do you need any directions getting to the country club?"

"Well, Todd thought I could just follow behind you all. That would make everything so much easier. I might want to stop all of you to get some outdoor shots somewhere, though. The sunlight is perfect for that today."

"Good idea."

And now, as the carriage continued through the pristine wintry whiteness, its driver, donned in a bright red jacket and black top hat, took a short side trail through a veil of lush evergreens, each branch drooping from the weight of the wet, sticky snow.

"Dennis wanted me to give you the scenic route around the mansion. We can double back onto the main road. It will just take an extra minute or so," he shouted to them.

Sara's blue eyes widened with excitement. She slid closer to her side of the carriage and stretched her neck out, so she could see beyond the high-backed seat. "Dennis is keeping up with us just fine. I think I'd like to own a Jeep, too, some day." She settled back into her seat and shivered from the sudden cold wind whirling around them. She shook her head gently.

"What's wrong, Sara?" Desiree looked concerned.

"Oh, I was just thinking about the taxi cabs you ordered for your parents. They won't have to worry about all this snow, or how to get to the club. I never would have thought of that."

"I got a cab for Dawna and Gordon, too. I don't think any of them will be staying late tonight. But our driver will be waiting for them all. I want them, at least, to enjoy *going home* in this colorful carriage."

"Yeah. Mine insisted on taking their own limo."

There was a look of contempt in her new husband's dark eyes and Desiree silently questioned its depth. His parents had not once interfered with any of the wedding plans, and no involved retailer had yet complained of any unpaid bill. She thought Mr. and Mrs. John Sommers deserved that small preference, at least.

"I heard that a chinook is coming tomorrow," Sara added moments later, finally breaking the silence around them. "What more could you ask for?"

When their driver steadily pulled at the reins and brought the carriage to a gentle stop, they were all silenced by the unspoiled view around them, and for a long while their hearts seemed to be singing along with the flock of sparrows perched in a nearby lodgepole pine. Thin, lacy cirrus clouds hid the low winter sun, and there was a periwinkle blue tinge to the quiet foothills valley in front of them. To the north, the ice fog had filmed the spread of harvested fields with a silvery veil. Facing west, on a slight rise in front of a wide cluster of snow-covered spruce trees in the distance, the two-story brick mansion nestled beside a swift-running creek looked as welcoming as a quaint country inn, secluded and private.

"Everybody, stay where you are." Dennis stepped into the large winter boots he had purposely brought with him, quickly getting out of his Jeep. He flung an old canvas bag over his shoulder and walked down a slight dip. "The snow's too deep for any of you to join me, but I can take a few pictures of you all from over here." In front of a heap of large rocks, he quickly rummaged through his knapsack, assembled his equipment, and started shooting just as the long whistle of a red-tailed hawk, soaring above, caused heads to turn.

Later, after watching the uniformed driver help the foursome out of the carriage at the entrance to the clubhouse, Dennis continued taking pictures. Only a skim of snow whitened the parking lot, and an old dying spruce tree, its twisted trunk curling around a large, sharp boulder, had caught his eye.

"One, two, three," he began, remembering that Desiree wanted no *obvious* candid pictures taken. And he was good at what he did, keeping everyone informed of what he wanted from them. He was able to get a few shots of Desiree just inches from a noisy red squirrel collecting cones, its bushy tail perfectly arched.

Immediately inside the double oak doors of the front foyer a wide aisle of green helium-filled balloons, weighted down by sprigs of waxy snowberries, would lead the guests through the short receiving line.

"You realize, of course, that this event has cost John and me a small fortune," Katherine Sommers stated with her usual flagrant flair as the small wedding party organized their positions only moments before the first guests were guided in. "But, Desiree, I personally want you to know that every penny you or Jon have spent for this day has been more than worth it. You have great taste, I must say. I am rather surprised but very pleased." And Desiree shone from the endless compliments soon given her from everyone there. Her face was aglow all the while.

The aisle immediately led the guests into the large dining room, where each round table was covered in scalloped white linen with wide gold trimming. The gold-plated flatware was wrapped with rich green velvet ribbons. Centered on the head table was a cascade of Dendrobium orchids, baby's breath, and lilies of the valley. Poinsettias in dark green planters and Norfolk Island pine, twinkling with tiny green lights, had been evenly placed throughout the room. In a corner beside the head table, the four-tiered wedding cake of tapering roses and ivy over creamy colored latticework was surrounded by hundreds of rose petals and eucalyptus leaves. In the opposite corner, centered on a raised bed of artificial snow and sprinkled with holly and ivy, the huge ice sculpture of a baby grand piano had Desiree holding back tears of joy. Chiseled to perfect half scale, it was a masterpiece!

The meal of grilled Cornish game hens, wild rice with cashews, baby peas, and apple tarts with homemade vanilla ice cream served with caramel sauce seemed to satisfy everyone.

"I think I'd better take your mother home now, honey," Christian Bjornson announced quietly, as the catering staff finished cleaning the tables and the five-piece band started positioning their amplifiers on the tiny stage across the room from the head table.

"You couldn't even stay just a few minutes longer to see the bride have her very first dance as a married woman?" There was a tone of hope in her soft voice, but seeing her father's head turn towards his wife, Desiree already had the answer. Why had she even asked that stupid question to begin with? She was still waiting to hear that special acknowledgement, their approval of today's affairs. From the moment she saw her parents shuffling around the kitchen preparing breakfast, she had waited for either of them to approach her and give her their blessings. None had yet been given her. Time was running out. As the numerous guests were starting to mill about, the new Mr. and Mrs. Sommers guided the bride's parents out into the crisp night air.

As if on cue, the sound of horse's hooves grew louder and Jon and his new father-in-law approached them.

"Were you pleased with this affair, Mom?" Desiree wanted to know.

"It was absolutely beautiful. Far beyond my imagination, I have to admit. Quite opulent, actually, and rather wasteful, don't you think? You've certainly been blessed, Desiree." The squeeze of her mother's hand was firm, not loving at all. "You know who to thank for this lavish affair. And it isn't just the Sommers. Now, don't you ever forget that!"

And as the bride's parents were being helped up the single step into the carriage and getting comfortable in their seats, Desiree looked up into the clear starry sky and gave a weak smile. "Thank You again, Lord."

Turn! Turn! Turn!

When the bride and groom were back inside, the band, dressed in black tuxedos with dark green cummerbunds, acknowledged the newlyweds and began to play "The Girl from Ipanema". Jon gently took off Desiree's long-sleeved jacket and draped it over a corner chair as he eyed his new bride and her dress, that utterly simple princess-line gown of whisper chiffon, the fitted bodice beautifully enhanced with swirls of miniature South Sea white pearls. He guided his new bride to the dance floor and kissed her softly. "You know that you truly are my very own girl from Ipanema."

The lead singer, donned in a smashing sequined mini dress, reminded Desiree of her sister. "Erin," she whispered to herself. "I know you are here with me tonight. I can feel your very presence, just like at the church. Thank you for that."

The band was now beginning their next song. When feeling the warm squeeze of John Sommers' hand on her elbow, the beautiful bride smiled as she was led to the center of the dance floor, still barren of any other guests. Jon was walking over to the head table where Todd and Sara were still sitting, chatting with the wine server.

"You have exquisite taste, Mrs. Desiree Sommers," John began, his bright eyes glowing with pride. "And everyone here is actually floored by the fact that you designed and sewed all the beautiful gowns." John twirled her around and caught her gently at the waist.

Just then, Mr. McMasters interrupted the duo for the next song and, donned in the same tuxedo he had worn the evening before, surprised his young dance partner and many seated guests by dancing the Charleston so nimbly. He showed no sign of embarrassment or concern in his partner's slightly awkward spontaneity in trying a dance so new to her.

As the night drew on Desiree Sommers, beaming with confidence and satisfaction, wanted to continue dancing with the guests—the neighbors, the relatives, the family friends, the judges, the bankers, the lawyers, the architects. To her surprise, no one questioned her sudden disappearance the night before and now they only continued to shower her with sincere compliments.

And standing tall, never too far from his bride, Jon wanted her to stay and enjoy the attention, the whole affair; but as his mind kept picturing the countryside mansion that had been given them for the week, impatience stirred within him. He wanted to be lighting a crackling fire in the oversized stone fireplace. On the bearskin rug in front of it, he would softly kiss her waiting lips, her flushed cheeks, and her warm neck. His hands would slowly caress the delicate curves of her willing body. Gently he would touch her softness. And, sitting up slowly, she would turn towards the dimming coals and loosen the satiny ties of her gown, carefully and deliberately, enjoying the intoxication as her own fingers would circle her hardened nipples. Then those same tiny hands would cup the fullness of her breasts, would squeeze them gently at first, then harder. She would lean slowly towards him, her eyes closing, her lips parting. Her entire body would be trembling with anticipation.

But instead, after saying all their farewells at the clubhouse and arriving at the mansion much later than planned, Desiree fell asleep on the leather sofa before he could light a fire. Behind him, her wedding attire was a heap on the carpeted floor. She responded sweetly and totally to his longing desire, however, when she was gently awakened. The evening was perfect. It was late in the morning when they finally arose from their impassioned harmony.

With hair still damp from their first shower together and their bodies wrapped in thick terry robes, they nestled in the padded lounge chairs in the glass-enclosed balcony off the master bedroom and eyed the sunlit shrubby meadow around them. Snowdrifts were slowly shrinking. The icy clutch of several winters had rusted the wheels of an old farm wagon, now tipped onto its side beside a dilapidated shed. The sudden squawking of a wounded black-billed magpie, its left wing twisted and dangling over a faded wrought iron weather vane, had Desiree plugging her ears. Then looking southward to study some deadwood and remnants of that summer's barley field that had somehow collected around a crooked mailbox by the narrow gravel roadway, she could see a shiny new van approaching.

The young deliveryman had diligently placed the two plates of eggs Florentine, a shallow container of various Danish pastries, a platter of sliced melons, and a carafe of Colombian coffee onto the large cedar table. When the lad finally left the mansion with his generous tip and a thick wad of crisp bills stuffed in his uniform pocket, a proud smile graced his face. And the newlyweds ate contentedly, sharing each other's food while watching two long-tailed weasels slip across the icy creek to the bluff beyond. Now, only the black tips of their tails could be seen flitting through the sparse brushwood.

Later, at the gift opening affair, expecting an elaborate entrance staged by the elder Sommers, Desiree was relieved to be greeted only by Theresa, whose obvious pleasure showed in her sparkling hazel eyes and sincere smile.

"You forgot to take something home the other night." Theresa pointed to the antique curio stand beside her.

"The roses. Those beautiful red roses."

"Not to worry, Mrs. Sommers. I've taken good care of them."

"Call her *Desiree* in this house, Theresa." Jon's voice was low and stern.

With a look of understanding, Theresa nodded her head and proudly ushered the bride and groom into the living room, where a cordial welcome of ready smiles and raised glasses of champagne was awaiting them.

"You two must be hungry," Theresa said with a soft giggle. "Come with me. You can visit everyone later."

In the adjoining dining room ceramic platters and numerous silver trays of creamy crabmeat canapés, stuffed mushrooms and tomatoes, smoked salmon with wild rice, and spicy apricot-glazed ham in a bed of snow peas splashed the long table with color, and champagne punch was served immediately by the small catering staff. The large, orderly affair was comfortable and Desiree, charming and vibrant in her swingy dress of icy-blue georgette, chatted easily with the guests as Jon and his boss talked in the foyer.

While her glass of champagne was being replenished, she excused herself and slipped into the small alcove beside the front closet. She took off her shoes and rubbed her aching feet before rejoining her new husband and the criminal lawyer, Michael Henderson.

"As I've told you already, Jon, you have a most beautiful bride," Mr. Henderson said as he took Desiree's hand and gently kissed it. "And, Mrs. Sommers. Don't you ever let him forget that, all right?"

"Yes, sir," she smiled.

Thick unruly brows curved high above dark-rimmed glasses as he searched the huge living room again. "This is another successful gathering by your folks, I see. But I'm most surprised that James isn't with us again today."

"James? James who? I know my parents wouldn't forget to invite anyone that would ..."

"James Robert Sommers, of course," Mr. Henderson stated emphatically. He glared straight into Jon's eyes.

Jon's dark eyes blackened. "Michael, I have not heard of anyone by that name."

"Well, actually I am not that surprised."

"Why? What are you trying to tell me?"

The balding man turned to face Desiree. "This is quite personal, and very private. Would you mind if I take Jon aside for just a moment?"

A touch of annoyance caught at her throat and her slow smile obviously gave him the wrong impression. Michael Henderson took Jon's elbow and led him past the alcove and down a wide hallway.

Curiosity heightened inside her but Desiree leaned against the dark wall paneling, took a few deep breaths, and waited. She could hear nothing from the two men and when Jon finally approached her again, she could see the tight press of his lips, the bulging veins in his neck. His tanned face was suddenly flushed with rage, and the ominous look in his eyes startled her.

"What on earth did Mr. Henderson say to you?" she asked.

"Never mind, Desiree." He led her to the front doors. "Let's get out of here."

"What? We can't, Jon! We haven't opened our gifts yet, and that's what this affair is all about." She spoke softly yet firmly between her teeth. "Please don't make a scene. Not here. Not now." Desiree cringed at her own thoughtlessness and took Jon's hand. "Maybe we could go to the mansion for a few hours and come back later to open the gifts."

"No. You're right," Jon finally replied, standing tall, straightening the collar of his sports jacket. "We should stay to open all the gifts. But let's get this damned affair over with as soon as possible. I don't ever want to come back to this house again."

Soon gifts of jade, silver, crystal, fine china, linen, and rich tapestries were placed on the dining room table, which had been cleared of all the food. Desiree was delighted with the extravagance, but as Jon became more aloof and deliberate, she tried to hide her concern with smiles of gratitude.

Jon loved the poise exuded by his new bride but frowned each time he glanced at his watch. He wanted to pick Desiree up in his arms and carry her outside, to get away from the crowd and his parents, to be alone once again in the country mansion with his new bride. Maybe then he could erase Michael Henderson's haunting words … He felt the tiny squeeze of a hand on his arm. "Did you say something to me, honey?"

"Yes, I did," Desiree whispered. "Only our parents' gifts are left to open. We can leave soon." She laughed inwardly at Jon's long sigh, but when she saw the crisp thousand dollar bill that had been folded carefully inside the beautiful card from her parents, she had to force back tears.

Desiree took a deep breath and hurried to the seats by the fireplace, bent down and kissed her mother and then her father. Jon approached them slowly and soberly, hugging them warmly, but his hands were shaking when he returned to the far end of the table and opened the large decorative envelope from his parents.

Desiree was overwhelmed at the various brochures of world cruises, so brightly displayed. She wrapped her arms around Jon, but he quickly pulled away. He grabbed the mass of colorful sheets and hurled them at his parents. As glossy pages fell like confetti, he pushed through the silenced crowd and stomped out of the house.

"Damn you, Mother! Damn you, Father!" He kicked the tire of his father's new Rolls Royce parked in the driveway. "Damn you! Damn you! Damn you!"

Both chandeliers chimed in their busy sparkle while a mixture of emotions washed over Desiree's face. What had just happened? As horrid thoughts raced through her mind, she stood motionless in the murmuring around her.

"Excuse me," she said finally to all the guests. Her voice was loud and raspy, so she cleared her throat before continuing. "It's obvious that this weekend has been tiring for both of us, so I think it's best that Jon and I leave now. Thank you all so very much for coming to share this special time with us, and for your beautiful gifts." Somehow she managed to pass through the stunned crowd.

Outside she quickly buttoned her thick wool coat she had grabbed from the front closet and raised its collar to cover her bare ears. At the end of the block she saw Jon turn around and start walking towards the house. She ran towards him, but when he saw her approaching, he quickly turned away.

"Jon! What's wrong?" she shouted and grabbed his arm.

"I don't want to talk about it!"

Under the pale milky haze of the streetlight above them, she took his hands and felt their cold stiffness as she pressed them hard against her face.

<hr />

Jon smiled as he watched his new bride again eyeing the rustic decor of the mansion's upper living quarters. Each room had its own personality, with varying hues of cobalt blue, forest green, and burnt sienna. The shiny oak floor was cool against his feet.

"Can I rub your back tonight?" Jon asked lovingly as he kissed her forehead. She had been so quietly understanding in the car, often squeezing his arm on the long trip back to the mansion, reminding him again of her presence and understanding. The caressing look in her soft blue eyes had already swept away his initial resentment, but for how long? He needed her. Just how much he needed her he was only now realizing. "At least I could draw you a bath."

"I can't lock the door on you any more, can I?" She smiled a teasing smile and then let him go draw the bath. She loosened the satin tie around her waist and let the robe fall to the floor. When he told her that her bath was ready, she forced herself to ignore his gentle caresses and scooted him away again. After leaving the bathroom door open just enough, she stepped into the full tub. "Please wait for me."

His blood warmed as he pushed a leather wing chair further from the dark marble hearth. After building a large crackling fire, he stretched his long lean body over the bearskin rug in front of it and waited. Wanting to turn and study his teen bride, longing to touch and again explore the smoothness of her every delicate curve, he pulled at the long strands of white fur ... She had asked him to wait.

From the bathroom she had been watching him. The quiet drive into the country seemed to have relaxed him, softening the harsh tone of his voice, erasing the deep furrows from his brow. The champagne was puckering her lips with its tang, and her mind was swirling into a vivid fantasy as erotic as the many scenes she had envisioned while reading over and over again her wealth of smuggled romance novels.

Her moist pursed lips had already kissed Jon a hundred times. Now her tongue was beckoning for more. That tall virile man, her husband now, had just stepped out onto the balcony. Jon was finally hers. All hers. Forever. She wished now that he would come closer. She wished he would touch her again and share the absolute ecstasy within her own body and mind, erasing all but the present moments—so near, so beautiful, so overwhelming.

She would bring him in from the chilly December night and in front of the bright fire she would start unbuttoning the satin front of the negligee she had unpacked earlier and hid behind the towel rack in the corner. She knew Jon's wide eyes would follow the gentle fall of her gown and he would so lovingly examine her absolute nudeness. Her hands would leisurely stroke the curving smoothness of her own body. She would caress her full, firm breasts and let her long delicate fingers circle the hard jutting nipples. She would lean towards him and gently nestle her head on his shoulder and rest her arms on his pounding chest. She would absorb the bluish-purple warmth of the glowing fire, of his manly essence. But all this while, could she hide exposing her own lack of feminine artistry?

"Would you like more champagne?" Jon shouted as he filled his own flute again.

"Yes, please," she answered softly as she dried herself off and slipped into the satin softness.

Facing the fire now, Jon was lying on the bearskin rug and blowing smoke rings into the air. She approached him slowly as hot waves of excitement flushed through her veins. With quiet anticipation she felt the coolness of the satiny bodice before starting to unbutton her long gown. As Jon sat up, his dark, dreamy eyes caressing the fullness of her breasts, a surge of panic overcame her. How many romance novels had she read, losing herself in each erotic scene, each romantic word, and each arousing gesture? Last night had been perfect. Even in her fantasy just moments ago, each movement, each intention, had seemed so natural and so easy. But now there was a tiny ache in the small of her back and her legs were stiff. She couldn't take another step towards him and both hands dropped heavily to her sides.

"I love you, Desiree." His voice was as soothing as a baby's lullaby. He guided her down onto the rug and slowly unclothed her. He moaned with pleasure at her perfect nakedness and his tremulous mouth lovingly traveled the smoothness of her body. She helped him unbutton his soft silk shirt and teased his hard flat nipples with her wet restless tongue circling the hairless nodules.

"You are beautiful, my darling. Absolutely beautiful."

They were alone in the country for the next few days, eating scantily, sleeping deeply when the hours of passion were finally spent. In the middle of the week they flew to Reno where a rented Mustang convertible took them down the busy streets of the city. They had an unhurried lunch from the enticing buffet at the Peppermill Hotel, enjoyed a couple of cocktails before strolling through the busy casino, and, as Desiree absorbed it all with such a youthful spirit, Jon casually looked around, not wanting to spoil his bride's enjoyment by informing her that despite crossing the border she would still be considered a minor. Since no one seemed concerned, he said nothing to her about it.

Then, under a cloudless sky they drove through miles of whitened high mountain forests and around secluded pearly-blue lakes. Desiree could easily envision every color of the rainbow in the vast wildflower meadows and the scenic waterfalls that the springs and summers would bring the area each year.

The spacious rooms in their suite at Harrah's Lake Tahoe made it another haven; their bay window view of the lake was breathtaking.

Various outdoor activities were plentiful: touring, skiing, sleigh riding, and hiking, but Desiree most enjoyed the shopping, and her initial exposure to gambling. Beginner's luck befell the pretty blonde at the blackjack tables. She lost count of her winnings the first few nights. Because of her easy charm, Jon was soon relaxed about her being with him at the slot machines and gaming tables, and he remained silent about her age.

Under sensational sunlight that entire week they enjoyed nature's endless wonders with leisurely hikes through thick groves of trembling aspen and towering ponderosa pines. But skiing the panoramic slopes of Heavenly Valley was a true disappointment for Desiree. Jon had described the basic techniques, had shown her each movement. Because of her inexperience and utter awkwardness with the long skis, however, a true fear of the snow and the steep slopes soon grew within her. She hated the deep moguls. She hated the giant trees. And she hated the other skiers, swooshing by with such skill. But she quickly mastered appearing poised and relaxed, as she waited for Jon to help her up again, again, and again.

Later in the week, quiet chats with other vacationers and long strolls around their heavenly lodging filled the early evenings. One exceptionally warm evening they stopped to have a few cocktails in a quiet lounge near the Riverwalk. It was a rather large room but the cozy alpine decor welcomed them in and Desiree chose a seat near the console piano.

"Looks like there's live entertainment here," Jon remarked to the waitress when she brought them their drinks. Pleased that again his new bride had not been asked for any identification, he shuffled his body to get more comfortable in the low leather chairs.

"No." The waitress smiled. "I think the only thing that has ever touched that piano is an old dust rag. Feel free to play if you want to."

As the ice slowly melted in her Singapore Sling, Desiree entertained the suddenly growing crowd with her own renditions of current hits by The Byrds, Peter Paul and Mary, and The Beatles. Everyone seemed pleased with her choices and when she finished

"The Flight of the Bumblebee", by Rimsky-Korsakoff, wide eyes and raised highballs greeted her.

Jon loved his new bride's unashamed charisma. Appearing so skittish and helpless on the slopes where she epitomized the snow bunny, she exuded poise and charm at the piano. Talented and confident, she was the ultimate performer. Back in their suite, though, she was his girl from Ipanema... *Tall and tanned, and young and lovely, the girl from Ipanema goes walking...* There, she belonged to only him.

Nor did their photographer let him down. Only three days into their honeymoon trip to Reno, a box of wedding pictures arrived early in the morning at their penthouse door, and over a huge carafe of coffee and a colorful platter of sliced melons, Jon and Desiree sat at the round table by the windows and started selecting their favorites.

"There's not one photograph I don't like, Jon. But these five are *perfect* to send as Christmas gifts."

"I agree. Dennis is waiting for us to send them back by airmail. Let me take them downstairs while you draw our bath."

After sharing a long relaxing Jacuzzi bath, and dressed only in her short slip, she approached her handsome husband. He slid from the corner armchair and held out his hand, guiding her closer, pulling down the satiny straps of the slip, letting the silkiness fall to her feet. He gently kissed her waiting mouth. He bent down to feel the soft firmness of her round breasts against his cheek, his mouth, and his tongue. Her warm body molded into his when he carefully let her down onto the bed and his face flushed with pleasure when she moaned for more.

He had fluffed up the pillows and together on the blankets they finished the bottle of Italian wine they had ordered earlier. Then he set the empty glasses onto the headboard and cupped his hands around the back of her neck.

"I just hope I don't get pregnant right away," she whispered.

"Oh, honey. Let's not worry about that on our honeymoon. I've waited too long for these moments with you. Besides, I thought you might not be able to have any children."

"What makes you think that?" she started. Her voice was high with surprise. She couldn't ever remember telling him anything like that. "I thought we had agreed to wait for two years."

He hadn't meant to upset her. He cleared his throat and sat at the small table by the television set. As he lit a cigarette he wondered how he could change the solemn mood of the conversation. Desiree had sat up on the bed and fluffed up the pillows again, still waiting for his reply.

"When your mother was ill and you had just started teaching during the evenings, your father and I had many hours together, you know."

"Yeah, I know. What all did he tell you about Mom?" She found it difficult to believe that her own father would talk to Jon about something that personal, and tonight she thought she almost preferred her father's quieter, more introverted moods.

"He just mentioned that your mother had had four miscarriages before Erin was adopted." He gently took her into his arms and cradled her.

"Yeah, and she took some special pills so she could keep me, although I was six weeks premature."

He pulled her closer to him again. "Well, now I know why you have such a tiny frame." He kissed her nose and let his mouth caress her closing eyes and soft warm lips, and so quickly his gentleness kindled her passion, left her wanting more.

Chapter Six

Most of the Christmas travelers, looking lost, exhausted, or totally frustrated, seemed to be ignoring the bright fancy decorations on display at the various kiosks at the busy Reno airport that early wintry morning, but while Jon filled the only empty available cart with their heavy luggage, Desiree smelled the pine freshness of some tiny well-lit trees near the information booth in her best attempt to appreciate the special season. But her mind was as preoccupied as she felt the others around her were.

Back home, leaving a more familiar airport, the frosty windows of their cab reminded them both of the cold whiteness they had left behind a few weeks ago. Below zero temperatures apparently was the norm now all around the region, prompting Desiree to catalogue all the yuletide activities still left to effect, and Christmas was only a week away. She took a notebook from her purse and scribbled another item onto the lengthening list.

The numerous wedding presents, still in their boxes, would have to be put in the basement, and little time would be given the newly married couple to frame, wrap, address, and deliver over two hundred of the wedding photos Jon was going to pick up later that day. Initially he had wanted to do all this himself, but she finally persuaded him to get everything done professionally and then have each parcel rushed by courier.

"There's so much to do when we get home," she moaned as she stared again at the frosty windshield, wondering how their driver could see well enough through its icy coating to stay in their lane. "I don't think we'll be ready for Christmas this year, Jon. And you know I wanted this first one of ours to be extra special."

"It will be, honey. Please don't panic."

She didn't see the gleam in Jon's dark eyes or the growing curve on his lips because she was writing another item onto the page. When he leaned sideways to take a peek, she handed him the notebook and then added, "I spent so much time on the wedding preparations that I totally forgot about the duplex, our new home, and the beautiful furniture and decorations we have to fill it with. It could have been fun. You and I taking our time in deciding where to put what." She squeezed his hand tightly. "Now there will be such a rush. Oh, how could I have been so negligent?"

"You weren't negligent one bit. You asked me to take care of all that for you. And I did."

"What do you mean, Jon? I don't remember anything like that."

"Well, you did, and I got all the help from Dawna and Gordon. You'll see when we get home."

When we get home. When we get home. The words were a lullaby in her mind.

Jon insisted that he carry his new bride over the threshold, officially this time, and once inside the duplex she felt she was still on her honeymoon in their beautiful suite at Harrah's Lake Tahoe. The sofa and loveseat, the bentwood rocker, both leather recliners, and all the side tables were exactly where she had envisioned they should be in their oak-floored living room. Not one item was out of place. And in the dining room, only their new set of Royal Albert dishes remained in the original boxes, to be displayed later in the maple hutch and buffet.

"I can't believe Dawna helped us with all of this. How did you even get her to offer?"

"It was just in passing that I told her I wished all this could be done before we got home," Jon smiled as he led her to the upstairs bathroom, where thick matching towels hung on a brass rack by the shower door. Down the hall a chintz duvet of pastel blues and greens covered their king-size waterbed. "Yes, Dawna insisted on doing all this for us while we were away."

"But how did she know where to put everything?

"Once I showed her that red binder of yours, she became quite excited about following through with it all. She couldn't believe your detailed sketches of each room and each piece of furniture."

"And then she lost her baby."

"Yeah, I know. But she decided to do this long before that, once realizing how busy you were with all the wedding plans and your extra students. Or, maybe she absolutely needed this outlet after coming home from the hospital, to keep her mind occupied with nicer thoughts. I'm not sure if she was able to help much with moving the heavier furniture, though. They're down east now, celebrating the holidays with her sister. Won't be back until after the new year." Jon stepped down to the foyer and looked at his watch. "Dennis is expecting me at his shop any time now, so I'd better go soon. When I get back we can start addressing all the gifts. I'd like them ready by Friday."

From the living room windows she waved to him through crisp champagne sheers that hung perfectly from the valance. Then, smiling, she twirled around the room again and again as satisfaction swelled within her.

At the dining room table she spread out the five different thank you cards she had chosen with such care in a tiny card shop in Reno. Thoughtfully she wrote a special note of thanks to her parents, to her in-laws, to Todd and Sara, and to Dawna and Gordon. After addressing the envelopes she decided to send Lynda a nice note also, thanking her best friend in writing, for helping plan such a beautiful wedding, and for giving her the thick, colorful cookbook and huge chrome spice rack filled with exotic spices. She wanted to find a new recipe for her parents to taste at the Christmas dinner. And garlic *could* be included. In fact, she was purposely going to find an easy recipe that required garlic.

With zeal Desiree licked the envelopes and put them on the settee by the front closet. When sitting by the hearth, she eyed every inch of the huge living room. On the stereo cabinet in the corner she could see the decorative foil paper of Erin's last gift, still unopened. She hadn't noticed it there until now. Despite the specific written instructions to open the gift sometime while on her honeymoon, the new bride hadn't taken the present with her to Lake Tahoe. Had Jon placed it there earlier? Or had Dawna found it upstairs amongst so many other gifts when she was organizing their home, and decided to keep it safe somewhere else?

Desiree moved slowly over to the stereo where she touched the coolness of the wrapping and fingered the tiny, tight curls of the thin red ribbon. There was still no desire within her to open it, and again she wondered how such a pretty box could be so fascinating, yet so repelling at the same time. Some day she would open it. The timing would be better then. When she heard Jon getting out of his car, she put the tiny package into the drawer of an end table and went to meet him at the front door.

"How many photos did Dennis prepare for us? I thought we only ordered two hundred." She could see something large had been stuffed in the back seat of his car.

Jon laughed. "No, no. This is the entire order. And they've all been wrapped beautifully. Thank you again for persuading me to have someone else do that for us." He kissed her on the cheek as he walked by and then dropped the box onto the kitchen table. "I have a surprise for you later, though."

After enjoying a hot delivered pizza Desiree subtly reminded Jon of his sloppy handwriting and started addressing the numerous packages herself. Within minutes he was out to the car and back. Ripping open a huge cardboard box in the middle of the living room, he pulled out the contents. A large smile lit up his face and with just one flick of his hand his *surprise* opened up. "See. No assembly required." An artificial spruce tree, its branches coated with a thick layer of fake snow and its very tip bending gently at the ceiling, was taking up the entire corner by the fireplace. The tip of each branch had tiny clusters of clear blue bulbs which sparkled the second Jon plugged in the cord.

"Where did you get something so absolutely stunning, Jon? I haven't seen a display of anything like this."

"When we were walking around Reno and you were looking for special thank you cards at the Eldorado Hotel, I decided to browse through one shop's catalogue. The special order has been waiting for us at Dennis' shop since Tuesday." Jon picked up the pile of cardboard pieces and stuffed them into a plastic garbage bag. "Like you said in the cab, there's still so much to do around here before Christmas. But this will save us quite a bit of time. I also got some cute tree ornaments and other paraphernalia for around this place, too."

"It's absolutely beautiful, Jon. Thank you so much."

He opened a smaller cardboard box filled with ceramic elves, reindeer, Santas, and cherubs. He carefully lifted silver and gold bells and tiny parcels of different shades of blue from another box.

But creating her own similar ornaments was the most enjoyable part of the holiday season for Desiree. She felt comfortable in her new home, but when Jon slid his recliner across the floor and into the corner by the picture window just to make proper room for that gigantic tree, she questioned her deepening downcast mood. Placing some colorful gifts beside the fireplace did not lift her spirits either.

In a few large boutiques in Reno and Lake Tahoe, carefully selecting a few Christmas presents and having them all gift-wrapped in front of her had been an exceptional experience for Desiree. However, her kickoff to extravagance was now her regret. All her previous gifts had been hand-made, with love. Throughout high school she had personally sewn, knitted or crocheted various woolen items, or perhaps had painted or sketched different scenes on stretched canvas. Each of these personal items had been wrapped prettily and to be given to her parents, to Erin and Aunt Julia, to Lynda and her mother and father, to her music students, to each senior at the church, and lastly, to a few needy strangers at the Salvation Army. Yes, each fall, besides her love of music, her hobbies had filled her spare time.

And then, as Christmas neared, she thoroughly enjoyed choosing colorful paper and ribbons, taking more time to crochet little bells, candy canes, or Santa's stockings for the individual parcels. This year, however, planning her wedding had taken precedence.

Finally, she had every parcel carefully addressed and stacked by the front door, ready for delivery. Then, taking her time, she glanced through the thick cookbook Lynda had given her. Pleased that a colorful picture was available for each recipe, she was also amazed at the variety of ingredients required for some. But thanks to Lynda, she had every spice she needed for the special turkey dinner she was preparing, and she was so thankful that the recipes offered the option of using fresh or dried ingredients. To the cooking novice, attempting to use fresh garlic, rosemary, or sage seemed rather daring and presumptuous, so she carefully measured everything shaken from the tiny glass jars and used the dull end of a butter knife to level off the individual grains or powders. *Just follow the recipe, Desiree. You can't go wrong then.* She could remember Lynda's exact words of encouragement.

When silver garlands and numerous colorful ornaments were placed around the living room, and the lengthy string of tiny blue lights around the new artificial tree was again switched on, the Christmas spirit finally took hold as the bride and groom nestled in front of a glowing fire. From the stereo the music of Bing Crosby's "White Christmas" album softly filled the room.

Before Desiree awakened the next day, Jon further enhanced the duplex's charm by adding several sprigs of holly, fresh mistletoe, and poinsettias throughout the entire main floor. The huge turkey had been washed, stuffed, and put in the oven at four in the morning. Wafting from the kitchen now, the faint scent of garlic, sage, and the roasting bird itself was already whetting his appetite. He knew this Christmas would be a different celebration for his bride, for her parents, and for himself, too. Since his early teens he had usually gone skiing during the holiday season, spending a week or so in Whistler, Jasper, or Banff. Twice, he had gone down to Aspen, his favorite. So, this year, staying in town with family, was going to be unusual, perhaps even a challenge for him, too, but he was determined to make it enjoyable for all.

And when her parents arrived, as he was taking off his thick winter coat, Christian complimented the hosts on the beautiful decorations. "I made sure we brought your mother's antihistamines. Thank goodness. And what on earth am I smelling?" He took in a deep, long breath. "How aromatic."

"Must be the rosemary, Dad," his daughter said quickly. She would never admit to her father that garlic had been added to most of the recipes being served that special day. It wasn't to defy him, not at all. She had decided that it was more of a hint, her way of silently asking him what his long family tradition was all about, a chance for him to explain his aversion to something so natural and so common in most households. "I got all the recipes for today's dinner from the cookbook Lynda gave me. I hope you like it." She rubbed her hand on the oak railing before putting his hat on the front closet shelf. "I hope we all do."

The odd quietness from their older visitors did not spoil one moment of the opening of gifts, since the newlyweds had expected it. Later, at the dinner table, Desiree was thrilled that her mother's plate was empty and her father was already asking for seconds of everything. Jon poured a special yuletide punch of cranberry iced tea to finish off the meal as Desiree cleared the table.

"That was absolutely delicious, honey. Before we go tonight you must give your mother that same turkey recipe."

Mae gave a weak nod. "Your father and I were hoping you'd both come caroling with us."

Jon admitted to only knowing the words to "Jingle Bells". But when *expected* to help feed the needy at the Salvation Army that next day, he had to decline. "My parents always donated money to that cause. I could never stand behind a line-up counter and hand out a paper plate to anybody. Not even one full of Christmas goodies. Mother would never ..."

"A donation would be quite fitting." Mae stated.

"Let me get my bank book," Jon offered. When passing by the stereo, he turned up the volume to "The Little Drummer Boy". Mae wrapped a soft afghan around her legs as she nestled her body into the bentwood rocker, while Christian stood up from the loveseat and walked around the room.

"I guess you haven't had the chance yet to decide where you're going to put all your tapestries, huh?"

"Jon hinted that we just keep them all in the boxes they came in. He prefers my own creations. Can you believe that?"

"Yes, dear. I think I can." He gave a quick nod to the young man.

Jon wrote out a check, folded it carefully, and put it on top of Mae's purse by the front door. Everyone was quiet and relaxed, enjoying the warm atmosphere. When the telephone rang, Jon quickly answered it. Soon it was dropped into its cradle.

When it started ringing again, he ignored it, and motioned that everyone else do the same.

"Christian, it's getting quite late. Perhaps we should be going soon." Mae started folding the afghan as she eyed her son-in-law, then her husband.

"Who was on the line, honey?"

"No one important."

"The persistent ring is rather annoying, though," Desiree hinted at long last, eyeing her mother's growing concern.

"Just like …" His mumbling continued as he walked into the kitchen and grabbed the extension. "Hello." His voice was cross.

"Son, I know it is you who has been calling the house all evening, then hanging up once we've answered it. But why?"

"No, Mother, it has not been me, or anyone else here. How often do I have to tell you that I don't ever want to hear from you or see you or Father again? And I mean it! Believe me." He was pounding his fist on the kitchen counter. "And don't you dare bother Desiree whenever I'm up north! Don't you make one phone call to her while I'm gone." He slammed down the phone and marched back into the living room towards the fireplace.

"Would you like to talk about it, Jon?" Christian's eyebrows were high with concern.

"It's a rather unbelievable story that I was told recently," he began softly, placing some birch logs onto the grate.

"The day after our wedding?"

"Never mind, Desiree."

So vividly that scene came into her mind again—that disturbing conversation Jon had had with the lawyer, Mr. Henderson. Something about a man named James Robert Sommers was still affecting her husband. After all this time, whenever thinking about it, her husband could still get upset enough to stomp around the duplex, slam both back doors, or kick the pile of chopped wood by the fence, each time yelling at his wife to forget everything she had heard about James Robert. And Desiree was slowly learning to just let her husband be. She would have to wait for him. In time, she would be told.

"Jon, Mae is getting rather tired, and it has been a marvelous but rather long day for all of us. I think we should leave now." Christian was already helping his wife with her coat. "It was a most enjoyable visit here. Thank you both, again."

Turn! Turn! Turn!

When Jon packed his bags and left for camp later that same week, Desiree questioned the emptiness quickly enveloping her. She was a married woman now, a newlywed, so why was she alone in their new home, their new bed? Where was her husband? She had to keep reminding herself that Jon was away at work. He would be back.

Initially she was almost thankful to hear from Jon's mother, but the number of calls was increasing, twice daily now, coming at the most inopportune times for Desiree. And the same words, the same questions, the same haughty voice was heard each time. "Are you going to continue working in the office when Jonathon's on time leave? Who's going to cook his meals if you aren't home? Who's going to clean up the duplex? His father and I have discussed it at length and we both want you to get a maid. You'll need one when you start teaching again. Has Jonathon bought you a piano yet? Surely you still can't be thinking of making daily trips back to your parents' house so you can teach there, can you? How absurd."

Desiree listened to her mother-in-law with a steady tolerance, finally telling Jon, but letting him think there had only been a few calls.

"Hang up on her next time," Jon insisted.

Reluctantly, Desiree followed those instructions and, in time, the persistent phone calls stopped. Wanting to share with Jon some ordinary moments, some daily routines, she cried herself to sleep the night he phoned to say he would have to stay in camp until the middle of February in order to finish his latest assignment.

Loneliness quickly filled the duplex. The painted walls around her were suddenly too plain, but even her own oil paintings gave her no solace. She knew not to hang up the silk tapestry Mr. Henderson had given them. Maybe she should buy some wallpaper. Covering one or two walls by herself shouldn't be too difficult. Or, maybe she could soon go to the movies with Dawna and Gordon. They both had mentioned wanting to see *Thunderball*. She had never seen a James Bond movie before, but she rather liked the looks of Sean Connery.

Regular phone calls with Lynda, however, absorbed *some* dull moments. Her ailing father's mentality was now stable; his shooing away small children had stopped. She was working as a teacher's aide in a grade school now, just blocks from home, and was most enjoying the art classes with them.

"Some of these kids should be teaching *me* how to draw," she laughed heartily during one conversation. "Unbelievable work some of them create."

But when the phone was back in its cradle, that same eerie empty feeling enveloped her again. Sometimes Desiree thought for long moments about taking the ten-mile walk over to her parents' house, sitting down at their old upright piano, and playing it just like she had done for so many years. She could even envision Erin sitting on the sofa and listening to her, like she had done a few times before, but wishing she were outside instead, playing dodge ball with the new neighbors. That was so long ago, when they were both still in school, when Erin was still …

Admitting it to no one, the talented pianist often wondered how her music students were doing without her. Then one day her father announced that a new neighbor of theirs had offered to provide transportation to their own home so Desiree could teach the piano to his twin daughters. It was the perfect arrangement for all concerned and word of her continued teaching quickly spread.

A different household of lessons three times a week soon had Desiree with little extra time for phoning anyone, visiting a friend, reading a good book, cleaning house, or preparing a proper meal for herself. Music was slowly filling her life again.

But as several weeks passed, she was now back at the office, too, so adjusting to her new music teaching agenda made mornings most disorderly. She spent many long moments in the bathroom, emptying her stomach of what little she had eaten in the past day or so, until, finally, a visit to her family doctor confirmed that she was six weeks pregnant.

Elated, she called her parents and they came over that same day, just as the pale winter sun was kissing the distant white-capped mountaintops. There was an obvious twinkle in Christian's round eyes and while Mae was again examining the living room's rich furnishings, he turned his back to her and proudly opened his parka to display a bottle of fine French champagne to Desiree.

"Our new neighbor left this at our front door a while back as gratitude for helping them move in a pool table." His exaggerated whisper was almost comical. "And, well, you know we had no use for it… Until now."

With a rush of pride, Desiree quickly took three crystal flutes from the dining room hutch. She watched her father struggle with the cork before filling each glass.

"Christian!" A rather contentious tone was in Mae's voice as she tried taking the bottle from him. "I won't have you drinking that stuff here. Or anywhere."

"Come on, Mae. I know Desiree should only have a sip tonight, but you don't have to be such a stuffed shirt. A single glass of champagne is *not* going to send anyone to hell. God is love, you know. Why don't you *live* it, not just *preach* it? Come to think of it, *you* don't even do that." Christian lifted his flute as a silent toast before taking a long sip. He quickly poured himself another drink and Desiree was quite surprised to see her mother reluctantly taking the one being offered her. The bottle was soon empty, despite Mae's utter disgust at the whole affair. She fell asleep on the settee with her full glass on the table beside her. Christian, however, had never been so jovial, so relaxed, such a true delight. The champagne graced him that evening, apparent by his unexpected deep throaty chortles that seemed to disturb Mae's sleep, but her regular snorts only caused more hysterics.

The sonnet he spontaneously created for the mother-to-be was touching. Glee swelled within her.

Even her father seemed surprised at his own quick wit; his sparkling eyes were wide with satisfaction. "Now, Desiree. Are you sure you wrote down each word correctly? I certainly hope so because I think I forgot most of our song already. I don't think I'll remember much of this entire evening. Damn!"

She had never heard that expletive from her father ever before and Desiree smiled at his unusual openness. "Got it all down, Dad. Maybe tomorrow I could write some music for it."

"That would be fab, Desiree. Let's entitle it "Desiree's Dream". Yes. I would like that, honey."

Only the faint glow of a distant streetlight broke the cold night's blackness when the taxi driver expertly helped Mae into the cab where she lay still in the back seat while father and daughter said their farewells at the front door.

"Don't ever tell your mother, but I would really like to do this again. Rather soon, I am thinking." Christian took her hands and drew her closer to him. "I love you, dear. Please don't ever forget that."

The faint smell of champagne on his breath as he kissed her cheek sent a warmth so wonderful coursing through her veins. Was his heart throbbing as fully as hers? It had been the first hug from her father that she could remember, and never had he told her that he loved her. What an extraordinary ending to an evening.

As the taxi drove away, she could remember every lyric of their song, the constant squint of her father's eyes in his obvious mental search for a suitable melody, the gentle bobbing of his head as he hummed various notes, and his right hand swaying exactly as if he were directing a philharmonic orchestra.

Desiree found some blank sheet music in the piano bench and carefully filled the page with the musical symbols. Put in the key-signature of Major C, the melody for "Desiree's Dream", a soft ballad, had come easily to her and now, just as the dark walnut cuckoo clock on the wall above her was announcing a new day, Desiree carefully folded the sheet music and stepped over to the far end table. Opening its narrow drawer, she placed the lyrics and composition on top of Erin's still-unopened wedding present.

Her sleeplessness that night was gratefully accepted. Some cosmic force, a divine calmness, seemed to have mentally embedded that earlier scene with her father. What a glorious hug it had been—close, tight, warm, sincere. Perhaps it had been the booze affecting her father's emotions, she mused, but it felt so good at the time. And it still did, no matter what the cause. Yes, it had been a most remarkable evening. Unforgettable.

Those animated memories sustained her, despite the following days passing by so slowly. She didn't want many to know of her condition quite yet. Only Lynda would next hear about her pregnancy—until Jon was home. Lynda was ecstatic to hear the news, of course, but Desiree couldn't tell her husband something like that over the telephone.

On Valentine's Day he arrived home in a brand new sports car. It was hers, "just because." His eyes shone like black onyx. "Come on. Let's get you behind the wheel."

"Let me get you something first." Her excitement was shadowing his generosity. She deliberately led him to the dining room table where she picked up the yellow bootee she had been crocheting. "Isn't this just the cutest?"

"Hey, for Dawna? That's great. So, she's pregnant again. Didn't take her long, huh? But let's go for that ride now. We have to get the car broken in properly. I know you're going to love it."

"Jon! This isn't for Dawna. It's for *our* baby. *I'm* the one who's pregnant."

There was a long moment of silence before he spoke. "Oh, no," he sighed, finally, and slumped into a nearby chair.

"What?"

Only the steady ticking of the cuckoo clock in the other room was heard.

"Say it isn't so, Des. Please tell me that it is *Dawna* who's pregnant. Not you."

"Well, she's not, Jon. *I* am." Her loving embrace was ignored. She was hurt and confused as the eerie silence continued. "I'd like to see the new car," she finally offered. Her voice was only a whisper.

"Yeah, let's go have that drive."

He insisted that she get behind the steering wheel, but the standard transmission had her continually stalling the engine or grinding the gears. Besides, she was pregnant. She had other things on her mind. How could she concentrate on anything else? Jon had been so patient with her on the ski slopes at Lake Tahoe. Why was he so edgy now? She would learn how to drive the new car. Just not today! His continued disregard bewildered her. She was carrying a baby—their own child. What could be more exciting than that? Certainly not a new sports car.

She had finally managed to properly get out of first gear, but now she was driving too slowly. "Like an old woman," he remarked.

"Jon!" She finally lost her patience. "You've got to tell me what's wrong. I think I've waited long enough for an explanation." She slammed on the brakes and the car jerked to a stop. "You've been upset since the moment I told you I was pregnant. But why? What are you afraid of? That I might miscarry, perhaps? Or are you just not ready to be a father yet? Is that it, Jon? Tell me!"

His eyes met hers with a hot rage. "I don't want to talk about it. You just wouldn't understand. How could you?"

"Jon." There was a tiny question in her voice but Jon was gone now. He had jumped out of the car and slammed the door shut. He refused to acknowledge her when she ran after him and then, reluctantly, she let him continue on alone. She sat on the edge of the curb as surprise and alarm grew within her.

As night fell she walked back home, only somewhat pleased that she had not driven too far from the house, because the sidewalks were getting slick now and the cold evening wind was nipping at her face. She had left her scarf at home. If she hadn't told Jon about her pregnancy yet and they had gone to the mountains, she might have already enjoyed a horse-drawn carriage ride through the pristine woods and a pleasant meal in their favorite restaurant, instead of plodding down the slippery sidewalk through this unfamiliar neighborhood.

The Camaro was parked along the street and Jon was sitting on the hearth with a glass of rum and Coke in his hand when she finally opened the front door. He turned his back to her as she approached him. He didn't say a word when she questioned him again. Forcing herself to go upstairs, she went to bed, crying. What was wrong with her being pregnant? They had already discussed parenthood. Jon had once told her that he wanted children—a girl first, then a boy. What had changed his mind?

He said little to his pretty bride for the next few days, answering only a few basic questions, and his prolonged cold conduct stirred an unusual fear, a strange anger, within her.

"I have to know what's going on," she said, finally. After looking at the evening's pinkish haze through the large kitchen window, she carefully emptied the portable dishwasher. "I'm your wife, damn it! Don't you think I have a right to know what's going on in your head, so I can try to understand the way you've been acting lately?"

Jon quickly lit up a cigarette, wondering how he could begin to explain what had been eating at his conscience for so long now. "We can't have this baby, Desiree." His tone softened somewhat as his dark eyes widened, and he took her arm and guided her to the table. We can't have *any* baby."

She pulled away from him but his grip on her wrist tightened. "I didn't think I'd have to tell you this quite so soon, because I still find it devastating. I myself still can't believe that it is true."

"You can't believe that *what* is true? What are you trying to tell me?"

He cleared his throat. "Remember the day after our wedding, when I was talking to that criminal lawyer, Mr. Henderson?"

"How could I forget? He asked you why a James Robert Sommers hadn't shown up. But you both went down the hall right then, so I couldn't hear the rest of the conversation. Who is this James Sommers? An uncle? You never did tell me."

"No, Desiree. He's my brother."

"Your brother? I didn't know you had a brother."

Jon leaned heavily against the counter. "Neither did I. And I still can't believe it. Apparently I have a brother two years younger than me. I've never seen James, and until that afternoon, I'd never heard of him. My parents didn't even bring him home from the hospital. They sent him away. They hid him, Des. And they're still hiding him today."

"Hiding him from what, Jon?" She let him slide the dishwasher back under the counter as she put the last clean mug into the cupboard.

"Absolutely everybody."

"Everybody? What are you trying to tell me, Jon? No mother or father would ever hide their own newborn." She turned to face him again. "Unless there is something wrong. Is there something wrong with James Robert Sommers?"

Jon took her hands before answering. "He has Down's Syndrome."

"Pardon me?" Desiree slumped onto a swivel chair. She couldn't look up at her husband, and for a long moment she fumbled with the tiny buttons of her blouse. She could remember her father bringing home a thick medical textbook from his school library so she could study up on it before meeting their new neighbor's Mongoloid child. She was only in elementary school then. "People can love children who have Down's Syndrome, you know."

"I think you already know that my mother could never accept imperfection, especially in her own flesh and blood."

"It just means the child has an extra number twenty-one chromosome in his cells. Trisomy Twenty-one, it's called."

"Now, how would you know anything about that?"

There was an edgy tone to Jon's voice, and she scratched the vinyl piping of the chair before explaining. "A neighbor of ours adopted a

Mongoloid baby years ago. And I know many more couples in this world have done the same."

"But my mother could not believe that she had actually given birth to one, and she felt the right thing to do at that time was send it away."

"It can't be true. Your parents wouldn't do such a thing."

"Well, I know they *could*. I know they *would*, because they *did*. Here, look at this." Reaching for his wallet, he pulled out a plastic card and handed it to her.

"A birth certificate for a James Robert Sommers," Desiree said. "How on earth did you get this? Your parents wouldn't …"

"No, they still don't know that I've heard anything about James Robert. I wrote the government with the information Mr. Henderson gave me, and that is what came back." Jon wiped his moist eyes with his arm. "Since I found all this out, I've been thinking more about just the two of us being together and maybe even going to Europe or South America before any family came. Before we adopted. And now you're pregnant—pregnant with a baby that will need extra special attention for who knows how long."

"Jon. Don't talk like that. I feel very positive about this baby." After stepping around the kitchen and quickly wiping the counter with a new sponge, she went through the dining room and down the few stairs into the living room, where she grabbed a tissue from a decorative box and blew her nose. "Our child is going to be beautiful and healthy, and I know you're going to love it at first sight," she shouted, before realizing that Jon had been following her.

He shook his head. "No, I don't think so, Desiree. Not anymore. And you'll have to quit working and teaching."

"Not for a while." She wondered if she would get beyond the third month and still be carrying.

"You won't be able to teach the piano with a toddler around the house, you know."

"Why not?"

"Don't you see, Des? A deformed child needs extensive medication and total parental involvement. You wouldn't have the time, let alone the energy, to continue with your lessons. You'd be stuck in the house with your little idiot. I just hope you miscarry."

"Pardon me?"

"That may be the best thing to happen to us right now, Desiree." His voice was almost a whisper.

Disbelief enveloped her as she dropped into the bentwood rocker. She squeezed its wooden arms until her knuckles were stiff as she tried to erase the foreboding picture that was forming in her mind. "Things will work out, Jon. Just you wait and see."

Speechless, Jon stood behind the bar and stared at her stomach until, finally, she went upstairs to bed.

Under the covers she could hear Jon stomping about in the basement. She had heard its squeaky door being opened, and now she wished she could join him in the exercise room to talk things out. Her entire body was sore. Every muscle ached, throbbing in rhythm to his jumping rope, and as she drifted off to sleep she envisioned his form and marveled at his perfect discipline in keeping his muscular body tight and agile. In her mind's eye he had smiled so sweetly the instant he saw her beside him. His eyes were keen as he fingered the cracked handle of the jump rope and, behind him she could see the wall she had lovingly papered in narrow green and white stripes.

The dream was so vivid… "Want to join me, Desiree?"

"You know I can't."

"Well, I guess a mother-to-be should at least make sure she's healthy and strong, huh?"

"Yeah, but she's supposed to take things fairly easy, too."

"Then come on, honey. Let's get you in shape for motherhood. Slow and easy."

His voice was the softest of lullabies and she loved it. She let him help her onto the bench press. "Ohh, that's too heavy."

"Well, try these dumbbells. Five pounds shouldn't be too much. They'll strengthen your arms and chest muscles."

A devious look glinted his eyes and she was suddenly mindful of his every word and expression. "Jon," she said uncomfortably. "It's more important for me to eat well and get lots of rest. This isn't necessary."

But he added more weights to the bar and was urging her to use them. "This will help you both. Come on, help the baby."

"No, Jon. The baby doesn't need this. The baby doesn't want this. It wants our love."

"No, no, the baby wants to be free, Desiree. Free. Keep working out now. You've got to help the baby. Help the baby, Desiree."

"Jon! I know exactly what you want me to do, but I refuse!" The phone started to ring. She went to answer it, but Jon pulled her back and handed her the jump rope. "Start jumping, Desiree. Help the baby."

"No, Jon! I won't do it. I won't do it."

Her own screams awakened her sweating body.

The shrill had alerted Jon. Throwing the jump rope into a corner, he dashed up both flights of stairs. He wiped the beads of perspiration from her forehead and held her for a long time as he tried to understand why she was dreaming such weird things.

"Todd just phoned. He asked us to go skiing with him and Sara in Jasper this weekend. I guess you're not feeling up to it now, are you?" His mind, however, was saying, *Damn! Damn! Three inches of new snow have covered the slopes and Todd's already made hotel reservations for us at the Jasper Lodge. Why did you have to get pregnant? What are we going to do when our little one arrives, looking so different?* "I think I'll go to Jasper," he finally said out loud. "Without you, I mean. Maybe Sara won't want to go now either."

"But Jon. You haven't been home a week yet." She couldn't believe that she was going to be alone again, after such a short and unsettling visit with her husband. Her heart, her mind, and her very core were all begging him to stay, but every urgent word was caught in her dry, aching throat.

Having erased their family situation from his mind, realizing that Desiree would soon understand his point of view, early Friday morning Jon prepared to leave for Jasper without her. "I'll phone you tonight after we get settled in." He kissed her softly and again rubbed her belly.

"Have a good time," she said weakly. "Everything is going to be fine. Just wait and see." And then he was gone.

In a daze at the office, Desiree somehow managed to feign a complacent manner all day and she was thrilled to hear Jon's voice when he called that evening. She listened intently as he told her about the cabin he and Todd were sharing. Perfect snow conditions had been predicted for the entire week, and they had decided to stay longer. But she noticed a strain in his voice when he asked about her and, remembering the nightmare, his blank stares, and the deliberate pats on her belly, she wondered what he was thinking as they spoke. Does he really want her to miscarry? And would he tell Todd anything?

She was beside herself for the next few days, methodically going to work, giving lessons, cleaning house, declining dinner invitations, and making up excuses to her parents who were anxious to visit her again. She refused to let them see her looking so weak, so pale, so lost, and she was thankful that they both thought she was keeping herself pleasantly busy with constructive activities.

It was Katherine Sommers' unexpected phone call that brought a new awareness to Desiree, who sat comfortably on the loveseat and listened as her mother-in-law invited them over for dinner that evening.

"But Jon's skiing in Jasper until the weekend."

"Well, we could manage just fine without him for one evening, couldn't we now?"

"But my morning sickness is already becoming an all-day affair. I think I'd better stay home."

"You're pregnant?" Katherine's voice rang with excitement.

The truth had somehow slipped out. "No, I don't really think so. I'm sure it's just the flu." She laughed nervously at her spontaneous lie, but she didn't want to have to answer the hundreds of questions that would come steadily after that particular announcement. "I have a doctor's appointment tomorrow morning."

"Well, I expect you to tell me everything he tells you. Call me the minute you get home."

"Yes, Katherine. I will call."

Behind a worn walnut desk cluttered with macaroni-covered planters of tiny cacti, a yellow toy bucket filled with broken-nib pencils, a one-armed GI Joe doll, and an array of family portraits in various styles of frames, Dr. Styles listened intently as she explained Jon's unexpected reaction to her pregnancy. "I would like to talk to your husband as soon as possible," he said firmly, writing more notes in her manila file folder.

"Jon wouldn't think of coming to see you, sir. He'd be even more upset with me if I suggested anything like that."

Torn between her doctor's encouraging words and her husband's unwavering ideas, she walked down the shady side of Eighth Avenue and was soon oblivious to the time, the rushed shoppers, and the numerous sale signs in the long stream of display windows.

Blackness had overtaken the day's smoky-blue sky when she finally made her way up the slippery sidewalk to the duplex. To stop the cold, wet wind from lashing at her face, she bent her head and hunched her aching shoulders. She let the front door slam shut behind her. She had seen the swag lamps shining through the frosty windows of the living room. Jon had come home early. He had finally accepted her pregnancy. Without taking off her boots or coat, she dashed beyond the front closet to meet him.

Greeting her, instead, was an upright piano, its rich walnut grain perfectly matching the varnished wood of their chesterfield suite and the bentwood rocking chair.

"Jon, where are you?" She couldn't find him anywhere in the house and finally she decided that he had wanted it this way—for her to be alone with the piano for a while, and as she played Rimsky Korsakoff's "Flight of the Bumblebee", great pride swelled within her. She was beside herself and when the phone rang, she jumped to answer it.

"Hello."

"Hi, there. How are you feeling today? And what did the doctor say?" Her mother's soft voice suggested concern.

"Oh, hi, Mom. I feel just great and the doctor said that everything's in order."

"And when is the due date?" Her tone had lightened.

"The baby's due on September fifteenth, and Jon came home early from skiing today and surprised me with a piano. An upright Cable just like …" She suddenly stopped talking, realizing just then who actually had given her the piano. "Yes, just like *yours*. But how…?"

"Honey, we both know how much you miss having your own piano. We bought it from the parents of one of your father's students. The boy wanted an expensive electric guitar instead. The piano is secondhand, you know."

"Ohh, I don't care. It's beautiful. But how did you get it inside? I know I locked up this morning and you returned the extra set of keys at Christmas."

"Your father waited until he saw you at the bus stop, and then he took out a basement window and he got in from there."

"Pretty sneaky. Thank you both so much. I can start teaching right here at home now. I'll have to phone my students and juggle their schedules again, though. I hope I don't lose any of them because of this." She chatted a while longer and then sat at the piano again. But now her hands were heavy on her lap. Her desire to play waned as darkening thoughts of Jon crept into her mind.

His next call came the day before she expected him home. "I phoned the office this morning to find out where they wanted me on my return."

He had rushed into the conversation. She was surprised and hurt. "And I saw Dr. Styles again this week and everything is fine. He just wants me to gain some weight."

"They want me to stay here longer, until next Tuesday, at least. And since I'm closer to camp here, I'm going to stay with Todd and Sara over the weekend."

He hadn't heard one word she had said. "But you didn't pack enough warm clothes." She tried choking back her disappointment.

"No, I didn't, but I can buy all I need up here, and I'll only be gone for ten days maximum. Take care now." He hadn't meant to sound so uncaring, so callous, because he *did* care— about her. He just didn't like the idea of …

"Jon, our baby's going to be perfect. Our baby's going to be healthy and beautiful," she screamed out to him. But he had already hung up.

She tried to paint a peaceful winter scene on the stretched canvas she had discovered in a wooden box in the basement closet, but the long sable brush wasn't her friend that evening. Her strokes were jerky, her perspective completely wrong. The upright piano remained mute also and, with the dirty dishes from supper still in the sink, the ironing still unfinished, and the new paperback she had purchased at noon still unopened, she went to bed early.

But comfort eluded her and she flung the blankets onto the floor. Suddenly her limbs were flailing, her head jerking. She was dreaming again. Her mind was going deeper and deeper into the darkness. "No! No! No!" she screamed as her head tossed about. Her entire body twitched as the nightmare continued and those three-eyed orange heads with green fuzzy hair were all laughing at her and sneering at her armless son, who was being tossed into the air like a football. Just out of her reach, the ugly creatures kept throwing him around as they cackled in their play and in her fright.

"Let him go! Let him go!" she shouted. Beads of sweat dripped down her forehead and she shivered from the memory of the ugly, monstrous shapes verging upon her deformed son as he bobbed up and down in the air. When her eyes opened again, she realized that she had been walking in her sleep. She was in the exercise room with Jon's jump rope in her hand, ready to jump.

"No! No! No!" After tossing the rope high into the air, she brushed over her tender breasts and still-flat stomach. She cringed, tensing every muscle in her body, when she heard the rope drop onto the floor. She had given in to Jon. She had totally succumbed to his sordid suggestion, to the twisted ideas of her own subconscious mind, and she hated herself for it. "I want you both. I want you both!"

The phone rang but she didn't answer it, as every unsightly shape, color, and gesture portrayed in her nightmare continued to flash through her mind—a constant reverberation of ugliness, evil, and horror. And she prayed that Jon would come home soon to rid her of this frightening solitude. As the evening hours slipped closer to dawn, she sat curled up in a comforter at the bedroom hearth and stared out into the azure morning, her face sober, her eyes blank. She was pale, drained, and apathetic.

As she folded the laundry later that week, she saw Dawna and Gordon Greene unexpectedly at the front door. She could no longer hold back her emotions. Her hands shook from fatigue and she started to cry after spilling a cup of coffee on Dawna's lap.

"Desiree," Gordon began softly as his wife washed out her skirt in the half-bath by the kitchen. "Are you pregnant?"

"What? Of course not!" She knew her reply had been too hasty, too harsh, a downright lie. "What makes you think that?"

"Well, Dawna has told me about your tiredness the last little while at the office and she's come to that conclusion. She's been waiting for you to tell her, but you haven't said a thing. Not a word at all about *anything*."

Desiree dropped a wet paper towel into a large ashtray on the coffee table. "Well, she's right. I'm ten weeks pregnant."

"I knew it! I just knew it! Right from the start you haven't been yourself," Dawna declared with a broad smile as she walked back into the living room. She had been given a satin lounging gown to wear while her skirt dried, and her hands were touching its smoothness as she spoke. "It couldn't be anything else. But you certainly don't look too happy about it."

"Oh, Dawna. I am but …" She touched the crystal decanter beside the ashtray.

"But you aren't too sure about Jon's reaction to it, are you?"

"Am I that transparent?" She stood up, walked over to the piano, and dropped her body onto the keyboard. The jangle startled everyone. "It seems that with just one look the entire world knows exactly what I'm doing, what I'm thinking, and how I'm feeling. Jon could read me like an open book right from the beginning, too."

"I can't believe what's happening to you, Des. What did Jon say when you first told him?"

"Nothing." She didn't want to get into any details just then, not even with her new best friend.

"Well, somehow he's given you a strange but very strong impression that he's not too pleased about this pregnancy. Seems he wants you to lose the baby, and you can't get that idea out of your mind."

"It's not at all what …"

Gordon leaned forward and took her hand. "There's a new special pill available that could help you with all this, you know."

"What?" She knew he was a prominent pharmacist but she didn't think he would …

"Why don't you go to your doctor again? See what he's willing to do for you."

"Gord! Dawna! I can't believe what I'm hearing from either of you. What are you trying to tell me?"

"Calm down now, Des. We're only trying to help. Neither of us would ever agree to anyone taking those pills senselessly. We're not saying that we want you to lose the baby, but your sanity is worth a lot too, you know, and taking a few pills is much better than …" Deep in thought, she looked up at the ceiling. "The timing might be off, though. They just might complicate everything now."

"I'm so confused," Desiree offered. "I feel so good about this pregnancy and I want the baby so much." She took a long drink of water before continuing. "You believe me, don't you?"

"Yes, of course. But what I think you need right now is a good night's sleep." Dawna stood up and took her arm. "Do you have any sleeping pills?"

"No."

"Gord, can you get any tonight?"

"Of course."

"But …"

"No buts, Des. He'll make sure they're the right ones. And they won't hurt you or the baby. Just some mild tranquilizers. *Very* mild. Not like some of those other pills." And Dawna stayed with her that night. Only two pills were needed. Only two were taken.

"Now, Des, just remember what we talked about last night," Dawna whispered to the sleeping blonde early the next morning, after shutting off the alarm and carefully straightening the soft covers on the daybed in the room's cozy alcove. "You'll soon know exactly what to do." She washed up, got dressed, and stepped out of the duplex while Desiree remained in a deep slumber.

Awakening an hour later than usual, Desiree phoned the office and was instantly told to stay home.

"I told Mr. Morten that you had a touch of the flu. I hope you don't mind the little white lie. He didn't hesitate giving you some time off, but he wants you to see your doctor again. Soon. He thinks you've lost too much weight lately, and we're *all* concerned about that. Be sure to have all those tests we talked about last night, okay?"

"Yes, *Mother*," she laughed softly. "And thanks again."

When the telephone rang late that evening, Desiree Sommers answered it with a new confidence. Her aching heart was on the mend and her troubled mind seemed washed of all doubt. She was in love with Jon, and she was carrying *his* child, conceived in love, and that thought, that beautiful realization, had helped her continue through another busy day. He just told her he'd be home that next afternoon. She was overjoyed.

A changed man was sharing her life again and Desiree's days of loneliness and anxiety were soon forgotten. Jon agreed that the old upright piano added a special richness to the living room's decor, and he helped her move it a little further away from the fireplace. He especially liked the idea of her now teaching at home, and several times that week he slumped into the armchair and listened to the unmelodious sounds of the young students. Occasionally, however, to hide his laughter from some of the children, he went downstairs and exercised until he and Desiree were alone again.

"It is so nice and quiet here now, isn't it?" He smiled as he mimicked playing the piano like her last student had done. "I don't know how you do it. Never did."

"You know I love it, Jon, and it keeps me busy when you're not around. Just think, soon I'll be home all day and I can teach my present students, some nursery kids perhaps, and even our own child. Until it gets older, our baby will be sleeping most of the time, and if it causes any problems during a lesson, I just won't charge for any time."

Jon quickly got up from the bench press and turned to face her. Thick brows arched over his searching eyes. "Honey, because you haven't started to show yet, I thought you had lost the baby."

She leaned against the papered wall near the treadmill. "Oh, Jon. Don't you think that I'd let you know immediately if something like that had happened? I'd be on the mobile phone so fast."

"Yeah, I guess you would be, but I still thought …"

She wrapped herself around him and tried to remember, to relish, only the special attention he had given her since returning home from the rigs. She had only assumed his quiet acceptance of the unborn baby, while all this time … "I honestly thought I would have lost it by now. Mom had three miscarriages in her second month and one in her third."

"You mean to say there's still a chance that you can lose it?" He stacked the large chrome dumbbells on the floor in the corner before he turned to face her. "Or do you think you've gone beyond that point already?"

"It's hard to tell. I just hope." She was without words for a long time as doubt, fear, and shock grew inside her, until finally she stood up and faced him directly. "Jon, whatever our baby is, I'm going to keep it. And I'm going to love it."

"But *could* you love it, Desiree? Could you love a child that is so imperfect?"

"Yes! Yes! I could!" She hated his tone of voice, his choice of words.

"Well, I couldn't. Not for one moment. No, Des, if our baby is deformed in any way, any tiny little way, we'll put it in an institution somewhere and tell everyone we know that it was stillborn."

An ugly apprehension flushed through her mind, warming every vein in her body with a sudden fervor. "But Jon. Don't you see? That's exactly what your parents did with James Robert. You didn't even know you had a brother until just a few months ago."

"Don't bring that subject up ever again! Do you hear me?" He bolted out of the kitchen, grabbed his jacket from the wall hook near the back doors, and slammed them both shut.

She didn't see or hear from him for four days. Only her ill-fitting clothes gave any hint that something was amiss in her life. She still hadn't told anyone else about the pregnancy. At the office she purposely looked busy, despite her empty workbasket, and her parents gleefully thought her number of students had increased. She could still remember solitude as having been a fairly good friend, most times, but now it haunted her. "Where are you, Jon? Aren't you a little lonesome for me?" How often had she questioned herself about that?

And she was missing her sister more than ever before. At the most unexpected moments, favorite childhood memories would fill Desiree's mind—chatting with everyone they met on their daily walks to school ... the weekly music lessons that were such a bore to Erin ... sharing the same bedroom for all those years, until they moved into the new house ... performing their own choreographed dance routines out on the front lawn in the summer time, when the neighborhood youngsters were coerced into paying, if they wanted to see them. The sisters charged twenty-five cents each, and Erin made sure she received ... the wilted rosebud falling from behind Erin's ear onto the floor at Todd and Sara's the night she died ... and her sister's wedding present, hidden, still unopened. *Memories.*

In the living room now, she walked over to the end table, reached into its bottom drawer and took out Erin's unopened package. She stood up, and for a long moment she was motionless, her face somber as she stared at the shiny paper and bright red ribbon. She gingerly took the gift, and under the faint light of the corner floor lamp she sat in the wing chair and looked out at the darkening March evening. *Memories.*

Having finally unwrapped a tiny plaque of the finest crystal, she kept it in the palm of her left hand. So delicate was this small adornment, sparkling with every color of the rainbow—red, orange, yellow, green, blue, indigo, and violet. Breathtaking. Especially the band of indigo, so thin, so difficult to distinguish. It was intriguing. And then, with a slight turn of her wrist, the colors were gone: from perfect transparency to a pale gray opacity. It was utterly fascinating.

She read the inscription. *To every thing there is a season, and a time to every purpose under the heaven... A time to get, and a time to lose, a time to keep, and a time to cast away.*

The sky had darkened, but it didn't matter. The beautiful plaque was in its protective box again, hidden behind a stack of albums in the stereo cabinet. She had placed her favorite record by The Byrds on the turntable and she sat transcendent as she absorbed the beat, the tune, and the words over and over and over. She was lost in the absolute stillness of infinity, soaring above the earth, beyond all concern, beyond tranquility. "Turn! Turn! Turn!" Looking through the open sheers of the bay window, she was once again charmed by God's evening masterpiece. But when she noticed Jon parking his car out front, her mind instantly buzzed with anxiety. She wasn't sure of what to expect from him, or herself, that night.

"Hello," she said softly and her searching eyes lifted when she heard his creaking footsteps inside at the front door. A tiny smile and dark questioning eyes soon greeted her. She could only hear the sound of her heart pounding against her ribs as he handed her a huge bouquet of long-stemmed red roses.

"Why don't you put these in a nice vase while I set up the other gift I have for you? Please take your time in there."

Her distrusting mind flashed horror scenes against its wide screen and her heart beat fitfully against her ribs. Desiree inhaled the distinctive essence of the bouquet as she walked into the kitchen and carefully unwrapped the decorative paper. She snipped off the end of each thorny stem with her sharpest utility shears, hearing Jon fumbling near the stereo in the other room. She wondered what he was truly thinking and what the other gift might be. She spilled some of the powdery plant food that came inside the wrapping and took her time cleaning it up, until Jon called for her.

With exquisite red roses decorating the side table and fire logs spitting playfully in the hearth, Jon guided her to the stereo where he carefully turned up the volume.

"It's a Stan Getz single. "The Girl from Ipanema". I saw it in a little shop in Jasper and had to get it for you. It's not exactly a current sale item, you know." He took both hands in his and whispered, "May I have this dance, my little girl from Ipanema?"

The warmth of his large hands caressed her willing body, and the faint smell of his woodsy cologne intoxicated her once again.

"I want you, Desiree. And I want the baby that you're carrying." Carefully he swept a single tress from her face, and he bent down to kiss her waiting mouth before carrying her up the stairs where soon their naked bodies were entwined and his ample hardness probed deep inside her until their feverish hunger was satisfied. The moment was electric. The night was perfect.

Cleanly shaven and dressed in new blue jeans and a cotton T-shirt, Jon was whistling his own tune when Desiree awakened early that next day. "Good morning," he said casually. She watched with glee as he hung up the appliquéd wall hanging she had forced herself to finish one lonely night. She had left it beside the closet doors. "Have you finished the macramé planter yet?" He preferred only her creations around the house, insisting that all the wedding gifts of rich tapestries, still life oil paintings, and various pastels be kept in the storage area of their basement.

"Almost."

"Good." He jumped off the cedar chest he had used as a ladder, stood at the opposite wall of the bedroom, and eyed his placement. "I just hope you're carrying a girl."

"Why? Because of that?" Warmth tinted her face as she pointed to the Holly Hobby wall hanging she had made so many years ago. It pictured a little girl standing in a field of silk daisies and wearing a gathered pink gingham dress, her hair in soft ringlets of twisted yellow angora yarn dangling below her wide-brimmed bonnet. A white felt kitten, playing beside her, finished the scene.

"No, no. The will."

"What will?"

"I thought I already told you about it. Well, anyway, Mother's father, Grandpa Williams, eccentric that he was, has left over a million dollars to the first granddaughter when she turns twenty-one. Apparently nothing is to be given to any other grandchild. Absolutely nothing. How absurd, huh?"

"But I didn't think you wanted anything from your family anymore."

"Just not from my mother or my father. Grandpa Williams was okay in his own peculiar way. But I don't want any son of mine to be doted on like I was. Girls are for doting on. Now, I think the front yard needs a good clean up. First time for me, huh?"

Yes it was. And in a short while Jon was sweeping their front sidewalk. The rear crease in his new jeans nicely followed the rhythm of his long steady swings. Desiree phoned her parents. She wanted the whole world to know just how good, how complete, she felt today.

Jon also raked the winter's debris from the neighbor's front yard, took out the garbage, and fixed the leaky tap in the half-bath. Then, having finished his chores, he drove to the neighborhood liquor store and bought a bottle of the best champagne and some crystal stemware, in a pinwheel design that had been on display by the entrance. In a corner flower shop on the way back home, he bought a small Venus flytrap, just for Desiree.

The plant, however, was more of a toy for him. After dinner he picked a tiny piece of steak left on Desiree's plate, stabbed it with the broken end of an old swizzle stick he had found in the junk drawer and, teasing the plant, waited for its young claws to open. Slowly, deliberately, he let the meat touch the tiny plant. Patiently, he waited. The chunk was obviously too big, so he broke a smaller piece off before trying again.

Into the early morning hours, taking only a few tiny sips of the champagne, Desiree sat at the hearth and watched her handsome husband, who still squatted in front of the coffee table. He was staring at the new plant, still waiting and occasionally poking the jagged leaves. He started laughing when he finally realized that she had been watching him all this time.

"Just don't ever be like my haughty mother, with all her orchids and roses, or her money, or any of her possessions. Would you promise me that?"

"Yes, Jon. I promise." Desiree smiled.

Chapter Seven

Wondering how she could survive the unrelenting heat of the long, dry summer, Desiree worked in the office until the Labor Day weekend. Her stomach was so large now, the baby so low, she found it difficult to sit up straight at any time. Her last office duty was to somehow settle herself in the boardroom to peruse various travel brochures for the owner of the company, who was planning a Mediterranean cruise later that year with his wife and two teenaged sons. It was a constant reminder of the fabulous wedding present they had received from Jon's parents, and Desiree often wondered when she and her husband finally would be on their own worldwide tour.

She could eat almost anything, could read the colorful brochures or any sized book directly from the huge hump of her belly by simply leaning further back into her seat. And it seemed the office staff had chosen to be her personal and vigilant caterer. During her last week at the office, every morning and throughout the entire workday, she would be guided to the large leather recliner in the far corner of the company boardroom, and be told to *just lounge there*. While using her bulging stomach as her own desktop, she quite enjoyed the various fruits and goodies brought to her.

In less than two weeks her baby would arrive. She was going to be a mother. Her big, round belly would be flat. There'd be no more waddling to get around, no more struggling to get out of bed, no more discomfort to sit up or to sit down again, no more dizzying trips every half hour to get to the washroom in time. And, hopefully by then, Jon would be starting an accounting job downtown somewhere, with only a twenty-minute drive from home—no more mobile phones or two-way radios or lonely evenings. Desiree was excited.

Despite her busy schedule and being the only unaccompanied mother-to-be attending the weekly prenatal classes recently set up at the hospital, Desiree did not miss one lesson, although, because of missing the bus transfer, twice she had entered the hospital's cool theater-style room in the middle of a documentary film or a special exercise session. One particular morning, however, as she heard the constant chirping of hungry chickadee nestlings from the poplar tree outside their bedroom balcony, Desiree sat on the cedar chaise lounge and struggled to remember everything she had been taught in those classes.

Contractions were inevitable, perhaps only varying in degree of pain, but hers had been coming every sixteen minutes for the past two weeks without any pain, cramp, or backache—just an annoying little pull from within—nothing excruciating at all, but certainly bothersome. She was still watching the clock, still waiting for that expected grab, but there was only a slight twitch again, and moments later, a sudden pull, another tiny constriction. Then, she was in the bathroom again, waiting.

She had been up and down both flights of stairs all afternoon, trying to catch up on all the laundry, to have the house spotless. The half-bath next to the kitchen soon became her middle ground where she would sit and wait and wait and wait. Then up, around, and down. Up, around, and down, again. It was becoming a routine now, a tiresome and uncomfortable routine. But she wanted the duplex totally ready for her new family.

Somehow during her many jaunts around her home, finally getting all the laundry cleaned, folded, and put away, and the vacuuming and dusting finished, she miscalculated her timing. Only five minutes had passed since the last contraction, and when the telephone started to ring, she could feel another tiny pull.

"Hello."

"You haven't left for the hospital yet?" Dawna's voice rang with surprise.

"No, Dawna. Not yet. I feel a little restless today, though. There's still no pain but the contractions seem to be coming even more often now."

"How often?"

"I've had two in the last eleven minutes."

"Phone Jon on the mobile and get him home fast! And then call your doctor."

Desiree laughed heartily. "I'm not in labor, Dawna. I don't feel any pain whatsoever. Just that same little pull and then that same little pinch. And it's still more than a week too soon."

"Has your water broken yet?"

"No, but when it does, I'll phone you."

"Well, all right then. I'll accept that. But make those other calls anyway. Put everybody on notice. Please."

Not thinking it was necessary to phone her doctor quite yet, Desiree did leave a message for Jon on the mobile. The operator had asked her to hold for a short while so she could get him on the phone, but Desiree hung up on her because she had to go to the bathroom again.

Most of her evening was spent either sitting on the cold white commode or pacing the large kitchen floor, because it was getting too difficult to sit down in a comfortable chair somewhere else, only to have to get up again to go to the bathroom. The contractions were still very weak, but constant, only five minutes apart now, and she had to go to the bathroom again. Was she actually in labor? She had to ask herself that repeatedly. Feeling no truly grabbing pain yet, she wasn't sure. After hearing a busy signal from her doctor's office, she decided to have a cab come in another hour.

So, this really could be it, she mused, as she wiped herself dry from the warm shower, taking her time brushing her teeth, applying makeup, and styling her long blown-dry hair. Then slowly, as she got dressed, the anticipation of motherhood enveloped her. When she toddled over to the phone to call Dawna and her parents, she remained exceptionally calm. She was very still in the cab, a little surprised that she felt so relaxed in her first stage of labor, her first pregnancy, one she had gone through to full term with absolutely no complications. No physical complications. Shouldn't she be a little more excited than this, perhaps even slightly afraid, at least a little apprehensive? How often had she made this same trip before to attend those weekly prenatal classes? Why did this same road seem so bumpy, so uncomfortable tonight? She needed a washroom soon.

"Slow down, sir, or I'm going to have an accident."

"What's wrong, ma'am? Are you going to have the baby already? Here? In my brand-new car?"

"No, no. But please hurry."

And he obliged her by speeding down the thoroughfare, changing lanes to pass a few slow-going vehicles, veering left and veering right, braking, accelerating. Veering again, braking again. As the horn blared, Desiree's body sank further into the back seat. They wouldn't make it to the hospital safely, she was sure of that, but the driver didn't hear her pleas. He wasn't listening to one word she was saying.

"You should have called for an ambulance, ma'am," she thought she heard him say. "You told me that you had lots of time."

They pulled into the emergency entrance, and Desiree felt relieved that she could walk in by herself. Quickly guided to a small corner room, she sat with her full overnight bag beside her chair—a chair so hard, so narrow, and so uncomfortable.

As the young nurse placed the previously completed admittance sheet directly in front of Desiree, the nurse leaned over the desk and started asking questions. Soon she was tapping the desk with the eraser end of her short pencil. Impatience seemed to unnerve her as she waited for the answers, while Desiree shifted her weight during another contraction.

"You've got the admittance sheet right there, filled out in neat printing, I believe. My doctor told me it has all the information about me that any of you would need. So why don't you just read the darn thing first? Then, if you have any more questions, I will certainly answer them. But please hurry. And where are your washrooms?"

Ten uneasy minutes elapsed and Desiree was so cramped, so ignored, so anxious. "Why can't you just tell me where the washrooms are? I really have to go. Now!"

The prim nurse stood up, strutted around her desk, and opened the door. Her hazel eyes were wide with annoyance. "Someone get a wheelchair for me. Fast!"

"I don't need a wheelchair. I just need a washroom." But by then, three nurses were in front of her. One nurse was already starting to unfold the foot stand.

"I can walk. Really, I can. Just show me where to go."

But they all insisted that she be wheeled around. The oldest nurse among them helped her into the chair and pushed her forward. At the nearest elevator they waited until finally the nurse realized that it apparently was stuck on the third floor.

"Where are the washrooms around here? I can't hold it in any longer."

"Someone! Get a doctor here! Immediately!!" Nurse Jacobson's full lips tightened and when no one appeared, she shook her head and helped Desiree down the corridor. Arm in arm, they walked up the two flights of stairs.

The pressure on her lower abdomen was increasing, almost intolerable. Desiree had to grab the railing. "Oh, please hurry. Why doesn't a hospital have any washrooms on the main floor? There should be several of them around here, you know."

She was helped onto a table in the prep room. Seven nurses quickly crowded around her.

"Is it always this exciting, this engrossing, to see a young woman in quiet labor? This is the maternity ward, isn't it? You should all be used to this by now, and all I want to do is go to the washroom. It won't take long and I'll come right back. I promise. Just tell me where it is."

"She's completely dilated."

"Where's her doctor?"

"When did she say she phoned him?"

"I tried phoning his office, but the line was busy," Desiree interrupted. "I thought I had lots of time. Until I got here."

"Call her doctor at once," the head nurse called out.

"When did your water break?"

"It didn't"

"What?"

"When did your baby drop?"

"It didn't."

"Pardon me?"

"Well, maybe it dropped just a bit tonight, about twenty minutes or so ago. I've carried it so low right from the beginning but it seemed much lower when I was walking around here tonight."

"When was your last contraction?"

"Oh, I don't know. A few moments ago, I guess. I can't feel any of them, okay? What is this, anyway? The interrogation room?" She was starting to hate the unrelenting voices, the muffled laughter in the background. "May I please leave the room?" She felt like a little kindergarten student, having to ask.

"Ma'am there's no time for that. Is your husband here?"

"No."

In the delivery room only a few minutes before midnight she was covered with thin white sheets, her feet hastily put up in the stirrups. She was still waiting, still holding back. There was no pain yet, just an ever-growing pressure down below.

Only three nurses were with her now, all watching the clock, while she eyed the various pieces of equipment along one wall. Concern slowly absorbed her, until she saw Dr. Styles marching down the long hall towards the room. His curly peppery-gray hair was mussed and his long trench coat flapped with his quick strides.

"Didn't you take those particular prenatal classes I arranged for you, Mrs. Sommers?" Irritation spurted from his mouth as he dropped his coat onto a corner chair.

"Yes, you know I did. Why?"

"Didn't someone there tell you to phone me when your labor started?"

"Sir, I …"

"Don't you feel like bearing down? Pushing?"

"I've felt like doing that all day, sir. But …"

"On your next contraction then, please push. Push hard."

She took a deep breath, shifted her body for more comfort on the thin mattress, and waited.

"You missed it. Let's try it again."

"How do you know if I've missed a contraction or not?" Her dry eyes glared at him.

"Take another deep breath and push… *Now*!!"

She pushed—hard—and suddenly she felt the gripping pull of a *true* contraction. Ohhhhh!!!

"One more time. Pushshshsh!"

The pain. Excruciating pain! "Ohh, Lord! Help me! Please help me NOW!"

Moments later the announcement came. "Good girl! She's here."

"What?" Hushed by the thrill of the moment, Desiree leaned forward to get her first glance of her newborn baby, but too many arms and hands and shoulders were in her way, and a rush of doubt overcame her. "Where's my baby? Let me see my baby."

When a nurse finally laid the tiny human being onto her suddenly flattened stomach, Desiree's eyes widened and she started to cry. "Ohh, no." She wanted to scream, to push, and to kick, then curl up under the sheet and go to sleep, not to be bothered by anyone ever again. Her first child, the little girl she had been hoping for all this time, was not the perfect package she thought all newborns would be. She was not pinkish-purple and slippery. Instead, her baby girl was dry, wrinkly, and flaky-white, as though an entire jar of baby powder had somehow been spilled over her. Both wrists and ankles were cracked, and bleeding. She was sickly white while her mother was sickly blue about the whole affair. Desiree moaned to herself in despair. "Where are you, Jon? Don't you know that I need you here with me right now? But please don't look at the baby. Please don't be upset. And please don't ask any questions."

In spite of numerous visitors when the regulations permitted, Desiree rested well in the hospital. She had lost every pound she had gained during the last few months of her pregnancy, and the soft, rosy color in her cheeks had stayed. Her face glowed. Her daughter's wrists and ankles were healing quickly; the color and texture of the tight skin was normal now. Yes, her little baby girl was picture-perfect.

Blankets, sleepers, dolls, and plush toys cluttered the side table and window ledge nearby, and still more visitors and more gifts were appearing, but Desiree had never expected to see Todd Remmings there.

"Sara's got her Samoyeds in the dog show here this weekend, and I took time off work just to see your new addition. Is Jon in town?"

"No. He couldn't get the time off but he phones here every night. He told me to expect something special from him today, but it hasn't arrived yet."

"I saw his parents in the parking lot. They look quite happy."

"It's just a façade, I'm sure."

"Why? Because it's not a boy?"

"Yeah. To continue the family business, I guess. And since Jon refuses to become an architect, his father can't wait for a grandson. I just gave them my extra house keys so they could have a brass crib delivered before we got home. Isn't that something, Todd? I never dreamed of having a brass crib for my baby."

"Well, you know they have the money. Oh, and speaking of money, Sara's making a small fortune breeding her dogs. I might be able to retire soon." He winked just as a young nurse was bringing in the newborn. "I know what else would be perfect for this little darling." He tweaked the baby's tiny nose.

"I think she's got more than she'll ever need."

"Not pick of the litter."

"What?"

"Well, maybe not for a little while yet, but in three or four years, a puppy would be an excellent companion. Have you thought of a name for her yet?"

"Jon has had one picked out for months. He insists that it be Jodi. Just Jodi. No middle name. I think his grandfather told him years ago that he thought that name was beautiful. Jodi is Hebrew for *the praised one*, you know."

"Jodi Sommers. Short and sweet. I like it. But of all the times for Jon to be still out of town, huh?"

"We both thought that we had planned everything so perfectly around her scheduled arrival, but we should have known that babies set their own time."

"Your obvious glow proves that it was more than worth it, though."

"Oh, yes. No doubt about that."

As they spoke, another nurse placed a bouquet of long-stemmed red roses on the bedside table and Desiree stretched her tired body to pull out the attached card. The unfamiliar handwriting said, 'To my darling mother, Love Jodi'. In the lower corner a scribbled note with smaller writing, more crooked than the other, had been added. 'I'm all done up here. Be home tomorrow afternoon, about four o'clock.' Desiree pressed the card close to her swollen bosom.

"He'll be home tomorrow, Todd." Desiree smiled. "Just like us."

Jon had offered to arrange for a limousine to take mother and daughter home, but Desiree preferred a less conspicuous ride by taxicab for just the two of them. She was planning to show Jodi around the duplex and rock her in the bentwood before putting her in the new brass crib she herself had yet to see. She would sing and play and talk to her newborn daughter within the quietness and comfort of their duplex.

"There you go, ma'am. Everything's inside now," the taxi driver announced early that next day. He set the last plastic bag, stuffed with various gifts, onto the loveseat in the living room and waited. "Do you need any more help with all this?"

"No, no, not at all. Thanks." She was rushing him by having the fare ready, including a handsome tip, and almost pushing him away with the closing door. But she was home now— home with her brand new baby girl. And welcoming them both was a beautiful baby grand piano, centered perfectly in the living room.

She could see a wrapped parcel, about the size of a cradle, under the main body of the piano, but she decided to open it at another time. "And we got this *including* a brass crib?" Her smile was wide. "And it's all because of you, Jodi. This will be yours when you come of age ... if your father lets us keep it, that is." Desiree touched the rich dark varnished wood, which so perfectly reflected her delight. Carefully she laid her tiny baby onto it and began to play Brahms' "Children's Lullaby".

"Will you let me keep this, Jon?" she questioned herself. "Will you let me keep it for our daughter?"

Later, to delay the expected verbal confrontation with her husband concerning the piano, Desiree filled a huge picnic basket with various cheeses, breads, and fruits. Jon's favorite bottle of wine was wrapped carefully with some folded paper napkins. She wrote him a short note of their whereabouts that afternoon and taped it to the back outside door.

For the very first time, within the hour, he would be meeting his baby daughter at the nearby park, at the same picnic table, nestled around newly-planted evergreens, where he and Desiree had spent many easy moments sharing a banana split or bag of jelly beans.

A skinny black squirrel, its scraggly tail kinked at the tip, chased a piece of shiny paper that whirled in a sudden gust of wind. Its eyes flitted nervously as it bit into someone's discarded chocolate bar wrapping before scurrying across the picnic table that Desiree was just about to set. In a split second, it had jumped onto the hood of Jodi's stroller, sat up, and started to rip the foil. Jodi slept soundly.

Smoothing a vinyl cloth over the table, Desiree heard the slamming of a car door. Proudly she lifted her daughter out of the stroller, unwrapped the pink blanket, and let it droop on the handle before turning around to face her husband. But instead, an older couple was emptying their hatchback of various pieces of barbecue equipment.

The bright afternoon sun was slipping quickly into a pale yellow glow over the distant mountains and Desiree wondered if she shouldn't pack up the platter of cheeses and bread, the bowl of mixed fruit, and the wine bottle, and then walk back home. She could put Jodi in her shiny new crib and wait for Jon to phone, maybe to explain why he was running so late.

Being careful not to be seen while breast-feeding Jodi behind a thick cluster of bushes, Desiree finally refilled the basket with the unused picnic goodies. But as she was packing up the stroller, she heard the steady blasting of a familiar car horn. Jodi stirred slightly and then went back to sleep.

When Desiree turned to face him, Jon was standing right in front of her. Donned in a navy pinstriped wool suit with a plain silk tie and pale blue shirt, he was as handsome as any man could be, and their embrace was electrifying.

"I've missed you so much." His eyes were sparkling, as he gently straightened the collar of her cotton shirt. "But you know I haven't seen our little girl yet."

With a loving gesture Desiree stepped out of the way and eagerly watched her husband slowly approach the stroller. After squatting beside it and carefully lifting up the blanket, he was silenced by the absolute miracle of life. He remained still, as though every muscle in his body were frozen.

"We created this?" he whispered at long last. He picked her up, twirled her around as she cooed, and his spirited play continued until the picnic table was reset and Jodi's eyelids were heavy again.

"I burned all my old rig clothes in our barbecue pit before coming here," he admitted freely, after taking a large piece of cheese from the wrapper and breaking off a piece for her. "I should have chopped up that piano and thrown it in, too. You know we don't need that monstrosity in our home. Why didn't you send the thing back the same day you got it?"

His voice was suddenly callous and Desiree sighed, certain that he was fighting the urge to explode. How quickly such a beautiful moment had past. "How would I be able to do that, Jon? I have no receipts."

"You could have had it sent directly to Mother and Father's house and then let them worry about what to do with the stupid thing. Tomorrow I'll phone for a delivery truck."

"Oh, but Jon. This could be the beginning of a family tradition. A baby grand for the first grandchild." She was trying to sound calm, to be poised. "What a wonderful idea. And it looks so beautiful in our living room."

"Honey, it almost takes up the entire wall by the front stairway. And you already have a piano. One that looks much better and much less conspicuous. We don't need that preposterous thing."

Jodi's whimpering quickly erased Desiree's disappointment.

"Oh, let me take her, honey. There's something for both of you on the front seat. Would you mind getting it yourself?"

And as Jon picked up the squirming bundle beside him, Desiree went to the car. On the passenger seat was a white plush bunny, almost as big as their newborn, with *I love you* embroidered on the pink bodice front. Beside it, still in its clear plastic container, was a blush-colored orchid surrounded by a tiny wisp of baby's breath. She picked up both items and walked back to the table.

"Thank you so much, Jon. It's beautiful. They're beautiful."

"Just like my new family." Yes, except for a brand new Corvette, he had been able to afford everything in his youthful dreams—a nice house, a motor home, a cabin cruiser. And he was a father now—a father to a beautiful and healthy baby girl. And he quite liked that scenario.

Chapter Eight

The long wonderful Indian summer had interlaced the usual urban landscape with variegated reds, oranges, yellows, and greens. As Jodi nestled in her arms, Desiree sat on the front steps of the duplex and eyed the loveliness. In the distance, a neighbor's lawn mower was chugging through the thick greenness. Across the way, an elderly woman was on hands and knees, pulling at the late summer's generous offerings.

"Hi, there." An unfamiliar high-pitched voice came from the other side of the caragana bushes that divided the property, and soon an auburn mop of short curly hair bobbed over the hedge. "I'm Carole Schrader. So many times I've waved to you through the front windows here, trying to get your attention, but you were always running to the bus stop."

"Hello, Carole. I'm Desiree Sommers and this is my daughter, Jodi."

"Yes, I know who you are. After the postman came one morning, I peeked in your mailbox and got your full name. Then I thought I might just as well phone *Information* to get your phone number. But you never seem to be home at night, either."

"I'm usually home then. I just unplug all the phones when I'm giving piano lessons."

"So you used to teach the piano, huh?"

"Oh, I still do."

"But how can you without a piano?"

"I have one in the living room. But ..."

"Ohhh, I didn't know that. When I saw that rich dark baby grand being wheeled out of your duplex and then into that huge van a while ago, I thought you were moving out. But when only the piano was taken, I wanted to come over and introduce myself right then. I just knew that you had bought the other one for the prestige, and soon realized that you couldn't afford to keep it. That's too bad. It sure was beautiful."

Desiree's eyes widened from disbelief.

"Well, Ken, my husband, you know, won't be getting home for a while yet, so I might just as well hear you play something for me right now."

The long impromptu performance satisfied them both, and then, the moment Jon's car door slammed shut each following morning, the front doorbell of the duplex would ring repeatedly. Carole was back, and Desiree's entire day would be ruined. She was *supposed* to be teaching pre-schoolers.

By week's end Desiree had already given her next-door-neighbor a thick self-explanatory book on the basics of oil painting and a few quick and easy patterns to crochet. An entire afternoon had been spent correcting Carole's initial attempts at it. Somehow there had been time between lessons to do all that.

The following Wednesday, however, proved to be most hectic for the young mother. Carole arrived at the usual early time, but even before lunch, her exceptional intrusion had Desiree at the verge of crying. The fourth student had been interrupted *again* as Carole questioned the cause of the different lengths in the edges of her square Phentex potholder.

"I just can't seem to keep my tension uniform, like you said was so important. Is there any way you can fix it for me? Maybe you could come over tonight, after dinner."

"Oh, no, Carole. Not tonight." She needed some distance from this woman. A million miles or so would be nice.

"But I told you last week that my mother-in-law will be visiting us on Friday and this has to be done by then. I told her she could take it home."

Desiree finally consented to go over later that evening, but soon she started doubting her decision. "She's driving me crazy, Jon," she admitted later as she prepared dinner. "Sometimes I just feel like picking her up by the scruff of the neck, hauling her to the back door, and kicking her right out of here and to the moon. I can't take it much longer."

"When she phones to invite herself over next time, just tell her that you're too busy with other things. Make something up if it'll make you feel better. If you think it would work."

"But she doesn't phone first. She waits until she sees you drive off in the morning and then, within seconds, she's ringing our doorbell."

"Well, I'm sure you'll dream up something to stop her. But you told me that you finally agreed to go there tonight. So, why don't you? Just to set things straight."

Desiree honored her commitment and as the neighbor's front doors closed behind the young mother, a dozen of Carole's friends were all suddenly around her. "Surprise!!" She was instantly pushed into an upholstered armchair decorated in pink paper bows and striped streamers, which had been moved into the middle of the room.

Then the questions began. "How long have you been teaching music? ... How long have you studied music? ... How old is your baby now? ... I hear that you sew and knit and paint and crochet, but with all that happening in your life right now, how do you find any time for the little one? ... Is it a boy or a girl? ... And what does your husband think about your crazy routine? ... He can't possibly be too pleased."

She sat through it all, answering everyone's questions with short breaths, soon becoming dizzy from the constant chatter.

"Listen, listen," Carole shrieked after the gifts were opened and coffee and snacks had been served. "Let's all help Desiree take these presents home and then we can see the baby, the crafts, and the old piano. Too bad the baby grand isn't there anymore, though. It certainly was handsome. Ken and I are going to buy one just like it, you know."

"But Carole," a small voice uttered from the corner. "You don't even know how to play the piano."

"Well, I can learn to play it, can't I? I might just as well take some lessons from Desiree. The extra money will probably help her out a little bit. Now come on everyone. Let's get our shoes and coats on."

Desiree could hold her tongue no longer. "But you shouldn't go over there now, Carole. Jodi could already be sleeping, and I don't want Jon to be disturbed, either."

"But we're not going there to wake up the baby. We just want to get a little peek at her. And I'm sure Jon won't mind us being there. For just a little while. We'd all like to meet him too, you know."

"No, Carole, maybe some other time, but just not tonight. Please." Her throat was dry. The back of her neck was stiff. She wanted to go home, alone, to peace and quiet, to a warm bed.

Carole patted her gently on the back. "If you're so worried about what Jon will think, I'll go over and check everything out with him first."

"But ..."

The persistent hostess returned minutes later to announce that no one was home. Everyone rushed to collect her personal things before parading next door.

Footwear was soon piled carelessly at the front landing. One open-toed leather pump had been kicked under the coffee table. Jackets and purses were piled onto the telephone bench near the stairs or onto the bentwood in the corner. Someone's acrylic-knit vest had caught on the rough corner brick and was left hanging on the wall. A plastic fork with pink icing and fruitcake remnants had been stepped on and broken.

It didn't take long before Desiree lost track of everyone. Who was upstairs in their bedroom now, trying to open the balcony doors? Who was downstairs, trying out Jon's exercise equipment? Who was in the sewing room next to it, snooping through all the patterns and pulling out folds of material from the cupboards? And who's now pounding on the piano or fingering the delicate oriental jade? And who is that over there, feeding Jon's Venus flytrap the piece of squashed fruitcake she had just picked up off the floor?

From the opposite corner of the living room, Desiree saw Carole stretching her arm to get something from the slightly opened drawer of the side table, and the young mother gasped. For some reason, though, even as tears welled in her eyes, she stood still and mute by the fireplace while her new neighbor carelessly dropped the sheet music to "Desiree's Dream" as she took the tiny white box out of the drawer, its loosely folded wrapping also falling to the oak floor. Two curious friends soon huddled around her.

"I can't read the scribbling on the card here. I think it says, 'Do not open until on your honeymoon. Love, Erin'.

"What a strange request. I wonder who Erin is. Maybe we should ask her. But let's see what's inside first."

"Ohhh my. Look at all those gorgeous colors, when you get it in the right light!"

"Why isn't this hanging up somewhere?"

"Be careful with that. I think that would shatter into a thousand pieces if you dropped it."

Desiree was benumbed and bewildered, feeling utterly alone even amongst the giggles and chatter, and only when Jon returned home an hour later, with Jodi sleeping soundly in his arms, did the women reluctantly gather their scattered belongings and leave. The acrylic-knit vest was gone, too.

"What a crew that was. Where'd they all come from anyway?"

"Next door." Her answer was a tiny sigh from total fatigue. "Carole had a surprise shower for me, of all things. You should see some of the nice gifts I was given for the baby. But I didn't know one person there, Jon. Need I say anything more?"

"Please don't make them your friends."

She smoothed the torn, crumpled foil on her lap as she tried to understand how something so beautiful could have been handled so carelessly, like a trinket, just another thing to dust. What all had everyone said about it?

"Is this one of the presents you got tonight?" Jon asked as he laid Jodi on the loveseat beside him and knelt down to touch the fine crystal now exposed by the open box. "It's a strange gift for a baby shower, isn't it?"

Her throat tightened but somehow she managed an answer. "No, Jon. This is a special gift from Erin. The last one she'll ever be able to give anybody."

"From Erin?"

The young Mrs. Sommers couldn't look up to face her husband just then. She touched the narrow box lovingly. "It was my wedding gift from her, Jon. Apparently she got it for me years ago and was saving it for exactly that."

"It's lovely. What dazzling colors."

"I didn't know before how to share it with you. I couldn't share it with you. I tried so many times before to tell you about it, but …"

His hand was tight on hers. "Keep it somewhere safe, honey."

Jodi had started to shuffle under the blankets and Jon cuddled her.

"I think our baby's hungry, Mama, and I'm afraid I can't help you with that." He grinned proudly as Jodi stirred in his arms. He was a doting father, spending many joyful hours with his firstborn. Twice already he had bathed her and four times he had single-handedly changed her diaper. He was mentally keeping track. What he enjoyed most, though, was taking her for long, leisurely walks after dinner through the neighborhood park. He was meeting several neighbors, and he knew that his young bride was getting some much-needed rest back at the duplex, before a couple more piano lessons would begin.

Yes, Jon understood why Desiree was exhausted by early evening. Because Jodi would tire out and fall asleep while still being fed, she was usually hungry every two hours or so and would start to whimper. Many times in the middle of the night Desiree hadn't heard her daughter crying in the bassinet at the foot of their bed and Jon understood why his wife occasionally thought herself to be an unworthy mother. He was thankful that *he* could hear Jodi's every whimper and every toss of her blankets, but he had heard Desiree crying again under the covers, had heard every loving word that she whispered to her daughter, and his saddened heart was throbbing again.

"You're a great mother, honey. You're just too tired to enjoy Jodi like you want to," he had said often, to deaf ears.

Not once did Jon complain about any of the interruptions around the house. "Let's have another baby right away. Maybe a boy next time." He had changed his entire lifestyle so he could relish the family existence. He seemed to thrive on it, but he still preferred being out in the wilds, being his own boss, basically. Gradually he felt that his new office job was actually pinning him down. He was attending night school, the one condition he had agreed to undertake when receiving his present accounting position. He studied earnestly.

And as the years raced by, if they weren't treasuring their leisure time by boating in their new cabin cruiser or camping in their new motor home, they would be flying over the deep dark blues of various oceans and seas before lodging in some romantic inn or world-famous hotel. Already they had toured most of Europe.

Desiree enjoyed those fabulous weekends and vacations, but each year as Jon's final examinations were approaching, his face drawn and his eyes dry, she became bothered by his having to study at the kitchen table.

"Jon," she began one evening after he had opened a thick textbook to begin his studies. "I wish you had a private room for that." She knew to choose her words carefully. "Why don't you change the exercise room into a den?"

"Some day, honey, I'll have my own study, you can have a huge conservatory, and Jodi will have her own nice bedroom, but I don't have the time to change things around here right now. I kind of like this place the way it is. It's roomy enough for the time being. I'm quite happy with how everything is already. Aren't you?"

"Yes, of course I am," she answered quickly and started filling the dishwasher.

The telephone rang and Jon answered it. "Yes, but Mrs. Sommers is busy right now. Can I take a message?"

As Desiree waited curiously, Jon scribbled something on the scrap piece of paper he had pulled out of his notebook. "Ohh, I'm sure she'll be very interested. We'll talk it over tonight and I'll have her call you in the morning. Thank you." He hung up the phone and snatched the dishrag from her hand before motioning his wife to sit down beside him.

"Who's Carmella Marinello?"

A quick smile came to her face. "She a world-famous singer. Why?"

"Hmmm. I haven't heard of her. But a Mr. Thornton was just on the phone." He was reading from his notes.

"That name doesn't sound familiar at all."

"He's a close friend of Mr. McMasters, apparently. You know *him*, that's for sure. And this friend just called to say that Carmella Marinello is having a concert at the auditorium this coming weekend. The regular lead-in pianist apparently broke her hip and right arm in a car accident recently and Mr. Thornton wants you to go there tomorrow for an audition." Jon looked her straight in the eyes and smiled. "You once told me that you wanted to be a concert pianist someday. Have you changed your mind?

"Oh, no." Already, beautiful visions of celebrity had flashed across her mind.

"Well, if you ask me, this sounds like a pretty good opportunity to get your foot in the door."

"But I have lessons all day tomorrow." She turned her head, not wanting Jon to see the disappointment in her eyes.

"Cancel them. This will be your first for such last-minute changes, I know, but who could blame you? And phone your parents to baby-sit. You know they won't mind."

"What piece should I play for them?"

"Maybe they just want you to play something brand new. Sight reading I think you call it. And you know you're good at that."

"I'm so nervous, Jon. But how can I pass this up?"

"Exactly. What really is there to lose? It's only for this Friday and Saturday night. Here's your chance to play in front of hundreds. Why not give it a try? I know you'll love it." He tweaked her nose and read his note again. "Have you heard this singer before?"

"Yes. Dad has a couple of her albums. She was once a world-famous opera star but she left the company a few years ago to get out on her own."

"Opera? No wonder I haven't heard of her."

"Yes, Jon. Opera." She smiled at his light mockery. "I think she's singing different types of music now. Her voice is so versatile. But I honestly don't think I have any chance at …"

"Now don't get negative on me 'cause of some fit of nerves. Come on, Des. Give yourself a break. I'll leave this note right here on the counter for you. Phone Mr. Thornton tomorrow morning and tell him that you'd be pleased to audition. Do it for yourself, Des. Or for me. Just do it!"

She made the call to Mr. Thornton the moment Jon was on his way to the office, and was told that a salary was also involved. Two nights of piano playing at the auditorium was double her monthly salary of teaching, and at the audition she performed Beethoven's "Moonlight Sonata" flawlessly. It had always been her favorite classical piece and that was what Mr. Thornton had asked her to play.

"Again, I must apologize for Miss Marinello's absence. She wanted to hear each contender personally, but she was delayed at the TV station this morning, and has another interview elsewhere in two and a half hours. She's a very busy woman, you know." Mr. Thornton's broad shoulders shadowed the papers on the table in front of him as he spoke. "There are eight other musicians scheduled for today, and later I'll be discussing each one privately with Miss Marinello. You know she doesn't have much time to make her decision."

"That won't be necessary, Richard."

"Pardon?"

Desiree recognized Carmella Marinello's dynamic voice and turned to face the portly woman, whose hand stayed on the brass knob as the door to the large oak study closed quietly behind her.

Surprise flushed Mr. Thornton's face as he shuffled some papers into his briefcase and stood up slowly. "But Miss Marinello, I've only had the opportunity to hear this young lady play and ..."

"Richard, I also heard her play, from the other room. And I want her. Please give me the list of other contenders and I'll personally phone them this morning to cancel their auditions." She set her large leather purse onto a side table and smiled at Desiree.

"I'd like to get to know more about you over lunch, but I have to leave here pretty soon, so let's make it before rehearsals on Thursday. Four o'clock. Would that be suitable for you?"

"Yes, that will be fine, Miss Marinello. Thank you." Desiree reached for her clutch purse before facing the woman again. "Do you have a particular theme you would like me to follow?"

"Yes, as a matter of fact, I do. Thank you for asking." Carmella eyed the large wall clock across the room. "I can spare a few minutes now. Let's find a comfortable seat and talk about it."

At home Desiree prattled on about the exciting audition. She told Jon about Carmella's tall, handsome carriage, her surprising naturalness, and her smooth speaking voice, which was as strong as her contralto. But she kept the salary aspect to herself, planning to put the money into their joint-savings account to surprise Jon one day with an expensive gift. She knew Jon didn't bother with that account any more. Perhaps he had already forgotten they still had it.

She was a huge success at the auditorium and received an encore each evening. Carmella openly praised her.

"I have a proposition for you, Desiree. One that I would like you to seriously consider," she announced softly when they were finally by themselves in the dressing room that Saturday night. "I called Joan Waverly's parents earlier this evening and, because of their daughter's particular injuries, they asked if I would find another lead-in pianist for my American tour. I would like you to join my entourage."

There was a wondrous sparkle in Desiree's eyes, a slight upward curve to her mouth. "Oh, Carmella. That's quite a ..."

"I know you have a lot of things to consider. All I want is that you think it over very seriously. Discuss it with your husband and anyone else you wish. And then say *yes*." The robust laugh was sincere.

"Jon almost insisted that I get an interview with you for these two evenings here in town, but he would never let me go on a tour. Never. I don't think I should even mention your proposal to him."

"I don't want to cause you any problems at home but neither am I going to let you slip out of my life that easily. You can be assured of that."

For months Carmella kept in regular contact with the young pianist. On her lined floral stationery, so picturesquely she had described each visit—the various concert halls, the proficient stage crews, the receptive audiences, and the hurried interviews. Desiree often wondered if she had made the right decision by keeping silent and staying home.

Resting between lessons or after taking her daughter to her best friend's for another sleepover, the talented pianist would often sit outside on the lounge chair and think about the total involvement of Carmella's musical world: the promoting, the necessary scheduling, the impressive performances, the critical acclaims, the ever-increasing television interviews, and the traveling itself. But at the same time, Desiree was apprehensive about the idea of so dramatically expanding her musical career. Perhaps she was slightly afraid of it all—the earnest patrons, the attending media, all strangers in unfamiliar places, and those thousands of eyes and discerning ears focused so intently on the pretty young blonde from the prairies. Now, those two evenings at the auditorium just seemed like a dream, a fascinating dream—one she would never forget. She decided to be satisfied with just that.

She had locked all of Carmella's scented stationery in her antique jewelry box, but the last letter was purposely placed on the kitchen table. Inside was an announcement of the western Canada tour beginning that coming July, and again Carmella, in her own bold handwriting and explicit choice of words, was asking Desiree to reconsider her previous offer.

It had been on Desiree's mind for a long time, and she wished now that Jon was aware of it. She wanted his approval and knew the discussion was long overdue. Yes, she would tell him tonight.

Jon, however, had bounded into the duplex later that same afternoon and dropped his textbooks onto the kitchen table. Plumping into a swivel chair, he stretched his brawny arms over the table. "Guess what?" Excitement rang in his voice. When his elbow brushed against Carmella's letter and the light green pages fell to the floor, he automatically reached down to pick them up.

"What, Jon?" Her curious eyes studied his wide smile.

"My application at Drummonds Oil was accepted today. Next month, I'll be their senior accountant."

"I thought you were looking for something other than an office job."

"But they're giving me an incredible salary increase and an unlimited expense account. How can I pass that up?"

"Will you be finishing this course?" She thumbed through a textbook as he watched.

"Yes, I will. That is the only condition given me." A sudden doubt clouded his eyes and he touched her hand. "I thought you would be as thrilled as me about this."

"Jon, I'm sorry that I don't seem very pleased about it, because I am. But I too have some good news." For a moment she hesitated and then, with a calm animation, she let Jon read Carmella's last letter.

"Is this her first proposal?"

"No."

"How long has she been asking you to join her?"

"Since her last visit here in town." Her voice was a soft whisper now.

"But why didn't you tell me about it before this?"

"I thought you wanted me at home." She picked up the small sugar bowl and started rubbing its gold rim.

"Only if you are happy here."

"I am happy here. You know that. And I don't ever want to lose any of this. But lately, something about Carmella's lifestyle, the whole affair, is stirring a little wonderment inside me. I can't pinpoint the reason for my restlessness but …"

"But you think you might be ready to give it a try?"

"I'm just not sure, really."

"I think you know that this tour is too promising for you to turn down. Or are you afraid that Carmella might start looking for someone else?"

"Maybe both."

"Then why don't you meet Carmella in Toronto, like she's been asking? Really. What harm can be done? I think it's a chance of a lifetime. Go for it, honey."

"But what about Jodi? We can take her on our weekend camping trips or our annual vacations, but I couldn't take her with me on the tour. You know that all my friends work during the day and we can't expect my parents to keep her all that time. And you certainly won't be able to."

"You're right about all of that, but you know your folks would love having Jodi around the house. She'd be no problem for them." He winked at her before walking to the back door to open it for his daughter, who had been in the back yard playing with their neighbor's cocker spaniel.

It was Dawna, however, who actually clinched the arrangement for the aspiring concert pianist. Visiting one night when Jon was at night school and Gordon was at the drugstore, she sadly announced having to have a hysterectomy in six weeks.

"But Dawna, if I go on tour, I won't be back by then, and you'll need all your family and friends nearby."

"Now don't you dare miss out on this super opportunity because of me!" Dawna slapped her friend's hand lightly before continuing. "Listen to me, please, and really think about what I'm saying. When I first met Gordon, I was so determined to have a career, asking him to wait just one more year before we started a family—then one more year after that and so on. Now, when I'm finally ready to be a mother, I am told that I can't be one. Ever!" She took her friend's hand before continuing. "We all have to decide what we really want to do in this life. But then we also need to go for it and not waste any time doubting. Des, do what's right for you and you'll soon realize that those who really love you will accept any and all of your decisions."

With an unusual calmness, as the soft light of the early summer morning played with her curly length of hair, Desiree waved back to Jon and Jodi and her parents. As if it were destined to be, every detail concerning the tour had been taken care of. The single drawback, however, was that Desiree might not be seeing her grade school friend in Toronto because of their conflicting schedules. A teacher's convention, Lynda's first, would keep her elsewhere.

Desiree excelled on the stage. Absorbing the attentiveness of each audience, she lost herself in the excitement. But each night, after the usual prolonged acclamations backstage, she would go to her hotel room, freshen up before phoning home, and talk for a long while with Jon and her parents. Then, trying to read a good book or some recent fashion magazine, she would fall asleep and dream of the fishing and camping trips, or the water skiing weekends that were keeping them all so busy at home.

But each and every morning she would awaken early, refreshed and eager to rejoin the entourage. Never the star performer, but having been immediately accepted by the talented and caring team, Desiree developed an excessive thirst for each new venture, and when they arrived in Vancouver weeks later, she was saddened at the thought of her last public performance.

Chapter Nine

Desiree caressed the crisp folds of the champagne sheers. Through the bay window of the duplex, her dry eyes examined the late-autumn tints of the neighborhood as she thought of her parents' long delayed six-month stay in Norway. Their dream had finally come true. She could envision her father's fascination with the billowing blueness, picturing him standing tall at the stem of the cruise ship, inhaling the balmy air, and scanning the rhythmic flow of the Atlantic. And her mother, no doubt standing proudly with her arm in his, would be looking up at him with smiling eyes.

They were gone now, in Norway. And she was home, in the duplex. Home—in a regular routine once again, no longer living out of the old suitcase, no longer having to tolerate such tight scheduling and countless interviews, or having to squirm again for just a single moment of comfort on the crowded buses that bumped along the highways. Home—where Jon was enthusiastic about his new job, about life itself, where her husband had joined a ski club, had taken up squash, was the skip on the office's first curling team, and still somehow managed to continue his studies, making excellent grades. Yes, home—Jodi was now going to kindergarten.

Interrupted by the phone ringing, Desiree was somewhat pleased to hear from Carole Schrader. "Yes, Carole. I know it's been exactly four months and three days since you and Ken moved across town. Jodi is on a field trip today and won't be back until late this afternoon. I'd love to have lunch with you and see your new house."

"I'll pick you up in an hour."

With perfect timing, Carole carefully parked her new Corvette in front of the duplex and, not wanting to waste any time in idle chit-chat at the front door, she rushed Desiree outside and then took her time proudly showing her ex-neighbor the latest in automotive advances. "Isn't it super? When are you going to get your own car?"

"Oh, I don't know. I'm managing quite nicely without one."

"But you wouldn't feel so cooped up in that little duplex of yours if you had one. And what if Jodi got sick or something? What would you do then?"

"I'd take a cab, as usual, Carole."

"I don't know why that doesn't bother you. But let's go now. I know you're going to love the house, and we just got new furniture last week. Thank goodness for charge cards. I have my own now, you know."

The dark brick bi-level on the east edge of town had once been a show home. Its carefully planned layout offered main-floor laundry, a sunken family room off the kitchen nook, three large square bedrooms, two full baths, and a huge balcony along the entire north side. Each room had been painted in varying hues of dusty rose, or papered in dark rouge stripes or bold floral patterns—pink, pink, and more pink. To Desiree, the modern furniture of glazed almond plastic only amplified the continued color scheme. She had always pictured each room in her dream home as having its own distinctive complexion, décor, and ambiance. Separate, yet harmonious.

"I've been saving the nicest room for last," Carole grinned as she led Desiree into the living room.

"A grand piano. I forgot that you told me you had one now. It's absolutely beautiful," Desiree gushed.

"And much bigger than your baby grand was, huh? Would you mind playing something for me?"

Desiree sat on the long molded bench and began to play a short concerto, not at all concentrating on the keys, the mood or the tune. Instead, she was remembering her last concert in Vancouver... Smiling, she thought again of Carmella who had always taken the prompt ovations and encores in stride. But that last night in Vancouver she had seemed anxious during the entire performance. She was leaving on a last-minute trip to London, England, that following week for a command performance in front of the Queen, taking only a small crew of musicians with her, and she wanted to publicly bid farewell to all the others. Then, at the end of her touching pronouncement, she gave Desiree the spotlight. "Except for a few recitals or local competitions, this young lady had never performed in public, and just by luck a mutual friend brought us together. But I deeply regret that this will be her last performance with me for a long, long time."

The audience had responded spontaneously with a lengthy standing ovation, but Desiree, taken by the moment, was overwhelmed to see Jon and Jodi waiting for her behind the curtains.

"We couldn't wait for you to come home so we decided to meet you here." Jon had admitted joyfully.

"Daddy said you would be on stage, Mommy. But he di'n't say that you would be all alone there. I wanted to sit beside you."

They stayed on the coast for an entire week, enjoying the luxury of the Sommers' penthouse apartment, celebrating Jodi's fourth birthday, and the beginning of their fifth year together. It was a perfect ending to such an unusually fulfilling summer.

"What's wrong, Desiree? Why did you stop?"

"Huh?"

"I thought there was more to that piece. You seem to have quit right in the middle of it. Your hands just seemed to suddenly drop onto the keys." Carole brought a tray of fresh sandwiches from the kitchen and placed it on a molded step table near the archway.

"Oh, this piano just brought back some very good memories. I'm sorry I ruined the piece."

"Now that you're back home, I thought I might just as well take some lessons from you. When can I start?"

"I'm not going to teach again. Not for a while, anyway. I just want to be with my family. This summer was pretty hectic."

"But won't you need the extra money?"

"Extra money? I don't think so, Carole. Jon just got another raise, and if he keeps up his studies like he's been trying to, he'll be a CPA this coming spring, and possibly vice-president of the firm as well. I don't think I have to worry about our finances."

"Jodi's four years old already. Pretty soon she'll want to have friends over to play somewhere, or have some pajama parties. Don't you think it's about time she had her own room? Sleeping in the alcove of your bedroom, at her age, must put a damper on your own privacy. Come on now, Des. Think about it."

"There has only been a few moments when ..."

"And poor Jon still has to study at the kitchen table. I'm surprised he hasn't complained about it after all these years. I'd start looking for a house pretty soon, if I were you."

"Oh, I couldn't do that. Jon loves it there and he'd be so upset if I even mentioned anything like that."

"This place has appreciated three thousand dollars since we moved in and it looks like the prices are still rising. Ken is seriously thinking about going into residential real estate because of it. Read the classified ads when you get home today and then study the prices in a couple of weeks. I bet you'll be surprised at the outlandish increases."

With Carole's daily reminders, Desiree finally checked some advertisements in the paper, and read a short notice on a half-duplex two blocks from their own that was selling for twice what Jon said he had paid for theirs. She started thinking that maybe she should approach him about it, perhaps after he had enjoyed his favorite meal.

"You look so tired tonight, love," she started, wrapping up the leftover beef. The tender roast with mashed potatoes, smooth gravy, and mixed vegetables had been her most tasteful meal yet, but soon after the dishes were put away, she didn't care to see her husband's steady yawning. "Why don't I put Jodi to bed early and we can have a couple of drinks in front of a fire before you tackle the books?"

"No, honey. I've got to study. I can't seem to grasp the last two chapters of this text." He slumped onto the kitchen chair and picked up the morning's newspaper as she cleaned the counter near the stove.

"Hey, what's this?" He had noticed the check marks penned in the real estate columns. "You want to move out of this place?"

"No, no," she laughed nervously. "Carole and I were just …"

"Don't like it here anymore, huh?" he interrupted, not looking up to notice her flushed face. "I love this duplex. I thought you did, too."

"I do." She grabbed the edge of the counter before continuing. "But Jodi's growing up so fast and we both want another child. Soon we're going to need more bedrooms." She had noticed the concern on his face, the fine lines deepening around his dark eyes, as she spoke. "I just thought we could look around for a little while and see for ourselves if the prices are rising as quickly as Carole keeps saying."

"And what does Mrs. Carole Schrader know about real estate?"

Desiree had almost expected that reaction, yet she had hoped that Jon might somehow be a little more agreeable. He was aloof, however, all during his time at home. At week's end, Desiree decided to go downtown to meet Dawna for coffee.

"Am I glad you phoned so early this morning," Dawna sighed, as she took off her light wool coat and hung it on the rack near their booth. "I'm exhausted already, and the work day has just begun. But Mr. Morten told me to take my time and enjoy this visit with you, and I'm going to do just that."

"I think you went back to work much too soon." The recent hysterectomy had saddened her friend's usually clear aqua eyes, had aged her smooth delicate face. The blue linen suit that had been Gordon's birthday gift to her last February now hung loosely.

"I don't know how you hold out so well with being at home all day, but of course, you have your hobbies and your beautiful daugh—"

"My good friends." Desiree smiled slowly.

"Will you be coming back to work? The entire office wants you to, you know."

"That's sweet, Dawna, but Jon likes me to be home."

"Even if Todd were transferred down here? He'd need his own secretary, you know."

"Todd is getting transferred?" Elbows soon were on the table.

"Well, it's in the makings right now. I'm pretty sure that it'll go through before summer."

"Dawna, if you need my help, any time, or if Todd's transferred, please let me know and I'll certainly consider working there again." Desiree carefully poured more cream into her freshened cup of coffee before reaching into her shoulder bag. In Toronto, during one of her few free afternoons, she had purchased a delicate pearl necklace, and now proudly opened its silk pouch. "I thought this would look smashing with your black wool suit."

"Desiree. It's lovely. Thank you so much."

"I just hope I'll find something special for Jon today."

A questioning look was distorting Dawna's pale face.

And Desiree looked up with widening eyes, setting her fresh butter horn back onto its plate, before explaining.

"Just give him some time and I know he'll forget all about those marked real estate ads. Sometimes I think you worry too much," Dawna admitted.

Later that morning, tightening the wool scarf around the stiff collar of her leather coat, Desiree stepped off the bus toting a small plastic bag of newly purchased cosmetics. She had browsed through several shops downtown, trying to find something nice for Jon, but nothing had appealed to her.

The warm west wind of a chinook had earlier prompted her to wear her new dress shoes, to break them in, but now the wind was cold and gusty and the unexpected snow was almost an inch deep already. Over patches of ice that had so quickly formed, she knew to be careful with each step, and with head bent to protect her face she brushed against the caragana bush of their front yard.

Inside the duplex she dropped her fluffy wool toque and let her coat fall onto the floor. Jodi would be home any minute. Lunch had to be prepared. While a small pot of leftover stew was heating on the stove, Desiree sauntered back into the living room to pick up her neglected winter attire. When she looked out the window for Jodi and her friend, she saw the For Sale sign in the middle of their lawn. She wondered how she could have missed it earlier. Besides, she had only suggested to Jon that perhaps they could look at some houses. There wasn't any rush to put the duplex up for sale. Their anniversary, Jon's mid-term exams, and Christmas were nearing, and she didn't want her family to be interrupted by realtors or prospective buyers. Why couldn't Jon have waited until the New Year? Why couldn't she have kept this entire issue to herself?

"I thought that was what you wanted," he told her over the phone later that afternoon. "Besides, the duplex should sell fairly soon, according to Mrs. Carole Schrader. Right? And you'll still have a few weeks to look for another house before December comes, before you begin all your Christmas preparations. You can start packing while I'm at work and none of us will be disturbed too much."

She understood what he was trying to say. Leaving everything to her was Jon's silent retaliation, his quiet revenge. And yes, she could do everything herself. She would *have* to.

Over the next few days, how often had she just turned on the dishwasher, or had Jon just opened his textbook, when the front doorbell rang again and another of Mr. Staut's clients appeared, eager to see inside?

To Desiree's delight, the duplex sold within a week for the exact price Mr. Staut had suggested, and Jon had started studying at the office, giving Desiree more time to organize the move, to find them a new place to live.

It was her turn now to interrupt other people, but she purposely scheduled each appointment for the early afternoon before the husband or school children returned home.

By the first of February the Sommers were to be in their new home. But where would that be? Desiree became more concerned as the days and weeks went by without any satisfying prospects.

Celebrating their fifth anniversary in the revolving restaurant overlooking the city, they sat quietly watching the early sunset gild the horizon. Despite the pleasant meal and smooth French wine, there was an uncomfortable air of tension between them. Jon would only speak about his concern of the upcoming exams, and Desiree could only respond methodically with a smile, weary from her activities involving the move, but worried most about Jon's obvious anxiety.

By Christmas the duplex was almost void of their various ornaments and artwork. Most of the individual touches that had made the duplex their home were now carefully packed in boxes in the basement.

She hadn't disturbed the living room, though. She would empty that room last, because that was where the beautiful upright piano would always comfort her, where the rhythmic swaying of the dark bentwood rocker could still ease her mind, where she could sit beside the red brick hearth and restfully gaze at the handmade silk cushions, her oil paintings, or her pastels, and the numerous family portraits. Yes, the huge living room was where her scanty collection of first-edition bestsellers rested neatly in the dark wall unit… Where she would snuggle up in the floral chaise lounge under an afghan to read one of those good books… Where she would listen undisturbed to Chopin, Beethoven, Roy Orbison, The Beatles, Bob Dylan, Stan Getz, or any other musician at her whim. Yes, the living room was her place of serenity, her sphere of peace, solitude, and contentment. She couldn't deprive herself of all that quiet pleasure by moving a single item, not until the holiday season was over. Not until it was an absolute must.

It was Christmas Eve now. The beautiful spruce tree, heavy with ornaments, twinkled with the numerous strings of tiny blue lights. Jodi was upstairs, sleeping soundly, and Jon was cracking some stubborn walnuts in front of a smoldering fire. Somehow, though, Desiree felt desperately alone. She still missed the usual festivities of caroling in the snow somewhere downtown, or visiting shut-ins at a few seniors' lodges. This time of year Jon let her do whatever she wanted outside the duplex, as long as it didn't involve him.

Earlier, she had heard from her parents, had listened to each of them describe the Norwegian Christmas traditions they were enjoying, the fabulous tours they had experienced, the particular fjords they would be seeing in the New Year, and the culture shock they were going through. But despite their happiness, she longed for them to be home. Perhaps it was the assemblage of bags, boxes, cartons, and crates now placed in any once-bare area around the duplex, the constant reminder of various undertakings still unfinished, which added to her despondency. She needed something more.

That following morning, however, having had an unexpected good night's sleep, she watched Jodi squeal with excitement as the little girl opened her gifts, and Desiree felt more spirited, almost anxious now to accept the quiet day ahead.

"Hey, I don't see anything under the tree for me from your mother, Jodi." Jon feigned annoyance as Jodi scrambled around the huge tree to help her father look for his present, while Desiree listened intently from the kitchen.

"Here it is, Daddy. I found your present. But it's kinda small."

"Let's see, now." Jon couldn't imagine what would be in such a tiny package. A ring or pair of cuff links, he guessed. Jodi was also curious, sitting in front of him, wanting to rip the pretty paper, but politely keeping both hands on her lap. "Hey! It's a Dinky Toy. A Camaro Z28, just like the one I bought for your mom a few years ago. But this one's newer, of course." He was puzzled, perhaps even a little disappointed, but hoped Jodi couldn't notice.

"Why would Mommy want a Dinky Toy like that?"

"No, Jodi. I bought her a real car like this one, but she didn't like driving it."

"How come?"

"You wouldn't understand," he laughed quietly.

"But how can anybody drive *this* one? The wheels are stuck."

Desiree joined in the laughter and quickly dried her hands before answering the telephone to hear Todd's deep voice from the other end.

"Jon," she shouted, away from the receiver. "Would you please take out the garbage? … And Merry Christmas to you, too, Todd," she said, after returning to the phone.

"Des, I've been so busy looking for a house in your fair city that I couldn't spare any time to visit with you last week," Todd admitted. "Moving is just too involved."

"One big headache, isn't it? We're still looking, but have you found one?"

"Yep, a cozy bungalow just across the reservoir from you. We're moving in three weeks."

"What?"

"Yeah. Head office wants me down there as soon as possible. Thank goodness they're paying for the packers too, or we'd never be ready in time. But what's up for you guys today? Got any company coming over?"

"No. And Jon couldn't see me roasting a turkey just for the three of us, so we're going to a nice restaurant later. He found one across town that will be open today. But the reservations aren't until four o'clock."

"Hey, that's not very traditional, is it? Why don't you folks come up here and have dinner with us? It's just a couple of hours drive. Sara has a huge turkey in the oven, and there's too much of everything else for just the kids and us. The roads are good, so why not stay the night?"

Jon bounded into the kitchen from outside and, without letting Desiree put down the phone, grabbed her and pressed his cold, moist body hard against hers. "I love it, Des. And I love you. Thank you so much."

"Jon!! I'm still talking to Todd. He wants us to go up there for dinner this afternoon and maybe ..."

Jon grabbed the phone. "Todd. My Christmas present is parked out back. It's a brand new Z28. It's already licensed and insured. Desiree obviously arranged everything. The papers are all on the front seat. I can't wait to get behind the wheel. We'd love to come up and see you."

After canceling the Christmas day dinner at the restaurant while Desiree rushed to pack a large suitcase for the three of them, Jon gave a melancholy sigh as he closed the trunk of his shiny new car. "I wish I had given you a nicer gift," he said guiltily, starting the ignition.

"But, honey, this diamond and sapphire ring is beautiful. Absolutely perfect." Desiree knew the rest of the holiday would be, too.

The first full week of the new year saw Desiree scurrying around the city in her continued search for a new home, and time was definitely becoming her greatest concern, because just that morning Mr. Staut had phoned to announce that an urgent family matter was going to take him out of town for at least two weeks. If she could take the time that very afternoon, however, he would be able to show her his next prospect.

"I'll have to bring my daughter. Jon's still at the office."

"Yes, that would be quite all right."

He had picked them up within an hour. "This place has been on the market for six months now without an offer," he had begun, noticing Jodi through the rearview mirror squeezing her plush toy.

"Why would *we* be interested in it, then?" Desiree retorted, shuffling her shoulder bag between her feet.

"Because I think it's just what you've been looking for."

"Could you give me some details before we get there? You didn't want to take the extra time over the phone."

"Definitely. It's a decade newer and twice the size of the duplex. Its only downfall, really, is the gaudy decor and lack of maintenance. But with a little bit of work, it would be worth thousands more. The owners have been in Montreal since the summer and can't afford to have someone fix it up."

"Why didn't they do it themselves before moving out?"

"It's beyond me, Desiree. But I know you enjoy decorating, and any problems I spotted are only minor ones. Jon could fix them all himself in just a few days."

The rest of the drive towards the outskirts of town was rather quiet, because Mr. Staut's young client had fallen asleep within blocks of her home, and her daughter was sitting quietly in the back seat, holding her plush animal gently. As he parked his station wagon in front of the brick split level, the headline news announcements on the radio gently awakened Desiree. Quick to adjust to her surroundings, she noticed the tall evergreens and bushy golden-tipped junipers breaking the whiteness, and she liked what she saw. Soon all seat belts were loosened.

Disappointment overtook her instantly, however, when Mr. Staut unlocked the front doors and they were all greeted by a long wall of torn orange and gold paper in a hideous scroll-like pattern. The burnt-orange shag carpet, now badly stained in several areas, ran throughout the living room and dining room. Below the bold yellow prints and murky brown and gray stripes, three broken baseboards stuck out from the walls.

"Oh, my, Mr. Staut. Who would want this place?"

"It does have good potential, Desiree." The ceiling-high fireplace of rich Italian marble, centered between two long, narrow windows in the square living room, softened the décor and he purposely stretched his arm over the shiny oaken mantle.

"Well, this fireplace certainly is attractive," she agreed reluctantly.

He took a crisp sheet of paper from it. "The flues were cleaned before the previous owners moved out. The bill here is the proof."

"But this ugly carpet was ignored? How odd."

"I can't argue with you there," Mr. Staut replied, and let her continue with her careful survey.

The narrow, drab partition wall that halved the large main floor also blocked the dirty bleached oak kitchen. Condensation and accumulated house dust had deposited a muddy mosaic on the cracked lattice windows, and the filthy floor tiling had lifted in several places.

Jodi showed her doll the weird design she could make on the filthy oven door. "Kinda looks a lot prettier now, doesn't it, Suzie?"

Through a painted archway, creaky French doors in the dining room opened out to a cedar deck, which extended around one corner of the house, and there was a double-car garage at the rear of the once nicely landscaped back yard.

Mr. Staut remained silent, following a few feet behind Desiree. He lit up a cigarette.

Upstairs, the same ugly orange carpet covered the long hallway floor and Desiree took particular notice of the distinct contrast of wall colors that the top level exhibited—the wide navy stripes of the hall, the solid deep purple of the smallest bedroom, and the rose and avocado prints of the other. She overlooked the faded mauve walls and the scratched hardwood floor of the master bedroom, however. Instead, a long mirror-tiled wall and the huge white French windows, exposing the railed cedar deck outside, caught her attention. She peeked behind a partition wall of peeling paint to see a long, narrow dressing room. The spacious en suite was papered in dark purple stripes, much like those in the hallway.

Jodi was soon dancing with her plush animal in front of the mirror tiles.

Mr. Staut hadn't said another word. He took the last puff of his cigarette and, as they were led downstairs, Desiree wondered where he was going to crush the butt.

The third level boasted a large family room with a corner wet bar and glazed-metal acorn fireplace against a feature wall of dark pecan paneling. The thick cinnamon-brown carpeting looked almost new, spreading into another smaller room, which Desiree thought would be perfect as her sewing area. The musty furnace and laundry rooms were large but unfinished. Mr. Staut pressed the butt on the cement floor by the drain hole and left it there.

The fourth level had been completely developed into a handsome games room of rustic tongue-and-groove cedar and cinnamon-brown shag carpeting that stretched over to the built-in cabinets and oak bar along the far wall.

"Now, this makes everything we've seen worthwhile."

"And you'll like the price."

"Let's discuss that in front of Jon, okay?"

"I hope he has time. Remember, I only have tonight to get this finished."

Jon arrived home later than usual, and remained very distant. All during the warmed-up dinner, apprehension tightened his face. Desiree found it difficult to start any conversation. Quietly she took a long, deep breath as she approached him. "I know something's bothering you," she said, finally. "Want to tell me about it?" She kissed him softly on the cheek.

"Oh, something happened at the office this morning that has me quite upset."

"Yes, I could tell. What is it?" She sat on his lap.

"A close friend of the president moved to town recently. He came in to see Mr. Lewis today, looking for a job. Just because he's already a CPA, he was hired on the spot as the new vice-president. Now there's no room for my advancement unless someone leaves or retires early. I got a private secretary instead."

How could she tell him about the other house now?

"If I didn't like it there so much, I think I would just up and quit."

"Oh, Jon, you know you don't mean that." How could she tell him that she needed his signature for the other house? "Have you met this new secretary yet, or is that also in the future?"

"Krystal Brooks? No, she was there long before I came on the scene. She used to be the receptionist. I think she'll do fine." He sounded more relaxed now; the tightness in his face was slackening.

"Good." Now is the time, she thought, and poured him another cup of coffee. "I found us a house today. Mr. Staut and I didn't go into too much detail about the finances, but with the sale of this place and most of my savings, I'm sure we can go cash to mortgage."

"Most of what savings?"

"The money from my lessons and all the concerts. I've been saving it for something special."

An eerie silence suddenly filled the room as Jon's dark eyes raked hers with a hot glare. "You bought me a brand new sports car at Christmas. You paid cash for it and got all the insurance on it. Now you're telling me that you have enough money saved up to go cash to mortgage on our first house? Wherever that might be?"

"I thought it would be a nice surprise for you," she said softly.

"Surprise isn't the word for it." He was stomping around the kitchen now, a lit cigarette burning in his hand. "What's the point of me working all day long, going to classes twice a week and studying every night, just to find out after all this time that you can bring in enough money, from one concert tour and a few years of piano teaching, to buy a house? I can't believe this!" He crushed the cigarette into a saucer before continuing. "I feel like I'm back at the mansion living with my mother and father again. It was *her* money that bought the mansion here in town, the apartment complex in Vancouver, the condominium in Phoenix. It was *her* money that bought the Rolls Royce and the Mercedes. It was *her* money that bought their yacht in Florida. It was *her* money that made Father who he is today. *Her* money, *her* influence, *her* everything."

Her inheritance, Jon, Desiree wanted to declare. *That's what it was. Just her inheritance!* But in a timid, low voice, she was only able to say, "It was *both* of your parents who gave us such a beautiful wedding. And we still haven't gone on the world cruise they paid for."

"Don't ever think that *they both* paid for that? No, no, Desiree. *Everything* originates with Mother." Sweat was cascading down his face, both jugular veins were bulging, and he was pacing the floor with quick heavy strides, hitting the countertop with his fists at each turn.

Desiree cowered in her chair. All memory of his particular upbringing had escaped her thoughts, until now. How long could Jon keep such anger? How long could he exude such hatred for his parents?

"Jon, you wanted me to go on that tour. You even persuaded me to cancel all my lessons.

"But you never said anything about being paid for it."

"I thought my surprise would be a little more appreciated." As her mind searched for exact words, her throat strained for a proper tone of voice. "Would you please come with me and Jodi to see the other house? I promise not to keep you there for long."

"You've got to be kidding me! You know I'm having trouble with my studies. You know I had a bad day at the office. How dare you ask me to spare you all that extra time!"

"Jon, I've worked hard too, in my own way, to give you this surprise," Desiree responded with only a hint of guilt in her soft voice. "I've come this far on my own, without anyone else's money, help, or involvement. You know we have to be out of here by the end of the month. We don't have much time now and that house is already vacant. We can choose the possession date ourselves."

"I just can't believe you didn't tell me about your salary," he repeated. "This house better be something special, Desiree.

She took a deep breath. "Well, it needs a lot of work, but I know I can do it all myself. And I will. But Jodi fell in love with the mirror tiles in the master bedroom. She danced in front of them almost the whole time we were inside."

It was a long, dispirited drive from the duplex. A continued tightening of Jon's face was all that was offered Desiree as she carefully described the other property. Would he create a scene there, in front of Jodi and Mr. Staut?

After being greeted by their realtor at the front door and seeing the overall appearance of the main floor, Jon shook his head in disbelief.

"I think we should show him the games room next, Mrs. Sommers."

"Forget it, both of you! I don't want to waste any more of my time here tonight." Jon walked into the kitchen and yanked at a loose floor tile. "You want this dump, Des?"

"Well, I told you that it needs a lot of work, but ..."

"Then you can have it. Where are the papers?" He scanned the few sheets handed him, shook his head as he eyed the nearby rooms again, and signed the contract. He shoved it into Mr. Staut's hand and stomped out the front door.

"Mommy, Daddy doesn't like this place very much, does he?"

Turn! Turn! Turn!

Jon didn't complain about the rows of taped boxes now piled high in the basement or having to ask where something was. He continued his daily studies at the office, letting his wife do all the cleaning, the wrapping, and the packing. He didn't know yet about her increasing bouts of nausea.

Yes! She was pregnant again, had been since their anniversary, and the thought of having another beautiful child within her gave

Desiree silent encouragement to continue preparing for the move. But when would be the right time to tell Jon about *that*?

She hadn't expected to see so many people arriving at the duplex to help them move. Dawna and Gordon had dropped off their half-ton before leaving for the airport to attend a health conference in Chicago. Todd and Sara had also offered to help somehow, but Desiree had insisted that they concentrate on getting their own new home in order. With the help of Jon's co-workers, by mid-afternoon all the bags, boxes, and crates throughout the duplex were gone.

Finally, familiar names were given distinct faces, but Desiree had pictured Krystal Brooks so differently. Her striking charm was difficult to ignore. The golden flecks of her green eyes accentuated the light streaks in the coffee-brown hair that softly curled at her shoulders, and the way she carried her tall, angular frame exuded a cool confidence. Desiree wished that some day she would have the same aura of sophistication.

Despite having all of the vehicles loaded and gone, with Krystal so near, Desiree found it difficult to concentrate on the last minute cleaning. She felt like a rag doll with her now-tangled hair knotted up at the crown, an old denim jumpsuit stained with bleach, and her dry rough hands stinking from vinegar and pine cleansers. Desiree dusted the large window frame in the dining room where she had heard Krystal giving instructions to the men and was now helping Jodi pack her various dolls and plush toys into a cardboard box for the last trip. She and Jon would be taking Jodi to the house, because Desiree wanted the duplex spotless for its new owners.

As the bright winter's day was quickly darkening, Desiree closed the front door of the duplex for the very last time, and with a deep sigh she locked the heavy wooden door, dropping all the keys no longer needed into the mailbox. Various memories flashed through her mind and with increasing apprehension she drove the Camaro to her new home where she was welcomed with a warm hug from Jodi, who had been waiting by the front windows for her mother.

The stereo was blaring somewhere downstairs and Desiree soon realized how easy it had been for Jon to persuade his cronies to hook it up before anything else got done, before anything else concerning the move was even started. She was aghast, however, when she saw that every box and crate had been placed in the living room. Only the furniture was in the proper rooms, despite everything else having been carefully packed and labeled. She refrained from joining the other merriment upstairs; she could see their old garden hose snaking from the main bathroom into their new bedroom. The waterbed would take hours to fill and she was thankful that someone already had thought of that.

"Mommy, Krystal told me that I could watch her and Daddy curl tomorrow. That'll be fun, won't it?"

"Yes, it will, honey, but I'll have to stay here and get the house organized."

Now donned in black dress pants and a beige button-down silk shirt, Krystal joined them. "I guess when you have Jodi with you all the time, it's easier to accept Jon being away so often," she said.

"She's great company for me." Desiree gently mussed her daughter's hair.

"Jodi, why don't you open that box we left by the front door, take out one of your favorite dolls and show it around the house? Maybe they all want to see it."

"Mommy! They're not my dolls. They're my children!"

"Yes, of course. Go and get your *children*. Maybe they want to see their new bedroom." Desiree wiped a fallen strand of hair from her daughter's face. "And where's your husband today, Krystal?"

"Oh, the body shop's open until noon on Saturdays, but Brent likes to tinker with his roadster 'til dinner time. We're separated now, though."

"Oh, I'm sorry. I didn't know. Jon didn't tell me about that."

"It was just two weeks ago. But I can manage quite well without him. He'll find out soon enough that it's his loss, not mine." She fumbled for something in her purse. "Would you like a joint?"

"Oh, no, thank you."

"You've been working so hard with this move, you should slow down a bit. Everything is out of the duplex now. This might help."

Desiree grabbed the edge of the dining room table. "Erin?" she gasped.

"Pardon me?"

"Oh, I'm sorry." Krystal's tone of voice and choice of words had caught Desiree quite by surprise. For a split second she thought she was with Erin again, talking with her older sister like they had done so many times in the past—like they had the day Erin received her honors award, like they had the same day she … A rush of sadness enveloped her but Krystal was still nudging her to have a toke.

"No, thanks, Krystal." She swallowed hard to help ease the sudden tightness in her throat. "I think I'd better start getting this place in order, if that's even possible. Why don't you go downstairs and keep Jon and the others company while I clean out these filthy kitchen cupboards?"

Krystal followed her into the kitchen and fingered the greasy counter. "After getting this place fixed up, I think you're both going to need to get out of here for a while. For a few months, maybe."

"What are you trying to say, Krystal?"

"I thought you'd be more excited about getting a free cruise around the world. Your wedding present from Jon's folks, remember? I would have gone the same week that I picked up my passport."

"Jon doesn't talk much about it," Desiree admitted quietly. Again, she had forgotten about that wedding present. "Too busy with his studies, I guess. I'm surprised he mentioned it to you."

"Oh, he didn't, really. But when his father called the office a couple of weeks ago and I had to take a message, I was too curious not to ask a few questions."

Desiree remained silent as she washed another shelf inside the cupboard.

"I never saw Jon that upset before," Krystal added.

"What do you mean?"

"He had had a bad morning, I remember." Krystal slid her foot over a loose floor tile before continuing. "He couldn't balance an account for a client, or something like that. He took an exceptionally long lunch, by himself, and after reading his father's message when he got back to his desk, he crumpled it into the wastebasket and stomped out of the office, ignoring everybody. When I caught up to him in the parking lot, he told me everything."

Everything? The word caught Desiree.

"But I think I did an excellent job of persuading him to accept the gift."

Desiree couldn't see out of the living room windows the next morning because bags, boxes, cartons, and crates were still piled in front of them, but she knew it was bitterly cold outside. She had had to close all the bedroom windows before finally getting to sleep, only to be abruptly awakened when Jodi crawled in beside her. Then, finally, while Jon was curling, they tidied up the games room and unpacked the boxes of dishes and kitchen utensils. Pleased to have her own bedroom and quite unconcerned about its dark, ugly colors, the little towhead unpacked the remainder of her dolls and plush animals, while her mother rested in the bentwood rocker that had been carelessly shoved against the piano on the long wall in the living room.

The smell of roast beef in the oven had her stomach churning again and she wished that she hadn't started preparing dinner. She had decided to tell Jon that afternoon about her present condition, but she didn't want to be interrupted by a sudden need to go to the washroom.

Jon was two hours later than usual when she heard his car door slam shut. She stood near the large closet in the front foyer, greeting him with a wide smile as he neared the house, but with the curling broom still in his hand, he marched passed her and stood in the kitchen.

"Go get a cigarette. I want to talk to you."

He knew she didn't smoke. His harsh tone, however, alerted her that something was amiss. She stood in front of the piano and waited.

"I'm going to be away for a little while," he started, still wearing his bright toque and down-filled jacket.

"Where are you going? I didn't know you had to go away on business." She watched him walking around all the cardboard containers, obviously looking for a particular label. He grabbed a small suitcase from the wing chair in one corner and put it onto the piano bench nearby. She watched him unzip it while he continued to look for something else. Finally he emptied an old shopping bag filled with some of his shirts and pants into the luggage. He found some of his socks and underwear in another bag and soon the suitcase was full. He tugged at the long zipper before saying anything.

"I'm not going on a business trip. I'm staying here in town, with some friends." Wanting to make a quick exit, he picked up the suitcase and walked around her. He didn't want to see the pained expression on her face. He didn't want to look into those pale blue eyes and have her persuade him to stay. He wasn't going to let anyone or anything change his mind.

"I just need some time to be alone. I'll be in touch," he continued. Grasping the handle of the suitcase, he edged out the front door. "Will you wait for me?"

"Yes, I'll wait for you, Jon. You know that."

With a hodgepodge of cardboard or wooden containers crowding her, her husband's offhand, obviously rehearsed words still troubling her, the bewildered blonde sat in the rocker. She was too shocked to move a single muscle. But he was gone now. He said he was staying with some friends. *Who, Jon? Who will be seeing you tonight? And for how many other nights?* She had been alone many times before, and now she was alone again, but this time it felt like a jagged knife was piercing her. There was more hurt inside this time.

The roast was burning, clouding up the air in the kitchen, making her gag, but she started rocking, still thinking about his last words. He was gone. She hadn't been given the chance to tell him about their new baby inside her. And he had totally ignored Jodi.

"Mommy, I can't find my pink bunny. I thought I put her in my bed, but she's not there now." Upset at herself for misplacing one of her favorite toys, Jodi came down to the living room and, seeing her mother cry, ran up to her with open arms. "What's wrong, Mommy? How come you're crying?"

Part Two

A Time For Decisions

Chapter Ten

Saturday, March 9

Her blue eyes sparkling, Desiree fingered the loose curls pinned carefully at her crown. Waltzing in front of the long mirror-tiled wall in the master bedroom, she watched her teal silk dress swirl around her hips, exposing her long, thin thighs. She could sense an aura of sophistication about her and she eyed the reflection with satisfaction. But when the wall clock above her chimed off another half hour, she sat cross-legged on the corner of the waterbed and laughed at the idea of thinking she could be so cosmopolitan. Those moments of contentment had been so few lately.

She enjoyed seeing the soft green freshness of the other walls, the printed green sheers and matching bedspread she had sewn one weekend. Somehow, she was going to prove her worth to Jon, despite the constant nausea and dizziness. She was pregnant again, into her second trimester already, and was absolutely thrilled. Her body was simply reacting to the physical strain of the renovations and the lingering odor of paint. During her last visit with Doctor Styles, he had hinted that *this* pregnancy might be different. And she couldn't deny that. She hadn't been this sick ever before, and she knew that her ability to go full term, again, was certainly in question. Maybe there was a pill she could take to help her with this. Yes, yes, she remembered. Her mother had been given a prescription just for that, to carry her through.

She softly rubbed her belly as thoughts of seeing her husband any minute now, after all this time, made her feel whole and spirited once again. A dinner party with his company's new executives was on the agenda. Earlier that week she had nervously accepted Jon's verbal invitation to join him and, after regular lengthy rehearsals in front of the forgiving mirror tiles, she felt that she had finally perfected her posture, her walk, and her talk. She was determined to be Jon's ideal escort that evening.

Ignoring the loud giggles from downstairs, Desiree tiptoed into her daughter's pink floral bedroom and eyed the room's new femininity with pride. She realized how selfish she had been with her time today, but Todd had arrived quite unexpectedly and was more than willing to finish stripping the torn dining room wallpaper for her. Besides, she really did have a special function to prepare for, didn't she?

In the den across the hall she sat on the edge of the sofa bed, pleased with the room's new masculine décor. She opened a large cardboard box by the leather recliner and instantly realized how much unpacking was still left to do. As she placed an old, thick scrapbook and her Polaroid camera onto the new roll-top desk, a framed photo fell onto the carpet. She couldn't remember packing that particular portrait of Erin, and now it arrested her. She placed it on the desk as the phone started to ring.

"Hi there," Dawna's chipper voice greeted her. She was a changed woman since she had visited an adoption agency and learned that she and Gordon would soon be parents. "I hope you're finished painting now."

"About an hour ago. Todd is still stripping the dining room walls, though, and Jodi is keeping him company. They don't want me down there. Jodi says *they have a system*, and she just doesn't want me to interfere."

"Are you ready to go, then?"

"Yeah, but my stomach hasn't settled down at all."

"I think *anybody* would feel sick from all the paint fumes in your house. Too bad it's so cold outside that you can't open a few windows. And you know it would have been smarter if you had waited until the summer to do any of that type of work."

"In the summer, you know I would rather be outside with Jodi."

"It just might be your nerves acting up. Maybe you're overly excited about meeting Jon's bosses for the first time."

"Yeah, I'm sure that's all it is." She wanted to tell Dawna everything, but couldn't. Still, after all this time, no one had questioned her much about his absence, because she had announced that he was away on just another business trip. But keeping the secret, hiding her anxiety and frustration, or remembering what little white lie had been said to whom, was draining her now. In a moment of despair she had agreed to help in the office the following week, while Dawna was attending a conference in Toronto. But now she was regretting that offer. How often had Jon scowled at her going back to the office? He did not believe in working mothers. She was sure that once he was aware of her new daytime activities he'd be gone again—no questions asked.

"Well, I just called to thank you again for offering to help us out next week. There are a few proposals to be executed and some dictation, but I know you can do it, so don't get frazzled. And for *my* sake, please don't do a better job than I do. Not just *yet* anyway, or I'll be unemployed before the baby comes." She laughed heartily before continuing, "Mr. Morten hopes you'll come back permanently."

Desiree gently rubbed the gilded frame of Erin's portrait. Dawna's voice grew faint.

"Desiree, are you all right?"

"Huh?"

"You haven't heard one word I've said in the last few minutes." There was a worried tone to Dawna's voice now.

"I'm so nervous about tonight, and Jon still isn't back." Back from where? She couldn't remember what she had told Dawna earlier.

"Go have a glass of wine and try to relax before he comes," Dawna suggested. "I'll phone you early next week to see how things are going. Have a great time tonight, and I'll see you on the eighteenth. Maybe sooner."

It was a long while before Desiree hung up the phone. Her mind was in another world, another time, as she stared again at the portrait. Her memory was vivid and she was overwhelmed by her feelings as she focused on that day in September, over five years ago now, when she first met Jon, when …

She was going to vomit again. She dashed into the main bathroom. Later, in the living room, she sat on a large crate still filled with her treasured first editions. She filed her shortened nails again, refusing to turn her head towards the foyer to steal another glance at the wall clock.

She was waiting for Jon, as she had promised she would. She hadn't seen him for over a month. One month, two weeks, and two days—all the time knowing he would be back, even though her patience and endurance had been weakening lately.

Her back stiffened at the sound of crunching snow outside the window. Was it Jon? Had he finally come home? This time she wasn't going to look out. She wasn't going to run to the window like all the other times, only to see some strangers shouldering the north wind. She would wait. But was it her husband? *Oh, let it be Jon. I have so much to show him, so much to tell him.*

Cuckoo! Another half hour had passed and she was still waiting for him, getting more jittery and doubtful as the clock ticked away. Her knee joints cracked when she stood up, stepped over to the end table, and pulled the clock cord from the wall socket. "As if that would stop time," she grunted to herself and stared at the brass prongs, almost wishing it were that easy. She let the cord drop onto the carpet and, dodging several stacks of cardboard boxes, she opened the narrow sheers with a quick sweep of her hand and pressed her tense forehead hard against the frosty window. She moaned. Outside, the streetlights created a milky halo in the purple-gray sky, and she could hear the late winter's wind whistling through the tall evergreens. A wooden birdhouse had fallen from the neighbor's mountain ash and now only the tip of its roof could be seen through the drifts.

Up the street another pair of headlights shone. She stepped away, not wanting Jon to see her waiting and watching eagerly for his arrival. As she stood in front of the mirror that was still propped against the front closet, she straightened her dress and examined her reflection. She sensed that she was losing all her poise. When the blurred taillights finally disappeared around the turn she walked deliberately over the bags and around the boxes and crates. She gripped the arms of the rocker with shaky hands as she sank into the bentwood and leaned her head heavily against its high, caned back. Staring beyond the large dining room, she noticed the numerous unopened cans of paint still piled near the back entrance. She sighed when she heard hushed tones and more giggling near the French doors.

In the far corner, Todd was still pressing the heavy steamer across the yellow and gold papered walls, peeling off the ugliness and letting it fall onto the carpet, while Jodi sat cross-legged on the floor a few feet behind him, being careful not to get in his way. Her round hazel eyes followed his every movement as she waited for her special cue—the click of the switch and an exaggerated wink. Giggling, she would then wriggle to the wall, pick up the soggy strips, and carefully drop them into a garbage bag Todd would hold open for her. She hadn't left his side from the moment he walked in the front door earlier that afternoon.

Desiree decided to remain in the rocker even as the steady buzzing of the steamer reminded her of the many chores still undone, the work she had envisioned would be finished long before Jon came back. But there just hadn't been enough time to do it all. Only now did she realize that perhaps she should have carried all the boxes and crates downstairs before painting the three bedrooms and that she should have concentrated on the main floor instead. But no one else could have done any better or gone any faster. She shouldn't have even suggested they move. She had uprooted everything and everyone.

"Mommy, when's Daddy coming?" Jodi asked impatiently. As Todd had finished stripping the dining room walls and was now washing them down with a large wet rag, Jodi had nothing to do. "When are we going to Gramma's?"

Desiree smiled and lifted Jodi onto her lap. Since she had last seen Jon, an obvious reconciliation had been made between him and his parents, and Katherine Sommers had been phoning the house regularly. They would be baby-sitting tonight. But how much did they know?

"Daddy will be here very soon, honey. Why don't you go upstairs and feed your dolls?"

"Mommy!! They aren't dolls. They're my *children*!"

"Yes, of course, your *children*." She peeked around the corner to see Todd still washing the newly stripped walls. She wanted to help him but the phone started ringing again. "It has to be Jon saying he would be over very shortly," she whispered to herself, and as she dashed towards the kitchen to answer it, she realized how quickly her excitement could grow with the thought of seeing him again.

"Hello," she said softly.

"I was rather hoping there would be no answer."

"Sorry, Katherine. We are all still here."

"But I thought you told me that the dinner was to begin half an hour ago. Is Jodi still awake?"

"Yes, she's feeding her dolls." *Her children.*

"John and I are planning to take her to the Anderson's cottage tomorrow. Let me talk to Jonathon. I won't keep him long."

"He's still out of town, Katherine." That lie was as spontaneous as all the others.

"Pardon?"

"He's not here yet. I'm expecting him any minute, though."

"He's not there yet? What do you mean? Jonathon wasn't out of town at all today. He called us this afternoon from his office to say that he would be leaving there early so no one would have to rush around the house tonight. And now you're saying he was out of town and still hasn't come home?"

"Yes, I did say that," she moaned, as her thoughts rambled on. She wasn't prepared to listen to the questions she presumed were about to be torpedoed through the wires, tormenting her, remaining unanswered until a later time, a *better* time.

"Well, I hope everything's okay, but Jonathon never mentioned anything about being away today."

"I'm sure Jon's all right," Desiree sighed. "He most likely just got caught up in some extra office work or something." *Or something.*

"Please have him phone me the instant he arrives there."

"Yes, Katherine. I'll make sure he does." In front of the chipped porcelain sink the tired blonde clutched the telephone receiver as she stared out into the blackened sky. So, Jon was lying, too. Now she knew.

A horrid thought flashed through her mind. Had Jon concocted this entire executive dinner just to test her reaction? And had she sounded grateful or too eager, perhaps, when so quickly accepting his unexpected invitation? She wasn't sure now. After that particular phone call, all she could remember was her lightheadedness.

When Jodi saw her mother at the doorway of her bedroom a few minutes later, she pressed a finger onto her pursed lips. "Shhh. Don't wake up Suzie. I just got her to sleep."

"I know you want to see Daddy tonight, and then go to Gramma's, but why don't you lie down with Suzie until he comes home? He'll be here soon." With a tiny smile, Jodi nodded and carefully picked up her doll, put her in bed beside her, and blew a quick kiss towards the doorway.

Downstairs, Desiree plumped onto the swivel chair Todd had moved from the corner of the kitchen. As he started to stick masking tape on the inside French door frames, the phone rang again.

"Hello."

"Have you phoned Mr. Thornton yet?"

"No, Katherine." She rolled her eyes at Todd.

"Surely you have decided to go on tour again."

"Well, I ... *we* aren't sure about it yet."

"I'll call Mr. Thornton first thing in the morning for you and tell him that you'd be honored to accompany him to New York."

"No, please don't do that. I just need a little more time to think things over. There's a lot involved, you know." *More than you realize, Katherine.*

"And I also know that Miss Marinello is returning from Europe at the end of next month and Mr. Thornton would insist on ample preparation for the American tour."

"I promised to phone him by the end of this week, and I will. Okay?" She was beginning to lose her patience with her mother-in-law.

"If Richard Thornton agreed with that, then, of course it's all right. Now, would you mind dressing Jodi for the car ride? I'm sure Jonathon will be there shortly."

Todd had finished taping the doors. He leaned against the side of the buffet and hutch, admiring his efforts. He lit up a Colt and took a long slow drag. "Was that twenty questions from your mother-in-law?"

Desiree laughed. "You know, that woman could drive me to drink. Jon and I haven't talked to her for so long and then, all of a sudden, she starts phoning me three or four times a week just to see what I'm doing or what I'm planning to do."

Todd smiled, nodding his head as Desiree continued.

"Her haughtiness one day and then her constant intrusion the next is something I never expected from Jon's mother. And she insists that I call her Katherine."

"Sara's mother used to be like that. We had our first argument over that woman. I guess it just comes with the title *mother-in-law*. She's mellowed considerably over the years, though, I must admit."

"Speaking of Sara, don't you think I should finish stripping this myself? She'll be home early tomorrow and I think you're going to fall asleep on her before she's even unpacked."

"No. *Next* Sunday she'll be back. She's got three more stops to make before she comes home. She's determined to get grand champion with Aurora this year, you know."

"Won't she ever let up on showing those Samoyeds? And to think she was going to send the twins to boarding school because of those dogs."

"Thank goodness I found the perfect nanny before she had the chance to register the boys there. Twins are a handful to care for sometimes." He took another long drag, whistling softly as he blew the smoke out of his pursed lips. "But at the time, I think she was just showing us all that she didn't want to move to another city. She was quite depressed for a while. She said if the twins weren't sent to private school, she would leave. With her dogs."

"She couldn't have been serious, though."

"Would you bring me an ashtray, please?" There was a sudden strained control to Todd's deep voice as he picked up some sticky strips of wallpaper that Jodi had missed. "If I get right back to this, it's only going to take half an hour or so to finish stripping the front wall. If Jon isn't here by then, we can enjoy that bottle of wine I brought over."

The phone was ringing again.

"Hello."

"My, aren't you the great talker tonight?" Carole Schrader's staccato delivery resounded in Desiree's ears. "This was my third and last attempt to reach you. I thought that since you haven't called to invite me over since you moved, I might just as well call you and invite myself. Ken has gone skiing again this weekend with a few of our new neighbors, but it's too cold for me so I might just as well come over and check out your new place."

"Carole, I *do* plan to have you and Ken over for a nice long visit, sometime soon, after everything's unpacked and cleaned up. But right now I have company, and tonight Jon's office is having a formal dinner party and we're already late for it. I should go now but I'll let you know when everything's done."

"Well, you know I wouldn't mind helping you unpack and put things away properly. I might just as well, for something to do. I'm so bored here. We could spend all day tomorrow moving furniture around, tidying things up, and chit-chatting. We can make a whole day of it, if you like. I'll phone you in the morning and let you know what time I'll be there."

"No, Carole. I'm ..."

"If we work together, everything will be done in half the time. We could be finished by noon tomorrow. Can't you see that?"

Desiree slammed down the phone, still not ready to admit to anyone that it was her own swelling anxiety that had brought her family to this house. Carole would just have to wait a little longer for an invitation.

"Have you seen a doctor lately?"

"Pardon?"

"Have you seen a doctor lately?"

"Yes, I have as a matter of fact." She rubbed her belly. There was no obvious hint of expansion yet. "But why do you ask?"

"Well, I've seen you get sick three times already today. It almost looks like you're pregnant, again. And doing so much work around here, by yourself, it seems." He shook his head in mild disapproval.

"I think it's just the strong smell of paint that's getting to me," she admitted. She hadn't told Jon yet, and she didn't really want to until she got a prescription from Dr. Styles that would eliminate all her symptoms. She knew Jon wouldn't tolerate her being so sick. Besides, shouldn't the husband be the first to hear about a new pregnancy? Or maybe it should be the parents. *How are you doing, Mom? Dad? I hope Norway is no disappointment to you like this house is to me.* "Sometimes I wonder if all this is really worth it."

"These renovations?"

"No. Moving. Moving into this house of shambles, uplifting our roots just to give Jon his own study, a room that he didn't even want in the first place. It looks like I was just trying to keep up with Carole and Ken Schrader."

"And so what if you were? You know, I saw her last week at the courthouse and she talked to me for half an hour, just as if we were the best of friends. I think I've only met her twice and that was at your duplex, if I remember correctly. And she's still bragging about her new house, her new Corvette, and that new grand piano she can't even play. Won't she ever quit?"

"I doubt it, Todd. But what really upsets me is that when she phoned the night Jon and I signed the mortgage papers I felt so smug, so relieved that we had finally done it. But look at this place!" She turned around, eyeing the mess around her. "Compared to the duplex, the only good features here are the size and the layout. The walls have never been painted underneath that ugly paper. There are seven different layers on some walls. Can you believe that?"

Todd gave her a tiny smile.

"And most of the light fixtures on the ceiling have been torn out. The kitchen sink drips, and that ugly floor took me a week to tear up and replace." She took a long breath before walking into the living room. "And who in their right mind would want a burnt-orange shag carpet on the main floor, on a level as large as this one, yet? No wonder this place took so long to sell. But who bought it? Good old Desiree. And why? Because the price was right and I was getting so tired of snooping into other peoples' houses, sometimes even interrupting dinner preparations or nap times. This was the twenty-seventh house I looked at!"

"You kept a record?" He tapped the lit end of his Colt against the rim of the glass ashtray.

"Sure did. It's all in that black binder. I'm never throwing that away." She stepped around some small boxes and sat on a swivel chair in the dining room.

"You sound bitter."

"You know, Jon never wanted to leave the duplex. He moved here just for me."

"But didn't you tell me that after you suggested looking for a new home, he had the duplex up for sale that very week?"

"Yes, I did."

"Well, he wouldn't have done that if he'd been happy where he was."

Desiree shifted her body and turned the chair in order to face Todd. "My timing was just a bit off. Adjusting to his new office job and finding the time he needed for all his studies was hard enough for Jon, but that unexpected delay in the promotion clinched it for him."

"That definitely would change things."

A sudden pattering of feet alerted the adults to Jodi running down the hallway of the upper level.

"Mommy. Suzie won't go back to sleep. She wants to wait up for Daddy. Please come and help me."

"Bring her here, honey."

Crunched together on the chair they swayed to the soft humming of a children's lullaby while Todd went back to his work.

"Maybe she needs more milk," Jodi whispered. "I go fill up her bottle again. You stay here and keep her warm, okay?"

Desiree set the doll onto the chair when the telephone rang again. Would she answer it this time to hear Jon's voice? Or would it be another curious busybody? She was counting each ring now. *Two—three*

"Mommy, don't answer it. I want you here with me. You been on the phone all night."

"But it might be Daddy." *Four*

"But he's 'posed to be here by now. Where is he, Mommy?"

"I don't know." *Five* "Maybe something went wrong and now he's trying to let us know. I'll see who's on the phone." *Six* "Hello."

"Is it Daddy? Is it Daddy?"

"I don't know. No one was there."

Jodi started to cry. "Maybe he won't be coming to get us now."

Desiree knelt down and caressed Jodi's soft chubby hands. "If the phone rings again, let's answer it right away, okay?"

"Could I answer it, Mommy? Could I?"

"Of course you can. If you answer it right away."

"Oh, goody. Now I better get Suzie so we can tell the other children."

As Jodi tiptoed back to her bedroom, Desiree wished that she herself could be so easily uplifted that evening. She stared at the clean shine of the new kitchen floor while hoping, almost expecting to hear the phone interrupting them all again. But the phone was silent and she walked towards the rear foyer as her mind was spinning with various possibilities of Jon's whereabouts.

She felt a deep churning inside her stomach and her lungs still ached for fresh air—air no longer cloudy with the heavy odor of paint. But she couldn't propel her stiff, cramped legs outside into the crisp March evening. She would rather be sick indoors.

Despite her clammy hands and sweaty forehead she held her chin high in an attempt to contain herself. Jon had still not arrived. Her wan face tightened as she pulled the hairpins from her crown and let her long curly tresses fall against cold bare arms as the pins dropped to her feet.

She watched Todd continue pressing, swaying. The thick layers of wallpaper were peeling off easily, displaying more ugly gray drywall. Only one more wall was left to strip and after the washing was done, she would have to start painting all over again. She moaned to herself. After the primer, two coats of eggshell would be needed in the two rooms. More work, more backaches, more nausea "Dr. Styles, please let me have those special pills. There's still so much to do around here, and I don't want to lose my baby," she softly said to herself.

Todd was washing the walls now. She was biting her lips. Her fingers tapped the top of the stove and her toes wriggled in rhythm to Todd's continuous movements. What could she do tonight to occupy her mind with constructive ideas? To keep her hands busy? She scrambled upstairs towards the bedrooms, her eyes surveying the bold papered walls of the upper hallway.

"If you come now, Mr. Jonathon Sommers, you can damn well wait for me!"

Her silk dress soon dropped to the floor and she gently massaged her abdomen as she tried to see even a hint of swelling in her belly. She wondered what this pregnancy would bring. It was already so unlike the first—that simple, healthy eight and a half months, the perfect pregnancy.

Soon clad in an old pair of blue jeans and a faded cotton blouse, she sat atop the stairs and let her eyes travel across the living room, where Todd was again picking up more soggy strips. Had she told him yet about how good he looked since losing all that weight?

Soon he would be finished and the drab ugly paper would be gone forever. Tomorrow she would strip behind the piano and then prime the entire main floor. Tomorrow she would buy Jodi a new spring jacket and take her for a leisurely walk in the neighborhood park to get some fresh air.

Todd seemed preoccupied; his temples were twitching. He had done so much for her today. They had done so much together. As he washed the living room walls she wiped the dusty canisters, which had been left on the refrigerator. As he swayed back and forth she wiped and wiped, almost glad now that Jon hadn't shown up. Her desire to socialize that evening with a group of well-heeled strangers had definitely ebbed.

She had rubbed the decals off the entire set of canisters. Damn! Now she would have to buy new stickers. She took another deep breath. Again she was rushing things, still finding it difficult to concentrate.

"You certainly are no quitter, are you?" Todd confirmed as he carried another full garbage bag into the kitchen and saw her trying to move the table back against the wall.

She looked at him drearily and sighed. So opposite Jon, she realized. Renovating and decorating had always been *her* job, every bit of it.

"When I first arrived here this afternoon you looked so ghastly pale," he began. "You walked around the house like a zombie. Your eyes were black and puffy from strain. You even told me you felt a little tired. But then you went ahead and painted the downstairs bathroom. But that *still* wasn't enough. Oh, no. As soon as the kitchen walls were bare and thoroughly washed you couldn't wait to get your little hands into the paint again. And only then did you tell me about having to get ready for an evening out with Jon." He scratched his chin while looking around. "Now listen to me. I can move this furniture around without any help from you. Go find something to read while I finish in there."

He took her by the shoulders and pushed her firmly into another swivel chair. She was too stunned at his harsh tone to shift her body for more comfort. She had used him today to do things she should have done herself and now after all this time Todd was letting her know exactly how he felt about it.

His long gaze kept her still but when he lifted one end of the kitchen table shoved beside the buffet and hutch, she noticed a leg caught in the twisted threads of the shag carpet. She jumped from the chair to raise the other end but when she heard the grated sound of spinning tires outside she looked toward the front windows. Too many boxes, bags, and crates were in the way. Despite standing on her tiptoes she couldn't see anything. The engine revved louder and louder.

"*Jon, is that you?*" her mind was shouting.

The car sped off. Was it Jon? Had he finally come home only to recognize Todd's company car out front? Her left knee buckled as she lifted the table again and she fell against the buffet and knocked over a wooden bookend. Her ankle throbbed when she stood up.

"Let's both quit now and have some wine," Todd started with the familiar voice of *I told you so*, as he massaged her ankle. Suddenly he started to chuckle. "You know, if I had thought of this before, I would've let you help me move this table hours ago."

"I don't know what you are getting at."

"Well, if this had happened then, you wouldn't have been able to do all that painting in the kitchen. Its table and chairs would all still be there. You'd only have been able to watch Jodi and me working in here. I don't have anything to do tomorrow, so I'll come over again and we can finish this off." He paused, placing her foot back onto the floor. "Hey, what's wrong?"

She turned her head. "You wouldn't understand if I told you." That was another lie. She was sure Todd would understand if she told him about her new single life. The sad point was, she couldn't tell him. She didn't have the guts.

And Todd had his own concerns that evening. How could he get Desiree to confide in him? He was aware of what was happening in her life, had been for quite a while, but she remained very evasive about it. He could sense a quiet force about her and if she ever did tell him, he would be there to listen and to comfort her.

"That was Jon out front before, wasn't it? Why would he take off like that?"

"Pardon?"

"You heard me, Des. Why would Jon take off like that when he knew my car was outside?"

She straightened her back and ignored his glare.

"Why would he do that, Des?" he repeated more firmly.

"I don't know what you are talking about, Todd."

"You know damn well what I'm talking about. Why wouldn't Jon come in?"

"Todd, really. What would this look like from the outside?"

She was frowning, almost in disgust, and Todd wondered if he might have pushed the issue too far that evening.

"Why don't we have some of that wine now?" He squeezed her elbow, hesitating momentarily before starting downstairs towards the bar.

Was that the doorbell? Desiree strained her ears. She panicked at the idea of Jon seeing her in her old torn jeans and wrinkled blouse. If only she could run upstairs and put her silk dress on again. But he was knocking at the door now. After running her fingers through her now-tangled hair, she straightened the collar of her faded cotton blouse. The doorknob started to turn. Her stomach started to churn. Suddenly, there he was.

Rushing into his arms, she kissed his cool, stubbly cheeks, squeezed his thick chest closer to her pounding heart, and poured all her love into the embrace.

"Hi," he said lightly, letting his arms fall quickly to his sides. Searching the front closet for an empty hanger but finding none, he dropped his leather jacket onto the telephone bench nearby and stepped around her. His wide jaw tightened as his dark eyes flitted across the untidy room. "Where's Jodi?"

She had waited all this time to hear that? She limped back to the piano, grabbed the top ledge for support, and eyed Jon in disbelief as he stared down the hallway towards the bedrooms as though expecting to see his daughter come running out to see him.

He was wearing beige cords and a terry cloth T-shirt that opened slightly at the neck, exposing his tight hairy chest. And those old hiking boots should have thrown in the garbage years ago. There was obviously no dinner party tonight. What was happening? She fiddled with a bobby pin in her jeans pockets and waited for him to say something.

"I thought you'd be finished with all these renovations by now, Des." A look of disapproval widened his eyes.

Words eluded her.

"The dinner was cancelled," he said flatly and turned to face her. "I tried phoning you earlier to let you know that I had invited my boss over here for a few cocktails instead, but you must have been out. I can see why you'd want to be away from this place."

"I've been home all day, Jon. You didn't phone me. And why was the dinner cancelled so late?" Hearing footsteps behind her, she cringed as she tried to block the archway to the lower level. She knew what Jon would think.

"Here's your drink, Des. Nice and cold." Todd's casual expression changed to a look of caution when he saw Jon standing beside her. He carefully set the glasses onto the piano top and walked closer to the couple. "Hi, there," he began, his voice friendly but not too eager. "We were starting to get concerned."

Desiree's eyes narrowed when she saw Jon glaring at Todd and then back to the wine glasses.

"Your good wife told me she was starting to renovate the house while you were away so I decided to come over today and help her tear off some wallpaper. But I think she's done an awful lot herself, don't you?"

Todd's voice was soft but Jon wasn't listening. Desiree couldn't understand his cold stare and his straight, stiff stance in front of the still-opened wooden door, which was chilling the room much like his very presence. And wasn't there a little glint of laughter in his wide, dark eyes? When she looked up again, Jon's face was tight, his eyes now ablaze.

"Excuse me, Todd," Jon said finally. Firmly and deliberately he took Desiree's arms and briskly led her into the kitchen. "So, you've got Todd coming over now, huh? I leave you to have a little time for myself and you find someone else to keep you company. A good friend of ours yet. Some friend. Some *good wife*."

The small of her back was pressed hard against the counter, its sharp edge gouging her spine. Jon's exasperation was shooting red-hot barbs of fear to her brain while it seemed he was actually enjoying the discord. She twisted, pushed, and shoved for freedom but his grip on her wrists only tightened, held her captive.

"You want to know something, Desiree?" Jon squeezed harder.

Her eyes widened with shame. Jodi had awakened and was teetering sleepily towards the kitchen. "Todd! Help Jodi! Get her away from here!" She could see Todd picking her up and quickly turning away.

"Did you hear me, Desiree?" Jon shouted.

She twisted, pushed, and shoved again somehow managing to pull away from him. In the far corner of the living room she leaned against the fireplace and watched desperately as Todd tried to block Jodi's view of the kitchen. Jodi was squirming to get another glance at her father or maybe even a hug and kiss from him.

"Daddy. Daddy. Wait for me!!"

Jon's face reddened, his dark eyes narrowed, and his fists clenched. He stomped back to the foyer and was reaching for the doorknob as Desiree struggled to restrain her daughter, who was now almost out of Todd's arms.

Jodi broke away and scurried towards the closing door. Desiree was too stunned to move, however. She wanted to bring Jon back inside. Back to stay. She shouldn't let him go. Not now. Not like this.

"Jon!!"

"Daddy! Daddy!"

Chapter Eleven

Monday, March 11

The alarm had been blaring for several minutes, but Desiree remained motionless beneath the covers as beads of sweat trickled down her forehead and tangles of long hair framed her milky face. Her mind was heavy with fatigue after another sleepless night spent reliving the recent events of her life. At times, the vivid memories turned into nightmarish dreams.

Her dry eyes were open, yet the vision was still so clear—three-dimensional and in Technicolor. In front of her the hanging plants, with their long macramé tassels, had again transformed themselves into dark, bearded monsters that flapped their jagged wings around her. The cattails and stalks of wheat, bunched together in the tall earthen pot beside the bed, lurked from the corner like entranced cobras, flustering each nerve center until total fatigue allowed her a few moments of rest again.

"Oh, just to have ten minutes of precious sleep," she moaned to herself as she turned off the alarm before burying her head in the thick soft pillows. "Just to have a little more time to figure things out." But it was Monday and she had to go to work.

Remembering her instant nausea from any quick move, methodically she slid her feet onto the cold hardwood floor and lifted her tired body off the bed.

The closet doors had been carelessly left open the night before and now she could only see Jon's clothing so neatly hung up, unlike the day he had left. Every item, including his many silk ties, had been dry cleaned and perfectly organized inside his half of the closet. During a short fit of anger and disbelief, however, she decided to pack everything of his and give it all to the Salvation Army. Soon his sweaters and a wide assortment of underwear were piled high in disarray on the corner dresser. It was then that her father-in-law had greeted her at the bedroom doorway early yesterday afternoon.

"You should never, ever, leave the front doors unlocked, young lady," John Sommers had begun as his eyes darted across the bright, cluttered room.

She whisked a loose strand of hair from her face as her mind filled with questions. Why was Mr. Sommers here? Why hadn't he asked where his son was? Or did he already know? Had Jon finally approached his parents, confiding in them both? She had purposely left the front doors unlocked for *Todd*, who should be here at any moment to help finish the painting. Now what was she going to do?

John eyed the freshly painted walls of the upper hallway and his head shook slightly in wonder. "Jon told us that you have been doing all the renovating here yourself. You've done a superb job, but you know I could have hired a contractor to do all of it. There seems little left to do now, so why not wait for Jon to help you with the rest? The playoffs will be finished tonight and he'll have more time."

Playoffs!! She had forgotten about Jon's curling league. So that's where he had been last night before coming over. But how did his father know so much about Jon's present affairs? She closed the closet doors with a quick swing of her arm.

"There's a huge roast in the oven and this morning Katherine instructed Theresa to make a fresh batch of chocolate chip cookies for Jodi to bring home. Where is she?"

"Still sleeping."

"What? At this time of day?"

Desiree turned away from him. She didn't feel that she owed her father-in-law any explanation. He should have realized that Jodi would have gone to bed later than usual the night before. Then, of course, she couldn't get to sleep right away, because ...

"Wake her up and get yourself properly dressed while I shovel the walks."

"No! Jodi needs her sleep." She couldn't let Mr. Sommers Sr. stay to help her with any chores, because Todd was coming. That had already been planned. That was more important.

"Come on, now. You both need some fresh air. And an afternoon with us, topped off with a roast beef dinner, will do you both good. Write Jon a note so he can join us all at the house later."

The note she wrote, however, was to Todd apologizing for her absence. She phoned his house while John and Jodi waited for her in the car but when she received no answer, she taped the short message onto the front door, again leaving it unlocked.

It was nearly two-thirty when they arrived at the Sommers'. With Jodi the obvious center of attention, Desiree found the atmosphere somewhat relaxing. The visit was comfortable enough and Theresa was her usual cute self.

At the candlelit dinner table, however, as butter melted on the mound of scalloped potatoes and blood oozed from the thick slab of beef on her plate, her stomach knotted. Both Katherine and John were watching her from either end of the long oak table, but she remained quiet and still.

"What happened last night? I thought you were going to have Jon phone us the minute he arrived home."

That didn't take long. Desiree sighed and slowly started to chew the tender meat, purposefully counting each bite, before placing the silver fork on the edge of her Royal Albert plate. But she was ready. She had mentally rehearsed this scene in Mr. Sommers' Mercedes. "Jon came home at ten o'clock last night. I should have had him phone you then, but I was rather upset by that time and I obviously got *him* upset. We said a few harsh words to each other and he left the house. Alone." There!! She had told them. She had finally admitted to someone that all was not too serene at home.

"But where did he go last night? And where is he now?"

"I have no idea, Katherine. I thought you might know." She was feeling faint and she leaned into the upholstered high back of the chair and closed her eyes.

"Well, perhaps he just needs some time to be alone," Katherine suggested.

"Yeah, perhaps."

Desiree wiped the sleep out of her eyes. She could remember yesterday afternoon so clearly—every single tense moment of it. But that was yesterday. And now at the doors of the walk-in closet in the master bedroom she tightened the thick towel around her still-wet body before pulling at the hangers until, finally, a navy wool pantsuit fell onto the floor. She suddenly felt rushed, almost hyper. A second wind had quickly come upon her. Soon she was a whirlpool of nervous energy. The hot shower hadn't helped relax her.

At the bottom of the stairs she re-read Todd's reply to her scribbled note from the day before. 'Drove by just as you were leaving the house with John Sommers, so I decided to try to get the living room done before you returned. Help you move the furniture back sometime this week. Sorry that I didn't have time to do it all today.' He had placed the note under the aged Venus flytrap on the piano.

She studied the note. *Sorry*. After all he had done for her already, why should Todd regret not getting all the furniture moved back?

She pivoted awkwardly around the main floor, which now seemed so much bigger—no more clutter and no more faded oranges or yellows or golds. No more drab grays and tans. Just a mile of bare white walls ready for her personal touches—personal touches that she had planned for Jon, filling each room with her own creations which he had once loved so much. "Jon, come and see what's been done to this house now. Come and see your den, your own private room—so new, so big, so masculine, so you. Jon, please come home and ..."

As she opened the front door to get the morning newspaper, she felt the quiet, eerie cold of the morning. *"More damn snow,"* she moaned to herself, wishing that she had let her father-in-law clean the sidewalks as he had offered to do yesterday.

"Oh, Mommy. There you are. I been looking all over for you."

"Honey, I didn't mean you to get up so early. You look so tired." She rubbed the sleep out of Jodi's half-opened eyes and gave her a tight hug. "I love you so much, Jodi. Why don't you get dressed while I make some breakfast? I think we have time for French toast this morning. Your favorite, huh?"

"Are you going to take me to day care before school again today?"

"Yeah. I promised Auntie Dawna that I'd go to the office all this week because she's out of town. Remember? She needs someone to do her work while she's away. Uncle Todd might need my help there, too. But you can walk to school from the day care with some of your new friends and I'll pick you up as soon as I can. Now please, get dressed while I get busy in the kitchen. I put your clothes on the top of your dresser."

Outside in the icy darkness, she struggled to carry her daughter over the freshly snowed-in sidewalk. Jodi's squirming body quickly weakened Desiree's aching arms as she continued up the slope carefully testing each step for ice before putting down her foot. Still tight from their newness, her leather boots had blistered both heels. She persisted, however, leaning slightly forward for better balance, holding Jodi tighter for protection. Then they fell.

In front of their neighbor's house her ankle twisted on the curb's edge and she lost control. Jodi sprawled, face down in the deep snow. Desiree screamed and crawled towards her and they held each other tightly on the edge of the sidewalk.

Then they plodded on through the snow and ice to the bus stop where they stood and waited. Gusty cold air whistled down Desiree's neck. Once inside the bus, however, the air was suddenly too hot and stuffy, so uncomfortable. The temperature had changed from bleak iciness to smothering fervor, and there were still several blocks to travel before they would reach their destination. Mesmerized by the seated crowd and the hum of the bus engine, Jodi remained still and quiet. Something intrigued the youngster about riding the bus, while Desiree just wanted off before she threw up.

Inside the day nursery, finally, Jodi shook and screamed and clung to her mother again. "Mommy, don't go. Please don't go!" Her quavering voice hushed the other children who began to gather around the couple. Desiree knelt down to kiss Jodi's cheek before a stout supervisor ushered them both to the wide front window.

"See, Jodi. Now you can see your mother walking down the sidewalk. And you can wave good-bye to her. And you know that she'll be coming to get you later."

Desiree rushed out. Still hearing the screeches from the front landing of the nursery, she forced herself forward. She didn't look back, didn't wave. She didn't throw a kiss. She had to catch another bus. She had to go to work.

Just then she gagged. *Damn.* She was going to vomit right there on the front sidewalk—right there among other mothers who were rushing their kids into the daycare, who were perhaps also concerned about getting to work on time. She took slow, deep breaths and continued walking. *Oh, where is that alley?* Gagging, she tried to breathe deeper, to gain some strength with each new breath and each single step, but finally she had no more energy, no more will to stop it, to hold it back.

The carpet layers were measuring Dawna's office again and two painters had just set their equipment on her walnut desk. Desiree had been disturbed so often that morning, she was surprised the five proposals left for her had already been typed out, and now she paused to relax in the large blue office.

The Boston fern had wilted over the weekend and Desiree sprayed the plant lovingly. She studied the cozy office with its pale blue walls, dark wooden furniture, and royal blue upholstered chairs. Two philodendrons covered opposite corners. Their vines, creeping along the ceiling, would soon be touching each other. Baby's breath adorned the brass planter and she wanted a slip of the purple passion plant on the credenza beside the portrait of Gordon. She touched the satiny finish of the picture and warm thoughts of Dawna quickly filled her mind. It was easy to waste time in the comfortable office, but she finally decided to check Todd's dictation because his young secretary had phoned in sick that morning and the concerned blonde immediately offered her own time to finish it.

"Got another tape for you, Desiree," he stated softly when he saw her at the door of his large office. "Gwen won't be here tomorrow, either. Are you sure you can spare the time? I'll have several more proposals for you to type up by then. My tapes are in that pile." He pointed to a wooden tray on the credenza. "And even though Mr. Morten was out of town this weekend, he's probably got quite a few filled himself."

"I'm sure I can manage it all. Dawna already asked me to work the entire week anyway. She must have known. But you'd better leave for the airport soon. Mr. Morten's plane will be landing any time now. I don't think you should keep him waiting."

"I know, but I've been interrupted so often this morning by those carpet layers. I wish they would do their work when the office is empty." He put on his thick wool coat and grabbed his leather briefcase from the corner of his desk. "Let me take you out for lunch tomorrow. Anywhere you want." Together they walked out to the reception area and as the office door squeaked shut behind him, Desiree glanced at the telephone messages the secretary handed her.

She sank into Dawna's chair as she reread the last message. The bottom note, with Pamela's ornate handwriting, had been taken hours ago. 'Krystal called. Wants to have lunch with you today'. And Desiree knew why—because she wasn't home when Jon, no doubt, had phoned her earlier. He would have assumed she would be back at work by now and he was getting his secretary to verify his hunch. He just couldn't accept his wife being a working mother. But why hadn't Pamela given her the message earlier?

She returned the calls immediately, but Krystal had already left and no specific rendezvous could be confirmed. Too tired and too hungry to question anyone about anything when twelve o'clock arrived, Desiree quickly got her coat and left the office. She panicked when she passed the lobby's corner smoke shop and saw Jon being handed some loose change at the counter. She had no desire to see him at all that day.

She hurried out into the gusty chill, hoping he hadn't seen her, hoping somehow she could lose herself in the maze of the lunch hour crowd. *"Where are you now, Jon?"* she asked herself as she rushed on. *"Can you see me running from you? Hiding from you?"* For an instant she turned her head to look back, but only a gray blur greeted her.

In a small deli several blocks away, and later back in the office, she tried to gain her composure, but the message from Krystal and Jon's unexpected visit had all but shattered her businesslike façade. All afternoon she kept to herself. She could almost hide in Dawna's blue office, transcribing Todd's tapes, and she was thankful that she somehow managed to concentrate on them.

Later, after a meal of thick juicy hamburgers and crisp French fries at a nearby café, the pale sun slipped steadily behind the silvery horizon as Desiree lifted her excited daughter over the short wire fence of the neighborhood park. At the curb's edge Jodi jumped into the fresh snow and whirled it high into the air. She lost her balance and fell. Desiree, still wearing her new boots, limped towards her daughter and pulled her up again, brushed her off, and tightened the scarf around her neck.

Two frisky terriers scampered by and Jodi dashed after them. She fell into the snow again but picked herself up to continue the chase. The dogs, however, had disappeared down a narrow back alley. While Jodi skipped along the curb looking for them, Desiree hobbled to a sheltered bus stop where she dropped her tired aching body onto the wooden seat and leaned against its high back. "I could stay here all night," she sighed. "This feels so comfortable."

"Are you gonna pick me up late tomorrow too, Mommy?"

"No, love. Today was just a little hectic for me. I was interrupted so many times I thought I'd better work a bit late. Uncle Todd had lots of work for me to do and I didn't want to disappoint him by not having it all done. Tomorrow I'll be there for you on time."

"Can we eat out again? And then come here after? Please, Mom?" Jodi started to shiver.

"If it warms up a bit and my feet can take it, we sure will."

"If I rub them tonight for you, would it help?"

"Yes, honey. It would help, but you know you don't have to do that. Now, take my hand. I don't want you to fall again."

Held in her mother's firm grip Jodi struggled to keep up with those long jerky strides. She wanted to be set free so she could jump or play or skate just a little bit longer in the fresh snow.

In front of the split-level, at last, Desiree reached into her purse for the house keys. A large parcel had been left on the landing but, as she bent down to get it, she heard a strange, unsteady shuffling behind her. Turning around instantly, she noticed a short and bulky figure approaching. She grabbed Jodi's arm.

"I'm Mr. Mussel-White from across the street," the man began instantly. "And I've seen three people slip on your sidewalk already today. I think you'd better get it shoveled before somebody gets hurt."

"Thank you, sir. But right now I'd like to get my daughter into the house, out of the cold." Still sensing his piercing eyes on her, she forced her key into the slit of the doorknob and pulled, but nothing budged.

"Mommy. That man is still here and I'm scared."

Desiree pulled again, and finally the door opened. They tumbled inside where the stale smell of paint greeted them. Mr. Mussel-White had disappeared, and after hanging up their coats, Desiree turned up the thermostat.

"That man wasn't very nice," Jodi suggested.

"No, he wasn't. But he's right about me getting the sidewalks shoveled soon. We don't want anybody getting hurt. Why don't you go upstairs and take care of your babies while I make some hot chocolate? Then it's bedtime." And as Jodi skipped upstairs, Desiree stepped outside to see what the postman had left for them.

Noticing the Norwegian postage on the large brown package, she smiled and placed it on the piano bench before entering the kitchen and turning on the burner.

Downstairs again, Jodi noticed the large parcel and ran into the kitchen. "Mommy, can we open it now? Can we, Mommy? Please?"

"The parcel is from Grandma and Grandpa in Norway. It's for Easter and we should really wait until then to open it. Let's have our drinks now."

Still chilled, she donned an old cardigan she had left on the loveseat and buttoned Jodi's sweater before filling the mugs. "I wish a chinook had come today so all the snow would melt away. I wish it would warm up a little so I could open some of these windows, but right now I have to go and shovel the sidewalks before someone else slips. Before Mr. Mussel-White comes over again. Before I get too relaxed and fall asleep right here in front of you. Why don't you give some of that hot chocolate to Suzie? Then you can stay in your bedroom and feed all your children."

"No. I want to stay here with you, Mommy. I want you to stay here with me. You been gone all day." Pleading hazel eyes looked up at her.

Desiree bent down and held a tiny hand. "But I must go outside and clean the walk. That old man just told us that some people have already fallen in front of our house, and remember this morning when you and Mommy fell? Well, maybe tomorrow *all* the sidewalks will be clean so we won't fall again either. Okay? I won't be long." She put on her thick wool pea jacket and struggled to get into her tight boots again, but Jodi still clutched her pant legs.

Immediately the young mother got the large parcel from the living room, found the good pair of scissors she had earlier placed on the buffet, and started cutting the thick strings of the brown package from Norway. The neatly wrapped box held a soft beige afghan, crocheted in a pretty cable pattern. Wrapped carefully inside the folds was a plastic troll doll, its sprightly face smiling at her.

"Mommy, what is that?"

"It's an elf. A troll. A special pretend creature that lives in the country where your grandmother and grandfather are visiting."

Jodi studied the funny-looking object. "Does he bite anybody?"

"Oh, no. He's quite mischievous and would rather play with us."

"He's kinda ugly but I like him. I think he wants to color in my new book. Could you get me my crayons so I can keep him warm down here?"

Seeing Jodi shiver, Desiree checked the thermostat again. It had not risen one degree.

Soon wrapped under a wool blanket with Jodi's coloring book opened in front of them beside the piano, they laid together on the thick shag rug. Pages of the cartoon sketches were soon being filled with bright colors.

"I think I should shovel the walks now, Jodi. Finish that pretty picture and maybe later we can share another quick mug of hot chocolate."

"I can help you, Mommy. Suzie and me can move the snow, too. And Elf can help, if he wants to."

"Yes, I know you can, but not tonight. It's too late for you to still be up and too cold outside for you to be with me out there. Tell you what, though. I'll put the piano bench in front of the window so you can see me shoveling. Then while I'm outside why don't you teach your children some nursery rhymes? Suzie might know most of them, but I don't think Elf does. Or maybe you could sing some new songs you learned at the day care? Okay?"

"Yeah. Okay. We can do that."

In the front yard, as the fierce evening wind whirled around her, she waved lovingly at Jodi. Her eyes watering from the cold, the anxious mother propped herself against the wooden handle of the shovel and thrust with all her strength. The flat edge of the shovel was catching on some broken portions of the public sidewalk, but she continued digging, lifting, tossing. Just a few more feet of deep patches and she could go inside for warmth.

Pushing hard again, she turned the blade onto its side and let the gathered snow pile up along the curb. Continually coughing, sniffling, and blinking, she rested on the shovel and examined her efforts. The narrow path behind her would have to suffice for the evening. "Endless snow!" she shouted. "Damn winters! Damn cold!" She pushed against the shovel and groaned again as she lifted the heavy load one last time. Glancing toward the house again, she noticed Jodi waving through the window. She was laughing and jumping, excited to be able to see her mother and knowing that she hadn't gone far away, that she hadn't left her. Desiree waved back and shouted, "Hi, honey. I'll be inside soon."

Anticipating comforting warmth inside the house, she was disappointed to discover that she had to zip up her jacket again, had to rub Jodi's cold hands and face, had to wrap the new afghan around the tiny, shivering body, and had to hurry downstairs to the utility room.

The furnace pilot light had gone out and the emergency line to the gas company kept ringing busy, even after four attempts. In a while all the burners on the stove were red with heat, the oven door was open, and the old drippings of an apple pie wafted through the kitchen. The marble fireplace was soon filled with two compressed logs and crumpled newspapers she had found in the den. When the tinder ignited, both mother and daughter had to turn their heads from the sudden heat and glare. Jodi, fascinated by the glow, the flickers, and the popping sounds, sat motionless on the floor until sleep finally closed her eyes. When Desiree picked her up and placed her on the loveseat between the folds of a thick wool blanket, the plastic troll doll was tucked under her limp arms.

In the wing chair Desiree cupped the ceramic mug with her cold hands and sipped the sweet hot chocolate, enjoying its warmth. After spreading the crocheted afghan around her legs, she opened the large envelope from her parents. Jodi's card was put aside to be opened in the morning, but hers exhibited a single tea rose. Roses were her mother's weakness—any size, any shape, any color. Inside the card, tiny sprays of red and pink buds splashed the shiny paper. A new brown bill was taped to the upper left corner. As she peeled off the tape, Desiree read the card: 'Easter Greetings to a Lovely Daughter and Her Husband'. Printed in both English and Norwegian, there was a handwritten note from her mother underneath. "Jam, you can't imagine the exciting time we're having here. Wish you were all with us. See you in June. Love Mom and Dad."

"*Jam*. You actually wrote down the name *Jam*," Desiree whispered. "You and Dad have been gone for how long now? And you are calling me *Jam* again. Thank you, Mom." She gave a tiny smile as her eyes stayed on the various pinks and reds. She rubbed the crisp bill absently. No one knew about her new singleness yet, or her pregnancy. Both topics were still too difficult for her to express. It would be too complicated for her parents to absorb, whatever words she chose. While her father's roots were being re-seeded, she felt hers were being destroyed.

"You wanna na'kin, Mommy? I get you one." Jodi yawned. The slits of her eyes were heavy with sleep. She pressed the tiny troll doll hard against her chest and teetered to the buffet. She quickly pulled a few tissues from the box. "Here you go. I think my new elf needs some, too. He looks so sad."

Desiree wondered how her husband could have left such a beautiful human being—so tiny, so innocent, and so loving. Abandoning his only child so guiltlessly. Desiree carefully picked her daughter up, laid her on the loveseat by the piano and began stroking the fine blonde hair, now wet at the temples.

Long gray shadows flickered against the walls of the living room as she stretched her aching bones but when Jodi started to cough in her sleep, Desiree forced herself up the stairs with a desperate spurt of energy. She was too tired to take them two at a time as she had done before.

In the den again, she slid open the closet doors and dropped some worn sheets from the upper shelf onto her shoulders. Back in the living room she dumped the contents of a small box onto the carpet and tucked the cardboard under her arms. Soon grocery bags filled with toys and pencils and stationary were emptied and old cotton drapes were snatched from their box on a nearby step table. She sorted packages of paper towels and paper plates from another box and heaved them towards the fireplace. She grabbed the old sheets and one by one ripped them into shreds before throwing them onto the grate. She grabbed, shredded, and hurled until the fireplace was full.

Again the blaze was breathtaking and again she nestled beside Jodi.

"Mommy, my throat hurts. I don't feel too good." Jodi's voice was croaky. She was suddenly panting, gagging. Warm vomit swept down Desiree's sweater sleeve.

"Jodi! Jodi!" she screamed. She picked her daughter up, but the flaccid body was as limp as a rag doll.

Desiree dialed the nightline to Jon's office. Once she told him about Jodi she knew he would come home immediately. He would help them. He would know what to do. But, she heard only static between the long, steady rings. "Where are you, Jon? Why aren't you at the office tonight? Why aren't you home here with us?" She let the ringing continue until finally she slammed down the phone.

"Damn you, Jon. Damn you!!"

Chapter Twelve

Tuesday, March 12

The early morning sun streamed through the long narrow windows, softening the living room's dark complexion. Worry swelled within her after she called Dr. Styles' office and was told that he wouldn't be in until noon. She had finally reached the gas company and was told a serviceman would be there shortly. She had also spoken with her boss, telling Mr. Morten she wouldn't be at work that day because she was going to take Jodi to the doctor's. But what was keeping the taxicab?

She finished her hot herbal tea and skimmed over the glossy kaleidoscopic pages of another Cosmopolitan. She leaned back, rested her aching head on the thickness of the high-backed wing chair, and let the magazine fall to the floor. She could still feel the stiffness in her shoulders, the numbness in her arms, the tingle in her fingertips. She could picture what was happening at the office. Todd's dictation was piling up, Mr. Morten's financial reports were still on his credenza, and the painters and carpet layers were disturbing everyone, as usual.

"Desiree, I can't understand a single word you're saying," Mr. Morten had said earlier, after her third attempt to explain. "Are you all right?"

Did she hang up on him? She wasn't sure. But she had phoned him. She had tried to tell him.

Jodi was still curled up in the thick wool blanket on the loveseat. Her tiny body was stiff now, like a plastic doll, like that little troll still tucked under her arm. Today she wouldn't be playing hide-and-seek under the bedcovers, she wouldn't be clinging to her mother at the front door of the house, she wouldn't be screaming at the day care. Today she was sick—short of breath, burning, freezing, coughing, and vomiting.

"Scream, Jodi. Pull at my pant legs. Tug at my sweater. Spill milk all over your new clothes. Or break a toy. Just don't lie there panting and choking."

She phoned Jon's office once again. Surely, he would be there now. His line was busy. Yes, she would hold. Soon he would be on his way to pick them up, to take them to the hospital.

"Mr. Sommers' line is still busy. Perhaps I could take a message."

"Yes. Could you tell him to call his wife? *At home*, please? And it's extremely important that he gets this message as soon as possible. Jodi is very sick and I'm taking her to see the doctor this morning."

When the doorbell rang, thankful that the taxi had finally arrived, Desiree hung up the phone and ran to the front door, but was surprised to see Todd standing there, his thick wool coat unbuttoned.

"Todd. I don't understand. Why are *you* here?"

"Syd said that you sounded rather frantic over the phone earlier so he asked me to come here and check everything out."

She pointed at Jodi. "The gas company's sending a man over to fix the furnace but …"

Todd dashed to the bundle on the loveseat, felt her damp forehead and knelt down to put his head on Jodi's bobbing chest. "Get your coat on," he stated flatly. "We've got to get her to a doctor right away."

"But I've already called our doctor and he won't be in until after lunch. I'm waiting for a cab to come and take us to the hospital."

"We can't wait for a cab. I'll take you both to see my old family doctor. I know he'll accept us without an appointment. Who knows when *your* doctor might be free? And the wait at the hospital could be even longer without any prior arrangement? Get Jodi wrapped up nice and tight. That wind is chilly. And leave a note for the serviceman." As he made a quick phone call, Desiree prepared Jodi for the car ride.

They had been in Dr. Mitchum's waiting room just long enough to remove their coats when another of Jodi's vomiting spasms alerted the doctor himself. Within minutes she was examined. The doctor immediately gave instructions for her to be taken directly to the children's hospital, and later, at the admittance counter, the friendly and efficient nursing aides required only a few moments to gather all necessary information.

Despite her short and raspy breaths, Jodi looked peaceful in her mother's arms. At the edge of a long vinyl bench in the brightly colored lobby, Desiree waited for Todd to park his car. She stretched over to a pile of magazines on the coffee table beside her and took an old issue of *Women's Day*. Nothing on the pages particularly caught her interest, and soon she was distracted by Jodi's next short spell of coughing and gagging; only the doctor's quick prognosis filled her thoughts. Somehow she remembered that a specific pneumonia, acute lobar pneumonia, was going to keep Jodi in the hospital for a few days, under strict supervision.

When a slow scraping sound alerted Desiree to her immediate surroundings, she noticed a small boy approaching the wide window across the room. He leaned against the bare pane of glass and was rubbing his left hip, while ill-fitting crutches kept him propped up.

She watched him intently and, as the sun streaked his short flaxen hair with gold, she could almost feel his yearning, his determination to be outside where most children could be even on a cold day like this. Her face flushed when he turned around unexpectedly and caught her staring at him. She quickly returned to the magazine, feigning interest in a glossy makeup advertisement. As the shuffling continued, her dry eyes scanned the wide assortment of lipstick colors on the picturesque layout. Quite unconcerned about their variety, Desiree was suddenly rather fascinated at the imaginative talent involved in naming the numerous shades.

The young lad stopped directly in front of her and was stretching his tiny bodice in an effort to see the same magazine page. Blushing now, she forced her eyes to stay fixed on the diamond stud earring of a blonde model wearing *Passion Plum* lipstick.

"Why do women wear all that gunk?"

He was rubbing his hip again. She wanted to help him sit down, but wasn't sure how. "I have heard that *any* makeup can improve one's look," she replied with mock sophistication. Hearing the cheerfulness in his chuckle and seeing the clearness in those large azure eyes, a soft invisible nexus absorbed her. It was beautiful. "You seem to have mastered those crutches," she added finally. "How long have you had them?"

"Exactly two months, one week, and four days." He proudly nodded his head, smiling. "Way too long for me."

"I think I'd keep track of that, too."

"I come here now just for the exercises." He straightened up, slightly turning one crutch for a better grip, and a tiny frown wrinkled his young face. "I don't want these for the summer time, though."

"I don't blame you," she continued softly. "What's your name?"

"Bradley Munsham," he smiled proudly, scratching a thin arm. "But all my friends call me Buck. After Buck Rogers. You know him?"

"Not personally." They laughed together and in that moment of gaiety, Desiree noticed how much this young lad's face reminded her of Jay North, the popular child actor in the television series *Dennis the Menace*. The resemblance was almost uncanny. "Bradley, my name is Desiree Sommers, and this is my daughter Jodi."

"That's a nice name. But you can call me Buck."

She wanted to take him home. "How old are you?"

"I'm seven years old and my mother will be here soon. She's talking to the therapist right now."

His short, frail frame belied his age. Desiree searched the room for someone else, but they were alone in the lobby.

He looked again at the magazine she was reading. "You don't really wear that stuff, do you?"

"Oh, just some of it. Sometimes." Jodi's sudden whimpering interrupted the conversation. Desiree dropped the periodical and held her daughter tightly.

"She's kinda young to be visiting anybody here, isn't she?" Carefully he leaned forward and lightly touched the exposed forehead. "Boy. Is she ever hot! And her face is red. But it's so dry. She's not sweaty at all. I always sweat when I get hot."

Not wanting to leave Bradley alone to stare out the large bare windows again, but seeing Todd at the main doors brushing a clump of snow off his coat sleeves, Desiree stood up to meet him.

The lad shuffled his thin body to face the newcomer. "Once your daughter gets well, I hope I can come over to your place and visit with her. I think we could have some good fun together." Bradley's soft voice was pleading as he followed the new arrivals towards the elevators and he got so excited by their positive reply that he almost tripped over a metal chair someone had left unattended.

As the old elevator chugged up two floors before its heavy doors grated open again, shaky hands checked the body swathed in the blankets. Each breath was rapid and shallow now. There was an obvious increase in the pulse rate too, but when Jodi started to convulse in her mother's arms, hysteria soon filled the nearby nurses' station.

"Can't any of you see that we need your help? I have a very sick child here. Come on now! Someone! Do something! Anything!" With Jodi now supported in her mother's left arm, Desiree picked up an extension phone, raised it high above the nurses' counter and then released it. The receiver fell from its cradle and crashed onto the floor. "*I'm* sure not the nurse around here. And why are you all just gawking at us? Get some help for me if you can't do it yourself!"

Her screams had alerted various nurses from several private rooms and Todd finally decided that he should now interfere. It was a true struggle for him, however, to loosen Desiree's tight hold of her daughter. When he scooted down one hallway, with babe in arms, Desiree rushed after him, still screaming.

"Todd! How dare you take her away from me! Bring her back! Bring my daughter back right this minute!" Uncontrolled anger spurred a noisy dash down one hallway where some janitorial equipment had been carelessly left beside the opened door of a storage area. Desiree's flailing arms hit a metal garbage can and knocked a wide assortment of cleaning implements onto the floor. Rubbing the pain in her wrist, she spotted a wide commercial broom and instantly selected it as her weapon. As she picked it up, a flurry of white uniforms gathered behind her suddenly scurried away.

The babe in arms was nowhere to be seen or heard. Only mother remained, her face turning scarlet and her eyebrows arching high above wide, frightened eyes. "Where's my baby? Where is Mr. Todd Remmings?"

"We'll get him for you, Mrs. Sommers."

When Todd returned, empty-handed, he took her in his arms and held her tightly against his chest. The pair was immediately asked to follow two concerned nurses to a nearby empty room, where more fright created more frenzy.

❦

The house was warm and stuffy. Desiree's heart was cold and heavy. "How are you doing now, Jodi?" She began talking to herself as she circled the large kitchen, pondering earlier moments with a woeful mind. "They all sent me home. The head nurse and one of the hospital doctors said I couldn't stay there with you because I was making too much noise for everyone else. They said that I was knocking things off desks and tables or whatever was near me because I was trying to get to you, to hold you in my arms again. No one liked my little fit of fright and Todd was even asked to help them. And he did. Yes, he even helped them take you away from me. I don't know where they took you, honey, but when Todd came back, he held me so tightly."

She reached for a tissue on the short counter of the kitchen and wiped her eyes before continuing her monologue. "I'm not supposed to come and see you without phoning the main nurses' station first. As a warning for them, I guess. Well, I certainly am going to phone them and if they don't want me there seeing you, the least they can do is let me know how you are doing. Yeah, honey, you are going to have to stay in that hospital for the next little while. They'll be giving you penicillin or antibiotics of some kind to help get you well. But you're too little for any of that. No child should ever be sick enough to have to take pills that strong. They almost gave *me* one. I think it was a tranquilizer, because I heard a nurse telling everyone else around her that I needed something to calm me down. Yes, I know I was panicky. What mother wouldn't be when seeing her child so sick? I didn't mean to upset anyone, Jodi. I just got scared."

Folding her tired body onto a kitchen chair, she stared at the service bill, which had been left for her. One hundred and three dollars. She wanted a cup of fresh coffee but there was no cream or milk in the fridge. And she wondered where her husband was now. Why had Todd been with her all morning instead?

Her restlessness heightened by early afternoon. She had already attempted to perfect more of the right hand melody of her own nocturne, her very first opus. It was a childhood aspiration, her very own fantasia, but the notes and the rhythm still needed drastic improvement. After making a full pot of coffee, she filled a crystal mug and stirred in only sugar. Then she walked downstairs into the bright yellow sewing room where she eventually found the particular patterns and box of remnants she was wanting.

With sewing pins in one hand and her best pinking sheers in the other, she studied the various swatches of material she had carelessly dumped onto the cutting table. Yellows, blues, and crimsons, florals, stripes, and paisleys, flannels, felts, chintz, and linens were all astray now. Another Holly Hobby wall hanging was soon to be in the making, to be hung somewhere in her daughter's bright new bedroom. But as tiny pieces of pink gingham fell onto the table, Desiree started wondering where her husband might be. What was keeping him so busy? He had no excuse for not returning any of her earlier calls. Suddenly, she could feel her blood warming, could hear her noisy short breaths deepen. A stark realization had finally come to her.

"Oh, Jodi. I'm so glad that you have other people taking care of you today. Maybe the doctors and nurses were right, after all. I don't know what I'd be doing for you now if..."

Hearing the lid to the mailbox squeak open, she took her time pouring her now-cold coffee down the kitchen sink before opening the front door. One envelope was a reminder notice from the mortgage company. She was two months in arrears.

After making another call to the hospital a short time later and being assured that Jodi was sleeping soundly, Desiree locked the front door and started marching up the street. Despite the bandaged blisters still tender inside her new leather boots, there was an increasingly obvious purpose in her steady stride. Jodi was in the wonderful state of dreamland while her mother felt as though she were walking directly into a state of anxiety. She slumped onto a cold wooden seat in a bus shelter and enjoyed the short rest.

Painting the horizon with its usual darkening smoky-blue tinge, the short chinook arch beautified the western sky. Soon the sidewalks would be dry and safe, needing a good sweeping. The grass would be plush and green, starving for nourishment. The air would be clear and fresh, smelling of pine cones and lilacs. Soon Jodi would be playing in the front yard, pulling out stubborn dandelions and chasing the sparrows that had once again nested in the neighbor's young mountain ash. Soon mother and daughter would be together at home again, talking, laughing, and loving. Soon she would have some money in her own account again to start paying the bills herself.

Entering the large shopping mall, finally, Desiree hobbled down the wide corridor. All around her teenagers giggled, obviously pleased with themselves for having skipped some afternoon classes. Small tots scampered from one small kiosk to another, squealing in their delight. Mothers, fed up and exhausted, sat on the wooden benches, no doubt dreaming of quiet solitude and some well-deserved leisure. Elderly couples strolled arm in arm, observing everyone with a slight hint of consternation. While strolling around that main walkway, heeding the fits of laughter, the expanse of spotless display windows, and the myriad of mosaic faces, Desiree somehow felt involved, included.

At the bank she handed the lone teller the withdrawal slip she had filled out at home. Two thousand five hundred dollars had been carefully written on it. "Do you have a pair of scissors?" she asked moments later, and when the teller handed her a small pair, she cut her bankbook in half.

"What are you doing? You still have some money in your account."

"But that money isn't mine," she replied, returning the scissors and stuffing the thick wad of bills into the zippered compartment of her shoulder bag.

At the open glass doors of the bank, however, she hesitated. Maybe she should have closed the account completely. The little money remaining wouldn't help her with much. It was Jon's part of their savings, though, and she would let him have it.

Sparkling jewelry displayed on plush blue velvet in a nearby showcase window lured her into the small shop where a row of sapphire rings, Jodi's birthstone, had caught her eye. She wanted to buy her daughter a pinkie ring for Easter, or perhaps save it until her sixteenth birthday as her parents had done for her. She touched the tiny Australian opal on her right hand and kept walking.

In a discount store she reached for an aqua-green shirtdress of slippery soft jersey in her size, her style, and her price range. Excited, she carefully took it off the hanger and looked around for a dressing room.

She found two huge Easter baskets filled with gaily-colored straw and candy, and in the toy department she had fun squeezing some plush animals, and quickly chose a pink stuffed bunny for Jodi. Further down the same aisle she picked up a detailed modeling kit that she was going to give Bradley the next time they met. Further down the store, there was a long counter where Easter lilies and a wide assortment of indoor plants were on sale. How could she resist buying a small one of each? If she took a cab home, her carefully packaged purchases would not get damaged.

After a while she called the hospital from a handy payphone inside the mall. Learning that Jodi was still sleeping soundly, she decided it was time to rest her aching feet again. She laid down her bulging parcels at a booth in a small corner cafeteria. She quickly ordered a cup of coffee and a butter horn before pulling out a pen and some scratch paper from her purse to start listing her regular monthly payments—utilities, day care, groceries, and now the mortgage. She sipped the hot coffee and stared again at the red figures on her most recent invoice—one hundred and three dollars. The fee was forty-five dollars just for the service call.

As her wondering thoughts continued, a young pregnant woman, whose delivery date seemed very soon, paraded in as her two young sons followed eagerly. She slouched into the booth in front of Desiree and was quickly waited on. The woman's faded trench coat hung sloppily over narrow shoulders. She appeared worried and pale and her small brown eyes looked tired. The oldest boy constantly scratched the corner of his eye patch while his sibling complained that the other had taken a bigger bite of the cheese sandwich they were sharing.

"Mom, I'm still hungry. Can I have some chips and a hamburger?"

From Desiree's point of view, she could see the young mother hiding her face behind the large menu she just picked up again and slowly pressing her index finger over her mouth, as if to silence her boys.

After finishing her butter horn, Desiree rustled her smaller paper bags into two larger plastic ones. Reaching for her purse and unsnapping the billfold, she took out the small wad of crisp twenty-dollar bills and grabbed her parcels before slipping out of the booth. Approaching the cash register at the front of the store, she felt a tug at her coat.

"Excuse me, Miss. My mother saw you drop this money when you got out of your booth just now." The lad with the eye patch was craning his neck so he could get a better look at Desiree as he handed her the bills.

Desiree smiled and closed the boy's small hands around the bills before ushering him back to his booth.

"Hi, there," she said quietly, as she wondered what story she could quickly make up so the boys could keep the cash. She turned to face the mother. "It was very nice of your son to return the money I just dropped," she started, standing there in a stupor with her bulging parcels. Act One. Scene One. Where was the rest of the script? Was this to be a mime? She hadn't envisioned that, but correct words weren't coming to her very quickly. Finally, though, her mouth opened and words started coming out. "I greatly appreciate your son's honesty, but I just won a little money in an office pool and was wondering how I could spend it on something special for Easter. Your son reminds me very much of my little nephew down east. And since I won't be able to see him again until sometime this summer, I'd like you to keep these bills. You could buy a little something for yourself and each of the boys. For next Sunday, maybe.

Home again, cheerful and buoyant despite her aching back and blistered feet, Desiree twirled in front of the piano. She had phoned the hospital once more before calling a cab to take her home from shopping, and she was thrilled to learn that her daughter was awake.

"She was asking for you just moments ago," the nurse admitted. "But she didn't stay awake long enough for any kind of answer. And Mrs. Sommers, we don't feel it would do any good for you to see her tonight. She still needs *us* for the next few days. And please try to get some sleep yourself. Having a rested and calm mother to come home to is also very important. You know that's better than perhaps interrupting things here again."

"Yes, of course."

So, as the late afternoon sunlight beamed into the living room, she pinched the leaves of the tiny new coleus she had placed on the mantle. Desiree thought of Krystal, who had sounded quite concerned about Jodi during their short telephone conversation just moments after she had struggled to take off her boots. Jon had asked her to make the call, to let Desiree know he would be seeing his daughter later that same evening.

"He suggested that I come over after work to keep you company," Krystal had said. "I'm really looking forward to seeing the house again, with all the improvements I hear you've made. I'd like to see some of your crafts, too. Would you mind?"

"Umm. Well, I guess that would be all right," she had replied in a slightly bewildered voice. "Is Jon coming here after he sees Jodi?"

"No. He'll be playing squash with his boss afterwards and then he's meeting some executives from Montreal at the clubhouse."

"How will he be able to spend any time with Jodi then?"

"Oh, don't worry about that, Desiree. He'll *make* the time. See you soon."

Krystal arrived within the hour.

"You know, Jon just told me about your musical talent. I think that's fascinating. Are you going to be performing at any more concerts here in town, or will you be on tour again?"

Both coffee mugs were filled to the brim. "I loved working with Carmella and the entire crew," Desiree replied proudly. "They all want me to join them for a tour of the States this summer. But the schedule is so tight. I'm a little hesitant to get involved this time." *And I'm pregnant,* her mind continued.

"When do you have to decide?"

"I promised them an answer by this weekend. I just hope I make the right decision for me and for Jodi. For everyone."

"Well, what's left of these renovations shouldn't take long."

"No, thank goodness. And I must admit that I'm pretty pleased with all the changes. Once the new carpets come, I know I'll be able to enjoy this place."

Krystal stood up, walked into the living room and studied the decor, touching the rich marble of the fireplace, the cotton twill of the loveseat, and the soft leather of both wing chairs.

"Just a few large plants in that corner where the tapestry's still rolled up would finish this room off perfectly." She touched the new softness of the afghan, and continued. "Jon gave me a rubber tree plant for my birthday last month. It's slowly dying, but my Creeping

Charlie and variegated spider plants are thriving. You can have some slips if you want. I'm having my passport pictures taken after work tomorrow, but maybe this weekend I can bring them over." She suddenly noticed the time on the cuckoo clock and hurried to put on her leather coat. "I had no idea it was this late already. We were too busy talking, I guess, and I didn't hear the chime. I have to go now. Thanks again for the visit, and I'll try to bring those slips over this Saturday." And with a quick turn, she was out the door.

Desiree waved through the frosty living room windows and when the telephone rang, she walked into the kitchen.

"Hello."

"Hello, Desiree." Jon's deep voice was calm and deliberate. "Is Krystal still there?"

"Uh, no, Jon. She left just moments ago. Why?"

"I *have* to talk to her. Would you mind going outside to see if she's still out there?"

"Well, yeah. I would mind. Why are you more concerned about talking with Krystal than being told how your own daughter is?"

"I'll be seeing Jodi later. Come on now, go and stop Krystal before it's too late."

"Before what's too late?"

"Oh, Des. Never mind." Jon then hung up his phone.

Chapter Thirteen

Wednesday, March 13

In Dawna's freshly painted office Desiree shifted her body in the new plastic chair, so hard, so unyielding. Her fingers tapped the corner of the new plastic desk, so big, so bare, so ugly, as continued thoughts of her last nightmare set her mind whirling with confusion—those horrid thoughts that Jon had kidnapped Jodi, that he had come into the house and taken his only child away with him.

She couldn't recall how she got to work that morning, having awakened again and again, tossing and turning in bed, searching all the bedrooms, the hallway closets, and every inch of the house, until nausea forced her in front of the commode in the main bathroom. She had to find Jodi. And didn't she phone Dr. Styles' office, insisting on an appointment that very day to have another thorough exam, to get some pills for her morning sickness? Didn't she take a cab to his office? Yes, she could remember doing that, but the doctor did not give her a prescription. Dr. Styles simply said he first was going to rush the results of that morning's tests. She could recall a strange, almost concerned look in his eyes as he wrote several notes in her file.

And now, after whisking off some dirty film from the large office window, she peered outside. Soon the young beauties in the new high-rise apartment across the alley would be donning their bikinis, she mused. Soon the young men in the offices nearby would be ogling the almost-naked scenery around the pool. Soon she herself would ...

Even today Dawna's once-comfortable office was lacking warmth, despite its newness. Today, the soft blue pile rug was sickly red-orange broadloom, of commercial quality. Today, the walnut desk and high-backed upholstered chair had been replaced with low, white modular pieces. Today, all the desktop plants were gone; only the philodendron remained.

"What's the frown all about?" Todd asked as he put two mugs of fresh coffee onto the new desk.

Her eyes flitted across the room. "Oh, Todd, look at this place."

He downed his coffee before lighting up a Colt. "Apparently this is just the beginning," he offered. "With Mr. Morten moving this weekend to open another office in some small town in Ontario, and Mr. Bracken taking his place here, things won't be the same any more. Syd hasn't even found a house yet."

"And his three children are still in school, aren't they?" she asked softly. Through the windowed front wall of Dawna's office she noticed the construction foreman saunter by with his robotic work crew following closely behind.

"We've got a lot to talk about, you know. See you later." Todd tiptoed out, winking.

Squatting on the ugly new carpet, Desiree touched a broken stem of the philodendron and thought of Dawna again. Returning to the desk, she picked up a few loose pages of a thick file and thought of Todd, then of Mr. Morten. Eyeing Gordon's portrait, she thought of Jon, of her parents, of Jodi. Proudly, she walked out to her own new desk in the main area, rummaged through a shopping bag she had placed in the bottom drawer, and took out a framed picture. Then, back in Dawna's office, she placed the photograph of Jodi beside the other frames.

Calling the hospital again, she was relieved to hear that Jodi was sitting up now. Her breaths were slow and heavy. There weren't any more raspy pants. Her fever was down and she was eating … There was a sudden rumble just outside the office door, and Desiree couldn't hear what the nurse was saying anymore. "Pardon?"

"Jodi's been asking for you."

She placed the receiver onto its cradle. *Jodi's been asking for you.* She felt like she was going to be sick again and she darted out of the room. Dodging the painters and hopping over their scattered materials, she ran down the side aisle towards the washrooms where her dizziness and nausea continued. It seemed an eternity had passed before she was able to return to her office, and just as she got comfortable behind Dawna's desk, Dr. Styles' phone call was put through.

"Mrs. Sommers, I have just received the results of your various tests, and I would like to see you as soon as possible to discuss them with you. How soon might you be able to get here?"

"I can leave right now, sir."

"Good. I'll be waiting."

The frazzled young secretary organized her work for the next day, scribbled a short note to Todd, called for a cab, and then left the office.

She no longer cared that Mr. Morten had left the city as suddenly as he did; he had his young family, and they could all adjust to the change. She no longer cared that Todd's dictation was piling up; Gwen had been assigned to finish it and she could do it today, tomorrow, next week, or whenever Todd decided to push her enough. She no longer cared if Dawna would be shocked at her gaudy new office; she would get used to it in time. None of that mattered now. She had her own concerns, hidden behind her frozen smile, as she was immediately ushered into Dr. Styles' private office. She settled into an upholstered chair while he skimmed through her file. She was studying him now, unlike her last visit when she had been in a daze. His hair, no longer streaky gray, was pure white now, though just as thick. And his leathery face was ashen. She thought it odd how her mind had ignored something so obvious just that very morning.

"Mrs. Sommers," Dr. Styles began slowly. "My calculations make you twelve weeks pregnant. Your blood pressure is considerably higher than normal, so I'd like you to take it fairly easy for the next month or so. This pregnancy may not be as easy as your first."

"Can you help me with my nausea? It's …"

"Of course. That is the least of my concerns right now."

"Pardon?"

He shifted his body in the high leather chair. "I …"

"Dr. Styles. Am I going to lose this baby?"

"It's more compli—"

"You can give me a prescription that will help me go to full term, can't you?" she interrupted, leaning forward in her chair, looking more eager now. "Like my mother needed in order to keep me?"

"You know that's definitely possible." He scanned the lab sheets again, before continuing. "But first, I want to line up some special tests for you."

"Special tests? What kind of special tests? What are you trying to tell me, sir?"

"I just want to make sure all the extra steps are taken during this pregnancy."

"Extra steps? What do you mean by that? I didn't go through any extra steps when I was carrying Jodi."

"No, you didn't, but you must admit that this pregnancy hasn't started out the same. This child may be different." He turned his chair and drew some brochures from his credenza. "Usually an amniocentesis isn't given this early, unless …"

"A what?" she interrupted again. She hadn't heard that word before and couldn't even guess what it might mean. "You are thoroughly confusing me today, sir."

"And I sincerely apologize for that, Desiree." He shuffled the loose pages into a neat pile on his desk. "It's a special procedure rather new to the medical field. It is given only when there's any question about normality *in utero*, the pregnancy. When there's a history of congenital abnormality. And you know this is the case from *both* sides of your family."

"When there's any question about normality *in utero*. When there's a history of congenital abnormality? What are you trying to tell me, Dr. Styles? And why are you even concerned about *both* sides of my family?" She sat up straight and waited for his reply.

Dr. Styles thumbed through the folder, quickly rereading some notes in his file. "It says here that you have a brother-in-law who…"

She gasped. Concerned only about her mother's weakness, about the possibility of not being able to go full term, she had completely forgotten about James Robert.

Doctor Styles raised his eyebrows as he continued. "There could be some major drawbacks with this procedure. I have some brochures here that I want you to read." He put the stack of pamphlets at the edge of his desk for her to take home. "Yes. This pregnancy hasn't started out the same. This child may be different. I would like to schedule an amniocentesis for you but I need your consent. Please read these thoroughly and discuss them with all your loved ones before advising me of that choice."

A wave of anguish flooded her mind when she caught a glimpse of a Mongoloid baby on the front cover of one brochure.

"Ohh, no." She slumped in her chair.

Dr. Styles saw the instant fright in her eyes and quickly put her file on the credenza. A deep frown etched his face as he walked around his desk and stood beside her. "I know you must have a hundred questions to ask, but right now it's too soon for me to have all the answers. I just want you to be aware of the possible turn of events *this* pregnancy might bring you. The amniocentesis will suggest what direction to take. But I must stress that there's a lot of risk involved, and I…"

"But what am I suppose to do *right now*? How can I help the baby? Is it too late for that?"

"I'm not sure yet. Would you like me to bring in your husband?" Dr. Styles started to walk towards the door of his office.

"Jon isn't here with me today. He's still at work." Her voice was just a whisper, her mind a steady whir. "He's going to make me lose it. With just the possibility of anything being different with our child, I know Jon's going to make me lose it."

"Pardon me? I can't make out what you are trying to say, Mrs. Sommers."

"Jon's not going to accept any of this, sir. How can I even begin to tell him? How can I tell *anybody?*"

"Have you got someone to take you home? You should have family or friends with you right now."

"No. I came by cab, straight from the office."

"Could I phone your parents, maybe?"

"No, no. They're in Norway."

"I'm quite concerned about you, Desiree. I remember your husband's reaction with your first pregnancy. Nothing's been confirmed yet, you must realize, but…"

She quickly looked at her wristwatch. "Jon still might be at the office. Would you talk to him now, to explain everything to him?"

"Certainly, Desiree, I can do that."

After her third attempt to get an answer at her husband's office, she decided to phone Krystal who would surely know where Jon was. Desiree thumbed through the phone book just handed her and dialed the number.

"Hello."

She gasped and slammed the phone into its receiver. Jon had answered the phone. He was at Krystal's.

With calm, clear eyes, Dr. Styles waited.

She felt invaded upon when he pulled a chair over and sat down beside her. Her knuckles were white from her firm grip of the armchair, and when she felt the doctor's hand on her shoulder, she refused to look at him. Her eyes stayed on the wall behind the credenza where numerous portraits of his six children caught her attention, and her mood suddenly changed.

Jodi's been asking for you.

She grabbed her purse, twisted her body, and stood up tall. "My husband is having an affair, Dr. Styles. With his private secretary, apparently."

"Oh, no. Please sit down, Desiree." He pulled a chair closer for her. "We have to talk about all that's happening to you right now, or could be happening."

"I can't talk about anything right now. I just want to see my daughter."

"But you must ..."

"I must what, Dr. Styles? Tell me. What is it? What *must* I do?"

Flushed with anger, anxiety, bewilderment, and hatred, she ignored his obvious surprise and stepped outside. A distressing heat had already coursed her face, her entire body, but somehow in the waiting room, despite a few pairs of unfamiliar eyes watching her, she was able to lift her jacket purposefully from the wall rack and casually feel its leathery softness. She was able to push each brass button through its respective hole and straighten the collar, all before stepping out into the hallway. She was going to see her daughter. "Jodi. Mommy's coming."

With long, steady strides she pushed her way through a crowd of people waiting at the nearby elevators. As fright and disbelief clouded her eyes, she turned her entire body. The doors to the maintenance area were just up ahead, and with a sudden surge she marched forward. Her eyes were watering now. She wanted to be out of the building, away from everybody. Groping for the door handle, she pulled it open and dashed inside. She didn't see the edge of the top step, and she tumbled down. She saw only sparks of color—narrow streaks of the rainbow— bright reds and oranges swirling into indigos and violets, then into grays, browns, and finally to black, solid black—smooth and soothing ebony.

Much later, tasting blood in her mouth, she slowly became aware of the damp cold concrete around her, to the crick in her neck, and to the shooting pains in her abdomen. She spit at the concrete stairs beside her, wiped her mouth in disgust, and whisked her long, tangled hair behind her shoulders. She stood up and teetered towards the slit of light around a double door nearby and pulled to open it, finally plunging out into the gray dusk of the evening. She was in a back parking lot, somewhere dark and eerie. Her jacket flapped open in the gusty cold wind and she stepped out onto a side street. Brakes squealed suddenly and a car horn honked, and she found herself dodging, limping.

A bus shelter was just up ahead and in a few moments she would be able to sit down and rub her aching body. Only a few more steps and she could catch her breath. She tripped on the curb. The palms of her hands were bleeding, her knees were pulsating, and she couldn't get up. She unzipped her boots and threw them onto the sidewalk ahead of her. She crawled to the bus stop and dropped onto the bench.

She sat there, her eyes blank, her mind frozen. Then, with both hands on her abdomen, she stroked the softness tenderly, and a smile slowly erased the creases of her face. She was pregnant again, pregnant with another beautiful baby. She was sure of that. She didn't care what Dr. Styles had hinted. And as the starry sky steadily spread its inky wealth around her, she stood up. With a new sparkle in her eyes she straightened herself up and went to get her boots. She was going to see her daughter. "Jodi, Mommy's coming. I'll be there soon."

Turn! Turn! Turn!

The steaming soapy water in the main bathroom tub slowly quashed the tightness in her legs as she soaked, motionless and unmindful, in the deep suds. She blew gently at the handful of bubbles and watched the clusters of rainbows soaring around her head, each popping quietly as it hit her face. She picked up more bubbles and blew at them until she was in a tiny cloud of pastels.

She was exactly where she wanted to be that night. Her own choice was to remain secluded and undisturbed, to let time float by, to give her a chance to blot out all the dark shadows of her mind. The bubbles slowly disappeared as the water turned cold. She smiled as she remembered Dr. Styles' earlier comments. *I'd like you to take it fairly easy for the next few months or so. This pregnancy may not be as easy as your first.*

"That's what I'm doing right now, Dr. Styles," she said out loud. "I'm so tired and I know I need a good night's sleep, but I still have so much to do here. So many things are still unfinished around the house. But this bath sure feels good."

After draining some of the cold water, she turned on both taps and sank back into the tub. "Maybe if I just do some of the work each day. Or maybe Jon would come back and hire help. Or perhaps Todd will offer to help finish a lot of it for me. Yes, I'm sure he will. Oh, I'm tired. So, so tired." Her words were almost a whisper as she closed her eyes, sighing, drifting off into a dreamlike state where she could see a brand new box of dry mustard in the soap dish by the taps. The large package opened easily, and she emptied the powder into the nice hot water. Swirling it around with her hands, she watched the water quickly change color, and she laughed maliciously at the purpose she had for it that evening. Then suddenly boiling water spewed from the faucet and ugly yellow ocher eddies bit at her nakedness, piercing sharp needles into her skin. She rubbed her abdomen. The heat was stifling and the steam caught her breath. "Let me out! Let me out!!" she screamed, pulling at her long strands of hair. She gasped for cool fresh air and reached for the sliding door. But it wouldn't open. Pushing and pulling, she was still in the pool of blistering lava that burned and suffocated her.

An eternity went by. She was in another world now—foreign, distant.

Drained by the total absurdity of her twisted imagination, her offensive subconscious mind, Desiree pulled a huge towel around her wet body. Despite now being able to easily open the shower door, and seeing no ugly orange residue, she found no solace. She thought she heard the phone ringing. Or was it a car horn blowing in the distance? Her husband had left her and she was pregnant again. Pregnant with a child who could be so different. She stared at the flaxen clump of tangles in her hands as thoughts of that yellow ocher repugnance in the bathtub converged again in her mind. Years ago, she could not remember exactly when she had heard, or perhaps had read, that hot mustard baths could quickly bring on a miscarriage.

Something about raising the blood pressure, she recalled. But why had that strange thought entered her mind tonight? And why was it still arresting her?

She couldn't let herself be idle any longer, to risk triggering another frenzy. She would have to keep busy, doing anything. She let the thick bath towel fall to her feet as she sat on the cold lid of the commode and started tapping the marble counter of the vanity. Slowly becoming animated, she was like a robot pacing the floor— over to the linen closet, between the vanity and the commode, and beside the tub, re-walking that same simple pattern. She wiped the long vanity counter before crowding it with large sponges, clean rags, cans of cleansers, jars of disinfectants, and a metal tray of various aromatic sprays. Later, she scrubbed the tub, the sink, the toilet, and then each wall, until the room was spotless. But she wasn't satisfied. The clean room still looked so drab. It needed painting.

Her dizzy, aching body was petitioning her to take a rest and she finally decided to take one. After getting the new can of paint, the stir stick, the tray, the rollers, and the paintbrushes from the back landing, she lined them all under the towel rack before walking down to the living room, where, as though finding a long lost friend, Desiree sat at the piano, that dark walnut upright still positioned slightly askew, dividing the living room and the dining room. She started playing one of Carmella's favorite songs, Ferrante & Teicher's "Midnight Cowboy", the opening piece for the entire Canadian tour.

She had purchased a thick book of sheet music by various popular artists during a rushed lunch hour, finally deciding to add even more variety to her repertoire. She had mastered so many genres of contemporary music—folk songs, pop, and country— but tonight she felt the strongest urge to be adventuresome, just to keep her own sanity. As her dry, rough hands touched the cool keyboard, "Desiree's Dream", the soft ballad that she and her father had created when celebrating her first pregnancy so many years ago, came so gently from the long, tight strings of the piano. She could sense her father's proud presence there. It was totally therapeutic.

With increasing interest, she read the forward of her new book, along with the individual histories of each contributing musician, and was quite taken by the write-up on Thelonious Monk, the apparent founder of bebop. Several of the following pages were filled with a fabulous combination of rhythm and blues and jazz. Realizing that bebop was simply a harmonic and rhythmic complexity of jazz, her initial efforts tonight would only be a small challenge for her. But that might be all she needed. She straightened her back, eyed one particular page, and began playing. There was a hint of disappointment, however, in her sudden burst of laughter. Sight-reading, note for note, had always come easy to her. The chosen tune was definitely correct, but the harmony, the rhythm, the entire sound seemed a little off. Shouldn't it be just a little more soulful?

She persisted, and after a few attempts the melody was finally right. She was perfecting her style with each note, each chord, each slur, and then the cadence. She now loved the beat, the pulse, and was improving the entire sound with a quick, masterful effect. It was the only break she needed. Relaxing into the music, she decided that, during lunch some day that week, she was going to go to the main library and get as much information she could about amniocentesis, because she had left the brochures on Dr. Styles' desk.

Suddenly energized, and wanting to get the painting completed before her daughter was allowed to come home, Desiree again opened the shower door of the main bathroom and smiled. The white porcelain tub was spotless.

She soon discovered that the cramped quarters in the tub made the work more difficult than she had expected. She carefully placed Jodi's old high chair where she could use it as a ladder. She didn't want to fall. She didn't want to miscarry.

She pressed the wet roller against the bare wall and forced it up and down, stretching and bending. Up, down. Left, right. Exact, rhythmic, constant. *So, you've left me, Jon. You said you were staying with some friends. Yeah, some friends. You couldn't admit that it was your own secretary. Coward!*

Was the front doorbell ringing again? Wondering who had the patience, or perhaps the stubbornness, to stay at the front door for so long, she hobbled downstairs. Dressed only in her old cotton smock, now splotched with a pale harvest gold semi-gloss paint, she opened the door to see a look of surprise washing over Todd's face.

"So what are you painting now?"

"Oh, Todd. I'm so close to being finished with *everything*. The main bathroom is almost done. I just have to fix the baseboards in there so I can clean up. I want to have everything done before Jodi comes home."

"Did you see her today?"

"Yes, I did."

"How is she?" He hung his wool jacket in the front closet.

"Oh, Todd, she's so ghastly weak."

"And I suppose you want to bring her home tomorrow?"

"Of course I want her home, but I know I'll have to wait a few more days."

"Yes, at least that, I'm sure. And by then you'll probably be dead in your boots if you don't let me help you a little more with this renovating. You've done so much by yourself, but I can finish the bathroom for you in no time. I really don't mind helping, you know." He gently took her arm and led her upstairs to the master bedroom where he carefully laid her on the waterbed. "There. You can have a little nap now. Just a short rest for your tired body."

She nestled under the afghan he had pulled over her. "Be here when I wake up, Jon. Please be here."

Todd's face tightened as he heard Jon's name being whispered so sweetly. "I will, Desiree. I'll be here when you wake up," he replied softly. He kissed her on the forehead before leaving the room.

She smiled as she heard the bedroom door close. Jon always kept their bedroom door shut. As her body sank into total comfort, her mind slowly drifted into another dream, a bright, colorful mirage where she saw Jon standing at the foot of the bed again, his arms reaching out for her.

"Get up, sweetheart," he whispered. "Get out of those dirty, baggy clothes and come with me. It's time to start your exercises."

"But I'm still so tired. So, so tired."

"No, no. You've had enough sleep. It's time to start your exercises."

In her dream she loved the soothing depth of her husband's voice, the warm press of his hands on hers. "Yes, Jon. I'm coming." Then, she couldn't see him anywhere but she knew he was nearby. The faint smell of his woodsy aftershave aroused her, and she started running on the spot to warm up. In front of the mirror-tiled wall, she studied her naked body, the tightness of her abdomen, and the pliable muscles in her long, lean legs.

"Let me see your entire routine, Desiree. Let me see how you keep your body so lithe and beautiful. Let me see."

"Yes, Jon, I'll show you." She touched her toes and reached for the ceiling, bending and stretching. She did twenty knee bends, pulling and straining. She stood up and started jumping rope but soon nausea stirred within her. But she couldn't stop now; she couldn't let him down. No. No. She had to keep going. Up, down, faster and faster. She stretched her arms high, then higher. She touched her toes again, bending and stretching. "I can't see you anywhere, Jon. Where are you?"

"I'm here, Desiree, right over here. Keep bending. Keep stretching. Keep jumping, and then afterwards let's walk out to the garage. There's something on the work bench I want you to bring inside tonight."

Dizziness enveloped her as she swayed down the hallway beyond the bathroom door. She dropped heavily onto the top stair and waited to catch her breath.

"Don't stop now, Desiree. Go out to the garage. I'm right behind you. It won't take long."

The cold March wind swirled around her and her lungs suddenly felt raw. It seemed as though the thinly frosted sidewalk was peeling off a layer of skin with each hurried step, and the musty bare expanse of the garage offered no comfort to her nakedness. Still unable to see Jon anywhere, she could sense his warmth on her shoulders, and her body mechanically followed his persistent instructions.

"See that box of spikes over there? Take out a couple of the long ones. Yes, the four-inch spikes. Now, grab that old hammer in the corner. Bring them inside the house, Desiree. We want to do it right. Do it for the baby. He wants to be free."

Her heart pounded and her chest ached as sweat dripped from her forehead, and she shivered in the dankness. Jon was pushing her now, pushing her back into the house. He had grabbed the new plunger from the hall closet before guiding her into the main bathroom.

"Here's the hammer, Desiree. Now nail those spikes into the end of this plunger." He had ripped off the plastic wrapping before handing it to her. "Pound them in real good, Desiree. Make sure they'll stay. It'll be so easy. Slide out the bath mat. I want you to feel comfortable. It won't take long, Desiree. Now lie down and spread those beautiful long legs or yours. Let me see you do it."

As her head swelled with fear and surprise, Jon knelt in front of her. Oh, how well he could massage her aching body.

"Give me the plunger, Desiree. It's right beside you. Yes, yes." He was slowly spreading her legs. "Bend your knees a little. A little more. We've got to do this right. Yes, that's good. Now, I'm just going to slide this up inside you. Nice and slow. That's it. We're doing it for the baby. Now let me jerk this in further. Jab. Jab. Jab. I'm helping you, Desiree. It has to be, you know. It's for the baby."

He ignored her screams and squirms.

"Deeper. Deeper. We have to make it penetrate. Let me see you bleed, Desiree. I've got a warm, wet towel ready for you. Ready to clean you up. Ready to soothe you. This will be so easy. Deeper. Deeper. Yes, yes. It's happening. It's happening. Oh, yes, it is good." With a sudden swing of his arms, he swooped her up and carried her back into the bedroom. Then, with no further words spoken, he was gone.

"Oh, Jon. Why? Why? Where are you, Jon? Where did you go so quickly?" She could smell the lingering woodsy scent of her husband. She could also sense an odd instant coolness and eerie emptiness of the room. "Jon?"

Suddenly he was in front of her again, looking so virile as he gently pulled her up, eyeing her so lovingly. His large hands caressed the softness of her face. His moist lips were eager, and she was melting inside again.

"Desiree." His bass voice was almost a whisper against her skin. "Phone Dawna. Phone your good friend right now and ask her to have Gordon bring you those pills, those special tablets. You know the ones. We have to be sure. We both have to be sure. Do it for the baby, Desiree. He wants to be free. Do it for all of us."

"Yes, Jon. I will. Of course I will," she said faintly, and took the telephone he had brought her.

"Desiree! Wake up! Wake up!"

"I can't do it, Jon. No matter what you give me or what you want me to do, I can't kill our baby."

"Desiree. Wake up. It's me, Todd."

"Todd? Todd? What are you doing here?" Her eyes welled as tiny hands pounded against his chest. "Are you helping Jon with this?"

"Helping Jon with what?"

"Where's Jon? Where is he? He was just here a minute ago. I have to talk to him. Right now! Jon! Where are you?"

"He's out somewhere but *I'm* with you now. *I'm* right here, Desiree. Everything is okay. You just had a dream. A very bad dream, obviously."

She sat up and nestled her head in Todd's arms. "Yes, Todd. I did have a *terrible* dream, another horrid nightmare that has me doing absolutely horrible things to my very own child. And to myself. When will they stop?"

"I don't know, Des." How could he begin to answer such a question? "Keep telling yourself that all those ugly thoughts are just flashes in your mind. You aren't a killer. You know damn well you aren't. You're not going to murder your baby. Jodi's in the hospital, remember? And she'll be home soon."

"Jodi. Yes. She'll be coming home soon. Yes, yes, yes."

He nestled her shaking body against his chest and held her tightly, smelling the herbal faintness of her long hair draped down her back. "Why don't you concentrate on me tonight?" he asked. "Good friends spending a nice, quiet evening together. I like the sound of that. How 'bout you?" He ran a bent finger down the bridge of her nose, not expecting an answer. "Let me show you everything I've done here tonight." He wanted to soothe her, to erase those ugly flashes from her mind. He was trying to understand the tremulous curve of her mouth as she looked up at him.

The bathroom was so tidy now. Clean. Fresh. The wide strip of masking tape around the ceiling and tub had been peeled off. The plastic sheets, once strewn over the toilet and vanity, were neatly folded on the countertop, and the loose baseboards had been nailed firmly into the wall. The mat was in place—spotless.

"Do you like it?"

"It's perfect, Todd," she said weakly. "Thank you very much."

They went downstairs to the family room where he had started a fire earlier. It was now bright and crackling. Two champagne flutes filled with white wine were on the coffee table. Todd lit up a Colt, watching her from the corner of his eye as she shifted her weight on the chesterfield for more comfort.

"You want to know something, Todd? I'm …" She stopped herself just in time, surprised at her own sudden desire to talk about her present condition. Hadn't she already said too much?

"You're what?"

She tried peeling some gold semi-gloss paint off her smock. How could she change the subject?

"I know what you are," he began. "You're confused and tired, and just too damn stubborn to do anything about it." He crushed his Colt and touched her bare arm.

Hot shivers shot up her spine, and for a brief moment she fantasized caressing his hard hairy chest, kissing his soft burning lips, feeling his total weight suddenly on her, and feeling him probe deep, deep inside her.

"Jon doesn't like you back at work again, does he?"

"Hmmm?" Wanting to continue with her fantasy, she sipped the tasty wine and looked straight into his pale eyes. There was a glimmer in her own as she realized that those recent sweet thoughts of Todd had erased the pain of some other horrid memories. She knew his eyes, those beautiful smoky-blue eyes, were still on her, awaiting an answer. He was letting her know that he would listen to anything she wanted to say. But what could she tell him tonight? What should she say to him now?

"Got some good news for you, Des," he started, finally.

Ignoring common knowledge about pregnancies and alcohol consumption, she finished her drink and poured herself another before Todd had the chance to stop her, before he could smudge the fading colors of her concentration. Yes, she decided, it would be so easy, so good with Todd.

"You've got Dawna's job when she leaves, you know. Syd's been very impressed with your work."

She looked over at him, silenced.

"Your face is still streaked with paint, you know." He smiled, tucking a fallen strand of hair back into place, rubbing her forehead with his warm hand. "There. Much better now." His eyes searched hers and she squeezed his arm gently. The dimple on his left cheek deepened when he smiled again.

"Why the frown, Desiree?"

"Let's fly to the moon, Todd. You and I could soar together up in the sky—so free and happy."

"What?" From the flickering lights of the fireplace he could see that strange look on her face again, could see her biting her lips as though searching for the right words to explain something to him. Tonight she needed a shoulder to lean on, and he thought he finally knew why. He wished he knew how to help, because lately he had had his own concerns. Sara's lawyer had phoned just before he left the office that afternoon. She was filing for a divorce and of course there was great concern over their twins. Yes, tonight both he and Desiree needed comforting.

"Would you mind rubbing my back for me, Todd? It's so sore." She felt a strong tugging at her heart as he guided her onto the floor cushion in front of the fireplace. The spicy smell of him was soothing her again; the gentle squeeze of his hand on hers was rushing a myriad of tingles to every pulsating cell in her body.

Drawn by the nearness of her, the softness of her skin, the scent of lavender in her hair, and the worried look in her huge snowy blue eyes, Todd knew he had responded too quickly to her request. He had been too obvious in his actions; he had to stop massaging her long soft back, because her warm body wanted more and he was longing to gratify.

"I've got a surprise for you outside. Go put on some warm clothes and I'll show you."

Out in the brisk evening air moments later Todd handed her a set of keys and guided her to an unfamiliar car parked in front of the house. "Well, how do you like it?"

"You *really* got this for me?"

He nodded.

She slowly brushed her hands over its hood and reached out for him, hugging him tightly. "Thank you so much. It's beautiful! But how did you know I was thinking about getting a car?"

"Something you said earlier this week," he offered, shrugging his shoulders in jest as he opened the driver's side door for her. "The pink card and application are in the glove compartment. All you have to do is complete and sign all the papers. And get your own plates. But you've done all that before, haven't you?" Proudly, he walked around the car and got inside.

"Drive on, my dear lady," Desiree thought she had heard him say as she turned on the ignition. "I think this car will suffice for my wings tonight," she said, laughing, putting the car in gear before checking over her shoulder.

"Some of the office kids are going to Sunshine this Saturday and I thought you might like to come with us. With me."

"Oh no, I can't, Todd. Jodi is going to be home by then. I want to keep her close for a long while.

"Of course you do. I forgot how soon she might be coming home."

"Besides, I don't really think I want to go skiing ever again. I hated skiing. I hated every minute on the slopes with Jon. Even when he was so patient with me up on the slopes, I just didn't get it." She slammed on the brakes, barely missing the stopped car in front of them. The long silence that followed was overwhelming. She had turned a corner too sharply, her hands gripping the steering wheel too tightly, her eyes staring straight ahead but only focusing on the darkness around them. Her perfect evening with Todd had been spoiled with just a moment's thought about her husband.

"Jon's left you, hasn't he?"

Oh, how she hated that name now. With gritted teeth, she straightened her back. She eyed Todd, the speedometer, the road ahead, and then the blackened sky. The bright full moon was in front of them. Her foot pressed steadily on the gas pedal. Yes, tonight she could reach the moon so easily.

Chapter Fourteen

Thursday, March 14

Squinting at the bright midday sun, Desiree put on her sunglasses, skipped over the short moist grass of the front lawn, and embraced the fresh spring air. She smiled, thinking about the previous evening. The long, comfortable drive to the mountains and Todd's quiet interest in her recent affairs had suppressed the confusion in her heart. It had been easy to finally express her innermost thoughts. She had had the best sleep she could remember. Today her mind was clear and refreshed. To her very core, she felt cleansed.

She had done so much that morning because Todd had given her the day off work. Now there would be no one around who might notice the scratches or bruises from her fall the previous night. At the office, no one would recognize her today because her shiny hair was up in a loose topknot, her makeup was flawless, her dress pants weren't ripped at the knees, and her face was glowing. A hospital nurse had advised that Jodi was improving remarkably well and suggested that Desiree visit her daughter that afternoon. It was almost an invitation.

The entire house was spotless now. The refrigerator was full, and the Cougar, royal blue with white vinyl roof and white leather interior, was now registered and insured. For the rest of the morning she drove around the quiet neighborhood, still quite unfamiliar to her, where she noticed many housewives opening doors and windows as though welcoming the long-awaited season. The warm glow of her excitement smoldered and the ruddy color of her cheeks deepened when she saw small children running, skipping, and jumping. Crocuses were sprouting. She had her own car now. Independence!

Later, at the hospital, Bradley was anxiously hiding behind the entrance wall to Jodi's room. One crutch banged against her bed when he turned to face Desiree and give her a hug. "I knew you would come today. I just knew it." Jodi had not awakened in the clamor and his loud whisper hummed with excitement. The forgiving twinkle in his azure eyes erased her recent absence.

But she had looked for him yesterday, had also asked where he might be and was told that he had already gone home.

There was a beautiful rosy color in Jodi's cheeks, and Desiree reached down, kissed her forehead, and stroked her silvery-blonde hair.

"She can go home tomorrow, you know," Bradley announced.

"Pardon?"

"I checked with Nurse Jacobson this morning. She can go home tomorrow. Could I come with you, too?"

Desiree could still see the gleam in his clear blue eyes, and his longing look softened her face. "We must check with your parents first, you know."

"Well, Mom's downstairs in the cafeteria. She said she would wait for us there. Is that okay?"

"That would be all right. Jodi needs all of her sleep and I'm in no hurry to leave here."

"She sure looks better today, huh?"

"You bet she does."

"And I promised her she could watch me do my exercises this afternoon. I told her all about them and she thinks they're funny."

Desiree smiled and carefully tucked the thin white blanket around Jodi's narrow shoulders before escorting Bradley downstairs to the cafeteria. A petite auburn-haired woman at a table across the room waved when she saw them approaching.

The women quickly introduced themselves as Bradley purposely chose the chair beside Desiree. "She's pretty, just like I told you, Mom. Huh?" His eyes were bright and inquisitive. "And maybe I can go see them at their place someday. How 'bout tomorrow?"

Both women laughed and soon Bradley joined in. "Well, can I go see them this weekend? That would be so much better than taking me over to Aunt Betty's, wouldn't it, Mom?"

"Bradley, please go and wash your hands before your chips come."

"Okay. Then you can talk about me going to visit Jodi. I won't be long."

After Bradley struggled with his crutches and left the room, Dianne Munsham set down her cup of iced tea and lit up a thin brown cigarette while Desiree sipped her coffee.

"I'd love to have him over this weekend, Dianne. It would help Jodi so much. But if you've already made other plans, maybe we should arrange it for another time."

"No, we can change our plans. It won't be any problem." Suddenly Dianne's deep brown eyes narrowed. "Bradley's pelvis was broken in three places in a car accident a few months ago," she admitted quietly. "I still can't bear to picture him staring out of these windows after his therapy, waiting for me to drive up in the van. He used to be so active in sports. Baseball's his favorite, and he was looking forward to being put on the community team this year. Since he was five years old, he insisted at every opportunity that I take him to the neighborhood park just so he could watch other teams play. He's our only child. And then, when the diamonds were empty, he would make his father the pitcher and me the catcher just so he could practice batting and running. He'd even run home from school to improve his speed." She fidgeted with a crisp French fry from the platter of chips the waitress had just brought them.

"Sounds like he's a very determined young lad."

"The doctors thought he would never walk properly again, and only last week Dr. Benson told him he didn't think he'd need the crutches much longer." Her soft voice now purred with pride. "He is still so self-conscious about his limp, but yes, he *is* a very determined boy."

"I've noticed him often rubbing his left hip, almost trying to massage it."

Dianne took a long drag from her cigarette and exhaled slowly. "Just yesterday, because of that, Dr. Benson told us that he is now more concerned about other possible health matters.

"Ohh?"

"He's lost so much weight just this past month. He has headaches now, which he just never had before the accident. And he tires so easily, so quickly."

"He's still healing, no doubt."

"The doctors here want to put Bradley through some special tests. Next week they are hoping to get them started."

The faint shuffling of crutches interrupted the conversation and as Bradley approached their table, Desiree pulled out his chair.

"Well, have you had time to decide?"

"If Jodi's coming home tomorrow, you may certainly join us. You can stay until Sunday, if you like."

"Oh, Mom, could I?" There was an instant glimmer in his wide blue eyes.

"I don't want to cause any problems for you or your family, Dianne."

"I know, but Robert and I had promised to take him and his cousin to see a matinee tomorrow ... Brad, how 'bout if we all go to the early show and we can drop you off at Jodi's afterwards? And then you can stay 'til Sunday night."

Bradley's eyes lightened. "Maybe we can go to the zoo, or to a park. Or we could go and see the..."

"Bradley!"

He slouched in his chair.

"First, let's see how Jodi's—" Desiree heard a familiar voice coming from somewhere behind her.

It was Jon, pouring coffee at the far end of the food counter, and Krystal was with him! Desiree quickly pulled a pen and notepad from her shoulder bag and scribbled down her address and phone number before ripping out the page. "You'll have to excuse me, but something's just come up and I have to go." She handed them the piece of paper. "Jodi and I'll be expecting you anytime tomorrow."

"Are you all right, Desiree?"

"I can't explain now, Dianne, but I really have to go. See you both tomorrow." She jumped from her seat but as she neared the exit, her jacket caught on the arm of a chair and it fell noisily onto its side. She couldn't turn around to pick it up because she was afraid Jon might see her. She pushed it away from the aisle with a quick jerk of her leg.

"Des. Des, wait!"

Damn!! Jon had spotted her. She continued down the corridor, quickening her pace, not wanting to see his face or hear his voice— ever again. He was catching up to her. She could hear each heavy step, so she started to run. She would kick her husband in the shins if he caught up to her. She would scream. She would hit him. She would punch him in the gut. She would smack him in the face!

He grabbed the long strap of her purse, stopping her. She turned to face him, ready to scratch his eyes out.

"What's gotten into you?" he asked

She stood there, muted, shattered.

"Can't I even come to see my own daughter in the hospital?"

"Of course *you* can," she spat.

He glared at her. "What do you mean of course *I* can? Are you upset that Krystal's here with me tonight? She's my secretary, you know, and she wanted to see how Jodi was doing, and Jodi will remember her." He let go of her purse strap. "As a matter of fact, I'm quite surprised Todd isn't here with you right now. Or is he at the house, waiting for you?"

"Todd isn't *anywhere* waiting for me." A sudden sense of defeat had softened her angry tone. Jon could harbor whatever thoughts he wanted, she decided. What did it matter, anyway? From the corner of her eye she noticed Krystal strutting out of the cafeteria. When their eyes met, the brunette's deliberate strides continued.

"Well, I'm not going to stay here any longer," Jon stated flatly. "Tell Jodi I'll see her again tomorrow."

"Just *you*, Jon?" Sharp blades of anger bolted from her dry mouth.

<hr />

While sitting in the rocker with a fresh cup of herbal tea on the end table, her new afghan draped over her lap, and a bestselling paperback in her hands, her mind filled with resentment. She could see Jon's car parked out front. Losing her concentration because of the persistent ringing of the doorbell, she finally decided to let him in before he used his key. She should get the locks changed soon.

"We were going to drive you back here, but I see you have you own car now. Wonder who arranged that for you?" He stepped past her and made his way to the living room, his eyes circling the walls.

A haunting quietness filled the air as her mind buzzed with apprehension.

"Why don't you spend more time with Jodi instead of using all your energy to redecorate this derelict house? I know you painted last weekend but it still stinks in here. No wonder Jodi got sick."

Through the long narrow windows Desiree could see dark clouds screening the full moon. Dark thoughts were filling her mind. She had nothing to say to her husband.

She sat down, nestling her weary body against the firm cane back of the bentwood, and rocked with uneven jerks. Jon was becoming increasingly annoyed at her silent determination.

Something moved in the front seat of his car and the curious blonde sat up, squinting her eyes for better focus. It was Krystal! Desiree scowled and grabbed the wooden arms of the rocker with her moist hands. Now it was *her* turn to interrogate. She pushed herself up, stiffened her shoulders, and clutched her hands. Following the same steps Jon had just taken, she walked slowly around the room.

Standing in front of him she glared into his dark brown eyes. "And where the hell have *you* been?" Her voice was almost a whisper. She had wanted to express more confidence, more defiance. "Have you been here, at home? Helping me? Loving Jodi? Hell *no!*" That was better.

Jon backed into the kitchen. When his hands touched the corner of the far counter, he stopped. She brushed him accidentally.

"Well, have *you* been here?" she continued with definite depth to her tone. "No! Not for over a month now! And why? Because you have a little chick waiting for you elsewhere. Just outside, as a matter of fact. I'm surprised Krystal hasn't come to the door asking her sugar daddy to take her home."

Jon slapped her face. When she smacked him back, the large veins in his arms bulged, the corners of his full mouth sagged, and the brow of his bronzed face furrowed.

"Look, Desiree. Let's talk this over sensibly." His voice was cracking, as though to show remorse, a tinge of guilt. It was too late for that, but Jon continued. "Look. If you need help, all you have to do is call us. We will pick you up and take you to the hospital to see Jodi. We will pick her up when she's ready to go home and we will bring her here. All you have to do is phone and let us know."

We, we, we. Us, us, us. What had he just said? She marched briskly towards him and he walked back into the living room as though preparing to leave. His surprise at her unusual defiance heightened as Desiree's long narrow fingers poked his chest. He stepped back, dodging. She stepped forward, jabbing, nudging, and pushing. "Get out! Get out of here this instant and don't even think of coming back. I don't want to see you again. Ever!" She threw his jacket out onto the driveway and moments later his leather shoes landed on the damp lawn. "There! Maybe Krystal will come and help you pick those up. Why don't you ask her to?"

Through the darkness outside, as Jon skipped over the cool dewy grass to collect his clothes, his eyes searched the silhouette of his car. How much longer Krystal would wait for him that night, he wasn't sure, but he still had things he wanted to discuss with his wife.

"Come on, Desiree." Both shoes were on, and, stepping back into the front foyer, he struggled to get an arm through the sleeve of his jacket. As he faced his wife again, his eyes widened with a look of urgency. "Calm down. Why don't we sit and talk about it over a cup of coffee, or a glass of wine? Whatever you want."

"Get out! Just get the hell out of here!" Surprisingly, the effort to lead him out was easy and short. She slammed both doors shut and set the deadbolt.

Her stomach was growling but she couldn't eat. After dropping a jar of grape jelly as she reached into the refrigerator for some apple juice a little while later, she sat at the piano and eyed her new music book, the prelude to her first opus, and the notes and lyrics to the pretty song her father had entitled in her own name. She needed to hear some music, something lively, symphonic, orchestral, or jazzy. It didn't matter. She had caught herself crouching on the piano bench; her fingers were limp on the keyboard. With a slow turn of her body, she walked up to the stereo unit and selected a Stan Getz album instead.

As soft music filled the room, she picked up one of Jodi's dolls—*children*—from the wing chair. "Jodi is going to be just fine. She's coming home tomorrow, Jon. But you didn't even ask about that, did you now? And she didn't get sick because of me." The despondent mother studied each corner, each wall, and every inch of the living room. "I did all of this for you, Jon. So what if you think I wasted my time? I don't care any more. You aren't living here now, so why should it matter to you anyway?"

But to her very core, she did care, it all did matter, and when she heard the soft opening chords of "The Girl From Ipanema", she walked over to the kitchen sink, lifted the eyelet lace curtains, and pried open the window. The fresh air was invigorating. She unlocked the front doors, swung them open, and rested there for a short moment, breathing in the cool fresh air. Then she went upstairs to open all the windows there. Up and around, pulling and swinging. She pried each lever with more and more rebellion. Pouncing onto the bed, she dropped her face heavily into a pillow, and was soon enveloped in total darkness, a vacuum of silence … but she had to breathe. She couldn't keep her face pressed hard against the pillow. She was too cowardly for that.

Sitting on the edge of the leather settee, she pulled both wedding rings from her finger and tossed them at the mirror. The wide gold band fell onto the floor and was lost in the twist of a scatter rug, while the diamond ring dropped beside the jewelry box on the vanity.

"Colors of the rainbow," she whispered, remembering the exact moment when she had accepted Jon's marriage proposal. *Remembering* the tiny Venus flytrap that Jon had once brought home, poking it, feeding it, teasing it. *Remembering* the wilted rose bud falling from Erin's ear when they were visiting Todd and Sara. *Remembering* her mother's single tear falling onto the white satin of Erin's coffin. *Remembering* her parents' departure for Norway, their last good-byes before they stepped onto the plane for Toronto. *Remembering* Jodi's tired smile and the weak squeeze of her fingers that very afternoon.

She looked into the mirror and saw the blurry image of herself. "How quickly reality can show its ugly face," she moaned to herself. Sighing, she rubbed her knees with her chin and let her long hair fall around her face to hide from the mirror's hideous impression. She almost wished it were that easy to disappear from the face of the earth.

She tossed a pillow across the room and a tiny vial of expensive *Joy* perfume dropped from the cedar chest. The sudden strong fragrance filled her lungs and queasiness gnawed at her stomach. She felt somehow forced to answer the telephone as its ring jarred her from her somber mood.

"Hello."

"Hi, Des." It was Dawna. "I just stepped into my hotel room after having a few drinks with some business friends here and I thought I'd phone you. Is there anything else you want me to know about your young friend that you might have forgotten to tell me last night?"

"What friend? What are you talking about, Dawna? I didn't phone you last night. Those seminars must really be getting to you. Or maybe it's the drinks."

"Of course you phoned me, quite late, as a matter of fact. I'd already been in bed for more than an hour when you called."

"I don't remember that, Dawna. Not at all." She had had that horrifying nightmare about her husband and his utterly sick demands, and in the dream she thought she had phoned her friend. But that was just in her dream—wasn't it?

"Well, although I wasn't quite awake at first, I *do* remember your voice sounding so different. You talked quietly and oh-so-slowly. There was a special depth to your soft voice, as though each word was written on a cue card in front of you and you were reading to an audience. There was a steady humming in the background, too. Not static, just an eerie buzzing that I've never heard over the phone before."

Trying to fathom all that Dawna was saying, Desiree paced the hardwood floor. "Did I say anything else?"

"I won't get into it right now, Des." Curious and concerned, Dawna continued. "Listen. The seminar is over with, thank goodness. I'll be getting into town about four-thirty tomorrow afternoon, but since Gordon has to work late and you and I have so much to talk about, may I invite myself over? For dinner, perhaps?"

"Yes, of course. I'd love to see you. Jodi will be here, too. But *please* tell me what I said to you last night."

"Well, all right. You told me about the younger sister of a high school friend being pregnant. You asked me to have Gordon send you a certain prescription so she could lose her baby."

"I *what?*"

"I talked to Gordon earlier today, and he said the prescription should be in your mailbox some time tomorrow morning."

Desiree didn't know what to think. "You mean he actually filled the prescription?"

"Well, he was hesitant, of course, but when I reminded him of how *you* were when pregnant with Jodi, he said he would do it." Dawna refused to admit that the pills being sent to the house were only weak tranquilizers. "Gordon just couldn't see a high school kid having to go through all the emotions involved with an unwanted pregnancy."

"Dawna! It's nothing like that. *I'm* the one who's pregnant. *I'm* the young girl you think is trying to …"

"Oh, that's fabulous. Congratulations. Boy, do we ever have lots to talk about tomorrow. But you don't sound very pleased. Again. And why would you let me think the *mom-to-be* was a friend's sister?"

"I don't remember talking with you last night, not at all. I just can't…"

"I believe you. But why are you making up such strange stories? What are you so afraid of this time? You had the perfect pregnancy with Jodi. And the *first* one is usually the hardest."

Desiree moaned loudly. The moment was wrong for explaining anything about James Robert, about any part of Jon's family background, or about the *special* baby she might be carrying. Those topics should not be explained over the phone to anyone, but tonight she wanted to tell someone about her concerns. She needed some guidance, some reassurance…

"Are you okay, Des? Suddenly you've become rather quiet."

"Well, this pregnancy is already different. And Dr. Styles believes that I might be…"

"What are you trying to say? Desiree? Are you still there?"

"Oh, Dawna. Dr. Styles said this child *might be different*. It's still too early to tell, but he wants me to have an amniocentesis as soon as possible."

"Wow! I'm assuming he explained what he meant by the word *different*. I've been collecting literature on just about anything concerning children, but I'm not sure what that procedure might be about."

"It's fairly new in the medical world. Apparently it can tell the doctor if there are any irregularities *in utero*." She wasn't quite ready to announce what particular *syndrome* was involved. "Dr. Styles just isn't sure if he wants me to take it because there is a definite risk involved. That's the problem."

"Does he honestly think you need to go through with it, though?"

"He told me that he wants to make sure *all* steps are taken during this pregnancy. I'm going to the main library soon to get more information about it."

"I'm collecting brochures on every subject. Let's read them over together."

She had spoken from the heart, admitting only what she felt was needed to help relieve her mind's doubt and confusion but now, sitting at the edge of the piano bench and eying the long pile of the old stained carpet, her heart started beating erratically. She could almost feel the throbbing against her ribs as she wondered about all she had said to Dawna in her dream the night before. Apparently she had requested one particular prescription. But how could she have done such a horrendous thing as involving her good friends in such a murderous scheme? Her nightmare had been an actuality, at least in part. She wondered if Todd had heard her on the phone. He was nearby when she awakened—still in bed. The phone was in the cradle, wasn't it? Yes, Todd would have made some remark if it hadn't been. And he would have placed it down properly.

She questioned what her sinister plan truly involved concerning that canister of pills. Had she actually planned to destroy an innocent, powerless child? She would be a felon then, a murderer. Could she actually take those crystalline tablets, crush them into tiny grains, and then toss them into her mouth and swallow them?

Trying to concentrate on the background music, her mind was still vividly picturing the ugliness. Yes, revenge was definitely in her own hands, in that clear plastic bottle, so tiny, so near. But her timing would have to be perfect, thought out to the exact hour, minute, perhaps second, so that she would be sitting in the rocker, waiting—waiting for Jon to come home and see her destroying his baby, his own flesh and blood. And she would grin as he heard her sudden gasps, as he witnessed each painful squirm and then the bloody mess. Shocked and bewildered, he would hesitate to touch her hot, wet body, so foul.

She went to the stereo and turned up the volume. Stan Getz was still playing and, from the soft sounds of the cool jazz that had earned him worldwide fame, the heaviness inside her slowly lifted. She felt remarkably calm, wonderfully free, and almost weightless. Yes, now she even thought she could fly.

Swooping up the afghan that had earlier dropped to the floor, she turned around and took a long slow stretch. Yes! The answer had finally come to her! All this time she thought her spiteful feelings were because she was still waiting for Jon, still waiting for her husband to return home. She had promised him that. And she would continue waiting for however long it took him. But lately the deep foreboding recesses of her subconscious mind had been looking for answers about her pregnancy, about her unborn baby. If it were different, she could still love it. She *would* love it.

Chapter Fifteen

Friday, March 15

Desiree watched her daughter with amusement as the tight blonde ringlets bounced with each hop, skip, and twirl. They had been home for over an hour already, and she hadn't yet told Jodi about their weekend visitor.

A blue van had pulled up in the driveway and Desiree opened the front doors of the house.

"Hi, Dianne. Hi, Buck. Come on in."

Dianne put the short crutches against the front wall. Bradley had walked in without them. His eyes sparkled as he leaned forward to peek into the living room, as though expecting to see Jodi, but she had run upstairs just moments earlier.

"Do you have time for coffee?"

"I thought I would have, Desiree, but my sister and her clan are coming over to visit later. I couldn't get out of it this time, and I have to straighten up the house before they all arrive, dust finder that Betty is. I hope you understand." She placed the small suitcase next to the crutches. "Thanks again for letting Bradley stay with you. I think it will be terrific for him." She was whispering, not wanting her son to hear her anxious voice, and moments later Jodi came down the stairs clad in her pink gingham party dress, white socks, and new black patent shoes.

"Hi, Jodi!" Bradley shouted excitedly. Jodi slowly walked toward him, her hazel eyes casting a curious look while Bradley remained still as anxiety colored his face with a nice shade of pink.

"Hi, Buck! I di'n't rec'nize you 'cause you're all dressed up. Just like me. Mom told me to get changed but she di'n't say why. But now I know." Jodi's tiny skips around the living room revealed her excitement.

"Jodi, I promised Buck he could come and visit you as often as he wants. He'll be staying here until Sunday night."

Jodi squealed with delight. "I got an elf from my gramma and grampa the other day. You gotta see his ugly face." She leaped towards him and Desiree braced the lad's back to prevent his falling.

"See you on Sunday, Bradley. I'll phone first to let you know when I'll be here."

"Thanks, Mom. See you then."

"He's going to be just fine, Dianne."

"Yes, I know, and thank you so much." She squeezed Desiree's elbow before stepping out the door.

"Buck, let's go up to my room. You can play with my children and pi'ture books and everythin'. Maybe Mommy will let me have my Easter present today so you can help me open it. I think it's a big coloring book." Jodi motioned for Bradley to hurry and, as he limped towards her, she studied him with curious affecting eyes.

"Mommy, Brad's got a funny walk. I can't even copy him. He's too hard to copy"

Bradley dropped the skipping rope he had picked up from the telephone bench.

Desiree rubbed her belly.

Jodi persisted. "Mommy! Did you see him walk just now? Kinda like a duck all the way to the piano."

Desiree quickly put her fingers on Jodi's mouth and held her hand while motioning for Bradley to join them on the loveseat. With head still bent he sat next to Desiree, who took their hands together in hers.

"Jodi," she started carefully, "Buck was in a car accident a while ago. I think he already told you that. His hipbone was broken in several places and he had to go to the hospital for an operation. He was in the same hospital that you were in this week but for much longer. And now he just has to go there for certain exercises and check-ups." *And some new tests, apparently,* her mind continued.

"You mean he could walk just like you and me before the acc'dent?" Her wrinkled face showed instant scorn. "He never told me that."

"Yes, honey. The car accident gave him that limp. Just because people *look* different, doesn't mean they *want* to."

"Yeah, Jodi," Bradley broke in. "I woke up one morning in the hospital and everybody told me that I wouldn't ever be able to walk without using crutches. Here, wanna try 'em?"

Feeling too sure of herself, Jodi stood high on her tiptoes, struggling to get the crutches under her armpits, but she fell and her giggling continued as she tried to stand up again.

"See. It's not so easy, is it? But if I had my way, I'd throw these out for good before you could count to ten."

"One, two, three …"

"Oh, come on Jodi. Give me a chance. My hip is kinda sore today. I'm still supposed to use these crutches but just not as much as before."

"The doctors had told Bradley that he would never walk properly again. He will always have that limp, but you shouldn't ever make fun of it. He likes to run and skip and play just like you do. And he will. But it's going to take a little time." She hesitated, squeezing their tiny hands harder, hoping she was telling the truth.

With eyes down and lips pouting, Jodi stepped over to Bradley's side and kissed his forehead. Bradley's thin arms wrapped tightly around Jodi's waist.

"Buck. Let me get my children. They're all upstairs. Then we can play house down here. Maybe Mom can pull out the coffee table for us. We can use it for anything, you know."

After slightly rearranging the living room, the children were happily engrossed in their own play. Knowing Dawna would be arriving in a few hours, Desiree placed the thick rib roast in the oven and soaked the freshly peeled potatoes in a pot of cold water. Not only to show off her new car, but also to take the children for a ride, Desiree had offered to pick Dawna up at the airport. But her friend had insisted on taking a cab all the way across town.

Now freshened up, still with time for a cup of coffee before Dawna arrived, Desiree joined the children. She had suddenly become a grandmother, according to the kids. She was to baby-sit all the other children while Bradley stayed with her in the hospital when Jodi was having her sixth child.

"See, Gramma?" Jodi put her teddy bear under her dress. "It's going to come out any minute now. You better get the children ready so you can take them home with you."

"Oh, I thought I was going to stay here with them." She went along with their game, pleased to have been asked to join in."

"Oh, Dad. I think it's coming. You better call the doctor right away."

Bradley mimicked a phone call while Jodi tried to push the teddy bear from under her dress, but it was caught around the elastic waist. She kept tugging at it but the stuffed animal wouldn't budge.

"Doctor. Doctor. The baby won't come out. You'd better hurry. I think my wife needs a Caesarean."

"That's quite involved, Buck." Desiree laughed softly at Bradley's quick wit. "How would you know anything about Caesareans?"

"That's how my mother got me. She told me what they're all about. Creepy, *I* think."

Jodi only bugged her eyes and tightened her lips with total disgust because the teddy bear was still stuck under her dress. "Dad! I need your help. Right now!!"

Bradley threw down the imaginary phone and came to his wife's rescue.

"Mom, what's a serean?"

"Caesarean, honey. That's a special operation that some women need when their baby is ready to be born." She wasn't quite sure how to explain it to a five-year-old.

"Did you have to have one?"

"No."

"How did I come out, then?"

"You came the natural way." Their little play was getting too involved, but Desiree wasn't sure how to change the story line.

"Did it hurt?"

"Only for a few seconds. And then, there you were."

"Mommy. Mommy …"

"Huh?" Desiree slumped into her seat and sighed loudly at her own reminiscing, so thankful that her baby had grown into such a little lady, so hopeful that the next one would be healthy. *Healthy.* She rubbed her belly again.

"Mommy! You aren't listening to me."

"I'm sorry but I was just thinking of the day you were born."

"Well, why don't you do it again? I wish you were going to have another baby. Then I could have somebody to play with me all the time and Bradley could come over to keep us both company."

The words resounded in Desiree's mind.

The doorbell rang.

"Oh, goody. Auntie Dawna's here." Before Dawna had time to put down her purse, Jodi was hugging her, pulling at her arms.

"If you can guess which hand your gift is in, you may have it. And this one's for you, Bradley. Or may I call you Buck?"

"How did you know my name?" His mouth gaped with surprise as he leaned against the telephone bench near the doorway and reached for his gift. "Thank you very much and please call me Buck. *All* my friends do."

"Buck walks a little funny, Auntie Dawna, but it's not his fault. He was in a bad car acc'dent."

A smile brightened Desiree's face as she watched her daughter rip the pretty pink wrapping while Bradley shook and squeezed his nicely wrapped gift, trying to guess what was inside before opening it. Soon the torn blue paper fell to the floor, and he smiled at the tiny rooster of white chocolate.

"You look so relaxed, Dawna. How do you do it?"

"I've made it a habit to sleep on planes. With all the traveling Gord and I do, there's no time for jet lag with this old chick. But I'm concerned about you! You look so pale and exhausted. I know you've had a lot on your mind lately, but straining yourself around the house won't solve anything. You've done so much already. There can't be anything left."

"Other than getting new carpets, there's just the laundry and sewing rooms, but that can wait."

"Yes, it can. I'm glad you're finally accepting that." Dawna turned around slowly, absorbing the decorating chores now finished. "You've done a fabulous job in here. Good on ya. And thank goodness Jodi's home again, and so healthy. You can spend some quiet time with her now. Well deserved quiet time, I might add."

The entire dinner was delicious. Bradley had eaten two pieces of hot apple pie, each with a large scoop of vanilla ice cream on top, and was asking for more. Later, with the children tucked in their own beds, Desiree piled more wood onto the grate in the family room as Dawna filled two crystal glasses with white German wine and snuggled into the upholstered chair in the far corner.

"I see you're making another Holly Hobby. I don't know how you can sew all those tiny pieces together to make something so pretty."

Desiree slumped onto the floor cushion, her eyes fixed on the fire in front of her. Jon had once said those exact words to her, and she could remember the morning when he had hung her wall hanging in the huge bedroom of their duplex. It was his quiet apology. It was her first pregnancy.

"Des!"

"Huh?"

"Do you want me to get the phone?"

"What? I didn't even hear it ringing. No, I'll get it. I'm expecting a call from Mom and Dad sometime this weekend … Hello."

"Hi. Are you busy?"

"Yes, Jon, as a matter of fact, I'm having some wine with a friend."

"Todd again, huh?"

She refused to give him the pleasure of knowing Todd wasn't there. "I'm with a friend, like I said."

"Well, I guess I could come over some other time."

"No, Jon. There's certainly a lot we should talk over, but not here. Ever again." She hung up. "Why does he always have to phone when I have company?"

"You would have let him come over tonight if I weren't here, wouldn't you?"

"I told him not to take another step in this house again."

"You know damn well that you didn't mean it, Desiree. And Jon knows it too … Is he helping you out financially?"

"No, not yet anyway."

"Hey, if he hasn't by now, he never will, at least not without a court order. I'd get a lawyer before I set eyes on him again if I were you."

"I can't, Dawna."

"Why not?"

"He's my husband, and I want him back so much."

"Oh, *do you*?" Dawna set down her glass. "After what he's put you through lately, do you actually think you want him back? Stop kidding yourself, girl."

"Oh, Dawna, I'm just so …"

"I know the security of a family unit is important to you and that you want Jon back because you think he gives you that protection. You don't need anyone but yourself, Des. I know a very good divorce lawyer. I'll make an appointment for you to see him next week."

"Dawna! Jon only asked me for time, and I'm going to give him exactly that."

"Have you had new locks put in the doors?"

"I can't get new locks yet."

"That should have been done long ago. When are you going to stop him from running your life?"

"Soon, Dawna. Soon!"

"You're just as edgy now as the first time, aren't you?"

A lengthy sigh was the expectant mother's immediate response. "I want this baby so much, Dawna, but I'm scared. I've been having nightmares about it. Each of them seem so real that when I awaken, I wonder if they actually *were* just dreams. They have me walking in my sleep, phoning *you* to ask for some special pills."

"I have to admit, your strange phone call had Gord and me quite concerned."

"But you know something? I can't remember doing that. I know in one dream Jon told me to phone you and ask you for those pills, but I can't recall *actually* doing anything like it."

"Did you get them?"

"Yes. There were in the mailbox this morning, just like you said." She took them out of her smock pocket to show her guest.

"You mean you haven't thrown them out yet?" She still wanted Desiree to believe they were the actual prescription.

"Nooo. I have to keep them."

"To use later?" Dawna quickly sat up.

"No, no. Just for now. To keep me focused."

"And Buck is your redemption, isn't he?"

"He has certainly brought me a lot of smiles."

"Is that all?"

"Pardon me?" Desiree put the vial of pills back into her pocket and started playing with an empty ashtray on the coffee table beside her.

"How long will Bradley have to use crutches?"

"The doctors aren't sure anymore. They're going to give him a few new tests to find out why he's not responding well to ..." Desiree saw her friend leaning forward in the sofa, could see a slight raise of her eyebrows. "What are you really trying to tell me, Dawna?"

"Well, what have your recent nightmares been about?"

"Jon and me."

"And who else?"

"The baby."

"What *about* Jon and you and the baby?"

Not wanting to answer any of those questions, Desiree kept spinning the ashtray until it dropped to the floor.

"Isn't there a common thread here?" There was a forceful tone in Dawna's voice now. "Come on, Des. In your sleep, isn't Jon trying to get you to lose your baby?"

"Uh, yeah."

"And why do you think he's doing that? Because your doctor told you that this baby might be *different,* that it might *not be perfect.*" She took a long sip of her wine before continuing. "But not perfect in *whose* eyes, Des? Somehow even your dreams are letting you think that you couldn't love your next child because it might not be healthy. Just like your first pregnancy. And look how beautiful Jodi is. But you would love her anyway, no matter what. Don't ever kid yourself about that."

"What has any of this got to do with Bradley?"

"Those ugly crutches, his tiny frame, and the possibility that he might have cancer didn't stop you from loving him right from the beginning, did they now?

Desiree's face tilted. "You're thinking *cancer* too, are you?"

"I'm not a doctor, but …" Dawna quickly filled her empty wine glass to the brim. "He is such a sweet little thing, you know. And you two truly do have some special connection, which only seems to be deepening. I find it quite remarkable."

"Yes, I know. I love it, and Jodi's so happy when he's around her."

"Keep him around then, as often as possible." The brunette swung her petite body off the corner chair, grabbed the nearby poker, and started prodding the dying embers. "Besides, Des. Nothing has actually been confirmed about this new baby yet. Maybe there's nothing for you, or anyone, to worry about."

Desiree was upset with herself for letting her good friend leave so early that evening when they both still had so much more to say and to share, but their mutual tiredness had easily contributed to that final decision. Later, submerged in a thick layer of iridescent bubbles, a slow, steady tranquility absorbed her and she started rubbing her abdomen. Pleasant thoughts of the healthy, perfectly formed baby she honestly felt she now was carrying calmed her mind. A boy. Jason. Jason Sommers. Nice and short, just like her daughter's, and again, she wondered if she could carry this baby to full term. She had abused her body so much lately.

She reached over the tub and got the bottle of pills from her smock on the commode. There were only five pills inside—thick and white and oblong. She stared at the label—*one a day for five days*. Then there would be *a couple of days of waiting.* "But only after being swallowed," she sighed.

"Hi. Is anybody home?"

Still in the tub, still soaking, still deep in thought, she heard Jon's heavy footsteps by the bathroom door. Dawna had been right. Getting new door locks was a must, a priority for her now.

After stepping out of the tub and tying a thick towel around her hair, she donned her terry cloth robe. Determined somehow to exude confidence and independence, to rise above her recent waves of spite and confusion, she dropped the pills into her pocket and went to greet her delinquent husband out in the hallway.

"What are you doing here, Jon?" She looked straight into the darkness of his eyes.

"Hi, honey," he replied as he held out both arms.

"Don't you *hi honey* me, Jon." She motioned for him to follow her downstairs to the family room, out of the children's hearing range.

He had thrown his leather jacket onto the armchair and, sitting cross-legged in front of the fireplace, he stirred the smoky coals with the poker that had been left on the hearth.

He was wearing a new outfit. She studied the hardness of his thick chest, his straight white teeth accentuated by the deep bronze of his face, and the white circles around his dark eyes that the winter sun had not been able to color through his ski goggles. He looked more handsome than usual.

How could she be so weak? How could she be so easily captured by his presence, by his warm hands that were now guiding her to the chesterfield? Her body was leaning toward his warmth, begging for more. "I love you, Jon," she wanted to say. Her heart was singing again and her every pore was tingling at the utter nearness of him, that woodsy scent around him, as he pulled her closer. A tiny voice within, however, as smooth as a lullaby, was whispering that she should be strong and ignore all those sensations. Oh, if she only could.

"Why don't you put on a silky lounging dress and I'll brush your hair for you tonight?" His voice was soft and casual as he stretched over to turn up the stereo.

"Please turn that down, just a little. You might wake up Jodi."

"This isn't loud."

Shaking her head, she gave a loud sigh. Another tender moment with Jon had vanished so quickly. Why was he studying the contents of the ceramic ashtray now? Was he looking for a butt from Todd's Colt? And what would his reaction be if he actually found one? She rubbed the container inside the pocket of her smock just as Jodi ran into her father's arms.

"Daddy, Daddy. You're here! Mommy and me have been waiting for so long. Where you been?"

With ears pricked, Desiree stood in front of the fireplace and waited to hear what her husband had to say.

"I've been away on business," he replied. "My, but you look thin."

She could slap him in the face right now but she didn't want Jodi to see the altercation or sense the estrangement between her parents.

"But Mommy said you was staying with friends so you could study better."

"No, honey," he said softly.

"Where were you then? You wasn't here with me and Mommy."

His lips tightened. How could he tell Jodi that he still loved her?

"Daddy. Where were you? You just said you wasn't with friends."

His daughter was interfering, prying into territory Jon found difficult to explain. He wanted to be honest with her. He wanted to be open and understanding, but he could sense Desiree's doubting eyes watching him.

"Daddy. Did you hear me? You keep looking over at Mommy."

An unusual discomfort overpowered him. He had hoped Desiree would leave them alone for a little while so he could discuss some things in private with his only child.

"Daddy!"

"I wasn't with friends, Jodi. I was living with one friend, a good friend. Do you remember Auntie Krystal?"

"Who?"

"Oh. I guess you don't." He looked rather surprised, but continued. "Well, she and her husband had a big fight and Krystal was left all alone, so I went to help her."

"But Mommy was all alone too, and you di'n't come to help her. You never was here when she was crying."

"Well, I'm here now, aren't I?" He turned his back to Desiree. "Since you've been cooped up in the hospital this week, why don't I take you on a picnic in the mountains tomorrow? We should be able to find a nice place somewhere there. The weather's supposed to be even better than today." There was an unusual gentleness in Jon's expression and in the way he lifted Jodi over his shoulders.

Desiree watched more suspiciously.

"Mommy can make a big lunch and you can bring your beach ball if you want. The three of us can be all together again. How does that sound to you?"

"What about Buck? Can't he come, too?"

"Who's Buck?" He looked at Desiree for the answer.

"We met a young boy in the hospital," she began slowly. "He's staying with us for the weekend." She bit her bottom lip, and rubbed Jodi's arm.

"Hey, that's terrific. Of course he can come with us."

"I wish I could tell him about it now but I think he's sleeping."

Surprised at Jon's instant consent, Desiree gently patted Jodi's head, hinting that she goes back to bed and, as she tucked the blankets tightly in again, the telephone started to ring. Hoping her parents were finally calling, Desiree ran to the phone in the master bedroom. Jon, however had already picked up another extension, and Desiree, disappointed at hearing the unfamiliar voice, stayed on the line.

"Hi, Rick. What a surprise," Jon started.

"We phoned you at Krystal's but she said you had gone home for the weekend. The gang is skiing at Lake Louise tomorrow and we all thought you both would like to come, but maybe now Desiree can go instead."

"What time are you planning to leave?"

"We're all meeting here at six. Would you like us to pick you up?"

"No, we'll meet you there. The usual place?"

"Yep. See you then."

Desiree dropped the phone and just moments later Jon loped into the bedroom where his sparkling eyes met her hot glare.

"Jon, I heard that conversation, *all* of it… So you're only here for the weekend, huh?"

"Honey. That's just what …"

"What did you just say?"

"That's just what Krystal's telling everybody." His dark eyes scanned the room. "She's upset with me right now and that's her way of covering things up."

"Covering *what* things up?" Her voice was faltering because Dawna's earlier comments had flashed in her mind. *Des, when are you going to stop him from running your life?*

"Well, we had an argument and …"

"And so you've come back home to your wife. To your daughter. To …" She was stuttering now. "And just for the weekend, huh?" She had to take a deep breath. Jon was walking away. "We aren't going to the mountains to ski tomorrow. You promised to take Jodi and Buck there for a picnic."

He was at the doorway now and as he turned to face her again, he saw her wedding rings on the dresser.

"Listen to me, Jon! We *have* to be with Jodi and Buck tomorrow. You promised. We can't just …"

"Well, you know we could drop them off at Mother's. She'll keep them busy with interesting things. She'd love the company, since Father is out of town all this month. You and I can still go skiing. Conditions are supposed to be excellent. You might start enjoying it. We can tell the kids something else came up and we just couldn't get out of it."

"How dare you! Jon, I'm not going skiing. With you or anybody. *I'll* take the kids on a picnic myself. Just get out of here."

He stepped back, hitting the edge of the door. "Are you kicking me out?" His eyes were suddenly shining like black onyx. "Are you?" he repeated.

"Well, yes. I guess I am." She felt like kicking him in the groin, but instead she snatched her wedding rings from the dresser and stepped closer to him. She grabbed his hand. "Here! Why don't you give these to Krystal?"

With a slow sneer curling the edges of his mouth, he walked downstairs, got his jacket, and left the house.

As the storm door creaked shut, Desiree constantly blinked her eyes, refusing to let any tears fall. But her mind was full of questions. *Oh, what have I done now? What have I done?*

She caught herself pacing the floor. Her heart was palpitating, her throat was tight, and her hands were sweaty. She sat still at the piano; her hands were idle on the keys while her insides were exploding.

Not wanting to miss the expected call from her parents, Desiree rushed to answer the telephone before the children awakened from the rings.

"Hello," she said weakly.

"Hi, Jam. Can you hear me okay? It's your mother."

"Yes, Mom. I can hear you very clearly." *Jam. Jam.* As a grand feeling of reassurance swelled within her, Desiree pulled out a chair in the dining room and sat down.

"Sorry we haven't phoned sooner, but our daily schedule is so packed with activities that when we get back for the night, we're too exhausted to talk to anyone. Yesterday we took a boat trip around the inner fjord archipelago. It was breathtaking, and so relaxing. The entire day was perfect. We both had a great sleep so we decided to call you now, before we head off for Lillesande. That's your father's birthplace, you know. I'm especially looking forward to seeing the white swans. They're all around the harbor, apparently. But what's happening at your end of the world?"

Desiree stood up and circled the clean spacious kitchen, tapping the countertops. Her mother's voice was soothing; the time seemed right. "I'm twelve weeks pregnant, Mom."

"Oh, how wonderful. That's exciting for everybody, isn't it? How did Jodi take the news? I bet she's looking forward to having a little brother or sister."

"She doesn't know yet. Neither does Jon."

"You wanted to tell us first? How sweet."

"Well ..."

"Well what? Don't keep me in suspense. Are you going to have twins, or triplets?"

"No, Mom. It's nothing like that. Nothing like that at all." Beyond the kitchen's café curtains, only the waning moon broke the expanse of blackness in that early spring evening. Proper words to continue this conversation seemed as remote.

"I think we're getting some kind of interference now. I can't hear you too well anymore."

"I can still hear you loud and clear, Mom." But her mind was still blank.

"Jam? What is it then? What are you trying to tell me?"

Silenced by the sudden reverberation of odd buzzing and whistling noises on the line, both mother and daughter waited, until finally, that moment of quietude clarified Desiree's resolve. Yes, now she could continue with her sad announcement. "I'm not doing as well this time, Mom." Her voice was a crackling whisper. "Dr. Styles thinks our baby might be different. He wants me to take some special tests. An amniocentesis, in particular."

"I think I would remember a strange name like that if I ever heard it, but I don't think I have. What's it for? Or what's it supposed to do?"

"Mom. Dr. Styles thinks our baby might be different," she repeated more emphatically.

"Different in what way? I don't understand, honey. Please tell me more."

"It might be a ..." All words had left her again. A loud steady hum filled the lines for a long moment, until Mae spoke up again.

"You've gotten quiet on me again, dear. Are you going to be all right? Should Father and I cancel the rest of our trip and come home?"

Desiree could only moan a negative answer to that offer. "It might be like Jillian and Bruce's daughter, Sandra," she blurted out. "You know, a ..."

"A Down's baby?"

"Yeah, Mom."

"Oh, Desiree. What have you been doing with your life lately?"

"Pardon me?" Tears were welling in her eyes. She put the receiver onto the counter, but could still hear each and every word proclaimed by her mother.

"You know that God punishes all sinners. What have you been doing with your life lately? Have you been going to church at all? Have you been praying for help? ... Desiree, are you still there? If you are saying anything, honey, I can't hear a word. Hello? Are you still there?"

Desiree could hear a click from the other end of the line and she gently placed the phone into its cradle. It would ring again, soon, but the dejected blonde wasn't sure if she would answer it.

Eventually she did.

"How sure is the doctor about all of this?"

With a deep sigh, Desiree answered. "He's not positive about my carrying a Mongoloid baby just yet, but he's sure enough that something is different this time. Those tests are not for *every* pregnant woman."

"Oh, Desiree. You've got to lose it. You've just got to. Look at all the pressure Jillian and Bruce are still going through with their little one. How old is it now?

"Mother! *Sandra* is twelve now. *She* is happy and doing very well in school. *She* is loved, Mother. That child will do very well when ..."

"But *you* couldn't possibly take care of a ..."

"Pardon me?"

"It takes a special person to raise those children. I thought you would know that. And what's Jon going to do when he finds out? We'll have to pray to God that He helps you lose it."

"Pray to God that He helps me lose it?" she shouted. "I can't believe what you are saying, Mother.

"God will know what has to be done."

There was another long stretch of silence over the wires.

"Desiree. Are you there? Are you still there, dear?"

Chapter Sixteen

Saturday, March 16

Desiree stretched her tired body between the new satin sheets that had bunched around her during the night, and again her restless mind returned to the setting, that same horror, where Jon was sitting beside her at the edge of the narrow hospital bed, his wan face tight and his moist eyes solemn. Writhing as she reached over to kiss him, she let her sore body drop heavily onto the bed. "Jon, I still hurt, and they won't let me hold our baby. They won't bring him to me or let me see him in the nursery. Please get him for me."

Alone once again because Jon had disappeared through the thick white walls of her private room, Desiree dropped her head against the thin pillows on the bed and eyed the dreariness of the room. Stretching a bare arm over the side table, she touched a glass vase that displayed a dozen red sweetheart roses. She stared at the moist, velvet petals and smiled weakly. Jon must have put them there when she was looking elsewhere, she decided, and with lightened spirit she opened the tiny envelope left inside and slowly read the message out loud. 'To My Dear Mother ... Love, Jason'.

She hummed the message over and over. "Oh, Jason. I love you. I love you." His features were so vivid in her mind. She had to see him again.

Staggering out into the long empty corridor she eagerly made her way down the hall, peering into each opened doorway to see who was there. All the beds had been made. All the curtains were open. All the rooms were empty. Where were the nurses? Just yesterday she couldn't get rid of the nursing staff. At least two of them had been beside her all day long, checking her pulse, taking her blood pressure, redressing her long incision, or injecting her with more painkillers. Now, unwatched, and feeling strong, satisfied, and important, she turned the corner towards the nursery. Yes, she was a new mother, again.

"Jason. I'm coming. Mommy won't be long. I'm coming to see you, Jason."

And there he was! Finally she could see her son, her newborn baby boy, so tiny, so beautiful, and so perfect. A nurse, whose robust frame faced the nursery window, was holding him up in the deep enamel basin, sponging him off. Desiree pressed her forehead hard against the glass for a better view. Soon her own hands were caressing him, bathing him, copying the nurse's every movement. Now he was being dressed in the cotton sleeper she had sewn for him, and she could feel his soft tight skin against her rough hands, could see the deepness of blue in his large round eyes. She stroked the thick dark hair on his tiny round head.

"Jason, I love you."

The nurse had wrapped him in a hospital blanket and was walking towards the door. He was going to see his mother who was anxious to hold him again, who was racing over to meet them. She turned the knob but it refused to budge. She tried again, without success. Soon she was pounding on the door, kicking it, lunging at it.

The nurse and baby were out in the main hallway now, prancing towards the distant elevators. Desiree darted after them. Her steps were long and rhythmic but the faster she ran the further away the twosome seemed to get. She was trailing behind. Soon everything around her was a darkening ugly gray blur, but she continued running and leaping. Her hands were flailing. Her arms were spread out in front of her. The walls were narrowing. Already, she could touch them. They were choking her now and she was gasping for air. The walls were upon her, collapsing just above her. She crawled on hands and knees.

"Jason. Jason. Come to Mommy. Come. Come to Mommy."

She could see her beautiful son at the end of a long narrow tunnel. Encircled in a sphere of wondrous illumination, there he was! Alone. Floating in the air. His eyes were clear, and little tufts of black hair curled gently on the top of his perfectly formed head. His chubby hands were curving inwardly. His arms were stretching out, extending beyond the bright white light. He was reaching out for his mother.

Suddenly that robust nurse reappeared, and Jason was in her arms again. She was feeding the tiny newborn nature's milk and stroking his head so gently. Her thin dark brows rose higher as her tiny smirk grew into a hideous smile, like the one worn by the Cheshire cat in *Alice in Wonderland*. But who was that in the distance? So obscure, approaching the couple from behind. Yes, the tall figure was beside them now. Who was it, watching the feeding so intently? Someone very poised, very elegant.

Finally the nurse turned slightly, and looked up. It was Krystal!

But now, who was behind Krystal? The tiny frail physique was nearing them all. When the figure shifted her fragile frame and those glaring eyes met Desiree's, the image fossilized … Mother!!

❦

Desiree struggled to untangle her long, tired body from the new satin sheets that had once felt so smooth and cool against her nakedness. Now bunched all around her, they imprisoned her restless body just as her nightmare afflicted her weary mind.

After dressing into a cotton turtleneck and pair of old jeans, she wandered quietly around the main level of the home, sliding her hands along some smooth surfaces, caressing a few valued ornaments. She sat near the piano and started to read *Valley of the*

Dolls once again. Still echoing in her mind, however, were her mother's recent comments, that eerie tone of voice so piercing to her ears. Why couldn't there have been a little static coursing through the telephone wires then? The paperback fell to the floor when she walked into the dining room.

At the trestle table, inattentive to the particular design her hand was creating on the thick sketchpad in front of her, her lackluster eyes followed the long curved strokes. My, how rough her hands looked. She needed a manicure. A pedicure. A massage. A chiropractor. A gynecologist. A shrink.

When two small hands covered her eyes, she gave a tiny smile. "Good morning, Bradley."

"Please call me Buck."

She put her arms around his waist.

"Hey. What are you starting to draw? Hmmm. Those eyes kinda look like mine. I don't think my lashes are quite that long, though." When he noticed a tear welling in his friend's eyes he kissed her forehead. "My mom likes to be alone when she's sad. How 'bout you?" He slumped onto the chair beside her. "Jodi and I can start on my new model ship this morning, you know. So we won't bother you."

Desiree had planned so many activities for that day, and the children were to be included in all of them. "Thank you, Buck, but this weekend is for you and Jodi. I can get a good sleep tonight." She closed the sketchpad and put it on the buffet. "Let's wake up Jodi and go out for some breakfast. I don't feel like making any this morning."

"Oh, she's already up, getting dressed."

Later, not able to finish the ham and eggs she had ordered, Desiree sipped her hot coffee and counted the red and white stripes on the papered walls in the quiet restaurant, thankful that Jodi had forgotten about the picnic with her father. Or had Bradley said something to her earlier?

Only a few blocks from the restaurant she was cut off twice by inattentive drivers, and was almost rear-ended when stopping for an elderly pedestrian. In the pocket of her tight jeans she felt the plastic container. She was uncertain about her nerves today, but the children were safe, still giggling in the back seat with the safety belts wrapped around them. They were all together, animated in their own separate ways.

The lawn of her parents' yard was patched with various shades of green. Buds were already forming on the huge apple tree she herself had planted in the middle of the front lawn that first summer in their new house ten years earlier. Healthy juniper bushes decorated the rock garden against the north side of the house and the youngsters tried to chase a lone black squirrel that had been hiding in one of them.

Inside the house, the faint smell of pine air-freshener lingered softly. Noticeably absent from the side table by the front door, however, was Erin's Bible, and Desiree assumed that her parents had taken it on their trip to Norway. The few bushy foliage plants were thriving as though no one had left. Mrs. Martin, a long-time neighbor, had obviously dusted recently; the reflection of the ceramic planters on the coffee table was clear and deep.

The children scurried to the piano and touched the keys with bungling fingers, laughing at their own clumsiness, while Desiree peeked into the kitchen and sighed when she saw the bouquet of dusty-pink silk roses on the table. She walked down the hall into her father's den where wooden framed pictures of various sailboats, trawlers, and ocean liners adorned an entire wall, reminding her of his love of ships and the sea.

In her old bedroom, walls of pale yellow paper and curtains of lacy white cotton lifted her spirits and she waltzed in front of the canopy bed before gently closing the door behind her. Nothing there had changed.

She sat at the edge of the king-size bed in the master bedroom, absorbing the richness of the room's French Provincial decor as the tuneless duet continued from down the hall. Numerous portraits of Erin, varying in shape, size, and frame, had been carefully arranged above the low headboard, but three familiar snapshots, set in new brass frames, soon drew Desiree to stand in front of the long vanity. The left photo had been taken when she was six months old, and the one to the right was of Jodi at the same age. Mother and daughter looked almost like twins, she decided, except for the color of their eyes. The original center snapshot, similar to the one of Erin that she had at home, had been replaced by one of Desiree, taken on her fourteenth birthday. She was so tall even at that early age, lanky, and with such ugly, knobby knees. Her hair was so short, chopped and sun-bleached.

She looked up at the large mirror before touching her thin cheeks, her long soft neck, her swollen breasts, and her soon-to-be bulging stomach. Several minutes lapsed before she touched the picture frames. "You were such a beautiful baby, Desiree," she said softly. "But look at you now. Look at what you've become."

<hr />

Jodi dashed up to her and pulled at the leather purse draped on Desiree's lap. "Mommy, come and watch Buck and me play Ducks and Drakes. Buck just told me how to do it. I want to throw more stones into the water, but I want you to watch me. Buck can make his skip two times."

"I'll be down in a minute, honey." The children's merriment had camouflaged Desiree's despondency that morning, but now she felt like an intruder, a nuisance to her friends. Todd wasn't home when she had driven by his house earlier, and she assumed he had gone skiing with the office staff. She wanted to see him, to thank him again for everything he had done around the house for her. She had also driven by the cemetery, planning to place her new Easter lilies on Erin's grave, but she had changed her mind when hearing Jodi and Bradley's spontaneous laughter in the back seat. And she wondered why she had driven across town to see the Greenes. Dawna and Gordon had been apart for an entire week and were now enjoying their own time together. She could have taken the children somewhere else. Today, however, she felt that she needed more than the children nearby. Her friends had welcomed them all inside, suggesting they take a drive to the foothills later.

And now the dense growth of tall evergreens swayed in the cool March wind like an elaborate ballet, and Desiree wrapped her jacket over her shoulders as she eyed the beauty around her. The damp ground sprouted tiny green shoots, and crocuses sprinkled the shoreline of the still, hazy green tarn. To the east the sky was cloudless, and only a few cumulus clouds broke the pale blueness to the west.

"Mommy, come here."

She stood up, stretched her restless body as if reaching for one of the clouds, and walked over to the alcove where Dawna and Gordon sat arm in arm on a boulder beside a fallen pine tree. Together they watched as Jodi threw a tiny stone into the icy water. Plop—two feet into the lake with a tiny splash. Bradley was by her side immediately, about to show her again.

Dawna and Gordon walked along the shoreline with arms still around each other, watching a robin feed its noisy young in a nest that the gusty mountain winds had tilted.

"Mommy, I wish Buck could live with us. I wish I could have a brother just like him."

Images of Jason again flashed through her mind. She picked up the bag of garbage left from their picnic lunch and dropped it into a nearby trashcan before walking back to the car. As one hand squeezed the tiny bottle of pills still in her jeans pocket, the other rubbed her belly.

Home again, she handed the children their glasses of orange juice and sat on the living room hearth as various questions whirled in her mind. Jon had gone back to his car to get something for Jodi, telling her that he had been sitting on the front steps for more than an hour before the Cougar had pulled up the driveway. He obviously had known better than to enter their empty house.

"I found this in the mailbox." He handed her a crumpled envelope and a heavy parcel that had apparently been quickly wrapped from the remnants of a used brown paper bag, its deep folds and double thickness obvious around the contents. Not one corner was wrapped tightly, and it seemed like an entire roll of packing tape had been stretched over and over that paperboard. No postage was showing either.

"What's for dinner?" he asked, finally opening the doors of the house with his own set of keys, walking in as though nothing were amiss between them. Handing Jodi her Easter present, Jon instantly announced that she didn't have to wait an entire week to start enjoying it. A pound of jelly beans, a heavy chocolate bunny, and three plastic dolls were surrounded in colorful straw that draped over a large white wicker basket. "We stayed up until two o'clock this morning to make this," he said, grinning proudly.

"But, Daddy. You promised to take me and Buck on a picnic today. Mommy took us instead. And Auntie Dawna, too. Why di'n't you come with us like you said you would?"

We, we, we. Here we go again, Desiree's mind brooded, ignoring the other comments. Jon hadn't gone to Lake Louise after all. He had gone back to Krystal's and then together, working into the early hours of the morning, they had made something special for Jodi, while all that time Desiree herself was alone in bed, trying to understand her mother's surprising comments before braving another succession of nightmares.

Melancholy nipped at her heart when she glanced over at Bradley, who looked dejected sitting on the piano bench, watching the strange man and his new friend pick up some jelly beans from the carpet. "Jon, don't give her too much candy now. Dinner will be ready soon."

Jodi stuffed a piece of broken chocolate into the closed mouth of one of her new dolls before standing up and offering some to her father.

Desiree watched in amazement. *Why are you getting all the attention now, Jon?*

"Would you please get me a tissue, Jodi? I think you missed my mouth." Jon laughed softly and placed the colored doll into the basket. Purposely facing only his daughter, he was trying to keep the conversation light and flowing. He had waited all afternoon for

Desiree to return home because he wanted to talk to her. He knew he would have to find the time later to clear the air with her. He would have to make sure the children were put to bed early.

As Bradley slumped onto the floor beside her, finger-pressing the slight crease of his blue jeans, Desiree squeezed his shoulder. Watching, hurting, hating, she felt so isolated and so desolate in her own home.

Jodi was still feeding her new dolls, offering more chocolate to her father, keeping a tissue ready for him as Desiree continued looking on. Yes, father and daughter. They were in their own circle, their own little bubble, and the tired blonde felt as if she were the intruder, the alien. She wished the bubble would break. Pop!! *Now I've got you! All of you. I'm pregnant, Jon. Damn it! I'm carrying your child again. Talk to me!!*

Jodi had just handed her some jelly beans and then bent down to share her candies with Bradley. His face brightened as he giggled.

"Shh, shh, shh. Don't wake up the children," Jodi whispered, and turned to face her mother again. She pressed her tiny index finger to her sticky lips. "Shhhh."

Desiree suddenly felt included. The spell was broken. With such a tiny gesture, Jodi had popped the bubble.

The smell of roast chicken prompted Desiree to the kitchen where she poured a flour mixture into the light chicken stock and stirred it vigorously. Only the soft whispers from Jodi filled the air and Desiree shrugged her shoulders, wishing she hadn't planned such an involved dinner. She would have preferred being in a quiet restaurant now, sitting next to Jon, with Jodi and Bradley across the table. All of them would be together there, talking and laughing, while someone else prepared the meal.

"Des. You forgot to open this envelope." Bradley was squeezing her elbow.

"Oh, I'm sure it's just some advertising junk. You can open it if you like." Desiree turned down the burner, poured herself a cup of fresh coffee, and sat cross-legged in a swivel chair.

Bradley tore open the envelope. "Who's Sara?" he asked immediately.

"Pardon?"

Bradley finished reading the message before handing her the note, and as she read it to herself, her face flushed with pleasant surprise. 'Had to coax Sara into letting me have the pick of the litter but I got it. Hope you're home tomorrow.'

"Will I still be here when it comes? I'd like to see the kitten."

"It's a *puppy*, Buck, a fluffy white Samoyed pup. I'll make sure you're still here when it comes, but let's keep it a secret for now, okay? I want it to be a surprise for Jodi. Please go tell her to wash up for dinner. It'll be ready in a few minutes."

"Don't forget about that brown parcel you left on the piano."

"Yes, of course. Maybe you can help me open it later."

Tiny elbows were soon on the edge of the wooden trestle table and then, waiting patiently for their plates to be filled, Bradley and Jodi draped their linen napkins over their laps while Jon sat at the other end and helped himself to some juicy dark meat.

"Walter Johnson gave his notice on Thursday, and he's thinking of moving to Alaska this summer," he began, spreading a thick pat of butter on the steaming baby carrots. "He couldn't get a raise so he decided to quit."

"Would you like more potatoes, Buck?" Desiree's voice twanged with annoyance as she reached for the bowl. *Is that all you can think of now, Jon?*

"Daddy. Will you play Pig-in-the-Middle with us tonight? It's Buck's favorite game. And it's fun."

"No, Jodi, not tonight. I'm a little tired and I think it's almost time for you to go to bed."

"But Daddy, Mommy always plays with me before its bedtime. And then she reads a story to me and all my children."

"Jodi!"

No games were played after dinner, but when Desiree recited the Children's Prayer in the soft glow of the nightlight by her daughter's bed, Jodi kissed her mother's hand.

"I gave Buck my new elf so he could have somebody to talk to when he goes to bed. Is that okay, Mommy?"

Desiree nodded her head, smiling, and tucked in the blankets before stepping out into the hallway where she could see Bradley stroking the long black hair of the troll doll as he sat on the leather chair in the den. She separated the blankets on the new sofa bed for him while he rearranged his Easter presents on the roll-top desk. On its corner was a portrait of Erin.

"Who's that pretty lady?"

"That's my sister, Erin."

"Can I meet her too, some day?"

"I sure wish you could meet her, but she died five and a half years ago in a car accident." Somehow the words were easy to say that evening.

His bright blue eyes stayed on the portrait for another moment and then lifted. "I'm sorry that Jon doesn't like me. I love it here, you know."

"And I love *you* being here." She bent down and kissed his cheek. "Don't you worry about anything now, okay? Have a good night's sleep and I'll see you in the morning."

"Good night, Des. Even though I'm going home tomorrow, we're gonna have a good time together before I leave. You just wait and see. And don't forget that a cute little puppy will be wanting to play with all of us before I go home."

"Why don't you think of a good name we can give it?"

"I would love to. Is it a boy or a girl?"

"Todd didn't tell us, did he? Well, why not think of two good names?"

"Okay. I can do that. Thank you, Desiree. Goodnight."

She made a tall virgin screwdriver for herself and, being careful to add only two drops of Tabasco sauce and one drop of Worcestershire sauce to the vodka, she also made a Caesar for Jon who was still sitting on the loveseat, his legs and arms crossed, the morning newspaper scattered on the floor.

Tapping the marble mantle of the fireplace, she sipped her drink as she stared outside at the waning moon and wondered why Jon had become so quiet and speechless. Or was his silence intentional, to unnerve her?

"Do you have any beer? Krystal makes the best shanties."

She shook her head. He was comparing her to Krystal and it sounded so callous, coming from his mouth. *So unfair, damn it anyway,* she thought. *We're two different people, Jon. If you like being with Krystal so much, why don't you just leave?*

As Jon sipped his Caesar, staring blankly at the upright piano beside him, her thoughts rambled on. As he tapped the lit end of his cigarette in the copper ashtray, she finished her own cocktail.

"You love her, don't you?"

"Pardon?"

"Come on, Jon." Angry lines soon wrinkled her brow.

"You mean Krystal? She's a beautiful person. I'll always love her."

"Then why are you still here? Why did you come here today in the first place?" She wriggled her toes in an attempt to concentrate on something other than her husband's handsome looks. "And why are you here telling your only child that you want to be with *her* and that you need to be *here*?

"Krystal's a beautiful person."

He was repeating himself now, lost for words again.

Desiree turned to face him directly. "Then why don't you go back to her?"

"Because when I'm with her, I still think about being here. All I think about is Jodi, this new home, and you."

"Oh, really now." Conscious of each word uttered, she took a deep breath before continuing. "What you really want is the best of both worlds."

He nodded his head as a tiny smirk curved his full lips.

"Well, I, for one, wish you the very best of luck with that arrangement. Have you mentioned this to Krystal yet? I bet she'd throw something at you."

"She probably would." Jon had thought everything would have been discussed and settled by now. In less than an hour he was supposed to take Krystal to a dinner theater, meeting her parents for the first time at the airport later in the evening. But he was still at the house, trying to tell Desiree about their plans. "I miss her already," he admitted, shuffling his body in the loveseat.

"And I suppose you persuaded her to come over here yesterday to entertain me."

He nodded his head.

Her great performance was nearing. *The Dénouement,* she had decided to call it. But why was she so doubtful about it now? She had rehearsed everything—each word, each movement. Keeping her gestures deliberately feminine, her soft voice sweet, firmly but politely she was going to tell her husband to leave. And she was going to help him pack. He wasn't going to get the best of both worlds. Not any more. With a sudden and rare look of confidence, she picked up her empty glass and went into the kitchen to answer the phone.

"Hello."

"Desiree, it's Krystal. I'm sorry to bother you right now, but my car won't start and I'm supposed to meet my parents at the airport later. I thought maybe Jon could come over and give me a boost. Is he still there?"

"Still here? Where else was he supposed to be? Hang on a second!" She threw the phone onto the counter and it fell to the floor as she walked back into the living room. "Krystal's timing always seems so perfect," she grunted while motioning Jon to take the phone. As her hands stroked the soft wool of the afghan, Desiree became aware that she had finally found the last few irregularly shaped pieces of her own life's jigsaw puzzle, and this realization alerted the blonde. She was ready for her curtain call, but what was keeping Jon? She leaned her entire body towards the kitchen.

"No, Krystal. I haven't had the chance yet … I do so know what to say. I memorized the note you gave me … Yes, I know exactly what time it is, but I'll need just a bit more … Well, take a cab then, if you can't wait for me any longer."

Still planning her attack, Desiree watched Jon walk over to the piano and drop one hand heavily onto the keys.

"She hung up on me."

"There's a first time for everything, isn't there?" She turned to face him directly. "I hear you and Krystal are going on a world cruise next week."

"No, not until the middle of June. We …" More keys were hit.

To hear such discordance from the piano just then was absolutely fitting for Desiree. Yes, at last the puzzle was complete. But she didn't care for the perspective. "I'm going to see a lawyer next week," she said frankly, as she played with a single hairpin in her jeans pocket. "And I'll arrange for Mr. Staut to put the house up for sale. Then I'll—"

"No, don't do that! Don't do anything like that!" He stood beside her and tried to take her hand, but she broke away. "Krystal and I have talked everything over. We've decided to find you a nice apartment. We'll pay the rent and all the utilities for you, so you won't have to worry about that."

"Pardon me?" She had envisioned the climax of this act, this finale, slightly wrong. Her field of view had somehow been distorted. Her husband was tapping his fingers on the edge of the piano now, looking frequently at his watch. But she had something important to tell him. Point-blank! It would be his very own choice to listen or not to listen.

"That's what we've both decided, Desiree. Let it happen exactly like that. *Please?"*

She hated him for using that single word in his usual low smooth tone.

"Are you listening to me?" he blurted.

"Jon, I think I've heard enough already."

"But there's more. Lots more."

"Oh, really?" There was a sudden urge, a strange pull within her suggesting that she listen to her husband, and she heeded that sensation.

"Krystal and I agree that *we* should move in here together. We both like how you've fixed everything up, but the house is way too big for you. And of course, what would be best for everyone involved is that we keep Jodi here for ourselves."

A rush of terror consumed the bewildered blonde. Nobody was going to take away her daughter. Not Jon. Not Krystal. Not *anyone!* She refused to listen to whatever Jon was uttering. With brisk long strides, she walked up to the master bedroom and angrily slid open the closet doors. She reached into the far corner for her old Pullman and wheeled it out.

Jon was at the doorway now, watching.

She twisted her long hair at the nape of her neck and wedged it together with the hairpin she had taken from her blouse pocket before lifting a handful of clothes hangers from the wooden rod. Soon suits, jackets, shirts, and pants were dropped into the suitcase.

"What are you doing?" he demanded.

She couldn't look at him. "You told me to wait for you, and I have. *And*, as you can see, I even washed or dry cleaned all the clothes you left here."

"But this is not how I wanted everything to …"

She grabbed the laundry bag nearby and soon a drawer full of his old sweaters was thrown inside. She then turned to face her husband. "I think all these are yours." She shoved the suitcase in front of him and handed him the over-stuffed bag. "You've had enough time to consider everything, and obviously you've made your decision. But so have I. You say you want to be with Krystal, and that's just fine with me. But it's not going to be here. Not anywhere *near* here. And you are certainly not taking Jodi from me. What made either of you even think that I would give her away? To you, or anyone?"

Jon took a small step out into the hallway. "Krystal would love to have four kids, but she can't have *any* children."

Anger, hatred, and disbelief converged in Desiree's mind, all taking center stage in her short melodrama. How could she quickly change the scene to focus on Jon's script, to expose *his* particular theatrical production? She glared into her husband's eyes. "So what are you trying to tell me, Jon? What exactly have you and Krystal lined up for me?"

"Your pregnancy with Jodi was so perfect, I think you could have a daycare full of your own kids." He cleared his throat to purposely soften his voice. "Why can't you understand me, Desiree?

Her lungs longed for fresh air. Her breaths were short as she stepped forward. "You're twisting things around just a slight bit, don't you think?" Sarcasm spewed from her mouth. "*You're* the confused one now, Jon. You've told me what you want. You want Krystal. All you think about is Krystal. Well then, go get her!"

"But it's …"

"Don't interrupt me, Jon. I'm not through yet." She pulled out a drawer from the corner highboy and emptied its entire contents onto the bed. "You know, your face shows such a soft expression of contentment when you have Krystal on your mind. Yes, it is that obvious. I know what she means to you and I'm setting you free. Now, is *that* not the epitome of understanding? Am *I* the one being unfair about all of this? I don't think so."

He quickly looked at his watch. "But you know that we …"

"You're interrupting me again, Jon." She eyed the clutter she had just made with his few remaining items. "I should have given all these nice clothes away instead of waiting for you to come back here and get them." She stuffed his entire collection of silk ties and a few leather belts into an old sports bag she had been planning to throw out, and tugged at its broken zipper. "Please be advised, you *and* Krystal both, that I will not, under *any* circumstances, *give* my only child to someone."

He looked at his watch again and spread out his long arms as an overnight bag was pushed in front of him.

"Jon! This is also yours."

Total bewilderment colored Jon's face an ugly shade of crimson but he knew he didn't have any time to argue. Straightening his shoulders, he looked at his watch again. He ignored Desiree's hot glare and carried his belongings downstairs. His jugular veins were swelling with resentment. His dark eyes were clouded with surprise. He truly hadn't expected such a reaction from his wife, but he hoped that Krystal might still be waiting for him at the apartment. He had to see her. He had to apologize to her for being so late. Besides, he could see his wife some other time to iron things out. Yes, Desiree would understand everything then. She always did.

Flushed with uncertainty, yet wrought with determination, Desiree brought down a large duffel bag filled with old golf shirts. She almost tripped down the stairs while carrying various toiletries in her hands. Her composure remained, however, as Jon took his belongings to the car.

He had everything now, and she watched him through the storm door. His walk was slow, his balance steady. Her stance was straight, her head held high. He hesitated before settling himself in the car, and blew his nose after starting the ignition. She cried a tiny tear for him, for Jodi, and for herself. He revved the engine momentarily, loose gravel flying as he sped off. She latched the storm door and leaned against the thick wooden door, letting it close gently behind her.

So, Jon was gone. She was without a husband now, and she finally had to accept it. Long moments passed as her tiny body rested heavily against the refreshing coolness of the front door, her wet eyes closed, and her steady breaths deepened. A calming, almost meditative awareness enveloped her. Loneliness seemed to be ignoring her just then and she gave a deep sigh as she finally locked the door. All bitterness seemed to have left her. Standing tall, she set the deadbolt, reached into her pants pocket, and pulled out the vial.

She set the tiny container of pills onto the dining room table and glanced at Todd's note, which she had earlier slipped under a doily.

She walked over to the piano and opened the parcel Jon had handed her outside. It was Erin's white leather Bible, still unopened since graduation. And in her large scrawled handwriting, Mrs. Martin, the Bjornsons' neighbor, had scribbled a short note on a torn piece of pink lined stationery. 'Got a frantic call from your mother early this morning asking me to bring this over to you as soon as I could.' Almost illegible, crammed in the tiny remaining space and circling around the edge at the bottom of the page, were the words John 14:27.

Desiree knew that exact verse by heart. "Are you asking for my forgiveness, Mother?" Her throat was tight now, her voice harsh and raspy. She sat at the edge of the loveseat and opened the Bible to a page in the Book of John, which showed a beautifully colored picture of Jesus and John the Baptist. She slid her hand over the cool smoothness and gave a tiny smile. With its pages still exposed, she set the Bible onto the piano. "I forgive you, Mom," she said out loud. "At least, I want to. I'm hoping that what I had to tell you over the phone just caught you by surprise and that those hateful words of yours were just a reaction to such unexpected news, before you really knew what you were saying." Gently closing the Bible, Desiree pressed it against her bosom. An understanding smile slowly erased the tightness around her forehead, and a soft peaceful quality returned to her heart.

Preparing to write her parents, to tell them *everything,* she stretched over and took the sharpened pencil and a thick pad of her favorite stationery from the top drawer of the buffet and sat down at the trestle table. But no words came to her. Instead, like earlier that day, she was marking the top page with long black strokes as her fingers moved so freely, so steadily… How easy each swirl appeared on the faintly decorated sheet.

"They wouldn't let me see you, son. They wouldn't bring you to me." A tiny tear splashed the corner of the paper where she had so perfectly captured the clear depth of the boy's round blue eyes, and now her hand continued drawing the soft curls of his long dark hair in such quick easy movements. The page was filling up with poetic rhythm. "My son, I saw you there in front of me. The vision was so distinct. But then you were gone. The moment fled so quickly. I remember your beautiful pink face and your bright blue eyes. Your tiny mouth was slightly open. I heard you calling me."

She blotted the page with a tissue. "I never got to hold you, son, or feel the warmth of your tiny body in my arms. I never got to feed you nature's milk. You were gone before I had the chance to give you any of my love. I saw you only once, my son. Maybe some day you'll see me." Carefully she tore the single sketch from its binding. The image of Jason, the name she and her husband had chosen for their first son, was remarkable and the uncanny resemblance to the child in her last dream held her for a few more moments. When she stood up and carefully eyed the newness of everything around her a rare feeling of satisfaction had somehow erased the lingering odor of paint, every ache in her body, and every doubt in her mind. Now a peaceful reverence was soothing her.

"Tomorrow, Jason, I'm going to buy a beautiful gold frame and set this sketch of you inside it for the entire world to see."

Moments later, however, as though driven by that same warm, comfortable force, with hammer and panel nails on the telephone bench beside her in the front foyer, she carefully hung the sketch, its thin wooden frame faded with age. Tiptoeing into the den where Bradley lay still, atop the blankets, she opened the desk drawer and carefully pulled out a binder of lined paper.

"Did Jon leave again?"

"Yes, Buck. He won't bother us anymore tonight."

"You still have me and Jodi, you know."

"Yes, I know. And I'm thanking God for the two of you. For all my good friends." A true sense of gratitude swept over her, and with a deep cleansing breath, she dusted the gilded frame of Erin's portrait with a tissue. "Now, where's the best place to hang this?"

"Above the desk so you can see it as soon as you come into the room. And maybe my mother will let you have one of me so you can hang it up there, too."

"I would like that, Buck. But I think you'd better try to get some sleep now, okay?" She mussed his short blond hair, tucked him in again, and closed the door gently behind her. She stepped into Jodi's bedroom and kissed her warm forehead. Tiptoeing into the master bedroom, she sat comfortably on the leather settee and caressed its smooth material with slow, easy motions. Then with calm deliberation, she stood up, walked over to the vanity, and touched the plush velvet box that no longer displayed her wedding rings. Slowly she closed the lid. Moments later she shut the sliding doors to the half-empty closet.

Downstairs again, as the soothing lyrics of "Turn! Turn! Turn! (A Time For Every Season)" played softly, she reached into the stereo's deep cabinet and took out a small white box from behind a stack of albums. Again, she carefully opened her sister's last gift. Crystal. How exquisite. Krystal. Jon's new love. His own wife's present rival. How ironic! Moments later, nailed above the piano and perfectly centered, colors of the rainbow winked at her.

At the trestle table again she addressed the envelope to her parents and proudly folded the thick letter inside. The words had seemed to flow onto the pages, unlike previous times. Her parents might not understand her choices or her decisions but ...

Listening to the cuckoo clock striking ten, she scribbled a note to herself to phone Mr. Thornton in the morning about going on the American tour later that summer. She would tell him how much she wanted to go, explaining that because of her present condition she would have to decline. She knew Carmella would understand, totally. And tomorrow she would be enjoying Todd's easy company again, and watching the children's surprise as they got their first glimpses of the soft white puppy. After Bradley was picked up, she would drive to the cemetery and let Jodi place the pot of Easter lilies on Erin's grave. She was going to phone Carole Schrader, too, and invite her over for lunch some day next week. She was also going to explain all the latest happenings to Lynda. She could do all that now. Yes, the time was right. And most certainly, she would order new door locks for the entire household.

Leaving the stamped envelope and lengthy list on the trestle table, the determined blonde picked up the tiny bottle of pills. With measured steps she walked up to the main bathroom. She leaned over the vanity and stared at her clear reflection. Desiree liked what she saw now. She emptied the plastic container and clutched the pills. As the white crystals started to crumble, an inner strength and quiet confidence enveloped her.

Then—*one*—*two*—*three*—*four*—*five*—she heard each separate splash in the commode. With a deliberate twist of her wrist, she pressed down the lever, and a single tear fell into the swirl.